...extraordinary thing.

...this time the crippled boy had sat unmoving in his stiff-backed chair, a black-garbed, silent mannequin. It was all the boy could do; Polty knew that. But the boy did not even seem to be hot, for all that the fire raged ever more brightly; it was as if the cripple really were dying by degrees, as Polty had said, and his capacity to feel pain was already gone. Was that why he would not even cry out, for all that Polty prodded and pinched him, slapped him, struck him?

But now, as the dwarf's music writhed around him, the crippled boy, smoothly and impassively, was rising to his feet. He was standing; his legs, that a moment before had been bowed and buckled, were all at once inexplicably straightened. The boy's limbs showed no strain, nor did he register discomfort or alarm as he crossed the narrow space to the hearth. There, the boy called Jemany knelt down, and thrust a hand unhurriedly into the centre of the fire.

And did not cry out.

TOM ARDEN

The Harlequin's Dance

First Book of THE OROKON

First published in Great Britain 1997
by Victor Gollancz

First published in paperback 1998
by Vista

This Millennium edition published 2000
An imprint of Victor Gollancz
Orion House, 5 Upper St Martin's Lane,
London WCWH 9EA

A catalogue record for this book is
available from the British Library.

ISBN 0 575 60192 2

Typeset by SetSystems Ltd, Saffron Walden, Essex
Printed in Great Britain by
Cox & Wyman Ltd, Reading, Berks

TO

Antony Heaven

The Burning Verses

1

THE CHILD WHO IS KEY TO THE OROKON
SHALL BEAR THE MARK OF RIEL
& HAVE IN HIM THE SPIRIT OF NOVA-RIEL:
BUT HIS TASK IS GREATER AS THE EVIL ONE IS GREATER
WHEN THE END OF THE ATONEMENT COMES

2

FOR SASSOROCH SHALL COME AGAIN FROM UNBEING
& HIS POWER SHALL BE A HUNDREDFOLD:
BUT NOW HE SHALL BEAR HIS TRUE NAME & TRUE VISAGE
THAT WERE HIDDEN FROM THE WORLD
WHEN HE WAS SASSOROCH

3

& BEFORE THE RETURN OF THE EVIL ONE
A TIME OF SUFFERING SHALL DESCEND UPON THE EARTH
& THIS SHALL HERALD THE END OF ATONEMENT:
& ONLY THE POWER OF THE OROKON
SHALL DEFEAT THE EVIL THAT THEN SHALL COME

4

& THE CHILD SHALL FIND FIRST THE CRYSTAL OF DARKNESS
FLUNG TO THE SKIES BY THE FATHER OF THE GODS:
& HE SHALL QUEST THROUGH THE LANDS OF EL-OROK
FOR THE CRYSTALS OF EARTH FIRE WATER & AIR
THAT HE MAY UNITE THEM IN THE OROKON

5

& IF HE SUCCEEDS A NEW AGE SHALL DAWN
& ALL THE LANDS OF EL-OROK SHALL LIVE IN PEACE:
& IF HE FAILS THE HORROR THAT HAS PASSED
SHALL BE AS NOTHING TO THE HORROR
THAT SHALL COME

Players

JEM, *a crippled boy*
CATA, *a child of nature*
SILAS WOLVERON, *her father*
UMBECCA RENCH, *great-aunt to Jem*
ELA (LADY ELABETH), *mother to Jem*
TOR (TORVESTER), *her brother; a wanted man*
THE HARLEQUIN, *a mysterious entertainer*
BARNABAS, *a mysterious dwarf*
XAL, *a Woman of Wisdom*
POLTY (POLTISS), *a bully; leader of The Five*
ARON THROSH ('BEAN'), *his best friend; member of The Five*
LENY, VEL and TYL, *members of The Five*
NATHANIAN WAXWELL, *surgeon and apothecary*
GOODY WAXWELL, *his wife*
GOODY THROSH (WYNDA), *mother to Aron; tavern-keeper*
EBENEZER THROSH (EBBY), *her husband*
OLIVAN THARLEY VEELDROP, *military commander*
EAY FEVAL (THE CHAPLAIN), *his chaplain*
NIRRY, *maid-of-all-work at the castle*
STEPHEL, *her father; old castle steward*
THE OLD MAID
MORVEN and CRUM, *soldiers*
OLCH ('WIGGLER') and ROTTS, *also soldiers*
SERGEANT BUNCH, *their immediate superior*
CHILDREN OF KOROS ('VAGAS'), *travelling people*
REVELLERS *in the tavern*
QUALITY-FOLK *at the ball*
VILLAGERS, PEASANTS, *more* SOLDIERS
&c.

SPIRITS OF THE UNCREATED, *creatures rejected by Orok*
TOTH-VEXRAH, *a mysterious enchanter*
THE LADY IMAGENTA, *his daughter*
PEOPLES *of El-Orok*
&c.

FROM THE MYTHOLEGICON:
THE TARN, *Creatures of Evil*
SASSOROCH, *greatest of The Tarn*
AON THE IRONHAND, *an ancient king*
QUEEN NAYA, *his queen*
RIEL (NOVA-RIEL), *her adopted son*
IXITER IRION, *first Archduke of Irion*
SOOTHSAYER
MOTLEY, *a court jester*
SWINE-WARRIOR OF SWALE
PRINCESS ALAMANE
PRINCE YON
&c.

Prologue to The Orokon

**OF THE FIVE GODS & THE CREATION OF THE EARTH:
OF THE JUVESCENCE & THE TIME OF ATONEMENT:
BEING ADAPTED FROM THE EL-OROKON
SACRED BOOK OF THE LANDS
OF EL-OROK**

1

In the time before the earth was brought forth from Unbeing, there was great warmaking in the realm of The Vast, which is home to the gods. In time the warmaking ended; but the god Orok, who had fought long and righteously, knew that he was suffering from a fatal wound. So it was that he withdrew to a far wilderness, as a god must do when his time has come to die.

And deep in the wilderness he came upon a rock. With his sword he struck the rock, and said, 'This rock I call the Rock of Being and Unbeing. This rock shall be the Rock of my dying.'

Around the Rock he raised a golden palace; and Orok withdrew into the palace he had made, to pass in silence the aeons before him.

For the dying of a god is a long slow dying.

Now it came to pass that the dying god grew lonely, and in his loneliness decreed he would have a son. He descended to the Rock of Being and Unbeing; and looking on the Rock, he saw its strength.

'Rock of Being and Unbeing,' he cried, 'give to me a son so great and strong.'

And the dying god raised his sword, and struck the Rock. There was a blaze of radiance; but as the radiance died away the god stood back, aghast. For before him there had come into being a creature hunched and twisted, garbed in darkness. And the dying god said: 'Creature, you are not comely. Tell me what you are.'

And the creature garbed in darkness said: 'Father, I am Koros of the Rock, and I come to you as your son.'

Then the dying god Orok knew despair. With his sword he would have slain the creature, but compassion welled in him and he decreed: 'Creature, you shall live.' And so that the creature could live and not be lonely, the dying god fashioned for him a sister soft as leaves. Her name was Viana.

And the children lived in the Palace of Orok, but their father turned his eyes from them.

The aeons rolled by.

And it came to pass that the dying god grew weaker, and decreed once again that he would have a son. He ventured to the Rock of Being and Unbeing; and as he raised his sword, he felt its swiftness.

'Rock of Being and Unbeing,' he cried, 'give to me a son so swift and fiery!'

There was a blaze of radiance; but again when the radiance died away the god stood back, aghast. For before him was a creature red of hair and eye, hovering on leathern wings. And the dying god said: 'Creature, you are not comely. Tell me what you are.'

'Father, I am Theron of the Sword,' said the creature, 'and I come to you as your son.'

Then it was that the dying god knew sadness. With harsh words he would have banished the creature, but compassion welled in his heart and he decreed: 'Creature, you shall stay.' And so that the creature could stay and not be lonely, the dying god fashioned for him a sister cool as water. Her name was Javander.

And the children lived in the golden palace, but their father turned his eyes from them.

And as the aeons rolled slowly past the dying god would venture many times to the Rock, and there he brought into being many creatures. But none of the creatures he permitted to live; for now he would have only perfection. Again and again he would strike the Rock; but again and again he banished his creatures to the Realm of Unbeing.

And the spirits of the Uncreated howled about the palace, but the dying god Orok did not hear them.

The dying god entered the last aeon of his age. The time of his creations soon must end, and he decreed that he must leave behind an heir. He looked on the Rock and then the Sword.

'Rock of Being and Unbeing,' he said, 'in the blaze of radiance when Sword clashes Rock, then there is beauty. Give to me a son so bright and beautiful.'

And this time when he struck the Rock the radiance did not die, and there stood before him a being apparelled in light. And the dying god whispered to the bright being, 'Fair one, you are comely! Tell me who you are.'

And the being apparelled in light said: 'I am Agonis of the Light, Father. I am your son.'

Then the dying god Orok knew joy, and took his son to sit by him in the throne-room of the palace.

2

One day the fair son was wandering in the gardens when he came upon his dark brother speaking to the air.

'Brother, to whom do you speak?' the fair god asked.

And his brother Koros turned to him and smiled, 'You cannot hear? All about us howl the spirits of the Uncreated. I had thought only our father could not hear them; I had not known, brother, that you heard with our father's ears.'

From that time, Agonis too could hear the mournful cryings. So it was that he said to his father, 'Father, the Uncreated are baying to be born. May I not make a world where they may live?'

And the dying god said, 'My son, your compassion makes me love you more. But there are creatures that should not be brought into being. You may create a world; but first you must separate the creatures of good from the creatures of evil.'

So it was that the fair Agonis set about the task, calling the Uncreated to him one by one.

*

Now, Koros envied the task of his fair brother. He said to him, 'Brother, let me aid you.'

But the fair Agonis only smiled and said, 'Dark one, I pity you, but you are unfit for this task. For though your heart may be good, your shape is evil.'

Then the dark fire of resentment burned in Koros, and he went to his brother Theron and said, 'The fair Agonis is making a world, and filling it with spirits only like his own. Our spirits, too, he would consign to Unbeing. Join with me, brother, to fight against him. For the death of our father is approaching fast, and soon a time of reckoning will be upon us.'

But the fiery Theron spurned his dark brother. 'Begone, misshapen one! I am not so fair as our brother, but I am fairer than you. My fiery wrath shall always be raised in the righteous cause of Agonis.'

So it was that the vengeance of the dark god came to pass. As his father slept, the first-born stole the Sword of Fire; and calling to him the spirits of the Uncreated, led them to the Rock of Being and Unbeing.

'Rock,' he cried, as he raised the sword, 'make for these creatures, the dark and fair alike, a world where all may live!'

He struck the Rock. An explosion shook the palace. Flames and black smoke filled the chamber and a black abyss opened in the floor. Through the abyss the Uncreated fell, and the dark god looked on the world he had made. Then it was that horror overcame him, for it was a world fashioned like himself. And the dark god hid in the chaos he had made, concealed among its vilest and most misshapen things.

Above, in the palace, his father trembled with fury. He called his children to him, and asked them what they would do.

Theron, red of hair and eye, would descend in wrath.

But the fair Agonis stepped forth and said: 'Father, our foolish brother has created a world of torment. Yet the sacrifice of a god may save it. Let me descend to the world my brother has made, and bring light to his darkness.'

Then the dying god looked on his son and said, 'My son, your

18

sacrifice would make all love you. But I am nearing the time of my ending. It is ordained that I should die into this new world, and that you, my children, should tend to it after me.'

So it was that for a final time, the dying god descended to the Rock of Being and Unbeing. When he had completed the enchantments he there wrought, the chaos of his dark son was resolved into order. He ordered the times and seasons of the world; he ordered the ranks of the creatures that lived there. The good he placed in a plenteous valley; the evil he banished beyond the far mountains. In the centre of the valley, which was the Vale of Orok, he planted the Rock of Being and Unbeing; and when his work was done, the god who had died appeared before his children for a final time.

'My children,' the dead god Orok said, 'this is not the world I wanted. In my dying I have divided dark from light; but darkness yet remains ever-present in this world. So it is that you must tend to this world.'

Then to each of his favoured children the dead god gave a province, and a crystal which embodied the powers of that province. First he called to him his two daughters. Blessing them, to Viana he gave a crystal coloured like earth; to Javander, one coloured like the sea.

He called to him his remaining sons. To Theron, Orok gave a crystal fierce as fire.

Then came the fairest son.

The lesser gods gasped.

For each crystal was a thing of rare beauty, but the Crystal of Agonis was rarest of all. Its colour shimmered and shifted like sunlight.

And Orok embraced his fair son, and kissed his eyes and lips. He said, 'Now, my children, the time has come when I must descend into this Rock of my dying. Know that I command you to live in bonds of love, and use the crystals only for good.'

And the living gods stepped forth to bless their dead father, when all at once came a cry of 'Hold!' For the dark Koros had come forth from concealment, and in contrition he knelt before his father.

'Forgive me, Father,' the dark god said. 'Bless me as you have blessed my sisters and brothers.'

The fiery Theron said, 'Father, let me destroy him.'

But the fair Agonis took the hand of his dark brother, and said, 'Father, he is contrite. Let him live and prove his worth.'

So it was that the dead god said to his son Koros, 'Misshapen one, you deserve only to die. But the pity of your fair brother touches my heart. You shall live, but your province shall be death. You shall be the guardian at the Gate of Unbeing. Yours shall be places where fear dwells, dark caves of night and spider-filled corners, bleak mountain passes and the catacombs of death.'

And to his first-born he gave a crystal coloured like night, glowing purple-black with a light that was like darkness.

Then he descended into the Rock of his dying; and when he was gone, the fair Agonis drew his sisters and brothers to him and said, 'Children, it is a great trust that our father has laid upon us. Let us swear to be true to that trust.' And placing his crystal atop the Rock, he bade his sisters and brothers do likewise, and said, 'Let us fuse our crystals into this Rock. And vow that for so long as they are here united, so their powers shall be used for good.'

So the five crystals were embedded in the Rock, forming the mystic circle called The Orokon; and for so long as the circle was unbroken, so the new world would live in harmony.

Thus it was in the first age of the earth, which women and men would call The Juvescence.

3

Now it came to pass that The Juvescence must end, and an age called the Time of Atonement begin.

When the earth was new, women and men would yield up their oblations to each of the five gods; but as time passed there gathered about each god a particular people, who were jealous of

20

their god. Even the dark Koros had his people, who did not shun him, but dwelt like him with darkness.

One day the fair Agonis called his sisters and brothers to him and said, 'Children, yesterday I spoke to our father, who lies in darkness in the Rock. Our father warned me that a time would come when the women and men of earth should not live in harmony. Thus it is that we must save them from themselves; we must bond them more strongly to the race of the gods.'

And when his brothers asked how this should be done, the fair Agonis told them it was decreed that a woman of earth should become his bride.

'Brother,' his sister Javander said, 'the life of a woman of earth is short. How should you find one to share your long life?'

'Brother,' his sister Viana said, 'the beauty of a woman of earth is fleeting. How should you find one who shall not fade?'

Their brother said he would search the earth for the fairest of its daughters; and when he had found her, he would make her a goddess.

Now it happened that in the Vale of Orok there lived an enchanter who wrought many spells. His name was Toth-Vexrah; and when he heard of the quest of the fair god he went to him and said, 'Great one, I can show you what you seek.' The enchanter brought forth a magic glass, and in the glass the god Agonis saw the image of a woman fair as himself.

'You speak truth, enchanter,' said the enraptured god. 'This creature might be a goddess already. Tell me where I may find her.'

And the enchanter replied, 'Great one, you have not far to seek. The name of this lady is Imagenta. She is my daughter, and I give you her hand.'

So it was that the enchanter brought his daughter to the god. Her face was swathed in a veil, which the god would sweep aside; but the enchanter called: 'Hold! Great one, there is a condition I would lay upon you. The glass shows but the shadow of this lady's beauty. In truth, my daughter is a creature so

21

radiant that no man may look upon her who is not her husband. Part not the veil until she is yours.'

The god assented; but asked only that he might possess the magic glass, that he might gaze upon it until the wedding. The enchanter gave it to him, and the god looked on the glass with a yet more ardent longing.

4

Now there was much joy in the Vale of Orok when the wedding of the fair Agonis was announced. Women and men fashioned rich gifts for the gods; there were sacrifices of blessing. Only the countenance of Koros was unjoyful; for when he saw the image which had so entranced his brother, the first-born of Orok burned with a dark fury.

So it came to pass that on the morning of the wedding, the Lady Imagenta could not be found. The fair Agonis was struck dumb with sorrow; so the fiery Theron called a council of the gods.

One god did not come.

'Sisters and brothers,' cried the fiery god, 'where is our brother Koros?'

Then it was that the enchanter Toth-Vexrah pounded at the doors, crying, 'Great ones, it is your brother who has stolen my daughter! For he has taken her to the feet of the far mountains, and there he has imprisoned her in a fortress of darkness.' And the enchanter made manifest an image of the captive.

'This cannot be!' cried the goddess Viana. 'My brother's powers are dark, but not wicked, and what we see must be an illusion.'

'Goddess, it is no illusion,' the enchanter replied. 'For look you on the Rock of Being and Unbeing, and you shall see that the dark crystal has been plucked forth from its place.'

The gods looked on the Rock, and saw that it was true.

Then the fiery Theron flamed out. 'Gods, our brother has broken our pact! Henceforth, he is our enemy. Fair brother, grieve not, for I shall destroy the traitor Koros.' And the fiery god plucked his own crystal from the Rock.

'Brother, I do likewise!' cried the goddess Javander. 'My powers, too, shall be raised against Koros! Sister Viana, will you join us in our fight?'

But the goddess Viana looked on them with loathing, and plucking from its place her own crystal cried: 'Sister, I do likewise, but my powers are for Koros!'

So it was that the first war of earth came to pass, when the forces of Theron and his sister Javander fought against the forces of Koros and Viana. To the standard of each god an army rallied, and destruction rained down upon the Vale of Orok.

5

And in all this the fair god intervened not, for he only stared, grieving, into the magic glass.

So it was that after long years, the enchanter Toth-Vexrah came to Agonis and said, 'Great one, the destruction which began at the feet of the far mountains is rolling ever closer to this palace of your grieving. Soon the whole of this vale shall be a wasteland. Even your fair people have gone to war in your name, wielding swords and axes. Yours is the most powerful of the Crystals of Orok. Use it now to bring an end to this war.'

'Enchanter, your words are evil,' said the fair god. 'Our father commanded us to live in bonds of love, and use the crystals only for good. Though I grieve for the loss of your daughter, my heart forbids me to disobey my father.'

'Then you are a fool!' the enchanter replied, and seizing the crystal of the fair god he spirited it away to the fiery Theron. So it was that Theron was victorious, blasting at last into the dark fortress of Koros.

'She is mine!' the fiery god cried; for through all this, in the secrecy of his heart, Theron had sought the lady for himself.

Inside the fortress, he assailed his dark brother, stabbing him in the thigh as a punishment for his lust. Then, his heart exulting, he leapt to the chamber where the captive had been held.

But in the chamber his joy turned to rage, for the lady had vanished, and could not be found. The fiery god wailed, and beat at the walls; he raised the crystal that was coloured like the sun, and called down destruction on all the world.

Then it was that the firmament darkened, and a voice like thunder bid the fiery god to hold.

'Father!' cried Theron, and sank to his knees; for it was the voice of his dead father, who had risen like a phantom from the darkness of the Rock.

And darkness spread lowering over the ravaged vale as the children of the dead god were summoned to him again.

'My children, you have destroyed this last of my creations. Were I still living, I should punish you mightily; but you have brought retribution upon yourselves. Your lives now must be lives of penance. It remains only that you retire to The Vast, and return this world to the Realm of Unbeing.'

And the god would have sunk back into the Rock of his death, but for his fair son, who called to him, 'Father, consign not this world to Unbeing! For though the gods, your children, have erred so grievously, the women and men of earth do not deserve to die. Let us live out our penance here, and build this world anew.'

Then the dead god rose again and said, 'My fairest son, my love for you has not waned. In the darkness of my death, I long for you to join me. But no, my child, the time has passed when the gods can live in this world; nor have its creatures deserved your care. Let it come to pass that this world shall live, but from now on its creatures must make their lives alone. Bring them to me.'

And the fair Agonis, sorrowing, gathered the peoples of earth to the Rock of Being and Unbeing; and there his dead father spoke to them thus:

'Women and men of earth, you can no longer live with the gods. Nor can your races, which have become warring armies, continue with one another. They must be divided, and you must go forth from this vale, once so plenteous, which has become now only a vale of destruction. Tomorrow, after a night of

24

mourning, my children shall return to The Vast, which is their home. Your fate lies beyond the far mountains.'

Then to each of the races of earth, the dead god gave a destiny. To the women and men of Viana, he ordained a journey to the east, where they would wrest new lives from a realm of dark forests. Calling to Viana for the crystal coloured like earth, the dead god entrusted it to the care of her people. 'This crystal is a symbol of your goddess. Bear it with you always, and she shall go with you.'

To the people of Javander and Theron he did likewise. Javander's people he would send across the seas, to the far islands of the west; Theron's, to the south, to blazing lands where the sun flamed high.

The dead god turned to the people of his fairest son.

'Children of Agonis, you have proved yourselves unworthy of him. Your journey is to the north, to mountainous lands of ice. There you shall live close to the vault of the sky, but yours shall be a sky that brings no warmth. Perhaps in time, as you look upon this crystal, you shall be brought to a proper atonement.' For the time that was to come, he said, would be a Time of Atonement, when all would live in sorrow for the errors of the past.

And then the dead god would have dismissed the races from him, but his fair son Agonis stepped forth and said, 'Father, you are just. But Koros stands here, too. What is to become of his people? Where is to be their home?'

Then the wrath of the dead god burst forth.

'Speak not to me of one accursed, deserving only of detestation! Creatures of Koros, you shall have no home!'

And seizing the crystal of his first-born son, the dead god flung it to the skies, high and far, so that none could see where it travelled or where it would land.

'Accursed tribe, it shall be your destiny to wander eternally through the lands of this world, searching for the crystal which alone might redeem you. And other races shall hold you in hatred, for they shall know it was your god who destroyed the Vale of Orok.'

So it was that the destinies of this earth's races were ordained. And that night, the night before the gods would leave the earth, the fair Agonis drew his sisters and brothers to him and said:

'Children, our father's wrath is just. He has decreed a hard destiny for the women and men of earth. But I have communed with him, in the darkness of his death. Our father has divided the five crystals; and yet, in time, they shall be united again. It is our task to look upon our peoples, watching over them until this time of redemption. Let us meditate on this redemption now, before the hour comes when we must ascend to The Vast.'

But the fair god did not spend that night in meditation. Instead, he called to him the enchanter Toth-Vexrah.

'Treacherous one, the time for recrimination has passed,' he said. 'But tell me, what has become of your daughter? My brother Theron told me she had vanished, but how can this be? Show me where she is.'

But the enchanter only said, 'My daughter is gone, I know not where, and all my magic is powerless to find her.'

And the fair god sighed, and looked once more on the magic glass, in which the beauty of the lady had not faded.

'This lady was to have been the redemption of this world. Had she been mine, this world would have prospered; because I have lost her, all has been lost.'

So it was that the night of mourning passed; and when the new day came, the five races gathered for a last time at the Rock of Being and Unbeing. The appointed time came; the gods arrived, and one by one bade their farewells to their peoples. But when it was time for the leave-taking of Agonis, the fairest of the gods was not to be found.

'Where is Agonis?' the cry went up, but the fair god had vanished, like the lady he had loved.

And to this day, his fate remains a mystery. Some say he descended into the Rock of Being and Unbeing, there to seek solace with the dead god, his father; some say he vanished into the magic glass.

Then there is the legend that he disguised himself that day, mingling with the peoples who were clustered about the Rock. They say he set out with them when they left the vale, determined to search the world for the missing lady. But in what disguise, or with which tribe he travelled, none can say.

And now, though aeons have rolled slowly past, still his worshippers look to the day when the lost god shall return to them, bearing his bride.

Only then, they say, shall The Atonement end, and a new age in the history of the earth begin.

The VILLAGE of and the WILDWOOD
IRION

KOLKOS AROS (The CRYSTAL SKY)

To the DALL RODER

CASTLE IRION

ROS of HXITER

OLD BARN

The LAZY TIGER

The LECTORY

The FORETELLING

The TEMPLE of IRION

OLD YEW

WALL of STICKS

WILDWOOD

BLOSSOM HOUSE

WOLVERON'S CAVE

CIRCLE of RUNES

MILL RACE

PALE HIGHT

KILLING ROCK

PART ONE

A Small Boy in Black

Chapter 1

TIGER IN THE WOOD

Deep in the Wildwood there is a green enfolding silence. Though the crazed peal of the cuckoo rings out, and the carillon of the nightingale, all sounds, soft or sharp, are claimed back by the forest. The hush possesses all.

There was a flicker of brightness in the deep green.

'Wood-tiger!'

Cata scampered forward, but the wood-tiger was gone.

'Oh Papa, make him come back!'

'Wood-tiger will do what he will, my child. He is a special fellow, and knows it. Should he show his stripes to silly little girls?'

Silly?

Cata stared indignantly into the gloom. She wanted all the creatures of the Wildwood for her friends. With just a look, without chanting or dancing, she could summon squirrels and robins, even the fat badger; she could converse with the wise damask owl and the sleek otter from the river. Only Wood-tiger would not come to her: still he remained the merest glimpse of gold, a flash of brightness in the dappled dark-green.

'Sometimes the brightest things are hidden from us, my child. But we shall see them when our time has come.'

Cata sighed. How many times had Papa said this? This time he had not even turned his cowled head. Left foot, right foot, planting his staff before him in the thick forest floor, the old man continued his stately progress, his dun robes unflapping in the stillness of the heat.

She called after him, 'Papa, when is my time?'

The old man only chuckled.

Cata's bare feet itched to plunge into the undergrowth. On another day, all else forgotten, she might have vanished into the tangled brackens and ferns. Today she only sighed again, said to herself the Wood-tiger rhyme, then scampered after Papa and grabbed his hanging hand.

'Papa, tell me again about the pretty fairings,' said the girl after a moment.

Again came a chuckle from beneath her father's cowl. Wood-tiger would wait, but the fair would not. All yesterday, and the day before, since the bright vans of the Vagas had lumbered into the village, the old man had spoken to the girl of the fairings, the stripy booths and raree-shows, the stones that flamed at the foreheads of the Vagas' turbaned heads. With beguiling words he had summoned gaudy images: the particoloured harlequin in his cap and jangling bells; the grizzled woman of wisdom with her flashing crystal sphere; the man with no head and a face in his chest and the woman with a fish-tail where her legs should have been. Had he raised the girl's hopes too high? Perhaps all these things, like so much else, now belonged only in that other world called the past. It had been so long since the fair had come; perhaps his own hopes were also too high.

'Poor Wood-tiger! So she has forgotten you already, my fickle child?' was all the old man said.

'Oh, Papa!' said the girl, and again scampered away from him.

She danced on the tangled path like a sprite.

So it was that they made their way through the Wildwood, the old man tramping like a pilgrim on ancient ways, the girl now dawdling, now darting forward, a restless familiar spirit in a grubby sackcloth shift.

The Wildwood encroached upon the village like a thief. The path was a sinuous, concealing tunnel.

Chapter 2

THE TOMBYARD

The village of Irion lies deep in the Valleys of the Tarn, the green hollowings in the foothills of those peaks that are called, in the ancient tongue of the Juvescence, the Kolkos Aros: the Crystal Sky. South of here, in the rolling Ejland downs, the white mountains might almost be a myth, some high-hovering symbol of an ethereal other world. To the dwellers in the Tarn they are a perpetual presence, if still not quite real: they hang at the horizon like a ghostly backdrop, white against the azure intensity of the sky. Even in the season of burning heat they are a reminder that the cold relents only briefly, here in this northernmost of the Kingdoms of El-Orok.

Yet at the height of the heat one might think the cold was banished permanently, even here. In that Season of Theron, Atonement Cycle 997*a*, as the calendar of the Agonists reckoned the year, the valleys sweltered as if the air were on fire.

It was the hottest Season of Theron since the war.

It was only when they reached the end of the tunnel that Cata took her father's hand again. The old man smiled sadly beneath his cowl. There was always this moment on the brink of the Wildwood; fleetingly, even now, for all the blandishments of the fair, Cata would have run back into the greenness. She caressed her face against her father's rough hand.

He pulled his hand away. 'Dirty-face! So, your Papa is your scouring-bark?'

'Papa?'

But the reprimand was only in jest. That morning the old

man had sent the girl to the river, to wash away her feral dirt; Cata, he knew, had communed with the sleek otter instead.

No matter: the girl must find her own nature. She was a child of the Wildwood, as he had been, before he had been forced to become something else.

It was a crumbling high wall that brought the Wildwood to an end. Through a breach they emerged into the tombyard.

Cata squinted.

The afternoon was bright. Mossy stones lay about them like dogs, slumbering shabbily in a neglected garden. There was an impending thick stillness, enmeshed with the heat, but from beyond the stillness came the clatter of drums, the scrape of the fiddle, the babble of voices from the crowded village green. The sound filled the circle of surrounding houses like a bowl, and rose, like steam or a strange offering, to the tumbledown edifice of the castle that presided, benignly on the bright day, over all.

White clouds dazzled in an azure sky.

'Oh, Papa!'

The girl forgot her fears. She danced out among the stones. Papa, still stately, planted his staff firmly in the grass between the graves and made towards the great yew in a corner of the yard.

Cata stared after him. 'Papa, not this time!'

'Every time, my child.'

She would understand some day. In the old man's heart the path to the tomb-slab was etched as deeply as the ways through the Wildwood; it was a path he must always follow. Stiffly, he bent to his knees. Twined above his head were the branches of the yew; beneath him, the roots twisted thickly in the grave-dirt.

'Ah, Yane,' the old man sighed, tracing his fingers over the letters of her name. A five-cycle had passed, and still it might have been yesterday when Yane, like a girl only sleeping, began the cold journey to what she would be for ever now: a frail cage of bones, lying beneath the earth.

The old man raised his head. He sensed the air. Nearby there were human presences, but none, he knew, could see them. His rough hand felt along the side of the slab. He clawed the moss and weeds from the mechanism.

The slab lifted silently, like the lid of a box.

Cata squatted impatiently on a grave nearby. She had seen the ceremony before and was tired of it. She could not see Mama inside the big box! There was only darkness. She stretched her finger to a strutting swallow; and the swallow, unafraid, hopped on to her hand.

> *Swallow, swallow, where have you been?*
> *My eyes in your eyes, show what you've seen.*

Cata closed her eyes, feeling the weightless pressure of the swallow's tiny claws. There came to her a confusion of greens and browns. She sensed the tap-tappings of beetles in bark and the slithering worms in the rich tombyard earth. Then there was a rush of bright blue. The weightless pressure was gone.

'Silly thing!'

Papa, standing above the tomb-slab, was mumbling now, his head bowed. Cata sprang up. She twirled twice for Mama, who lived in the earth; then lightly she ran through the sunshine, leaping across the tomb-slabs like stepping-stones. As she ran she burbled:

> *Stone, stone*
> *All alone:*
> *Earth, earth*
> *Death and birth.*

It might have been a prayer, but if it were, it would have been a prayer not to the god of the temple that rose before her, forbidding and grey, but to the spreading yew, to the soil with its tunnelling worms, to the green of the Wildwood that pressed, insistent, at the dividing tombyard wall.

'Child!'

The voice was sudden and sharp as a shot.

Cata started.

She turned, blinking. Between mossy slabs a fat form was waddling towards her from the direction of the temple.

'Would you desecrate the resting-places of the dead, child?'

It was a huge-breasted woman in a black trailing gown.

'Do you understand me, child?'

Puffing, the woman rose over Cata like a monstrous bird, too heavy for flight. A bonnet shaped like a coal scuttle was jammed on to her head and a golden pendant hung, glittering, from her neck.

'Some Vaga-brat, I'll warrant! I'll teach you respect for the Lord Agonis!'

The words meant nothing to Cata, who only stared blankly into the bloated face. The girl was standing on an ornate tomb; with a wrench the fat woman pulled her to the ground.

Then suddenly Cata was screaming and kicking.

'Let me go, let me go!'

'Let her go, Umbecca.'

'Papa!'

The fat woman relaxed her grip. Cata, after a last ineffectual kick, scurried to conceal herself behind her father's robes. She peered back at the fat woman. Piggy eyes blazed in the bursting face.

'Well, well. Silas Wolveron,' said the fat woman tartly. 'I should have known. This can't be Catayane's girl, surely?'

'I am Catayane!' Cata burst out.

But Papa's hand, smoothing her hair, seemed to bid the child be silent.

'You haven't changed, Umbecca,' was all he said, and turned to go. 'Come, child. The fair awaits.'

'Yes, take her to her kind,' the fat woman spat. 'Catayane's girl? A Vaga changeling, I'll be bound!'

'No, Umbecca. She is Yane's, can't you see?'

And turning back, the old man propelled his daughter forward. The fat woman looked the child up and down. What she saw was a scrawny urchin, a five-cycle old, with matted dark hair and a face black with dirt. The child's arms and legs were webbed with scratches and a sackcloth shift barely covered her thighs. But the fat woman saw that what the old man said was true.

Catayane's girl.

The huge breasts swelled with a slowly drawn breath.

'A disgrace.' The voice was an outraged whisper. 'A disgrace to her mother's memory, do you hear?'

'Oh, I hear you, Umbecca. I can still hear.'

Wonderingly, Cata looked back and forth between them. What did she mean, this fat woman in black? It was seldom that a villager spoke to Papa, and Cata had never heard one speak like this. For the first time there came to the girl the sense that her world, which she knew so well, was shifting, just a little, beneath her bare feet.

'Papa?' She had begun to feel a strange alarm.

But Papa only laughed. 'Oh, Umbecca, you are just the same! Come, my child.'

He turned again to go.

'You are a wicked man, Silas Wolveron!' the fat woman cried after him. 'The Lord Agonis will punish you!'

The old man's laughter ceased. As he turned again to the woman called Umbecca, he drew back the concealing cowl from his head. For an instant, the fat woman stared directly into his face: at the twisted scars that seamed his cheeks; at the empty sockets where his eyes had been.

'Can I be punished more than I have been, Umbecca?' was all he said. 'Now goodbye to you.'

And the woman called Umbecca, as she waddled away, gripped the pendant that swung from her neck and recited a prayer to the Lord Agonis.

'Papa?' Cata began, as they approached the tombyard gates. The old man had hidden his face again, and planted his staff before him with a grim determination. There were many questions the girl might have asked.

But a bright figure was somersaulting on the verge by the

gates. The village green was suddenly in view, with its milling crowds and laughter, its stripy tents and booths. Cata rushed forward, the tombyard forgotten.

The fair was upon them.

'Papa, come on!'

Chapter 3

BLUEJACKET! REDJACKET!

It was two cycles or more since the Vaga-vans had last lumbered into the village. Through the dark days of war and the cycle that followed, the Vagas had been nowhere to be seen in the valley. Some said they had retreated to the high mountains, biding their time in the thin sharp air; some said they had vanished into another world, as Vagas, some believed, had the power to do.

Cata believed it. Plunging into the alleys between the brightly painted vans, tugging eagerly at Papa's hand, she might have been herself in that other world. The crowd flowed about her like a deep, strange sea. There was incense, music, the glitter of gold. Marvelling, she pushed towards the inviting stalls, reaching for the trailing strings of beads and the spangled undulations of unfurling lengths of cloth.

'Take that! And that!'

Cata darted back. It was a little girl and boy, clashing wooden swords. Laughing, they skipped through a forest of legs. A big boy, at the coconut shy, hurled a bright ball. 'Got it!' he whooped, and leapt up in triumph. Everywhere voices called 'This way, dearie!' and 'Roll up, roll up!' There was laughter, there were jostlings, there were cheerful cries. To Cata it was all a bright world of wonder, and even the dolls on the shelves behind the stalls might have been about to break at any moment into a joyous, wild dance.

'This way, my darling!'

It was a Vaga-woman, calling her. Framed in a curtained gap between two vans, the woman was a vision of robes and flashing rings. She leant down towards the little girl.

'Do you want to see your future, child?'

Cata gasped, 'My future?'

The Vaga-woman laughed. The face beneath the turban was dark as elberries, as if she had stained the skin with the juice. In her hand she held a smoking pipe, and gestured with the stem towards the curtain behind her. It was dark blue and embroidered with stars.

Cata turned away, looking up at Papa.

'Papa, who are they?'

She meant the Vagas. There was something strange about them, Cata knew, stranger than their jewels and their dark faces and the bright dyes of their clothes.

'Papa?' Cata said again.

But the old man was silent. In the midst of the crowd, he had drifted into reverie. Intoxicatingly the alley, with its chaos of smells and sounds, brought back to him the last time the Vaga-fair had come. There it was, visible to him as if to an inner eye. Golden coins flashed in swarthy hands. Foam rolled whitely down the sides of silver tankards.

Oh, the beguiling sweet rottenness of it all!

Silas Wolveron, an old man even then, had felt none of the wonderment his daughter felt now. He had seen it all before and he had seen the truth: the chipped paint; the mildewing canvas; the faces of the Vaga-women seamed with pox. Yet on that day, the last day they had come, the shabby little fair had been transformed.

Yane, his darling girl, would meet him in the tombyard.

This way, my darling.

And for a moment as though he could really see again, the old man remembered the girl running across the tomb-slabs, her shoes in her hand and her white dress billowing back, wraith-like, as she ran. It was almost evening. Shadows fell blackly across the graves and the old man was waiting, concealed under the yew-tree. The girl gasped as she collapsed into his arms. Flakes of seed-cake clung to her lips and a rag-doll, won at the coconut shy, fell from beneath her arm to the ground.

Do you want to see your future, child?

42

And even as the old man held her in his arms, he might have heard, but for the revelry of the fair, the thud-thudding drumbeats that were coming ever nearer, converging on the village through the thick-wooded valley.

The Bluejacket army was on its way.

Silas Wolveron had the gift of night-vision. Even as a boy, when his eyes were green pools, fresh and brilliant as Cata's were now, he could shut them tight and walk in darkness. The Wildwood, with its entangling roots and branches, was etched on his senses as if on graven steel. Yet nothing could make up for the vision he had lost, and the horror of the last thing he had ever seen.

'Papa!'

He bent down to his little daughter, and Cata, looking into her father's ruined face, forgot her annoyance with the abstracted old man. She reached up, rearranging his cowl.

The afternoon passed.

Round and round the alleys they went, weaving in and out. From the coconut shy Cata won a plump rag-doll with a mouth stitched into a beaming smile. In a dark tent she gazed, intrigued and appalled, at the fish-tailed woman and her headless husband. Then Papa led her round the edge of the green on the back of a pony with a tinkling bell.

She raced back into the alleys.

There was a crazed shriek, 'Bluejacket!'

From round a twist in the alley, the shriek rang out again. It was an invitation. In the window at the top of a narrow canvas booth, a little blue man was leaping up and down.

Cata gasped, delighted.

The space before the booth was rapidly filling. There were broad backs, thick thighs, dusty trailing skirts. She craned her neck eagerly as a different cry came, 'Redjacket!'

The blue man was gone. Now a little red man was bouncing in his place.

'Bluejacket!' The blue again.

'Redjacket!' The red.

'Bluejacket!'

'Red!'

It was the Blue and Red Play. Wolveron, his hand in his daughter's hand, winced. He had not thought this sham-battle would still be fought by Vaga-puppets, so long after the real battle had been decided. To Cata, the puppets were only funny little men. What could he say to make her see? Faster and faster they bobbed up and down; first blue, then red, each shrieking out his name.

A pause; the stage was empty. Then suddenly:

Blue!

Pause.

Blue, blue, red.

When the stage was empty, Cata held her breath. To know which little man would bob up next seemed all at once the most important thing in the world.

She held up her doll, so her doll could see.

Blue!

Red!

A pause again. At the back of the stage was a picture of rolling green hills; high white mountains rose above the hills.

'Papa, it's the valley!' Cata cried.

From under the stage came the clatter of a drum. Then came Bluejacket, rising slowly. At first there was only his three-cornered hat; then his nose. How huge it was, how swollen! Then, slowly, up came the braided jacket. Flinging back his big nose, puffing out his jacket, the hideous puppet strutted back and forth. In his little hands he held a bayonet. As he strutted he boomed out proudly:

> I'm a soldier of the blue cloth
> The only true cloth!
> I serve the true king
> I serve the blue king!

There were hisses and catcalls; then laughter as the little man stared at the crowd malevolently, jabbing with his bayonet.

44

'Traitor!' called a voice.

The blue man seemed to grow uglier and uglier. His hat was squashed down over mean slits of eyes and his jacket strained over his misshapen form. He resumed, ever more swaggering and defiant:

> *Blue! Blue! The king that's true!*
> *True! True! The king that's blue!*

Only when the jeering had died down was the nasty blue man replaced by the red.

> *I raise my voice and I proudly sing*
> *Ejard Red is the rightful king!*

With his plump cheeks and his happy smile, the red man contrasted strikingly with the blue. His bayonet was not aimed angrily at the crowd; it was thrust back over his shoulder. His uniform was resplendent and adorned with medals. As he marched, his back was stiff and straight. The crowd cheered. At the climax of the song the alley rang out to a thunder of voices, joining in:

> *We raise our voices and proudly sing*
> *Ejard Red is the—*
> *Ejard Red is the—*

'Oh Papa, I do like the little red man!' Cata twisted her head back happily.

> *Ejard Red is the king!*

'Papa?'

Where was he? He had let go of her hand. Cata was wedged between the ample skirt and breeches of a fat old woman and a fatter old man. Red-faced and raucous, they swayed from side to side, her skirt and his breeches parting, then opening, like thick smelly curtains.

Cata writhed.

Cleaving the air above her head, a silver tankard in the fat man's fist slopped sticky foam down the back of her neck. She thumped at the smelly curtains, breaking suddenly free.

'Papa?'

Moments passed before she saw his cowled head, rising like a rock above the surface of the stream. By the blue curtain with embroidered stars he was speaking to the Vaga-woman who had said to her: *Do you want to see your future, child?* With a flash of rings the woman took Papa's sleeve. He inclined his head. The curtain billowed back as they vanished between it.

'Papa!' Cata stamped her foot. Why had he left her? On the puppet-stage, Bluejacket and Red were circling, snarling; there was a clash of bayonets, but Cata did not see. She turned fiercely, this way and that.

Then she saw the harlequin.

Chapter 4

THE TINY SUN

The harlequin's hands flapped alarmingly in the air. Bony like a skeleton's, at any moment they might have slipped suddenly free, skittering over the crowd like ungainly, ugly butterflies. A mad thing in motley, he was long-limbed and lean, each part of him tethered to the others, it seemed, only by the flimsiest of loosely knotted thongs. Bright bells jingled on his cap and a silver mask concealed his eyes. Twisting, writhing, darting forward and back, he careered through the crowd like a particoloured whirlwind. Villagers pointed and laughed. As he capered, he sang merrily; silly things like:

> *Double, double,*
> *The cat's in trouble,*
> *She's licked up all the cream!*

or:

> *Little bird, little bird, fly away quickly*
> *Here comes a boy with a stone!*

Between verses he snatched a green reed from the waistband of his breeches, piping soaring cadenzas. Behind him, huffing and puffing, there scuttled the podgy figure of a dun-coloured dwarf, his short arms turning frantically at the heavy hurdy-gurdy that was strapped across his chest. Children scampered in their wake; Cata scampered with them.

The harlequin sang:

> *Stir a cup of sparkling mead*
> *Drink it down and then proceed*
> *To tumble, jumble, in your cups*
> *Like a hog who greedy sups*

And rolls in mud like you,
Mistress,
Rolls in filth like you,
Master,
Rolls in dung like you!

The bright figure span back on his heels towards the children. He bowed low. They had reached the edge of the village green. The hurdy-gurdy made a last exhausted wheeze as the dwarf collapsed beneath a shady elm.

Go, go! he seemed to say, shooing away the children with his fat little hands.

The children only laughed at him.

The harlequin remained bent, fixed in the scraping bow. Then, rising slowly, still half-crouching, he paced back and forth with long emphatic strides. His head jingled as he swivelled in a mime of furtiveness, this way and that. He might have been a hunter, intent on his prey, if a hunter had gone forth in cap and bells.

He darted behind the trunk of the tree.

There was a pause; then the masked face peered back round the trunk.

'Barnabas, play!' came the hissed command; and the dwarf, with an exhausted groan, turned the handle of the hurdy-gurdy again.

From behind the trunk came a watery arc of gold. Glittering, it rose high, then gurgled, steaming, into the parched grass.

The children squealed and clapped.

'Harlequin, some magic!' a boy demanded, when the harlequin reappeared. The boy, a podgy, spotty creature, was bigger than the other children, and older; he was their leader. His hair was bright orange, the colour of a carrot.

'Magic! Magic!' the children chorused, and Cata, on the edge of their little group, joined them.

The motley figure obliged. Flapping long hands with a shushing motion, he pirouetted slowly, then stood poised, a bony index finger laid on his lips. The eyes behind the silver mask gazed up thoughtfully.

'Barnabas?'

The harlequin did not turn round. The dwarf, expiring after his last burst of accompaniment, had slumped back a little too far against the tree. Pinioned beneath the heavy hurdy-gurdy, he waved his little arms and legs helplessly in the air.

The children giggled.

'Barnabas, really!'

The harlequin grabbed the little man by the shoulders and shoved him impatiently back in place. Wearily, the dwarf's hands set themselves in motion. This time the tune was not a merry jig, but a meandering undulation of almost tuneless sound. It curled from the hurdy-gurdy like incense smoke, and set in motion by the strange sound, with long limbs slithering on the air like serpents, twisting and writhing, the harlequin danced.

It was beautiful and eerie, and as Cata watched, the thought came to her that the motley figure was leading her, in some mysterious inward way, into a labyrinth. She was frightened, but excited, too. She had thought the Vaga-fair was another world; but in the harlequin's dance she glimpsed another world again. The bright sun sparkled on his bells like gold; the dwarf's peculiar music seemed to curl round him like vines; and when the boy who had demanded magic called out impatiently for the magic to begin, Cata could only wonder what the boy could mean. It seemed to her that the harlequin's dance was the magic he had promised.

He arched back his head, his throat stretching taut. Jingling his bells, his motley limbs twitching, he might have been about to sprawl backwards on the grass. Only the music seemed to tether him upright.

He jerked forward suddenly, slumping to his knees. One hand he stretched skywards, fingers splayed; the other, he cupped beneath his open mouth. His shoulders shuddered and the outstretched hand clutched and unclutched urgently at the air. He retched loudly; then vomited a golden coin.

The children only stared, solemn like the harlequin, as he passed the coin slowly before their eyes. Cata craned forward eagerly to see. The coin, glistening with spit, was stamped with a swirling pattern.

The harlequin lifted his hand above his head. The coin rose like a tiny sun, and all the children watched it rise, silent and intent.

There was a last flash of flame and the coin was gone.

The harlequin displayed his empty hands. He shrugged. He prowled back and forth. Like a stealthy spider he retreated and advanced: then he pounced on the carrot-haired boy. For an instant the boy struggled, then was still, as the harlequin's bony fingers forced his lips apart. The coin, covered in drool, tumbled from the boy's mouth.

The boy sank to his knees, gasping.

Again the coin passed before the fascinated children.

Again it rose like a tiny sun, then vanished.

Three times the harlequin repeated the trick; each time he produced the coin from the mouth of a different child. And all the time the dwarf's music kept on playing, twisting and turning through its labyrinth of air.

Cata's heart pounded. Already she seemed to feel the coin in her throat, and the harlequin's fingers pushing between her lips.

She gripped her doll tightly.

She wanted it to happen.

But the music was winding down. The hurdy-gurdy gave a last tuneless wheeze and the dwarf fell forward in an exhausted slumber. Was the enchantment broken? The harlequin stretched. He yawned. He turned his back on the children and flung himself down beside his little companion.

The carrot-haired boy demanded, 'Harlequin, the gold!'

His voice was hoarse.

But the harlequin, propped against the trunk of the tree,

had closed his eyes already. His bells jingled as the boy shook his shoulders.

'Harlequin!'

Smiling, the harlequin opened just one eye behind the holes in his silver mask. Languidly, he stretched out a long arm and pointed the way back towards the crowded alleys. And though the children had not played this game before, they understood at once that the coin was hidden somewhere, further afield this time, and that they must find it.

They scuttled away; Cata followed.

Cata had been afraid of other children until now. On the few occasions when Papa had taken her into the village, she had held his hand tightly, and when the children had looked at her, she had looked away. But secretly, when they could not see her, she had seen them.

Many times, she had spied on the carrot-haired boy and his friends. They were older than Cata, perhaps by a full cycle; but the girl could not help longing to be one of them. In the Season of Agonis, peering over the frosty tombyard wall, she had watched them in their thick coats on the white village green, pelting each other with snowballs; in the hot days of the Season of Theron, the girl had shadowed them as they wound their way through the Wildwood. She thought of them as strange animals whose language she could not speak; and yet she wanted to join in their games. Only fear held Cata back; fear and an awareness of the barrier, like the tombyard wall, that rose between herself and them. But in the harlequin's dance there had been no barrier at all.

She was one of them; she could run with them.

She had not run three steps when the carrot-haired boy rounded on her, suddenly fierce. The milky face beneath the bright hair was spattered with freckles. The thick lips curled into a sneer.

'Go away, Vaga-brat!'

Cata was startled.

'But—'

51

The boy stamped his foot.

The children's high laughter echoed behind Cata as she blundered away, her eyes blurring.

Under the elm tree, the harlequin was sleeping.

Chapter 5

SCANDAL IN THE LECTORY

'Nothing?' the old man said.

'Nothing.'

But the voice was tender. With coarse fingertips, the Vaga-woman traced the seams of the mutilated face. She sighed. There were powers she possessed that the peoples of this land would call powers of darkness. There were bitter herbs, there were roots and sticky clays, which her tribe had come to know in the aeons of its wanderings; there were rare powders kept in pouches of leather; there were oils in stoppered vials.

None would avail.

Her touch lingered over the empty eye-sockets. 'Ah, half-brother! How weak we are, when we think ourselves so strong! The old wisdom holds sway over the errors of nature, but our power is helpless against the fruits of men's evil. I'm sorry, Silas.'

'No, Xal. No, I knew as much.'

Old Wolveron sought her hand. In his darkness he was aware of her robes, pungent as spice, and the tart tang of smoke from her pipe. With his night-vision he pictured the scene: in a gloomy tent behind the backs of vans, they sat at a small, round table. On the table lay a thick brocade cloth; on the cloth was a heavy sphere of glass. Golden lamplight suffused the acrid darkness.

This was the den of the Woman of Wisdom.

'Ah, Xal! It's been such a long time.'

'It is the destiny of our race to bide our time.'

'Do you still believe it?' said the old man after a moment.

It was a question that came to him sometimes, nagged at him, in his cave in the Wildwood.

'That we are only waiting? I believe that all things must pass. But half-brother, you are one of us. You have in you The Rapture. Can you not feel the change, in the fabric of the air?'

Xal's free hand hovered over the sphere; Wolveron sensed the faint surge inside the glass. There was a quiver, barely perceptible, in the air around them.

'I feel only the imprint of the past,' the old man said.

'Then all you feel will slip from you.'

And Xal's hand slipped from his.

They sipped their bitter, steaming tea.

'The Time of Atonement is ending, Silas. You feel that, don't you?'

'I feel something, Xal. I feel fear for the future. Not for myself; my life is done. But I feel fear for my child.'

A catch came into Xal's voice. 'Silas, I know the fear of which you speak. My own child is already a man, and strong; I am frightened for him, too. But half-brother, you must not weaken. The time is coming. You have a part to play.'

Pain welled behind the old man's empty eyes. It was a familiar pain. 'Xal, I shall try. But you forget, I am only half your kind. Half of me is an Ejlander.'

'I don't forget it, Silas. It is the central fact of your life.'

The old woman leaned back, sucking at her pipe. In memory Silas saw its ornate carved bowl, its sinuous stem. Silence fell between them and the muted sounds of the fair seemed to grow louder in the perfumed gloom: the wheezing melodies, the shrieks of laughter that might have echoed from a distant place.

Then all at once Old Wolveron laughed, too. His laughter was soundless, but deep, and coursed through his body in heaves like sobs.

It was alarming.

'I'm sorry, Xal,' he gasped. 'It struck me, that's all: the

comedy of it! All those cycles fighting back the Vaga in me. And now . . .'

He gestured about him; and Xal, seeing the joke, could not but smile. There flashed upon her mind a vision of her half-brother as she had seen him the first time, so many cycles earlier: a pallid, thin young man in a high-collared suit, the Circle of Agonis glinting against the shiny black of his chest.

Your camp has been the scene of lewdness and impiety. I have come to demand that your tribe move on.

Xal had been just another Vaga-wench then, serving at her father's table when her father was Vaga-king. Then, it had been Xal's turn to laugh; she laughed aloud, and her father did not check her. He propelled a spurt of Jarvel-juice from his lips and gazed wryly at the visitor.

So, so! The Lector of Irion! Boy, tell me: have you anything between your legs? Or do they cut it off?

The young man flushed darkly, angry and ashamed. He clutched his pendant. Could the power of his faith have struck down the Vaga-king, Silas Wolveron would have called on it then. He was filled with righteous fervour. How strange it is, the distance one may travel in a lifetime! The young Wolveron and the old man he had become were opposites.

Or were they?

His half-sister, seeing him that day, had felt for the first time the stirrings of her own power. She saw his future enclosed in him like a bitter, hard tuber, waiting to sprout. Then she ceased laughing, and felt tenderly towards him.

She had not known he was her half-brother then.

Silas Wolveron had been Lector of Irion for the length of almost eight cycles when the scandal had occurred which so shocked the village. It had not been wholly unexpected, it was true. Wolveron had been a good Lector, much admired, generous and kind and endowed, it seemed, with the expected fiery piety; but in his last cycle or so there had been signs, too many, of a growing oddity.

It began with the Glass Room, the curious edifice he had built at the side of the Lectory, with walls and ceiling alike made of panels of glass. He filled the room with plants and flowers; then he had his huge desk brought in and would sit writing his canonicals and tending to lectorate business in the middle of this artificial forest. He would even take tea there, with members of the congregated! One respectable widow reported that the Lector had barely looked at her throughout, instead gazing distractedly around him at the foliage and up at the clouds through the glass above his head.

Then there were those who said the Lector had been wandering in the Wildwood, muttering to himself and running his hands back and forth along the trunks of trees. One night in the local tavern, a young woodcutter even claimed that he had been about to set to work on a sturdy oak when all at once a creature in ragged robes had burst out from the undergrowth, demanding that he desist. This had been shocking enough; but imagine his horror, whispered the woodcutter, wide-eyed, when he had looked into the creature's face. *It was the Lector*. Some did not believe it, but next day the story had spread through the valleys.

Soon there were other stories, and some were worse. Some said they had seen the Lector coming back from a Vaga-camp; not dressed, this time, in the garb of the Order. The Lectory servants spoke of chantings behind locked doors and sudden changes of mood. The cook whispered to a neighbour one day that Lector Wolveron had refused her best herb-mutton, and declared that he would no longer consume the flesh of beasts! The poor woman had almost burst into tears; but the very next day, she said in wonderment, the Lector seemed simply to have forgotten what he had said, and called for his favourite pheasant-in-Varl-wine!

It was very odd. It was too odd.

Soon there were the times during the canonical itself when the Lector would seem to lose himself, becoming suddenly distant. The congregated would be left to sit in awkward silence, shuffling their feet and shifting their eyes to each other, back and forth, nervously. Was the Lector unwell?

Uneasy murmurings began. The Maximate would have to be informed. Irion's, after all, was a wealthy temple, an important one, endowed generously by the Archduke's ancestors. This could not go on. But Lector Wolveron had been a popular figure for many cycles. When the Archduke's sister-in-law, the pious spinster Umbecca Rench, was asked to intervene, she rejected the proposal violently, declaring her absolute faith in the Lector.

It was a declaration she would live to regret.

The crisis had come in an unexpected fashion.

In the Season of Theron just before the war, a young girl from Agondon had been staying in the castle. The girl, Yane Rench, was the cousin of the Archduke's late wife, Lady Ruanna, and her sister, Umbecca. Lady Ruanna had been a great beauty; and in Miss Rench, it was said, the charms of her dead cousin had been created afresh. The Archduke, clearly, would ask her to marry him. It was hardly thought that the girl would refuse. It would be a splendid match; and after all, the Renches were by no means rich. Think of it! The girl would be 'Lady Catayane'!

It was not to be.

The fact of Yane's refusal was bad enough, but when the truth of her affections came to light, Irion and all the valleys reeled in horror. It was, quite simply, the most shocking exhibition of immorality that any of the inhabitants had witnessed. Whether the worst depravity lay on the Lector's side, or the girl's, was a subject of much debate; though many found themselves agreeing that it was, surely, on the girl's. Wolveron was a Received man and sworn to celibacy; but he was old and mad and sick. Catayane Rench was a girl in her prime, loved by all and with splendid prospects before her – and all she could do was throw them away! The old man and the girl retreated to a cave in the Wildwood, to indulge their filthy passions.

Both, it was later said, received their just deserts. The girl died, apparently in childbirth. Wolveron, after the war, was arraigned as a traitor.

It was not for his guilt with Yane Rench that the old man lost his eyes; Ejland, after all, was a civilized country. Rather it was the case that Lector Wolveron was believed to have smuggled certain secrets into the castle during the Siege. His crime was one of war, against the Bluejacket victors; but even those who felt contempt for the victors could not quell a certain satisfaction in themselves that 'Eyeless Silas', as they now would call him, had at last received the punishment he deserved.

It was Umbecca Rench who had paid for Yane's slab in the tombyard.

But she had never forgiven Yane.

And she had never forgiven Silas Wolveron.

'Had I been always bound to fall, Xal?' the old man asked now.

'But, half-brother, of course. We can conceal ourselves. But not for ever.'

Xal took his hand again. Fondly she recalled the day when he had come to her in the Vaga-camp and declared, at last, his kinship with their kind.

And his kinship with her.

Poor Silas! How he had suffered! And how he would suffer! For it was now, as she looked into his face, that the Woman of Wisdom felt a new, disturbing awareness. There was a watery shimmer in the globe of glass. Could this be part of the destiny before them?

'Silas! Your night-vision—'

'Yes.' His voice was a whisper. 'It was what I meant, Xal.'

'You didn't say . . .'

'I knew you would see it.'

The old man bowed his head. A silent knowledge passed between the half-siblings, and Xal knew that a time would come when Old Wolveron would be truly blind. Perhaps not soon, but it would come. Already, his world was growing dim.

'An error of nature, is it not?'

'Yes, Silas. Nature. We are growing old.' The catch had come back into Xal's voice; Old Wolveron was aware, of course he was aware, that what she said was not quite true. The glowing metal that had seared out his eyes had seared his brain too. Tender, tiny connections inside him were fraying; in time, all his senses would be taken from him. He would die in a feelingless, dark silence.

Xal had retreated into the depths of her lair; when she returned, she pressed a small bag into her half-brother's hand. His fingers closed around it; it was strangely heavy.

'A sand, half-brother. Bright and glittering. Very rare; and all I have. From ... oh, a land far beyond the westerly islands ...'

Wolveron smiled. Was there a land beyond the westerly islands? Unknowingly, Xal had slipped into her Woman of Wisdom voice, rich in mystery and portent.

'Mix with earth from the Wildwood floor: earth plenteous with spores and the crumblings of dead leaves and the dry discarded carapaces of beetle-wings ...'

'The ordure of owls?'

'Yes. Make a rich, soothing mud. A lush viscidity ...'

'Yes. Yes.'

Xal desisted.

'But only when the time has come, Silas,' she added. She had been speaking lightly, to cover her pain; but Xal was not speaking lightly now. An awareness had dawned in her, one deeper than before. There was something that she knew.

The old man sensed it and nodded solemnly.

'I shall play my part, Xal.'

From outside, there came shrieks of laughter. There were cheers. The puppet-play was nearing its climax, in the carnage of a final conflict between Blue and Red. It would end differently from the one in reality.

Drunken voices roared raucous approval.

'I must retrieve the girl. I should not have left her.' Wolveron concealed the bag of sand inside his robes.

'Bring her to me, Silas. Let me read her.'

'Xal, she is young,' said the old man kindly. 'Let her be.'

The half-siblings embraced. They were standing at the curtain that was embroidered with stars, and Xal found herself wondering: could Silas see the stars? She had never quite known what his night-vision saw.

'They frighten me sometimes,' Xal said, as the crowd exulted in the Bluejacket's death. 'I wonder if what they want is justice. Or only death. And death. And death.'

'Don't you know?'

Suddenly, Xal pressed his hand. 'Silas, come with us. We can take care of you. And the girl . . .'

'We are creatures of the Wildwood, Xal.'

She nodded sadly; he was right. It had been one of her own moments of doubt. But how could she doubt? It was all beginning.

It was beginning now.

Xal swept back the curtain with her gnarled, ringed fingers. At once she cried, plucking at a stranger's arm, 'Good sir! Let me show you your future!'

'I have none with you, crone.'

'My friends, come! Ah, I see the silver glinting in your hands!'

'Child? Child?' Old Wolveron called.

Already the crowd had separated the half-siblings. Milling bodies surrounded the old man and he gripped his staff tightly, shaking his head as if to clear his night-vision.

It was clouding; there was no doubt it was clouding.

'Eyeless Silas!' a cruel voice called.

'Eyeless Silas!'

'Eyeless Silas!'

It was a chant he had heard before. At another time, he would have reflected sadly on the cruelty that children are taught, or know, so soon. Today the old man only moved on, oblivious, seeking his own child.

'Child?' he called again. 'Child?'

Chapter 6

FIVE FROM IRION

'So where is it, then? Bean?'

'I don't think we'll find it, Polty.'

'What's that, Bean? You're mumbling.'

'I said we can't find it.'

'*We can't find it!*' Polty imitated Bean's reedy, nervous voice. 'You're such a girl, Bean! Tyl? What do you think?'

'Search me, Polty.'

'What's that? You've got it, have you, Tyl?'

'No, I didn't mean—'

Tyl squealed as Polty wrestled her to the ground.

'Polty—' Bean attempted.

Taunting the old blind man had been only a diversion. It was time to resume the quest in earnest. The crowd parted, making way for the children. Some people laughed. Some looked annoyed. The little boy called Bean gazed down anxiously at his two rowdy friends, rolling in the dust. Where was Leny? Where was Vel? If he were a stronger boy, and a different sort of boy, Bean might have joined the fray, dragging Polty away from the girl. But Bean, like Tyl, was thin and light and weak; Polty was plump, heavy and strong.

Tyl's squeals grew louder as Polty ripped her dress. The ripping sound seemed to bring the fat boy to his senses and he sprang away from the girl. But he was unabashed. He grinned, dusting off his breeches.

'What are you looking at Bean, eh?'

Bean was looking at Tyl, who was looking at her dress. Her mother had made it specially for the fair. The little girl's eyes filled with tears.

'She said she had the coin!'

'D-don't be silly, Polty,' mumbled Bean.

'Bean, you're mumbling again! Hey, where have you two been?' This was addressed to Leny and Vel, who had straggled back through the crowd, arm in arm, giggling.

'We've been to the Woman of Wisdom,' said Leny proudly. 'Guess what she said, Polty? She said we'll be together all our lives, me and Vel. She said we'll be together even in The Vast!'

But Polty wasn't interested.

'You still had some coins?' was all he said, outraged. 'You didn't tell me!'

Wasting coins on the Woman of Wisdom! Polty would have used them at the coconut-shy. He scowled and kicked his foot against the side of a Vaga-van. He might have kicked Leny or Vel instead, but Leny, unlike Tyl, was a plump, sturdy girl, and Vel was the blacksmith's boy. He was strong.

'Hey!' came a voice from inside the van.

Polty grinned. He kicked the van again and took to his heels, signalling for his friends to follow.

There were five of them, so they called themselves The Five, or sometimes, The Five from Irion. Carrot-haired Polty had been their leader from the first. He had a kind of power, though sometimes Leny and Vel might forget it. They would get too wrapped up in each other, and ignore Polty. Polty didn't like that.

Polty would say he was strongest of The Five. He could say this, and get away with it, because Vel would never challenge him. They all knew this; but then, no one challenged Polty, unless of course you counted his father. Of all the children, Polty lived in the nicest house. His mother and father were the richest. But the other children wouldn't want to live in Polty's house. Polty was often punished cruelly, beaten and whipped. He would be punished tonight, Bean had no doubt, for running away to the Vaga-fair. Goodman Waxwell was very strict. Sometimes, when The Five went swimming, Polty wouldn't take off his shirt. They all knew why.

✳

'I want that gold,' said Polty when the five children flopped down, puffed out, on the grass. Weaving through the bright, pungent lanes of the fair, they had fetched up in a little gap between the tents and the vans, like a clearing in a forest. No one was watching them.

'Give it up, Polty,' said plump Leny. 'It was just some dirty Vaga-trick.'

'It was real! It was in my mouth!'

Polty was sulking.

Bean looked nervously at his carrot-haired friend. The afternoon had worn on and they were all irritable. They had looked at all the freaks and they had been to all the stalls. They had made themselves sick on sugared small-beer and sticky Vaga-bread; the girls and Bean had ridden the pony twice around the green while Polty and Vel ran behind them and jeered. Now the children had no more coins and they were all hot and tired. Polty might do something nasty soon.

Something else.

Shyly, Bean moved closer to Tyl, who was pretending she didn't really care about her dress. It was a very pretty dress, made of bright red cloth. Bean wondered if his mother might fix it, before Tyl went home. He didn't suppose so. Bean's mother kept the tavern, and had no time.

'You know how much you could get with that gold?'

'Shut it, Polty,' said Leny. She was picking dandelions and blowing them over Vel. Polty looked annoyed. He ripped up a clump of weeds and threw it at the girl. There was a clod of dirt attached.

'Hey!'

'All right for you, isn't it? You've got some coins still, haven't you, Len?'

'No!' The plump girl pouted defiantly. 'I've got none, Vel's got none, we've all got none. And you had more than all of us, Polty . . .'

It was true. Before the fair, Polty had stolen a whole bag of silver from Goodman Waxwell's desk. Polty was greedy, that was his trouble. But Bean didn't like to think that. Polty was his best friend, after all.

'Shh! Look!'

It was Tyl. She had found something.

Their little clearing was a very noisy place. In the lanes, they had started up the Vaga-play again, and the crowd was singing loudly. But Tyl, leaning against the back of a van, had heard a different, softer sound. A weak, plaintive sound. She twisted about and peered beneath the van. In the shadows, on a discarded sack, was a mother cat and her kittens. All the children huddled about to see.

'Aren't they lovely?' Tyl's elfin face was overspread with wonderment. She counted the kittens, out loud, on her fingers. 'There's five of them, Polty!' she squealed, delighted. 'We could have one each!'

It was a silly thought. Bean's mother would never let him have one. Nor would Polty's father.

The fat boy sniffed.

'It's only a mangy old cat,' he said. 'Do you want to see a joke?' he added, after a moment.

The children, a little reluctantly, turned their attention towards him. Sometimes Polty had secrets and sometimes he had jokes. The secrets were things he had stolen from Goodman Waxwell's. Goodman Waxwell had lots of interesting things. Funny bottles and potions. Once Polty made Bean drink from a purple bottle, and poor Bean had thrown up for the rest of the day. The jokes were things like the time they all hid on top of Farmer Orly's haystack and threw down rotten turnips at Goody Orly, when her back was turned. When she found out, she chased them off with a broomstick. It was so funny!

Polty's jokes were always funny.

His hand darted beneath the van. Tyl gasped. Polty was fat, but he was not clumsy. Swiftly he drew forth the mother cat, holding her up by the scruff of her neck. The cat clawed the air, wanting to scratch him, but his grip was too tight.

He grinned.

'Puss-puss . . .'

He stroked the cat's whiskers.

She was a skinny, flea-bitten, mongrel cat. There were bits of black in her and bits of white, but her coat was mostly made up of gingery stripes. The kittens under the van were mewing for her bitterly.

Put her down, Polty, Bean wanted to say.

But somehow he couldn't. He looked nervously at Tyl.

This was Polty's joke:

With one hand, he held the cat by the head, clamping his fingers tight about her jaw. In his other hand, he held her back legs. He raised his arms above his head and stretched them wide.

Bean looked between the faces of his friends. Leny and Vel were smiling; even Tyl smiled, too. They were all strangely entranced. They had seen the harlequin's magic: this was Polty's. The cat was extended like a concertina. She was so long!

But that was not the joke.

Polty counted to five.

Then Polty pulled.

The action was a swift, snapping jerk. There was a crack, like a shot.

The children were too shocked even to gasp.

Polty had broken the cat's spine.

He lowered her to the grass. Carefully, almost tenderly, he laid her on her stomach. The sound of mewing still came, wildly now, from beneath the van.

For a moment the gingery body heaved, convulsing. Then the front paws clawed at the grass. The cat was trying to crawl back to her kittens, but the back part of her body was a useless burden. Afterwards, Polty would imitate, with a grin, the scrambling, paddling action of those weak front paws, as the back paws trailed behind.

That was the joke.

Chapter 7

JEM VEXING

'Yane? Dance, Yane!'

Again the rag-doll raised her prone form; again she strutted the mossy stage, kicking her floppy legs weakly into the air. Forwards, backwards, backwards and forwards, Yane was dancing the dance of death.

She slumped down again. Her face, still fixed in its idiot grin, was stained green with moss. Her head lolled, twisted awry. Sand ran from a hole in the rough stitching of her neck.

Cata shook her.

'Bad Yane!'

But the game had grown dull. Squatting on the slab beneath the spreading yew, the girl looked about her. An hour had passed. The sun had begun its long downward journey; black shadows cut sharply over the tombyard.

Cata wiped her nose on her wrist. A grey squirrel was looking at her quizzically. She closed her eyes. For a moment she saw herself as the squirrel saw her: a little girl hunched on her mother's grave, forlornly tormenting a lifeless doll.

She sprang up.

'Damn!'

It was a word the village-brats would say; they thought it was a bad word.

She said it again.

'Damn!'

How she hated the carrot-haired boy! Again she saw him turning back to face her, his thick lip curling. The other children had turned, too. Two skinny boys and two girls, one small and one tall, they followed the carrot-haired boy in all he did. They sneered when he sneered. They laughed when he laughed.

Cata kicked at the tussocky grass, once for the leader and four times for the gang. She knew what they were like; she had always known. She had seen them sprawled by the river, tempting sleek fish with hooks and wires; she had seen them hurling stones at robins in the trees.

Cata forgot her tormented doll and scuffed miserably amongst the overgrown graves. The sun between the shadows in the tombyard was intense. There was a sharp-edged line between light and shade; it might have been a crack in the parching earth. Cata followed it, her head hanging.

It was when she looked up that she saw the flash.

There was a second flash; then a third. She screwed up her eyes. It came again, golden, pulsing like a signal, from the dark shadows of the temple portico. She turned her head, this way and that. Cautiously, Cata approached the temple.

It was a study in decay. Turned half away from the high tombyard gates, the temple rose from the overgrown path as if it were itself a vast neglected tomb, a grand vault in a city of humble slabs. The tilting spire looked set to topple. The heavy pediment sagged dangerously forward. Fronds of ivy clawed thickly up the façade and hung in ragged curtains between the high columns of the portico.

There was a soft sound of creaking.

It was not until she stood at the foot of the steps that Cata saw clearly what she wanted to see. In the shadowy cave between the central columns she saw the temple portals, rising massy and ornate; she saw the barricades set shabbily before them – the weathered planks, the rusted chains; and before the chained and boarded doors, moving first a little forward, then a little back, in time to the flashings of the golden pulse, she saw the dark figure, dozing in the rocking-chair.

It was the woman called Umbecca. The pulse of light was

a sliver of the sun, striking the pendant that hung from her neck.

Forward, backward; forward, back.

Flash.

Flash.

Cata ascended the temple steps. Sleeping, the woman filled her not with fear, not with dislike, but with a curiosity at once idle yet intent. The face beneath the bonnet was sagging and lined. Broken veins webbed the plump cheeks and there was a pale fuzz of fur on the woman's upper lip. Her mouth hung open, breathing in and out.

Cata moved closer.

A bee, heavy with pollen, meandered on the air. Bright-winged, it shimmered in the sliver of sun. With sudden spite, Cata cupped her hand. She reached up, impelling the bee towards the wet cave of the mouth.

The cave snorted.

Cata leapt back – but not before an object had fallen into her palm. She clutched it. From behind a curtain of ivy, she peered, more warily now, at the woman called Umbecca. Had she swallowed the bee? Still the chair rocked in an unbroken rhythm; the snort had subsided into a huffing snore. Looking down, Cata slowly opened her palm. The object she had clutched was round and weighty; it was glistening and golden; it was slimy as snot. Her heart exulted. She had found the treasure.

That was when a piping, imperious voice sounded from the shadowier depths of the portico:

'Who are you?'

Cata jumped, and the coin fell from her hand.

A small face was staring at her intently.

The face belonged to a boy, but one very different from the village boys that Cata had seen. His clothes were odd. He wore a black, shiny suit with a high, stiff collar. A head of colourless, lank hair was surmounted by a wide-brimmed, cylindrical hat. He was very pale. He looked very clean. Propped against the temple doors, the boy sat motionless, his legs jutting woodenly beneath a thick blanket.

'I am Jemany Jorvel Torvester Ixiter of Irion, nephew and direct lineal heir of Jorvel-Jorvel Torvester Ixiter, forty-eighth Archduke of Irion,' he said. 'Or I would be, except that I'm a Vexing. So they call me "Jem Vexing". Are you a Vaga?'

Cata's brow furrowed. Why did people think she was a Vaga? The woman called Umbecca and the carrot-haired boy had flung the word at her like an accusation, but this boy's tone was coolly unchanging, level and hollow as the pealing of a bell. Anxiously she glanced towards the rocking-chair, fearful that the sleeping fat woman might stir.

'Yes, what a pity Aunt is asleep. Shall we wake her?'

Cata stepped back. She was ready to run.

'I suppose you're afraid of the Circle,' said the boy. 'Aunt said you would shrink from the symbol of truth.' With a jerky hand, he indicated his chest. Hanging from a chain around his neck was a pendant like the one the fat woman wore, a gold inverted V enclosed within a circle. 'You shan't be permitted to desecrate the temple – you know that, I suppose?'

Cata did not. Curiosity impelled her; she moved closer to the boy. He could have been a species of Wildwood creature, but one whose mind was closed to her. Something in her wanted to laugh at him, at his silly names and pealing, precise voice; something else remained apprehensive. There was a ghostly quality in the boy, in his face and voice, and for an instant Cata wondered if he were quite alive. She shuddered. Might he, perhaps, be some strange half-and-half thing, some offspring of the dead who lay all around?

'I had rather hoped a Vaga would come,' the boy went on. 'Aunt said once there was no difference between a Vexing and a Vaga, but I don't think that can be true, do you? I think Aunt was annoyed when she said it, so perhaps she didn't mean it. Sometimes she says things she doesn't mean. When she's annoyed, I mean.'

'I'm not a Vaga.'

'Of course you are.' The boy's nose wrinkled. 'Aunt says Vaga-brats are never washed. Their hair crawls with lice and their clothes are infested with fleas. Or is it the other way round? Anyway, that's why I don't think a Vaga is a Vexing. Are you a girl?' he added.

Cata coloured. The otter, that morning by the stream, had told her she must bathe. She had denied it indignantly. Now, standing before this pale boy, she knew that it was true. Her face and hands were filthy. There was dirt under her nails. Her hair was matted with grease and sticking burrs.

Yet Cata would rather be dirty, as she was, than clean like this boy.

She did not answer his question.

'What's a Vexing, then?' she asked instead.

'You mean you don't know?' The boy was scornful. 'It's something special. Very special.'

The girl was unconvinced. She toyed with a frond of ivy. 'If you're so special, why aren't you at the fair?' she said suddenly.

The boy looked down. There was a crack in the level voice. 'The fair is evil. It is a defiance of Agonis. Aunt says—'

'There's something wrong with you,' Cata said.

She moved closer. She hovered over the boy, intrigued. When he looked up at her, the eyes in the white face were dark, deep pools.

They flashed fire.

'You stink, Vaga-brat! Leave me alone!'

Cata, the impulse of cruelty suddenly strong in her, only laughed. Then her laugh froze. The boy's thin arms were grasping at the shadows. He seemed to be trying to pull himself away from her, out from under the gaze of her mocking face.

Now Cata understood.

The legs beneath the blanket were brittle sticks, twisted at tortured angles.

She dropped back, abashed.

'You can't walk,' she said.

It was then, as if with deliberation, that the boy began to shriek. It was the bell-pealing, resumed at a higher pitch; it was the cry of a bird that some cruel, impervious hand was holding into a flame.

'What? What?'

The rocking-chair was still, and the face in the black bonnet swivelled towards the boy.

The shriek ended precisely as the fat woman awoke.

'You were sleeping, Aunt.'

'Nonsense, Jem. The righteous do not slumber in the service of Agonis.' She stifled a yawn. 'You called out? Someone was here?'

'No, aunt.'

There was a rasp of ivy.

'What was that?'

'A bird,' Jem said.

It was Cata's feet, shifting; she had plummeted into the shadows just in time. Her heart thumped. Already she seemed to feel the fat woman's grip, tightening on her shoulder.

But the boy said nothing.

The fat woman sighed. She heaved herself from the chair. 'I thought I heard a bird. Oh, dear.' Discreetly she adjusted her clothing, plucking at the cloth that stuck hotly to her thighs.

'Aunt, what is a Vexing?'

'Jem, really! Why even do you ask?'

'It's my name, isn't it? Jem Vexing.'

The fat woman pursed her lips. She might have been deciding to say nothing; instead, she decided that truth was best.

'*Vexing*, Jem, is a nice word for *bastard*.'

There was a pause.

'Aunt, what's a bastard?'

The response came inevitably.

'*Bastard*, Jem, is a nasty word for *Vexing*.'

'Oh.'

Pause.

'Aunt, when will the Vagas come?'

Cata stiffened. Was the boy playing a game? Would his thin arm, encased in black, point in sudden triumph to her hiding-place?

Urgently she wanted to burst into a run.

'They could come at any time, my dear,' the fat woman was saying. Her tone had become sonorous. 'Think of the Vaga. Think of his vileness. The Vaga sees our temple decayed like this, and his dark heart rejoices. He would plunder the House of Agonis of its relics. He would sacrifice to his evil god, Koros, in its midst. To the Vaga, all that is most sacred to our race is the merest cistern of his debauchery. That is why, when the Vaga-vans come, the faithful must gather in the temple portico.'

Dimly, Cata began to understand. It was a ritual, like Papa's at the tomb-slab; but there was much in the world, as it had been since the war, that was the merest shadow of what it was before. Much had been lost: much was diminished. Before the war, Papa had eyes to see, and Mama did not yet live beneath the ground. The castle, a tumbledown ruin, was a sturdy, noble bastion. In those days the temple, too, had thrived; and, in each season when the Vagas had come, the shadows of the portico had been filled with many figures, solemn in their black clothes and flashing golden pendants.

The fat woman waddled down the temple steps. 'I shall take another turn about the tombyard, Jem. One cannot be too vigilant. One cannot be too cautious.'

Only when she had disappeared round the corner did Cata emerge from behind the fronds of ivy.

'Why didn't you say something?'

'I'm not afraid of you,' said the boy.

'You were afraid. You screamed.'

'Go away.'

'You go away.'

The pale face flushed.

'You can't,' Cata said.

'I can!'

Cata laughed. She scampered to the foot of the steps. She somersaulted on the grass. She leapt up and down.

'Then come to the fair!' she called back. 'Come on!'

The boy did not move.

'I hate you,' was all he said.

'And I hate you!'

Cata turned her back on him. She had not meant to taunt him; he filled her with pity. Yet there was something horrible about the boy, something awful. If his limbs were strong and he could run and jump, he would be the same as the carrot-haired boy. He would throw stones, and wrestle, and yell tormenting words.

But there was something in his weakness too, something in his whiteness, that made Cata hate him. Her mouth set hard as she made her way back to the tombyard gates. She looked down at the overgrown path; at the cracked flagstones and tough, untrampled grass.

'Wait!' came the boy's voice.

Cata turned.

She started.

The boy had crawled forward to the edge of the portico. Straining, gasping, he heaved himself upright, clawing at the coarse fronds of draping ivy. He hung there, swaying, his legs twisted uselessly.

One leg was bowed and the other was buckled.

'You dropped this,' he said, as Cata came closer.

The boy bit his lip. He reached into the pocket of his black coat. In the palm of his hand he held the harlequin's gold, and when Cata reached for it, did not snatch it back. Wonderingly, Cata looked from the gleaming coin to the boy. The black hat had fallen from his head. His hair fluttered freely. Insects droned on the early evening air.

'Jem!'

Now it was the fat woman's turn to shriek. Cata jumped back, clutching the coin. The ivy tore away in the boy's straining grip and he tumbled down the steps like a doll.

Like Yane.

He lay there, unmoving. Then the fat woman was huffing forward; and Cata was running and running, sobbing, calling out to Papa.

'Child! Child!' Old Wolveron cried.

The old man had been seeking her, for he had been frightened, too.

Chapter 8

A GOOD WOMAN

The Castle of Irion glowers down darkly from a crag above the village. Haughty and sublime, suspended above the valleys like a hovering, strange sentinel, the great edifice has maintained its vigil through numberless cycles of the seasons. The rock on which the castle stands, dark against the backdrop of the white mountains, is the Rock of Ixiter, so named after the first Ejlander to command its imposing heights. Here, when history had barely begun, a rude fortress was raised from tree-trunks hauled up laboriously from the valley below. This was in the days of the Submissions, when the tribes of Ejland, pushing north, had wrested the foothills of the Kolkos Aros from the misshapen creatures of evil. In the long battle to subdue the valleys, before the misshapen ones were driven back into the Realm of Unbeing, the rude fortress had burgeoned, doubling and redoubling in size and strength, until it stood out at last in all its glory, monumental in its vastness of quarried stone. High slit-windowed towers rose imperiously. Battlements clawed at the sky. A deep moat lapped round massy foundations and threaded sibilantly beneath a ponderous drawbridge. A grim portcullis, with spikes like fangs, guarded the way into the interior strongholds, the inner bailey and the castle keep. This, at the northernmost limit of the kingdom, had once been the greatest of the castles of Ejland. It was from here, as epicycles passed, that successive lords of the Ixiter family, styled Archdukes of Irion, had held their despotic sway over the valleys; from here that invasion and insurrection were crushed, time and again. Yet it was from here, too, but a five-

76

cycle earlier, that the legions of the Bluejackets had over-whelmed the besieged forces of the rightful king.

Now the castle held only the remnants of its glory. The drained moat was a foetid marsh. The curtain wall lay in ruins. The shattered arc of the inner bailey exposed the keep, its great stones pocked with hurled boulders. The wreckage was deep and with each season that passed grew only deeper, as if the assaults of the Siege, not registered all at once, yet lingered in waiting about the ancient fabric, uncoiling slowly like a lazy spring. Walls crumbled; stones crashed; tormented timbers gave way in the end. To the visitor, gazing up curiously from the village, the castle might have seemed a place to be shunned, aloof and ill-omened, fit home only to cawing rooks, to clinging ivy and moss, to the winds that swept down, swooping and shrieking, from the white impas-sivity of the Kolkos Aros.

Yet life lingered in the masterless house. In the eviscerated chambers of the keep, fires burned. Voices sounded. And on that evening of the day of the Vaga-fair, as the bright sky declined into purple glimmerings, a ragged figure wended its way stealthily uphill to the ruinous castle, skirting close to the undergrowth on the precipitous twisting path.

'Disgusting.'

'That was your first thought?'

'Mm?'

'She must be such a lonely child.'

Aunt Umbecca gave an airy laugh. 'You'd hardly think her a suitable friend for *our* boy, I hope?'

'He has no other.'

Aunt Umbecca took a deep breath, but she held back her reply. She had, as it happened, arranged a friend for Jem; but now, perhaps, was not the time to mention it. Ela could be so touchy.

The two women faced each other across a small round

77

table, high in a chamber of the castle keep. The casement was open and the candles fluttered on a breeze.

Ela shivered.

'You're not cold, my dear?'

'I must see him.' The younger woman reached across the table, gripping the handle of the bell that crouched like an inverted goblet beside her aunt's plate. A sharp jangling sounded on the air.

'Ela, no.' Her aunt's plump hand stilled the jangling.

'You said he could have been killed!'

'A little fall, that's all. Now, niece, you mustn't upset yourself.'

The door clicked open.

'Ma'am?'

'Nirry, bring in Master Jemany,' Ela said.

The maid only snuffled and shifted her feet. She looked expectantly at the older woman.

Aunt Umbecca breathed, deliberately.

'Nirry—' she began.

She paused; she might have been sifting mentally through the prospects of deprecation.

She looked down, with sudden satisfaction, at her plate.

'This mutton,' she proceeded, 'is unconscionably tough. In a perfect world, Nirry, I would at this point remark that you might, as it were, *inform Cook* that I should speak to her about the matter; as it is, girl, you may consider that I have spoken to *you*. At length.'

A snuffle was the reply; perhaps the fourth since the maid had entered the apartment. She was a small, whey-faced creature with pallid, nervous eyes. Yellow hair, lank and greasy, trailed from beneath her discoloured cap.

Ela pushed back her chair.

'I must see him.'

'Niece, please.'

The younger woman took several decisive steps, then faltered. She swayed. Her white nightgown fluttered in the breeze.

'You see, Nirry, the mutton has upset Lady Ela. One should think it were made from Cook's old boots!'

There was a snuffle.

'And much, Nirry, as one might in principle commend such thrift, I am afraid I must advise you in this instance to find better uses for your late mother's things. Help Lady Ela to bed, girl.'

'No.' Ela slumped back into her chair instead. 'Nirry, my shawl—'

Aunt Umbecca sighed. It had been unwise, no doubt, to broach the matter of Catayane's girl. But how unpleasantly the afternoon had ended! The subject had burst, unbidden, from her lips.

She sipped from a tankard of small-beer.

'Our child is perfectly well, niece. Perfectly. One was merely remarking on the condition of that – that girl. Reprehensible, as I told Silas Wolveron. Still, the child was born in depravity. It is only to be expected that she should live in it.'

Ela adjusted her shawl about her shoulders.

'Nirry, close the casement,' her aunt commanded.

Nirry closed the casement.

'I note you have a snuffly nose, Nirry.'

Snuffle.

'Shall I take the mutton, ma'am?'

Umbecca waved the girl away.

'That girl is a slattern,' she observed, as the maid withdrew.

Sometimes, when Ela's aunt contemplated her life, she could weep: she could simply weep. That very afternoon was a case in point. She had to find Stephel to drive them home early. Of course, she was forced to retrieve him from the tavern by the green: from the Lazy Tiger! The wretched man was sodden with drink. His companions, coarse village fellows, had bellowed oaths and ribaldries.

The fat woman shuddered. She said aloud, 'In Agondon, one would have decent servants.'

It was a frequent theme. The Archduke, when he had departed his ancestral home, had left the two women with a staff of three: his old steward, Stephel, an irascible, shifty fellow, but fiercely loyal to the Ixiter family; the old steward's plump wife, known even to her husband as 'Cook'; and their daughter, who was to be maid-of-all-work. The arrangement, Umbecca had assured the Archduke, was a generous one, most admirably generous; she had always sought to impress Jorvel with her compliant, sweet nature. He could hardly have foreseen that his old steward, in mourning for the glory days of the castle, would have descended swiftly into a drunken haze; or that Cook, leaning one evening over a cauldron of rabbit stew, would be struck down with a sudden apoplexy, leaving her snuffling daughter to find her, face down in the scalding mixture, and sullenly and without competence to assume her mother's duties.

A year ago, Umbecca had written to the Archduke, inferring delicately that a new arrangement was needed; Jorvel, alas, had not replied.

'I frustrate you greatly, don't I?' Ela murmured.

'My dear?' Umbecca's knife sawed at the mutton.

It was an odd accusation. For it was the endeavour of her aunt's life not to be frustrated; to feel no discontent with her status in the world. Everything had a reason. One must submit to fate; and yet the failure of her appeal to the Archduke had started up a nagging in the fat woman's heart; and sometimes, like a temptation from the path of piety, the niggling thought would come to her that her fate was unjust. She was, she told herself, *a good woman*; the mission of her life had been to be *a good woman*. For her pains she had been consigned to a place denuded of society and even, in this aftermath of war, of civilization. When that wretched girl Yane had run off with Silas, Umbecca had held fond hopes that Jorvel might at last, at least, recognize the merit that had lain, all this time, so close at hand. He had not. Poor Umbecca! As the Archduchess, she would have lived in high style in the capital, where Jorvel now filled a prominent government post; but her lot, it seemed, was to squander her prime as the moral guardian of an ungrateful, immoral girl. Could it be borne?

Umbecca sighed.

Such doubts were wrong.

It could all be borne.

'That girl is a slattern,' Ela was saying.

She was repeating her aunt's remark about the maid; but whether satirically or sadly was hard to say. She looked up. She was sallow and thin. There were dark circles beneath her eyes and her golden hair had faded to the colour of damp straw. How altered she was! What a price she had paid! Yet, as her aunt would remind her frequently, she had brought it all upon herself. There was no denying it: Ela's fate was just.

Her aunt laughed again. 'Niece, really! I was speaking of the maid. There are many things for which I have reproached you, my dear, but I believe I have yet to describe you as a *slattern*.'

'You called me worse. After the Siege.'

'My dear! I'm sure I did no such thing.'

The Siege of Irion had been the bitterest chapter in all the annals of Ejland.

It had been in the bleak depths of the Season of Koros, AC 994*e*, that civil war had broken out. It was a war, some said, that had destroyed the old kingdom; which, said others, had brought it to the brink of its historic destiny. Ejland had been a realm racked by many wars; but always they had been against its neighbour, Zenzau. Then, at the end of Cycle 994, for the first time since the days of the early tribespeople, members of the races of Agonis had turned their arms against each other. It lasted through all of the cycle that followed, and would come to be known as 'The Ninety-Five'.

The war had been between two rival claimants for the crown: the Twinned brothers Ejard Red, called Redjacket, and Ejard Blue, or Bluejacket. It was an ancient custom in the Agonist lands that 'looking-glass children', as the Twinned were called, must be given the same name. Only the colours of the clothes they wore must mark them out, one from the other, for it was believed that in the Twinned were to be found two halves of a divided being. But each of the halves had a separate role to play. Ejlander custom had it that only one of such half-children, the one delivered first from its mother's womb, should move and live freely in the world. It was the task of the other to be a familiar, a companion; but that was all. There was no question that the young princes would reign together. Ejard Red was the rightful king.

Now it happened that Jagenam the Just, the father of the two princes, had been a great reformer; in his time many ancient privileges had been taken from the Order of Agonis, which had grown oppressive and corrupt. At court, the Temple Party had long sought to restore its time-honoured rights. To this end, the wily courtier Tranimel worked on the envy of Ejard Blue. Soon the blue prince, a staunch Agonist, believed that it was his duty to depose his impious brother.

After a cycle of bitter fighting, Ejard Red was besieged at last in Irion's high stronghold; only to be betrayed in the end by his erstwhile follower, the treacherous Archduke. Captured, the king was taken back to Agondon to be executed. Bluejacket, the puppet of the evil Tranimel, was king.

Ela set her plate aside.

'If it weren't for me, Aunt, where would you be?'

It was a question Umbecca had often contemplated; a question her niece had often asked. The replies, Ela suspected, did not quite reflect the truth of her aunt's thoughts. The fat woman laid aside her knife and fork and gazed into the candles in the centre of the table.

'I am a woman of no consequence, niece,' she said simply. 'Not in myself. You forget, my sister and I were from a humble home. It was Ruanna's fortune to captivate the heart of the Archduke; and mine, through the generosity of your noble father, to be her companion in her new life.' She sighed.

'Now Ruanna is dead, and I am companion to her child. The Lord Agonis has a role for each of us in this world, niece; this is mine.'

Ela sat silently, toying with her small-beer. She said, after a moment, 'But what is mine?'

'Niece?'

'My role. Is it my role to make you unhappy, Aunt? Is that what the Lord Agonis planned for me?'

'Niece, you know not of what you speak,' the fat woman murmured, looking down.

'You'd be in Agondon now if it weren't for me,' her niece pursued. It was an idle pursuit. In her voice was neither eagerness nor rancour, only a hollow sadness. 'We'd both be in Agondon. You'd be a leading light amongst the Temple ladies; I should be a great beauty, and receive many suitors.' She twisted a strand of her lank hair. 'Unless of course I had accepted one by now. Think how happy we'd be, Aunt, you and I, as we planned the wedding! We'd be so happy. Everyone would be happy.'

'I dare say.'

'Except Jem. Because Jem would not be born.'

'No,' her aunt said dryly. 'He would not. Eat your mutton, my dear. I have decided it is rather more tolerable than I thought.'

Chapter 9

A GOOD MAN

There was a knock at the door.

'Good women? If I may take the liberty—?'

'Goodman Waxwell, do come in!'

Umbecca's face, which had become pleated and pouched, was smoothed at once into an eager welcome. She rose from the table, sailing blackly across the apartment with outstretched, plump hands. There was a rigmarole of greeting.

'Mistress Rench, you overwhelm me—'

'Not at all, Goodman Waxwell! Ela, do ring for Nirry.'

But Ela was only looking at the new arrival curiously. It was not that he was a stranger to her; indeed, she had seen him many times before.

Too many.

Nathanian Waxwell was a spindle-shanked, crook-backed creature with sinuous soft hands and tufty whiskers that sprouted profusely on either side of smooth-shaven lips. On the bald dome of his head he wore an unravelling, discoloured wig. Advancing with a curious crabwise air, a twisty smile on his naked mouth, he held before him, like an uncertain offering, his battered leather instrument-bag.

'Yes, Goody Waxwell's wrist still gives her trouble,' he was saying. 'I'm afraid there was no question of the vigil—'

'No, no! No question at all!' The fat woman overwhelmed the visitor's words. She laughed; she pursed her lips; she glanced quickly towards Ela. Her niece believed that the boy had been taken not to the temple, but to the fair. Absurd, of course: but there was no point in upsetting her. No point at all.

'Ela, dear? Nirry!'

Ela did not ring.

'You shall pass on my fondest regards, Goodman?' her aunt went on. She had sunk beside the visitor on a sofa by the fire. 'Your poor wife! Ah, I fear she shall be taken from us before her allotted—'

The visitor laughed, too.

'Mistress Rench, no! Berthen is a woman of peculiar determination. I sometimes think her afflictions merely make her more determined to . . . live.'

Umbecca sighed. 'Indeed. And the boy is well?'

'Tissy? Oh yes. Indeed.'

The visitor's knees were pressed tightly together; upon them was perched his instrument-bag; upon the bag, twitching as he spoke, reclined a soft hand. His eyes flickered incuriously about Lady Ela's apartment: over the threadbare carpets, over the latticed, curtainless casements, over the canopied bed with its heavy, drawn curtains and the wormy panelling that ran around the walls. It was not a cheerful room.

'Why has he come?' Ela said softly.

'Ela?'

The voice was suddenly shrill, 'I said I wouldn't see him!'

Her aunt laughed again, a little too loudly, and tapped her forehead surreptitiously. 'You'll excuse my niece, Goodman Waxwell.'

Really, thought Umbecca, Ela could be so tedious. It had all begun a year or so ago, when the girl had become convinced that the physician was an evil man, and his medicines were poisoned. It was outrageous. Goodman Waxwell had never shown anything but a tender concern for the girl. He was wholly admirable. In Agondon, Umbecca often thought admiringly, he could have been what the world would call a great man, which is to say a rich man; but he was not a man in pursuit of gain. His wife had brought him an adequate income; with it, Goodman Waxwell was able both to live in a manner concordant with his dignity, and to bless the valleys with the fruits of his philanthropy. He was a man with a gift to give. It was the gift of healing.

He was a staunch Agonist.

❋

'I came, Lady Elabeth, to see the young Vexing,' Goodman Waxwell was explaining. His voice was kind; there could be no doubt that he was a very kind man indeed.

'Aunt! You said Jem wasn't hurt!'

'Jem is not hurt, niece.'

'Oh no, indeed,' smiled Goodman Waxwell. A pulpy hand waved on the air. 'To a tender and delicate constitution, of course, any shock must be a source of alarm. Your aunt did right to send for me; but under the circumstances, and allowing for the debilitation suffused from the misshapen lower parts, which we must consider incontrovertible' – the hand became expansive – 'I have thought that just a little bleeding, the merest trickle, was sufficient. The Vexing is stronger than one might expect.' The naked mouth snaked into a satisfied smile.

Ela rang the bell.

'Nirry, I must see the young master—'

Her aunt's voice rode over hers. 'Ah, Nirry. Goodman Waxwell must be rewarded for his labours. The best Varl-wine! And you'll try a little cheese, Goodman?'

'Indeed, Mistress Rench! That would be pleasant.'

'The Tarn Blue, Nirry. And the best Varl-wine.'

Nirry snuffled assent.

'I must go to him.' Ela was struggling up from her chair again. 'Nirry—'

But the maid had gone.

'Niece, really! Our child is sleeping.'

Umbecca turned back to her guest with a sigh. *My poor niece!* the sigh seemed to say. Goodman Waxwell had warned that she should not excite herself. It was her aunt's duty to ensure that she did not, but the physician could see, could he not, the difficulty? The impossibility?

Ela, who had succeeded in standing, advanced towards the door. But her steps were faltering; she staggered back, slumping disconsolately on to the wide window-ledge. She shivered, burying her arms inside her shawl. How she cursed her weakness! Her life, which had seemed about to open on to bright vistas, had instead become a dim, shrunken thing. She had brought it upon herself, her exile, her illness; and yet, if her life now were the punishment for what she had done, Ela knew that she would do it again.

She slipped back the catch of the casement. The long evening lingered; poised, it seemed perpetually, on the brink of darkness. She gazed down through the ruins of the bailey to the steep track that led up to the castle, twisting and turning; far below lay the village. Distantly the sounds of the Vaga-revelries drifted up on the empurpled air.

The voices behind her were a murmur, rippled with laughter.

'My good woman, an excellent Varl-wine!'

'You're too kind, Goodman Waxwell!'

Then, 'The Vagas, of course. Something *must* be done.'

'*Order*. What we need is order.'

'And faith, Goodman Waxwell?'

'My good woman, of course!'

There was a gasp. It came from Ela.

'Niece, don't sit in the chill.'

But Ela was standing again, gazing below with a new intentness. She closed the casement swiftly and turned back to the room. Was it some deception of the clear evening, or had there, in the moment before the closing of the casement, wafted into the apartment a hint of song, the merest snatched strain, from a source rather closer than the village green?

It had gone unremarked by the couple at the fire.

'One has hopes that we may bring her, in time, to repentance,' came the undertone of Ela's aunt, soft and cooing; Goodman Waxwell was nodding his shabbily-bewigged head.

There had been a sound. It was the whistling of a reed.

Framed against the lattice of the diamond panes, Ela struggled to suppress a smile.

Chapter 10

THE SECRET IN THE WAINSCOT

When Ela was a child, the apartment she now inhabited had belonged to her mother. It had been different then, a happy place in a castle bustling with life. There were hangings and pictures. There were glittering ornaments, little golden animals and porcelain figurines. There were tall vases enamelled with twisty stems; in the Season of Viana, the room was filled with flowers. It was an enchanted place; here, in the evenings when they were small, dressed in matching white tunics, Ela and her brother Tor would run and dance and leap. Lengths of cloth, pungent and lush, lay across the sides of ornate chairs; the children would seize them and wave them and roll in them; Mother clapped and laughed. In a chest by the casement was a box of jewels. Later, Ela would recall her hands, white like mice, slipping through the cool caverns of ruby and diamond and pearl, mingling with her brother's hands when his hands were small as hers. How the jewels had glinted!

On the wall beside the fireplace had been the best thing of all: an ancient, heavy arras that was unstirred even by the creeping chill draughts of the Season of Koros. The arras depicted the story of Nova-Riel, the kitchen-boy who had become king; but epicycles of smoke and the beating sun had faded the bright dyes to a mellow blur. It was a shabby thing, but in its shabbiness was a secret wonder. On their nameday, when they were five, Mother had decided to reveal it to the children. How her eyes had glittered! In the wainscot behind the arras was a secret door. Beyond the door, a narrow passage passed darkly between the thick castle walls.

The children gasped.

Mother bent down; she hugged the children to her. That had been on a long lingering evening like the evening it was now, with the sunset refracting goldenly through the diamond panes of the casement. Since then, the apartment had altered entirely; the vases, the jewels, the rich skeins of cloth, had been taken surely as Mother had been taken, never to return. Everything had gone: the bed, the table, the chairs that were here now were the merest dilapidated stand-ins, called up from distant, despised chambers of the castle. The arras that had hung unbillowing and impassive through the dark days of war was torn down after the Siege, and burnt. Ela had gasped and cried, but her aunt was unyielding. The arras depicted a heathen legend; besides, it was dirty.

But Aunt Umbecca had never discovered the secret the arras concealed. The door was fitted too smoothly into the panelling. Fondly, Ela looked towards the wainscot now.

'You'll call again soon, Goodman?' Ela's aunt was saying. She lowered her voice. 'And next time, perhaps, young – ah – Poltiss . . . ?'

'Tissy, yes. Indeed, yes.'

Ela did not hear the last part of the conversation. She only sighed with relief as the crook-backed creature made his way from the apartment, his naked smile twisting and twitching. At last! Her aunt would accompany him to his carriage.

Ela crossed to the wainscot. It was then that the melody came again, as she had known it would, this time from behind the dark panelling. It hovered plaintively on the evening like smoke; it was an old Ejlander air. Mother had sung it to them when they were children. Aunt Umbecca would say it was a Vaga-song, setting her face against it as if at an imprecation; but Mother would only laugh and sing it regardless. Ela stood trembling as she softly intoned:

> *Hey, ho! The circle is round!*
> *Where can its start and its end be found?*

A pause.

There was a muffled laugh. The panel slid open, then shut again behind the slender, tall figure who stepped forth, enfolding Ela in his arms.

'I thought that old fool would never go!'

Ela could only gasp, 'Tor! Tor!'

He stroked her hair. 'Hush. I said I'd come back, didn't I?'

'Tor, it's been so long.'

'Let me look at you.' He stepped back.

'I'm not strong, Tor. Not since . . .'

She would have turned away, but could not. She gazed at him. His face had set into firm angles, measured cleavings of cheekbone and jaw. When he smiled, it was with a new certainty. Could this be her brother? Only the bright straw of his blond hair was unchanged. Each time he came back he seemed taller, stronger: the gangly boy had become a man. There was a musket slung over his shoulder, its bayonet fixed and jabbing at the air; in one long hand he held a three-cornered hat. Ela's eyes travelled, marvelling, over his limbs; over his high boots, dusty and scuffed; his tight breeches, once white; his brass-buttoned jacket that was torn and stained. Scarlet, it burned with a dark refulgence. It was the colour of the deposed king.

'Redjacket,' she mouthed.

He returned, 'Redjacket.'

It was a game, of course. He must have travelled back to her in some other costume, and changed into this one only when he was safe inside the chambers of the castle walls. A Redjacket soldier would be shot on sight.

'It isn't over, sister.'

Now Ela turned away. This was not possible. This was too much of a game. She supported herself on the back of the sofa. Distantly, from the courtyard, came the sound of hooves. The surgeon's carriage was clattering away.

'Tor, it's over. It has to be over.'

Tor laid down the musket and the three-cornered hat. He

circled Ela in his arms again. 'Dear sister, how wan you are! Dear sister, how pale!'

Ela turned back. She returned his embrace. 'Tor. Tor.' It was as if her brother had absorbed the strength of them both. Yes: she had given him her strength, laid it at his feet like a sacrifice. On the day when they had parted she had said to him plainly, even boldly: *Brother, my strength goes with you. Take it. Take it.* And he had embraced her then as he embraced her now, and kissed her; and then – it was true – he had taken her strength.

It seemed so long ago. The cycles of the seasons had come and gone; the child had been born, a twisted thing; and the child and Ela, in the abandoned castle, had clung feebly to life, and wondered why.

Ela buried her face in Tor's shoulder. 'Tor, why have you come back? Why?' she murmured. In the cycle since the Siege, her brother had returned only twice before. Both times were brief; and both times, when he left, it had seemed to Ela that she would never see him again. Her brother's life, she knew, had become a dangerous madness: he was a wanted man, a rebel.

They called him The Red Avenger.

In the long intermissions between his returnings there were only scattered letters, cryptic and elliptical and without address. Ela would ask, keeping her voice level: *Who brought this letter, Nirry?* And the maid, her nose wrinkling, would answer: *Some ragamuffin, miss. He's in the kitchens now.* Then Ela would demand that the ragamuffin be brought to her; and once, one afternoon when her aunt was sleeping, the boy had been brought to her, his face hastily scrubbed. Ela was enthralled. Could this urchin be a member of the Resistance? *It's better that you know nothing, nothing*, Tor had said. Her heart pounded as she took the boy's hand. It was little and coarse; she felt the calluses and ragged nails. Tenderly she pressed into his palm a silver coin; the coin was wrapped in the folds of a note on which she had scribbled only: *Tor, I love you*. There was nothing else to say; or everything.

But Tor knew.

He was humming softly now, close to her ear, and Ela found herself humming too, stumbling in the wake of a sinuous tune. It was the refrain she had sung by the arras, but twisted and turned, made alien and wandering.

Why have you come back?

The question seemed to float evanescently away; and Ela, in Tor's arms, was shuffling across the floor. Was it her imagination, or was there soft music, floating into the candle-light from behind the wainscot?

'And they danced together till the end of the ball,' said Tor.

Ela laughed. Yes, she was dancing; only a slow shuffle, but it was the first time, after all, since the Great Masque, the red king's splendid gesture of defiance, held in the castle at the height of the Siege. Then she had danced! How she had danced! Ela might have sobbed. She revolved in Tor's arms across the threadbare carpets. Round, slowly round, went the barren wainscot. The candles began to blur; and the music, too, that at first was unfamiliar to her, seemed to be undulating into a different shape. It was almost as if she were drifting into sleep, entering a region at once known and unknown, familiar and strange. Then she knew where the melody was leading, through all the labyrinths of its twisting turnings, and she mouthed softly into her brother's ear:

'The circle is round!'

He laughed.

She laughed.

She whirled in his arms.

'No!'

It was a stricken cry. Moments passed until Ela realized that it had erupted from the black form of her aunt, bulking massively in the open doorway. Ela started. She might have jumped back, but collapsed, instead, on to Tor's shoulder.

Tor gazed, smiling, at the ominous figure.

'No.' The fat woman turned away. She wrung her hands. 'No.'

Tor said levelly, 'Dear Aunt Becca.'

His sister's face remained buried in his shoulder. She coughed, juddering. How frail she was! When she pulled away at last, Tor's shoulder was soaked with blood.

Chapter 11

'HUL, BANDO AND ME . . .'

'The Pillar of Death—'

   'That will be all, Nirry.'

The maid's heart sank. It was cruel!

But she had been hovering. Back and forth, unbidden by the bell she came, bearing the best delicacies from the castle kitchens; eager, Ela knew, once again just to see, to marvel at Tor. She had splashed more wine into brimming goblets. She had jabbed with the poker at the roaring fire. Now she could gladly have seized it again and struck her fat mistress between the eyes.

Reluctantly she made her way to the door.

'From the stormswept cliffs of Xorgos Island,' Tor was saying, 'the Pillar rises sheer. It has no windows. It has no doors. Blankly it soars to the skies like an obelisk. Only through the caves in the cliffs below can this most terrible of prisons be entered.' He sipped his wine. 'They say when a man first sets foot on the island, he is lost: that he has passed inexorably into the dimension of the dead.'

Jem's eyes shone. He might have been dreaming.

'It was The Red Avenger's most terrifying mission. Across the gulf creaked the prison-ship, heavy with its burden of the wretched. Condemned from the vile tongue of the traitor Ejard Bluejacket, a hundred more servants of the rightful king would soon be shut away in the vast tower. Even with my two loyal companions, how could I free them from this fate?'

Warm before the fire, Jem sank more deeply, more content-edly into his mother's arms. His uncle's voice was mellow but intent. It was like a spell; it lulled the boy into a state of trance. Could Uncle Tor be a magical being? Though his red jacket

94

was dirty and shabby, to the fascinated boy it could only seem resplendent. The story wound about his heart like a vine.

'We thought we were doomed, Hul, Bando and me. A ragged trio against the might of the Bluejackets! We had no weapons and we had no hope. Furtively our leaking skiff skirted across the waters. Bitterly, Hul execrated the conquerors. Bando bemoaned our fate.

'I was silent. Day after day I crouched with a spyglass to my eye, following the flutterings of the hated blue pennant.'

Ela might have been dreaming, too. She must have been dreaming. Time had passed and the scene, which had seemed to bode so ill, had rearranged itself as an image of happiness: Tor, by the fireside, telling stories; Aunt Umbecca benevolent and drowsy; Ela, content to sit and watch her brother, barely taking in the words he said. She was too happy. Jem was in her arms: Tor had insisted.

Lightly Ela toyed with her little son's hair.

'The prison-ship lay at anchor off the island. The great cave that was portal to the obelisk was barred by a vast grille. Only once in each moonlife, at the time of Hornlight, would the portal open, admitting new prisoners. A high wind had pushed our vessels rapidly across the gulf. Hornlight was four nights away. Curtained by the jagged edges of cliff that ring the island, like great rocky roots reaching deep into the gulf, we lay in wait and watched, Hul, Bando and me.

'Victory has rotted the fibre of the Blues. They loll like swine. They swagger. They puff with pride, bloated like the ballooning throats of toads. The prison-ship, we soon saw, was the scene of coarse revelry. The captain was a drunkard; the men followed his lead. While his prisoners languished in the squalors of the hold, each night the decks above them rang to roared laughter, to shouting and song. Heavy boots stamped, drunkenly dancing, on the thick timbers that confined the wretched cargo.

'On the first night the revelry was violent. The decks swarmed with men. On the second it was quieter; barrel after barrel of rum had taken its toll. On the third night the air was chill; the men were below. The revelry had resumed, but less intensely.

'This was our last chance. The hanging moon had almost reached its ripeness. Solemnly I glanced back and forth between my companions. How I had come to love them: Bando the Zenzan, squat and dark, round-faced with curly hair; Hul, an Ejlander like me, tall and blond. Never would I forget Bando's hearty laugh; his jokes; his good-natured taunting of the solemn Hul. Poor Bando! He understood little but he understood loyalty. In a time better than this he would never have left his village. He would have lived close to the earth and the rhythm of the seasons, fathering many children and growing fat. Round his neck he wore a red bandanna.

'Hul stared fixedly at the evil ship. I saw in his lean face the lineaments of a scholar. His mind was formidable and restlessly questing. How he would have flourished in the halls of learning, his fiery tongue turned to the disputes of philosophy! He could have been one of the great men of the age, had he not followed The Red Avenger.

'Noiselessly we slipped into the chill waters, our limbs smeared with pitch. I recall the slow shock of cold as I descended. I recall my iron, feelingless intent as I forced my numbed arms to cleave across the waters. The evil ship sloshed on the tide, its sails furled, its tall masts skeletal in the moonlight. I clambered up the anchor-chain, my teeth gritted and my every muscle taut.'

Tor paused, sipping at his wine.

'Uncle Tor!' Jem breathed. 'Go on!'

Ela laughed. The boy was dressed in a white linen gown. His twisted legs were tucked beneath him. Could he, she wondered, recall the last time Tor had come? The boy had been so small.

Perhaps it had all seemed like a dream, just a dream.

Aunt Umbecca felt herself falling.

She was not listening to her nephew's story, the second or third he had told that night; his words came to her as the merest succession of sounds, sweet and soft. A smile overspread her plump features. How handsome Tor had become! Even last time he had returned to the castle she had thought of him still as a boy, a fledgling thing. No more: he had not grown taller but he had grown into his height; he had acquired proportion and he had acquired grace. His lean frame bent intently forward; his eyes sparkled with fire. Long hands moved elastically on the air as if conjuring the images of his story like phantoms; in the mellow light his shabby uniform might have been restored to all its lost splendour.

Redjacket! Once, the very word had set Umbecca's pulse racing. Once, a parade of soldiers in scarlet was a sight to swell her heart. Dreamily, she thought of the uniform that the Archduke, Tor's father, had worn as a young man, in the days when red, only red, could be the colour of the king; and perhaps in the son, Umbecca thought, she imagined that the father had mysteriously returned, assuming again the form in which he had first called on her sister.

It had been so exciting.

It had been so long ago.

'Dripping, we crouched on the slimy deck,' Tor was saying, 'concealing ourselves behind a line of barrels. Our plan was clear. The sentries were on the bridge. They stamped and shifted in the cold. They laughed. They swigged deeply from a glinting bottle. We had only to creep up on them, Hul and I, one from the starboard, one from the port. Bando would watch the hatch that led below. In moments, we would break into the ship's arsenal. Then the Bluejackets would be at our mercy!

'Aching through the rigging with its swollen pallor, the moon etched a spider's web of shadows on the deck. My heart thudded hard. I crept towards the ladder that led up to the bridge. A raucous toast sounded from below: to the health of His Imperial Agonist Majesty, Ejard Bluejacket!

'A fire of anger burned my frozen limbs. I thought of the prisoners who languished in the hold, the valiant men whom the traitor-king called traitors.'

Yes, Umbecca felt herself falling. Later, she would burn and throb with shame. In the cell-like chamber where she slept on a mean couch, the fat woman would kneel before a gleaming icon. She would clutch the circle at her ample breast; earnestly she would move her lips in prayer. She had failed: she had failed. She must beg forgiveness. Yet what could she have done? It was as if young Torvester were possessed of magic. He had appeared in her niece's apartment as if from nowhere; he had suffused the dying evening with a strange lambency.

Umbecca felt an uneasy twisting at her heart. She knew what was right and she knew what was wrong. She knew it absolutely and she had no doubts. Yet Tor seemed somehow to sap her resolve. He left her helpless. In his presence, it was as if she must cast down, like unneeded lumber, all the things she knew to be right. *No!* she had cried, standing in the doorway; and wringing her hands, she had turned away.

To no avail.

Boldly, brazen in the forbidden uniform, Torvester had advanced on her, jaunty with his maddening grin. He had embraced her.

Oh, nephew.

He was such a beautiful boy!

There are children who are magical and children who are not. Ela was without magic: Tor had too much. He had been a scapegrace boy. His knees were always skinned. His face was black with dirt. He was an orchard-robber and a thrower of stones. He ran with the stable-boys and village lads. By his fourth cycle he was the terror of the castle. His mother saw only his beauty; his father saw only his fire. *Torvester! Torvester!* the Archduke would cry, when some new outrage came to his ears; but always the boy, summoned to his father, would only grin and shift his gangly limbs, irresistible with his haystack hair and his whistled refrain, as his father dismissed him, of *Hey, ho! The circle is round!*

The song shocked Umbecca. It was a Vaga-air; it meant, she believed, that nothing mattered, that everything that happened was the merest turning of a wheel, empty and meaningless. It was blasphemy. For this alone, the boy should have been punished. But he had never been punished.

Dear Aunt, he exclaimed, it seemed with joy, as he had squeezed her in the unresisted embrace. And standing back from her he had asked her, his eyes bright with mirth, whether she were aware that the Goodman was married.

'I thought you might have forgotten, Aunt. Oh, and I should tell you: he is a firm man. Rigid. Morally, I mean.'

'Oh, Torvester!'

She could not help but laugh.

Only later would a different impulse grip Umbecca's heart. Alone in her cell, she would reach up to the icon. Her plump fingers would tremble, it might be with fear; but all at once she would know that it was not. It was anger.

Curse the boy!

Curse him!

He was not a beautiful boy. He had never been beautiful. Torvester of Irion was evil, nothing more. It had always been in him but now it had burst forth, bright as fire and as terrible. The young man was a renegade; but she, Umbecca Rench, was a servant of the king. The rightful king. Would Umbecca Rench connive at treachery? She would not! She knew her duties to her king, to her god, and she would fulfil them. She would send word to the Archduke!

But she would not.

As she lowered herself slowly on to her hard couch that night, Tor's aunt would know that she would do nothing, say nothing, make nothing happen. Tor would go free. He would always go free. Torvester of Irion was the magical child.

And that night, alone, Umbecca would weep.

'The blue pennant fluttered from the mast above our heads. How slowly I crept! Time seemed suspended. I rubbed my frozen limbs. The toast came again, but it might have been the same toast, the very same, coming round again in a loop of time.

'Then all at once the loop was broken. There were raised voices from the bridge; a sudden struggle. "Give it me, give it me!" The bottle crashed to the deck. "Damn you!" One drunken sentry had launched himself on the other. Then came the shot. The body lurched forward and tumbled over the railing of the bridge like a sack.

'The murdered sentry had not screamed. But suddenly the deck was alive with cries. The dead man's shipmates were swarming up from the hatch. There was no time to waste.

'I broke cover.

'I ran

'Shots rained around me. I seized the dead man's musket. Madly I fired into the swarming Bluejackets. Two fell back. But there were more, then more. There was no time to load again. I lunged forward wildly with the dead man's bayonet.

'Meanwhile Hul was defending the bridge. Bando had broken into the ship's arsenal. How we defeated forty Bluejacket curs, I shall never know. They were bleary with rum, but enraged and strong. The battle raged on for what might have been hours.

'But it was only minutes before the deck was awash with blood, before the air was a chaos of shots and clashing steel. Then the captain lay lifeless at my feet, and the chained prisoners had broken from the hold. There was a flurry of splashes: Bluejacket after Bluejacket striking for the island, certain to be dashed against the pitiless coast!

'Hul took command. We cast up anchor. We unfurled the sails; and as we turned on the tide a rain of cannon-balls exploded suddenly from the rocky cliffs of the island. We had been watched! Great iron spheres splattered into the sea like falling stars. One, hurled high, almost snapped our mizzen mast. Bando the Zenzan sank to his knees, crying piteously to his goddess: "I am too young, I am too young!"

'Later we would rib him, and Bando laughed too. But it was nervous laughter. It had been so close! And in his heart every man on the ship that night gave thanks to whatever power might preside over the world. In the despair of defeat we had believed the gods were against us; now, how could we not believe their powers were raised in our cause? A hundred men saved from the horror of Xorgos Island!

'As we struck out for the Zenzan coast on a merciful high wind, the ship rang now to Redjacket songs, and the reverberation of manacles being struck from ankles and wrists. We lowered the hated pennant of blue, and Bando's red bandanna fluttered from the mast. The Red Avenger had triumphed again!'

'Oh, Tor!'

When the story was over, there were tears in Ela's eyes. She hugged her son tight. She kissed his forehead. But the boy had grown heavy against her breast.

Now Jem was really dreaming.

You can't walk, the Vaga-girl had said. But in his dream, Jem could run and jump. He could plunge into the sea in the deep Gulf of Ejland, where the Pillar of Death towered from the cliffs of the island above. With strong hands he could clamber up the barnacled anchor-chain. His blood beat in the cords of his neck. In a matter of moments, the battle would begin.

The boy had seen only pictures of the sea. But now he seemed to see it inside him, too. In his dream he lived in Tor's world; in his dream, Jem was Tor. He was The Red Avenger! And when his uncle lifted his slumbrous form, to carry the boy gently to his mother's bed, Jem in his sleep felt himself to be rising, as if by his own power, above the grip of the world.

'You'll be here in the morning, Tor?'

It was his mother's voice that Jem heard, as if from afar, as he fluttered down fleetingly from his buoyant dream. It must have been much later. Only a single candle was burning, and the sound that came, as if in reply to the question, was only a soft, lilting song. A lullaby.

Hey, ho! The circle is round!

Jem rose effortlessly back into the dream-world.

Chapter 12

THE NEW DIVULGED DESTINY

The story of the wars of Ejland was a long and bitter one, and the volumes which told it filled many chambers in the Great Library of Agondon. To the scholars whose task it was to tend to their country's history, the wars were a matter of perpetual dispute. That there had been wars, extending back to the earliest days of the Agonist lands, there could be no doubt; as to their nature, number and extent, this was somewhat more difficult to determine.

To one school of thought, that of the Intercessionists, the first war to be celebrated in Ejlander memory was that bloody skirmish on the eastern borders which had come to be known as the Intercession, or Intercession of Aon the Ironhand; Ironhand, they argued, being the first single sovereign of the lands of the Agonists, and therefore the first who could claim truly to have waged war in the name of the kingdom.

This was a view disputed hotly by two camps: the Pre-Aons and the Queen Elanists. Queen Elanists were those who believed that only from the time of the Holy Empress, Elabeth the First, could Ejland as a kingdom be considered to have existed; Elabeth being the first to reign over a united Ejland, as opposed to holding, at one and the same time, titles such as Prince of Down Lexion, Blood Potentate of Varbyshire and Holluch, Great Excellency of the Tarn, and so forth, in the manner of Aon and his successors. It was Elabeth's famous 'Three Campaigns', therefore, the great sea battles in the Gulf of Ejland, that must count in this view as Ejland's first true wars.

The Pre-Aons would have none of this; to them, even the Intercessionists were putting things far too late. The

Intercession, said the Pre-Aons, for all its importance, could be understood only with reference to the many prior bouts of enemy perfidy, and valiant struggles against it; eagerly they would cite the Varby Massacre, the Penetration of Varl, and a hundred other tales of the broadsword and the axe which, their opponents said, could hardly be thought more than the folklore of primitives. To the Pre-Aons, any description of the ancestral Agonists as primitive was one to be resisted vigorously. They would speak of the historic destiny of their race, which, they claimed, had been evident from the first.

Wasn't it all there in the El-Orokon?

There was no reconciling the three parties; but had it been possible to take a fourth view, this might have been that it was misguided to seek to number, as if one could truly number, the wars of Ejland. In truth, some might say, it was not a matter of one war, then another, then another; but merely of a series of episodes in a single, interminable war. From the time when the worshippers of Agonis, god of air, had first settled in what was now the kingdom of Ejland, they had never been at peace with their easterly neighbours. The eastern lands formed the Empire of Zenzau, home to the worshippers of Viana, goddess of earth.

In Zenzau, the Ejlanders were seen as a tyrannical, covetous people; to the Ejlanders, Zenzau was a primitive, dark kingdom, its races barely removed from the half-savage Vagas with whom, it was clear, they had more than a passing kinship. Ejland had annexed much of the territories of Zenzau, and intended to take still more; but to the successive kings of Ejland, and most of its peoples, this was wholly justified, given the nature of the Zenzans. One had only to visit the colonies, it was said, to take one's measure of a Zenzan. Ejlanders who returned from the occupied lands would testify eagerly to the rightness of their regime. In the regions known as the Agonist Deliverance – Zexal, Varl and the island kingdom of Tiralos – swarthy Zenzans waited on the tables and cleaned the muddy boots and laboured in the fields of the prosperous colonists. The notion that these servile peoples could govern themselves was laughable; while as for the rebels of the Resistance, their uncivilized violence said all that needed to be said. How much better off the Zenzans would be, when their entire empire was under Ejlander rule! Each year, in high Theron season, elaborate ceremonies in every occupied town marked what was called Deliverance Day, commemorating the time of conquest. In an ardent service of thanksgiving to the Lord Agonis, Zenzans in colourful national dress would abase themselves in homage to their enlightened masters, who had saved them from the dark hold of their own inferior god.

By the time that Tor had become a traitor to his country, the Zenzan wars had continued for some seventy cycles, if one were a Queen Elanist; three hundred, if an Intercessionist; or almost as many as a thousand, should one take the Pre-Aon line. There was no prospect that the war might end. Queen Elabeth had seen to that. Under the doctrine of the New Divulged Destiny, proclaimed by the Holy Empress in the Atonement Cycle 925*c*, it was the historic mission of the Ejlander peoples to subdue the followers of Viana, bringing them to the love of the Lord Agonis.

As the Zenzans seemed never to be wholly subdued, so it seemed that the war could never end. It could only fall into abeyance, here and there.

The war might have been blamed as much on the geography of the Lands of El-Orok as on the shared mythologies of its peoples. Scripture had it that there had once been a great diaspora called The Vagabondage, when the women and men of earth were cast out from the Vale of Orok; and in each of the Lands of El-Orok, there were legends of a great journey, epicycles earlier.

But something had gone wrong.

The peoples of the fire-god, Theron, had headed south, to

what were now the kingdoms of Unang Lia; those of Javander, the water-goddess, had crossed the sea, to the far islands of Wenaya. These were remote and widely scattered places, far from easy prospect of communication; but the peoples of Agonis, god of air, and of Viana, goddess of earth, had not similarly separated themselves. When the races had divided, the El-Orokon said, it was decreed that the followers of Agonis should make their way north, to the mountainous lands of ice; and those of Viana to the east, with its thick, dark forests.

But both tribes, in order to reach their new lands, must first have had to travel side by side up the curve of the Juvescian Peninsula. Viana's people, it was often observed, had failed to head directly eastwards; both tribes must first have travelled north, and found that thick, dark forests covered all the lands that awaited them. For long cycles, so legends told, the Agonist tribes had pushed ever northwards, through dangerous wild woodland, seeking their mythical lands of ice. At last they had come to the Valleys of the Tarn, where the great white wall of the Kolkos Aros rose above them pitilessly.

There was great sorrow amongst the Agonists then; for if this was the place appointed for their destiny, then theirs must surely be a destiny as cruel as the punishment of the despised Children of Koros.

But then they saw that this could not be so, for Agonis was the favoured of the five gods. Though the Ur-God Orok had punished all races, and justly so, could it have been his intent to withhold from the people of Agonis the indulgence he had shown to the god they worshipped?

The elders of the tribe, who were the first Lectors of Agonis, decreed that their race must travel no further. In the sacred parchments they carried, it was written that they must 'live close to the vault of the sky'. But what could this mean? The sky was so remote. Would one, on a mountain, be significantly closer?

So it was that a chasm opened between the words enjoined

in the El-Orokon and the deeds enacted upon them by the Ejlanders; and so it was that the doctrine of the Divulged Destiny, or First Divulged Destiny, as it was now known, came about. Spiritually, the Lectors decreed, it was in the white mountains that the Agonists would live, elevated far above the world below. The mountains, they said, were a vision vouchsafed to the fair god's people, expressive of his superiority to other gods, and the like superiority of those who followed him. It was the destiny of the race of the fair god to live not in the bleak mountains but in the rich valleys and plains; yet to aspire spiritually to the mountains, as to the loftiest of sacred ideals.

Time's cycles unfolded and the peoples of Agonis turned away from the Kolkos Aros, filling the great plains between the mountains and the sea with their prosperous cities and towns. Of their superiority to the Children of Viana they could have no doubt. Beating back the Vianans to the east, the Agonists could only despise those who looked not to the sky, but grovelled amongst the dirt and filth of the earth; those whose goddess, in the war in the Vale of Orok, had lent her strength to the dark campaigns of her brother Koros, the Vaga-god. The first destiny of the Agonists was a spiritual ideal; but from the beginning, the seeds of the New Divulged Destiny were stirring. There were those who believed that not until the fulfilment of this new destiny could the present degenerated age pass, and a new age begin.

By the time of Tor's visit to Ela, there was a strong sense abroad that the historic struggle of the Agonist peoples was at last reaching a climax. The year, after all, was 997a; the thousandth Cycle of Atonement loomed near.

Chapter 13

ADVENT OF BARNABAS

Silence.

Ela rolled her head on the long cylinder of pillow. Beside her, Jem slept soundly, his breath barely rising, his blond hair mussed about his eyes. She smiled. She would not wake him. Carefully she slipped out from between the sheets. She reached for her shawl. The apartment glowed with the luminescence of morning. The panelling shone darkly; the chill white light pressed, calmly insistent, through the closed, latticed casement. Ela opened it. She shivered.

Was the season changing?

But it was too early.

The casement disclosed a vista without colour or life. There were gathering clouds; and then Ela realized that there was silence too, from the village far below; and if at first she thought it was the silence of early morning, she sensed all at once that it was not so early.

'Niece, really, you'll catch a chill!'

Unstartled, Ela turned to her aunt. She did not close the casement. She said without emotion, 'The Vagas have gone.'

'Oh?'

It was as if a dream were over, but Aunt Umbecca showed no interest. Immaculate in fresh black garb, the golden circle glittering on her bosom, she bustled importantly about the apartment, tutting at the ashes that were all that filled the fireplace and the table that had not yet been laid for breakfast.

Disgraceful.

The sixth fifteenth of the day had passed already. Where was Nirry, that wretched girl? Umbecca's plump hand reached for the bell.

'No,' Ela said quickly. 'Jem.'

Her aunt would have ignored her and woken the boy, had not the maid appeared at that moment, her condition more than usually bedraggled. She had thrown on her uniform in a hurry.

'I think we've all slept a little late,' said Ela.

But her aunt was not listening, and Ela, her back to the pressing, chill light, felt inside herself a slow access of dread. Yes, it was as if a dream were over.

'He's gone, hasn't he?' she mouthed without sound.

The maid was making up the fire.

Aunt Umbecca sat expectantly at the table. 'Come, niece, and close that casement. Nirry will bring our breakfast soon.'

Ela, disconsolate, slumped into her place. Blankly, looking past her aunt, she stared into the centre of the shabby apartment. She might have been seeking out the dust that inhabited the air, exuded as if breath from threadbare sofas and carpets, woven epicycles earlier.

The room had become her world.

Ela shivered again. The chill, from the casement that still stood open, was travelling inexorably up each of her limbs.

He was gone.

Tears gathered behind her eyes; her aunt was speaking of the pattern of the seasons, matter-of-factly as if nothing had happened; and all at once Ela seized the bell, jangling it before her aunt's face.

'Niece!' The plump hand gripped Ela's wrist; the red, bursting face swooped suddenly forward. 'Foolish, wanton girl! Do you not see that it is right that he should go? He is travelling with those filthy Vagas, I see it now. What did you think? Did you think he would stay? Do you think he could stay? He is mad! He toys with you! Even here, at the far edge of the kingdom, could the wretched boy live beyond the reach of justice?'

'Justice? What do you mean?'

'Your brother is a traitor.'

'No, Aunt. That's my father. My father betrayed the king, had you forgotten?'

Ela's lips were white; her aunt's were merely pursed, stiffly for a moment, before she said quickly, 'The king is Ejard Blue. The Archduke is his loyal minister.'

Ela would have laughed; but she wanted to cry. 'Oh yes, Aunt. The rewards of treachery can be great, can't they?'

'I shall pray for you, Elabeth.'

'Damn your prayers!'

The two women faced each other across the empty table. Ela's aunt felt a dark emotion, descending over her in the chill morning like a pall. Her niece filled her with something that was not quite despair, that was more a gnawing, dulled rage.

What was wrong with the girl?

What had happened to her?

Umbecca thought back to the days after the Siege, when the Archduke was preparing to leave the castle. Everything was in tumult; there was excitement in the air. Clip-cloppings of horses, rumblings of carts had sounded continually from the courtyards below; hullooed commands of upper servants rang through every chamber of the devastated castle and mingled with the excitements of the departing nobles. The castle would be abandoned; yet did any but the old steward, Stephel, feel sorrow? There was a fever of expectation; even Umbecca, in her pious cell, had packed her few belongings again and again, ardent for the journey to Agondon to begin. What should she wear to the coronation? A new age was dawning!

But Ela was unwell.

Had the excitement had been too much for her?

It was at dinner on the last night, here in this very apartment, one of the few state-rooms that the Siege had left undamaged, that the girl had stood suddenly before her father and his followers, her chair juddering back, and declared, 'Father, I am with child.'

The nobles had gasped. The minstrels, who had been playing a sprightly jig, fell silent. Tor, flushing, overturned a goblet of wine, and Umbecca, gazing into the radiance of the Archduke's features, had studied as if with a strange detachment the overspreading, black cloud. And yet her heart had seemed about to break; and break it did, later, when the room was empty but for herself, for the Archduke and his daughter. First the girl had refused to reveal the partner of her whoredom; then her father's steely, controlled wrath had descended with the precision of a slow, deliberate blade. *Yes. Yes*, Umbecca had mouthed, as the Archduke decreed his daughter's banishment. It was right. It was good. But Umbecca could have wept; and how much more so, when seasons had passed and the news reached the castle that Tor, too, had sullied his father's name.

The Red Avenger!

How the colour had drained from Umbecca's face; she was stricken, as if with an illness. But *yes, yes*, was all that Ela said; and her niece, Umbecca saw, was smiling.

'You knew? Niece, you knew?'

That was when Ela, torn and twisted from the birth, had laughed. It was the first time she had laughed since the Siege had ended.

Weeping, Umbecca had sent for Goodman Waxwell. It seemed the laughter would never stop. That evening, Umbecca prayed with a new fervour; she prayed that the love of the Lord Adonis would descend and scourge her heart like a flame. The stone floor of her cell dug cruelly into her knees, through the thick fabric of her gown and her worsted stockings. Hate and love fought in her for predominance. She had loved Tor so much! Then, if at any time, Umbecca's faith tottered. The Archduke's face rose in her mind like a vision; tears ran down her cheeks. The Archduke was a man of such goodness, such virtue! What had he done to bring this reckoning upon him?

But perhaps, thought Umbecca, there was one thing.
One thing.

Now, staring at her pale niece across the table, Umbecca Rench felt an uprush of anger. Of course, she knew why: the events of the last evening filled her with shame, as if at some loathsome, some blasphemous debauch.

She had been weak.

She had been wicked.

She must atone.

A high-pitched wailing suddenly sounded on the air.

'What?' Ela turned, clutching her forehead. For a moment she had thought the sound was inside her skull.

Nirry screamed.

'Shut up, girl!' Umbecca snapped. Her heart lurched. What could this be? Some new trick of Tor's? But he was gone, gone. The commotion seemed to come from the courtyard below.

'Nirry, see what it is.'

The maid squatted, red-faced, by the still-cold fire.

'Haven't you lit that fire yet? Stupid girl! Give me that tinder-box!'

Nirry scuttled away.

'I shall be making the meals next, I have no doubt,' said Umbecca. 'Oh, curse this wretched life!'

Her bulk strained against ample corseting as she struggled to lower herself before the hearth. Disgusted, she eyed Nirry's inefficient assemblage of green logs and twigs. The maid was highly strung, and sullen with it, Umbecca thought. She blamed Ela. One had to set an example for the lower orders; this was what came of failing to do so.

Ela said nothing. She could think only:

Tor has not gone.

But he had.

A loud snuffle announced Nirry's return. 'Ma'am, there's the strangest little man—'

Umbecca was huffing energetically at the fire. She turned, her crimson features close to bursting. 'Little man?' she cried, outraged. 'You come up here to tell me about some filthy beggar, girl? Send him packing!'

The twigs would not catch fire; they were only smoking.

The wailing came again, closer now. Nirry turned, gasping. The little man had followed her upstairs. With a bowed head, doffing his cap, he entered the apartment. Umbecca gazed at him, transfixed in horror.

'Ugh, it's one of those Vaga-freaks! Nirry! Get your father!'

But Nirry did not move. With a shy, gummy grin, the freak advanced. A wizened little man, he was the size of a child. His gait was an awkward waddle, but whether this was because of the shortness of his legs, or the heaviness of the box that was strapped to his chest, was hard to say. The box was made of shiny wood, the straps of oiled leather; down one side was a row of keys, like the keys of a harpsichord. The instrument, evidently, had been polished lovingly; the dwarf, for his part, looked remarkably clean. The thinning hair beneath his little cap was brushed neatly and his cheeks glowed, a healthy pink. Standing before Ela, he essayed an ungainly bow.

Ela had stood, too. Smiling, she reached to steady him.

'Niece, keep away from him.' Umbecca was frightened. 'Do you have nothing to say for yourself, little man?'

There was no reply. Reaching into a pocket of his tunic, the dwarf offered Ela a parchment scroll. Turning, with pounding heart, she slipped off the ribbon that was tied around it.

'Niece, what is it?'

But Ela did not hear. Only later, when her niece was sleeping, would Umbecca reach for the roll of parchment that Ela would keep, like something sacred, by her bed. Now, reading it for the first time, Ela turned back to the casement. She was no longer shivering. In her white gown, she stood in a shaft of sunlight.

Beloved,

> *I had no choice but to deceive you. There is no time to stay longer and I must go. Whether I shall see you again, I cannot say.*

> *The Bluejackets are mustering for a new war against Zenzau. Some say it is the hundredth of the Zenzan wars; the First Minister has vowed that it shall be the last. He has declared it to be a holy war. A great revival of the faith is planned. (They see its utility!) Agonism at long last shall destroy its rival creed; or rather, the Bluejackets shall crush all resistance. They know that Zenzau, so wasted and decayed, has been all along the base for our operations. Their reign of terror, they see, can be purchased only in the utter abjection of the dark kingdom.*

> *Dearest, we thought we had seen the worst. We have not. The horror of the Bluejacket regime is just beginning. That is why I must try to stop them. I have never truly been a Redjacket soldier. Here, there were no Redjackets to join; it was only another costume I wore. Another game I played. But in Zenzau, Redjacket survivors lie in wait. Torvester, heir of Irion, must join them!*

> *Ela, my love for you shall remain with me till I draw my last breath. My love for the boy is a consuming flame. It threatens to burn my heart away.*

> *I must go.*

> *The bearer of this letter has been a faithful servant to me. He cannot join me in the journey I must now take. He cannot be part of the struggle that lies ahead. Take him to you; he is a talisman. Perhaps he may become a companion to the boy, for he is of the boy's size, and has much special knowledge, which in time he shall reveal. His name is Barnabas.*

> *Remember my love for you shall never alter.*
> > *Tor.*

The parchment shook in Ela's hands; when she read the last words, she let it fall. Tears streamed freely down her pale face.

But she bent down.

She was smiling.

'Barnabas,' Ela said softly, 'welcome to your new home.'

'Niece, what are you doing?' Umbecca cried out. She would have blundered forward, seizing the dwarf; but something prevented her.

Wildly she gazed towards the big bed, where the little boy, who should not have slept there, had hauled his torso upright. The eyes beneath his mussed blond hair were enormous as he took in the scene. His gaze seemed almost to hold it, to fix it in place.

Ela was asking, 'Do you speak, Barnabas?'

Her voice was kind.

The dwarf's reply was to open his mouth; and Ela, gazing between his open gums, saw not with horror, but only with compassion, that his mouth was not only toothless but tongueless. She nodded slowly, sadly, and her tears might have flowed again; but the dwarf's little hands reached for the brightly polished instrument. With one hand he turned a handle; with the other he pressed the keys.

There was a crackling in the fireplace. The smoking twigs had begun, at last, to burn.

Chapter 14

THE TAVERN-KEEPER

When the Archduke departed his ancestral seat, Bluejacket soldiers flanked his carriage and all his train. Villagers, and dwellers drawn from deeper in the valleys, lined the road that wound through thick woodlands to the south. Some were sobbing. Hulking farmers broke down. A whiskery washerwoman with leg-o'-mutton forearms, heedless of the rolling carriage-wheels, cast herself forward and implored that their lord remain. Others, in their hearts, longed to do likewise. The old, with trusting gnarled faces, could barely understand that their master could leave them. The young stared blank-eyed, sullen and afraid, comprehending not with their heads but with their hearts that what they were witnessing was a historic day. To some, it seemed that the Bluejackets were taking away their lord. They had thought that the king was in the castle. They had thought the Bluejackets were the enemies of the king. A hasty proclamation on the village green had told them that all they had believed was false. None could know then that, under cover of darkness, the rightful king had been spirited away in chains. But the cannons and gunfire had been stilled for some days.

Something had happened.

Time had seemed suspended.

At the head of the Bluejacket patrol rode their commander, a steely-faced man with magnificent curling moustaches and eyes hard as flint. Resplendent in a uniform glittering with brocade, an ornate scabbard hanging from his hip, he rode high and proud on a huge black stallion. His name was Olivan Tharley Veeldrop. He had made himself hated by the dwellers of the Tarn. There had been torture; there had been beatings: Veeldrop had ordered them. Sometimes he had performed them. It had been Veeldrop, with evident relish, who put out the eyes of Silas Wolveron.

The village had lived under a reign of terror. Now, the proclamation in the Archduke's name had announced that Veeldrop was not an enemy, but a friend. They could not know then that, to the Archduke, this was true. In the matter of a moment the king's betrayer had reversed all his enemies and all his friends, flipped them over like a coin in idle fingers.

He would have his reward. In the depths of his heart, the Archduke had aspired to greatness; now, greatness was within his grasp. No longer the provincial scion of a line of robber barons, in Agondon he would be Third Minister in the Bluejacket government; in time, he felt confident, he would become the first. The Archduke of Irion did not look back as he left the home of his ancestors, never to return. Perhaps his countenance was written over with guilt, perhaps with a carefree malevolence; but the Archduke, behind the curtains of his coach, could not be seen.

There was a small disturbance before the long train vanished at last on the winding road. A mess of offal arced through the air, splattering the coat of arms on the side of the coach.

'Traitor!' called a guttural voice.

Commander Veeldrop, an eyebrow arching beneath his three-cornered hat, stayed his magnificent mount, just a little. 'Kill that man,' he instructed blithely; and his guards, who were not quite sure which man was meant, fired several shots and killed several villagers, and the commander proceeded on his way.

The curtains in the coach did not stir.

That had been a cycle ago; in the cycle since then, the confusions of the villagers that day had given way to a chill, hard certainty.

Rumours spread.

The tavern-keeper of the Lazy Tiger was a drunken old man called Ebenezer Throsh; in truth, it was his wife, the redoubtable and long-suffering Goody Throsh, who ran the tavern. Her husband only drank; and seemed content to do nothing else. But now old Ebenezer had developed a new obsession.

One evening, slumped as usual at his table in the tavern, the old man began to mutter of the horsemen he had seen, deep in the night after the day the Siege had ended. 'Horsemen? What horsemen?' his wife called; but more to humour him than anything else. *Poor Ebby!* she thought. Returned from the latest of his bleary wanderings, he was filled again with incoherent tales. Nothing he said had any meaning.

Bluejackets, he was saying, *but without their blue jackets*.

'What? What does the fool mean?' Stephel from the castle demanded.

No one paid attention.

Stephel had shunned company of late; he would drink alone in a dusty corner, smoking a foul pipe. Fellows were saying there was something rum about Stephel; fellows were saying they had never much liked him. His question, shouted just a little too loudly, was the only one he would ask that evening. The steward merely sat, taciturn and frowning, as the hours wore by and the drunk began to burble now, ever less coherently, of a prisoner in chains, of a nobleman in rags.

'Bluejackets,' the drunk slurred, his tankard gripped tightly, 'Bluejacket soldiers with a noble prisoner!'

Later, none could say just who it was who first saw the significance of what the drunk was saying. The knowledge flared up suddenly, as a flame takes hold, all around the smoky, low-beamed room.

'The king!'

The murmur filled the tavern; in days to come, it would travel as if with the wind through all the Valleys of the Tarn. It seemed that bleary-eyed Ebenezer Throsh, lying in a ditch on the outskirts of Irion, had been witness to the enactment of his kingdom's tragedy.

All at once the denizens of the Lazy Tiger were gathered round Ebenezer. The old man's rheumy eyes glittered. 'They looked,' he hissed, 'as if they were going to slit his throat!' There were gasps. The landlady wailed. The old steward, Stephel, who had remained in his corner, slipped out of the tavern into the night, his frown deepening into a black, overspreading scowl.

Outside, a high wind was whipping at the branches of the tall, ancient elms that surrounded the village green. The Season of Theron was not yet over, and already, in the days since the Archduke had gone, the skies had displayed the disorder of the Season of Javander. Already the leaves on the trees were beginning to fall; they swirled round Stephel's feet as he drunkenly flayed his old grey cart-horse. People said the cold would come earlier that year; and it did.

That was in Cycle 996*b*, just after the Siege had ended; by the first year of 997, it had become an axiom in the Valleys of the Tarn that the seasons, once so predictable in their progress, had ceased to revolve in the old, orderly way.

Some said the world had fallen into the sere; that it was sinking at last into disrepair. Some blamed the decline of the ancient faith; as if in the temple, now barred and bolted, the villagers had driven the engines of the seasons. Some said it stemmed from the days of the Siege. In his treachery, they said, the Archduke had violated the very order of the world. The earth itself, they would say, and nod sadly, was protesting the betrayal of Ejard Red.

The Vaga-fair had been over but for a few days when the chill winds swept down from the Kolkos Aros.

Chapter 15

TREACLE

'Jem. Jem? Your friend is here again.'

Jem, dressed in his best black suit, sat stiffly in a stiff-backed chair, his useless legs arranged neatly before him. He did not look up. The scene was laid in the barren alcove where his aunt had decreed the boy should sleep at night, now that he was getting a little older. A cheerless place, a stony hollowing in the castle walls, it was redeemed just a little on this chill afternoon by the fire that leapt brightly in the blackened hearth.

'You remember Tissy, don't you, Jem? Goodman Waxwell's boy?' Aunt Umbecca said. She was holding back the curtain that concealed the alcove; and through the gap sidled 'Tissy'.

Or rather, Poltiss.

Or rather, Polty.

'Now boys, you play!' Jem's aunt called breezily, turning back with a little laugh to the physician, who waited in the taper-lit corridor.

Later, when Jem recalled his earliest life, he would be aware of a great and all-encompassing solitude. Life, it seemed to him, was unfolding at a distance. Isolated in the inertness of his body, there was an element in which he was imprisoned, as a fish might be imprisoned in a bowl. It was not until much of his second cycle had passed that Jem, for the first time, was to have a friend; but Jem's friend would not be the one his aunt endeavoured to supply.

The curtain, purple and velvety, billowed back into place.

'Master Vexing! Hello again.'

Jem's spirits sank. He could think of nothing to say. Later, Nirry would bring them tea; later still, his aunt would appear and say: 'Jem, dear, it's time to say goodbye to your friend,' or 'Come, Jem, all good things must come to an end,' and Jem would think: *as must all bad things*.

'See this top?' The boy spun it. 'Look, it's running down.'

It was Polty's second visit, and this time, he assumed more quickly what was, Jem had known at once, his true character. The restless phase was curtailed this time: no sitting with Jem beside the fire, gazing up and down at the stony ceiling; no pacing back and forth before the slit window, or shifting-about of the Zenzau checkers. The footsteps of their elders had barely faded before the carrot-haired boy was circling Jem's chair.

The top had run down.

'That's like you.' A pointing finger. 'What does it feel like?' The boy's voice was low, and as he spoke he brought his lips closer to Jem's burning ear. 'Is it spreading more? I'd say it would spread more and more, wouldn't you? Now it's your legs that are numb as planks. Soon it will be all of you. Father says you're losing all feeling. Can you feel this?'

First came the proddings of the plump fingers at the flesh of Jem's calves.

'Can you feel this, Vexing?'

Jem could. The pain was dulled, but definite. Then the proddings were higher, in thighs and ribs and arms. And faster. The pain was sharp. Afterwards, the bruises would be hard, dark little circles. Round and round Jem's chair went the carrot-haired boy, his plump face splitting into a broad, yellow grin.

'And this? And this? Tell me what you feel!'

Jem's mouth set hard. The boy was so much bigger than him. So much stronger. But Jem would not cry out. He would not cry out.

'You're a freak, aren't you? A stinking, rotten freak!'

A cry rent the air.

'No! I shan't see him!'

'Niece, really! I'm ashamed of you!'

Meanwhile, Goodman Waxwell had gone to Ela's apartment. Sighing, Umbecca turned from the bed where Ela sat upright, blazing-eyed. But Ela's resistance was only temporary.

'Perhaps a little sleeping-draught?'

'Ho, indeed!' Umbecca rolled her eyes; Goodman Waxwell made his crabwise way forward, smiling, inevitably, his twisted smile. By Ela's bedside he rummaged in his bag. From a clatter of calipers and scissors and knives, from amongst the pill-boxes and pouches of powders, the unravelling bandages and torniquets, the little leather thongs and uneven lengths of string and the crumpled handkerchiefs and spilt tobacco, the snuff and the hairs and the flakes of dandruff, the physician produced a stoppered vial. His moist lips bared back as he brought the sticky stopper to his teeth, extracting it from the neck of the vial with a sharp *pop!* Filling a teaspoon with a black, bile-like liquid, the physician held it to Ela's lips. The liquid slid slimily over Ela's tongue, and Ela slid again into the insensibility of sickness, lolling back, ashen-faced, on to her pillow.

'My wife calls it *sleepy-treacle,*' the physician remarked.

With a little laugh, one might have called it a giggle, he twisted back towards his fat friend. She smiled. A pleasant afternoon by the fireside was in store. Outside, the world was grim. The sky hung lowering with enswathing dark clouds and the roads were a sludge of grey, churned snow. The physician would be in no hurry to leave.

'The Vaga-dwarf! Well, well!'

It was the hurdy-gurdy that had made the cry. Moonlives had passed since the day of the fair, but Polty had not forgotten the strange little mute who had scurried back and forth behind the harlequin.

But he was astonished to find him here.

The carrot-haired boy moved forward, towering over Barnabas. Jem watched, sickened. Now was the time when he might have cried out; instead he could only look on, mute like the dwarf, as the little man's fingers coaxed a strange, undulating tune from the polished box on his chest. Like the slow, mysterious winding of smoke, the music filled the alcove; and as it filled the alcove it seemed that the dim light was growing unaccountably brighter.

Polty turned and saw that the increase of light came not from the narrow slit of window in the wall but from the hearth. The flames were becoming hotter, leaping higher. All at once the plump boy was tugging at his collar. Sweat rolled down from his carroty curls, bathing his plump, reddening face. He stumbled back towards the curtain, away from the incandescence.

That was when he saw the extraordinary thing.

For all this time the crippled boy had sat unmoving in his stiff-backed chair, a black-garbed, silent mannequin. It was all the boy could do; Polty knew that. But the boy did not even seem to be hot, for all that the fire raged ever more brightly; it was as if the cripple really were dying by degrees, as Polty had said, and his capacity to feel pain was already gone. Was that why he would not even cry out, for all that Polty prodded and pinched him, slapped him, struck him?

But now, as the dwarf's music writhed around him, the crippled boy, smoothly and impassively, was rising to his feet. He was standing; his legs, that a moment before had been bowed and buckled, were all at once inexplicably straightened. The boy's limbs showed no strain, nor did he register discomfort or alarm as he crossed the narrow space to the hearth. There, the boy called Jemany knelt down, and thrust a hand unhurriedly into the centre of the fire.

And did not cry out.

'Goodman, you'll try some seed-cake?'

'My word! Your maid reveals unexpected gifts.'

'Nirry? Oh no, Goodman Waxwell! The gift is mine.'

'My good woman! A thousand pardons.'

The physician's moist lips were stuck thick with crumbs. His soft fingers brushed the lady's hand, and more than once, as they sat side by side, he permitted his thigh to slither against the fabric of her skirt. A haze of laughter and chinking teaspoons enveloped them; Ela, sinking into a different haze, heard snatches of their happy conversation reverberating, like buzzing bees, just beyond her heavy head.

'A great revival of the faith, you say?'

'I have intelligence.'

Buzz. 'From the Archduke?'

Buzz, buzz. 'My poor niece.'

A longer, nagging buzzing. Then the voice suddenly sharper:

'How long shall she last?'

Buzz, buzz.

In the chill moonlives since the day Tor had come, Ela's illness had become worse and worse. Perhaps it was the cold; perhaps it was the fact that Tor had gone again; perhaps it was the waiting, the interminable waiting, for news to reach the village of the Zenzan war.

It was not to be expected that Ela should recover. It was not in nature. She had struggled against her illness, and struggled hard; but something in her had broken, snapped clean through, almost at the moment when the Siege had ended.

How long did it last?

The sweating Polty looked on, astonished, as the cripple, standing once more, then turned to him slowly; and slowly, ceremonially, held aloft in his hand the golden treasure he had retrieved from the flames.

It was an enormous, glowing coal.

The coal rested on the boy's unburning palm and the boy's eyes seemed to blaze bright as the coal as he looked steadily, triumphantly at his enemy.

It was magic.

Or an illusion.

All the time the strange, haunting music filled the alcove, and as the scene unfolded before the astonished eyes of Polty, Jem too was in reality only a watcher, motionless in his chair, flicking his eyes first from the dwarf's pudgy hands that made the music; to the sweating Polty; to the phantom Jem that stood and walked and thrust unburning hands into the fire.

Flick.

Flick.

Then suddenly the phantom Jem had closed his hand over the coal; then the coal had vanished.

Polty swooned.

Buzz.

'How long? Impossible to say.'

'They tend to linger?'

'Yes. They do.'

Ela's mind sank into the stickiness of the treacle; and it seemed, in the moments before oblivion engulfed her, that perhaps, after all, life had always been this way, and words had been only these bumblebee buzzings, blundering without meaning back and forth in the air. It was as if a thick gauze, humming and shooshing, had fallen into place around her like a curtain; and though the gauze was light, a cobweb that even Ela's hands could easily have torn, her arms were so weak that she could not raise them. The cobweb remained. Sometimes, fleetingly, it would billow back; but now, as the white chill of the Season of Agonis settled heavily on the world outside, it was as if the web were closing in tighter, thickening and hardening.

Like treacle.

Sticky treacle.

The next thing Polty knew, the cripple was sitting in his stiff-backed chair again; and all was as it had been before.

But it was not.

The music played on, and all at once a desperation seized Polty, coursing through him implacably like an urgent nausea. He stumbled forward. The flames leapt up sharply, goldenly again. Deep within the flames he saw the huge coal. It was the same coal the cripple had brought forth; it had to be.

But how could that be?

Polty did not know; he knew only that he had to have it. The blazing flames singed his eyebrows, his hair. His fat face was roasting. He plunged his hand into the fire. The pain was so intense that he did not even scream; did not even, for a moment, think to draw back his hand.

Then it was over.

The fat boy, silently screaming, was blundering into the curtain, thumping against the velvet to smother the flames that had caught rapidly at the sleeve of his jacket. Then he was gone, and Jem was alone with Barnabas.

The carrot-haired boy would not visit again.

'My, my. It is effective, isn't it?'

Once again Umbecca was standing by Ela's bed; once again she was speaking to Goodman Waxwell. Her niece had slept soundly all afternoon. 'Poor Ela! She is in such pain. I dare say, if she could slumber a little longer . . .'

'A little more . . . *regularly*?'

'Goodman, you have often mentioned the danger of hae-morrhage. And poor Ela will sometimes excite herself so . . .'

It could be most distressing. For long phases Ela would fight, fervently but uselessly, against the swooning depths that always lay in wait, ready to claim her. Sometimes she cried out. Sometimes she cursed her fate. Sometimes she would rise from the bed, refusing to return. Relentlessly, and for all her aunt's protests, the foolish girl would pace the floor of her apartment – even the chill corridors of the castle – until at last, and inevitably, she crumpled into unconsciousness. Then her fever would flame high again, and all her endeavours to cure herself would have made the wretched girl only worse than before. Perhaps the sleepy-treacle, her aunt thought, would help poor Ela to bear her fate.

The fat woman smiled, and suggested as much.

'Hmm . . .' Goodman Waxwell stroked his chin. His brow furrowed. When he spoke again, there was a sternness in his voice. 'I take it, my good woman, you are aware that such medicines must be used only . . . *sparingly*? The consequences of improvident dosage could be serious, I need hardly add.' The physician gathered up his bag again; the early darkness was falling and really, he must go.

Umbecca's red cheeks had become a little redder. 'I'm sure, Goodman, I did not wish to suggest . . .'

She accompanied the physician down the stairs.

'Barnabas, how did that happen?' Jem said later, after they had played a game of Zenzau checkers.

But the dwarf, of course, could not reply. Instead, the little man knelt by a corner of Jem's bed, retrieving the top that had rolled away from the hearth. He span the top in the centre of the floor; Jem watched.

And watched.

The fire burnt brightly. Snow was falling outside the slit-window.

'Goodman, I can't be sure,' said Umbecca.

'Our temple is barred! Bolted!' the physician cried. 'Perhaps the Revival may come; perhaps it may not. But it is incumbent upon those of us who keep the faith to gather where we can, for communal worship. Only thus can we survive this wretched time.'

They were standing in the archway on the brink of the courtyard. The physician, his soft hands already gloved, a long scarf wound about his neck, was fumbling to button an enormous greatcoat.

Light snow was falling and the physician's bony mare, tethered to a ramshackle carriage, was stamping. Stephel, red-nosed, held its reins. Already the physician's boy was sitting up on the cart. He was looking more than usually sullen, and occasionally moaning.

'Good woman, think of your faith,' the physician went on. 'Irion has fallen into ungodly ways. Mercifully, the Redjacket king is now deposed. But the infection lingers. Look around you! How long before it comes creeping, creeping, to possess you, too?'

It was nothing the physician had not said before. Until now, Umbecca had been doubtful. She had made vows. She had duties. With a furrowing forehead, she watched now as the physician pulled a woolly hat from his greatcoat pocket; and idly it came to her that Goody Waxwell – thin, stick-like Goody Waxwell – had, long ago and laboriously, knitted this hat, these gloves, this scarf. The thought caused the fat woman a curious pang.

Stephel hawked a gob of phlegm on to the cobblestones.

'At my meetings,' the physician was saying, 'we see – we *feel* – the value of the faith. But more must join us. Our numbers must swell; but it is not, of course, only a matter of numbers. Good woman, were *you* to come among us, you should be in the briefest of time a leading light. A *leading light*, good woman!'

Stephel studied the glistening phlegm. Polty looked at it too. In the almost-darkness it pulsed on the slushy stones like something living; but in a moment a carriage-wheel would smear it flat. Stephel could feel compassion for that gob of phlegm; Polty could not.

The carriage juddered as the physician, puffing, heaved

himself up into the driver's seat. 'In two days it is Blackmoon. Shall I send the carriage for you, dear lady?'

Umbecca looked down, biting her lip. Duties. Vows. And yet, might not Goodman Waxwell's meetings offer her the way to the deeper piety she knew she sought? The piety that underlay her duties, vows? *Oh, Goodman, I can't be sure*, she might have said; but already she had nodded curtly, and already the physician had whipped his bony mare.

The carriage rumbled away.

Polty was snivelling. Only later, when they were home, would Goodman Waxwell discover the reason why. *You put your hand in the fire? You stupid boy, Tissy!* the physician would cry, as he forced the boy, with his agonized hands, to tug down his breeches.

Thwack!

Thwack!

Afterwards, 'Tissy' would fall into a fever.

Troubled, Umbecca turned back towards the stairs. She hugged herself. How cold she was! Upstairs, Nirry had not yet lit the candles. At the criss-crossed casement, only a bleak light glimmered. A wave of loneliness swept over Umbecca. Ela was still sleeping; the guest was gone.

But on the little table by Ela's bedside, barely visible in the fading light, stood the sticky, stoppered bottle he had neglected to retrieve.

Chapter 16

THE PALE HIGHWAY

'Barnabas! Look!'

The boy was growing bold. In a wickerwork chair fitted with wheels, Jem whizzed rapidly down the long passageway. Iron bands bound the wooden wheels and whirred like thunder over the polished floor; Jem's hands, blistering, dashed again and again at the spinning circles that carried him. He squealed with delight. His blond hair billowed back and flashed like gold in lines of light from the leaded windows.

Flash!

Flash!

It was so exciting. Far from Ela's chamber, the boy and the dwarf were in the long tumbledown west wing of the keep, where Barnabas had found an unrutted, even floor. Still sleek from centuries of polish, glassy from generations of shoes, marvellously it had escaped the assaults of cannon-balls and flames and crashing, heavy stones. It was the Long Gallery, stretched beneath a low, arched ceiling of moulded plaster. On the wainscoted walls a succession of dark portraits hung in heavy, gilt frames. Most hung askew; some were slashed.

To Jem, they were a blur.

On and on he whizzed and whirred. He closed his eyes. He could go on for ever.

A flight of stairs brought the gallery to an end.

'Ouch!' Jem's hands clutched suddenly at the wheels. He knew just when to open his eyes. He lurched forward, laughing. Far behind him, the dwarf's applause rang; then came the slap-slap of little boots, scuttling back eagerly to the crippled boy.

'Barnabas,' cried the boy, 'I have never gone so fast!'

The dwarf nodded eagerly; the hurdy-gurdy wheezed. *Nor have I*, it seemed to say, and Jem laughed again. Pride shone in his friend's wizened face.

It had been the dwarf who found the marvellous chair. As moonlives passed and the dark Season of Koros gave way at last to the Season of Viana, the little man with his hurdy-gurdy roamed the castle far and wide, seeking out its mysteries. He had returned with untold treasures, abandoned in the Archduke's hasty departure. There were tarnished candlesticks, dented goblets, a shield emblazoned with the Redjacket arms; there was a bejewelled scabbard, a suit of mail, a moth-eaten cap lined with dark, sleek fur. There was a kaleidoscope that showed shifting patterns when Jem held it to the light; there were leather-bound books with cracking spines; there were animals made of wood or stuffed with straw. There was so much to discover; and Jem envied his little friend's journeys. In the alcove where he slept, the crippled boy would arrange the many treasures; but how he wished that he, too, could set out in search of them!

Then one day the dwarf lugged back the wickerwork chair that had been abandoned in a box room high in the castle. From then on, day after day, Barnabas would bring Jem to the Long Gallery, trundling awkwardly over other, uneven floors to this special, superior place.

Life in the castle had changed in many ways since the dwarf had arrived. More and more often, Jem's mother was sleeping, and often Aunt Umbecca was gone. Airily she spoke of duties. Vows. On the Canondays which initiated each phase of the moonlife, when the snow did not lie too thickly on the ground, a carriage sent from Goodman Waxwell's would rumble into the bailey and bear her away. At first, only hours would elapse before she would return; soon it became days.

In the last chill days of the year, in the time that the Ejlanders called the Festival of Agonis, Ela's aunt remained away from the year's last Canonday through all the intercalary days which followed. Only when 997c was over, and the first Blackmoon of the new year had passed, did she return. Her niece said nothing; she slept away the season like a princess in an old tale. Nirry tended her in her slatternly way; Stephel shuffled drunkenly between the kitchen and the stables; and Jem found himself more and more in the company of the dwarf.

Barnabas was Jem's first friend. From the moment when, raising himself up in his mother's bed, the boy had first gazed, fascinated, at the dwarf, Jem had known that a new era in his young life had begun. Soon Barnabas was filling his days, and Jem would have been astonished, had he thought to look back, at how empty, before the dwarf came, his days had been.

In Jem's alcove, the dwarf slept on a mat beside him, the polished box strapped perpetually to his chest; and in the mornings the boy would wake to the peal of the strange music, and the wizened face staring at him expectantly. In the beginning, before Barnabas found the chair, the day that followed would be a series of spectacles, of magic tricks and dumb-shows and games of chance; in between would come quieter, different games.

With a stub of powdery stone that never seemed to grow shorter, the dwarf's little hand drew markings on a slate, circles and straight lines and curving lines and slanting lines; and Jem, sure that there was magic in these markings, copied them carefully while the dwarf looked on. Only slowly did the boy realize that his mute companion was teaching him his letters. Then, with props salvaged from innumerable dusty nooks, the dwarf showed him what the letters meant. He held up a withered apple. A dead beetle. A crack-lipped cup.

Jem learnt quickly.

Barnabas applauded.

They ate magnificently. Back and forth, upstairs and down, the dwarf would scurry to the castle kitchens, returning with all his crippled friend could desire; and though Nirry would protest at the little man's raids on her pantry, she soon found, in truth, that she could not resist him. Much of her time was spent in baking for Aunt Umbecca; but now the supply of biscuits, cakes, pies and tarts increased both in quantity and in quality. Many of them were destined for the alcove. Nirry's skills, which she had thought merely dull, now delighted her. Jars of her mother's preserves, left to lie, were rescued from the obscurity of high dark shelves; willingly the maid, with sleeves rolled back, wearied out her arms as she rolled and kneaded dough or beat with her wooden spoon at bowls of rich, thickening cream. How she loved to watch the dwarf demolish a plate of her best Tarn-cakes, soaking them first in a dish of milk before he pushed them into his gummy mouth!

The dwarf had charmed her.

'It's not true that he can't talk,' she said once to her father. 'He smiles. He frowns. He rolls his eyes. He jerks his thumb and he opens his arms. And oh, the music of the hurdy-gurdy!'

Her father, in reply, only grunted.

Sometimes, in the chill evenings of that Season of Koros, Nirry would sit upstairs in the alcove with the young master and the dwarf, plying her needle and listening, entranced, to the strange sounds from the polished box. The box glowed richly in the flickering firelight and Nirry, her eyes cast down, her fingers working, would feel a wave of deep yet delicious sadness sweeping over her; then her tears would fall.

She would not snuffle. She sobbed without sound; it was almost as if the wheezing music had soaked up, like a sponge, all other possible noises. They barely heard the winds that whirled outside the walls and cascaded in scattered, mad raids through the cracks and cavities the cannon-balls had made.

Jem would huddle in blankets, lingering in wakefulness. The undulating tunes made him think of the future, of the life that stretched before him, mysterious and veiled. Before Barnabas came, life had hung suspended; or so it seemed to Jem. It seemed to him that he would always be a child, and live in the castle with Mother and his aunt.

Now he sensed that this could not be so.

Among the treasures that Barnabas had discovered was a small, discoloured picture in a chipped frame. A view from on high, perhaps from a hilltop, it showed a pale road, a highway, winding over a range of hills and far, far away into an unseen distance. Often, in the sleepy afternoons after tea, Jem had sat studying the little picture. He would wonder where the road might lead.

The dwarf's melody, meandering and unending, was like that road, Jem thought; and fancifully, as the music lulled him, the boy would see himself travelling that road, skimming its surface as a stone skims over water; and fancifully, too, as he was almost sleeping, he imagined that Tor was waiting for him on the road, standing patiently and smiling in the far, far distance.

Tor would call, 'Come on, Jem! Jem, come on!'

But then it would come to the boy that the far road was a road he could not walk. That was when Jem grew sad; and as he slipped into sleep he would think of the future with a rueful, injured wonderment.

END OF PART ONE

PART TWO

The Kingdom of the Castle

Chapter 17

THE CIRCLE OF KNOWING

The world was frozen into a bleak whiteness. Snow heaped heavily on the high battlements of the castle and the slabs in the tombyard and the tussocky expanse of the village green. Ice hung from the eaves of cottages and the barren branches of trees and clenched the river into a glassy immobility. It was the dark season of the year, when the sun peered only fleetingly through the hazy sky each day. Silence hung over the village like a pall.

'Hey! Vaga-brat!'

Cata sprang away from the wood-pile. Roaming the village in the brief daylight, she had been gathering firewood from the yards of the cottages. The heavy burden clattered from her arms.

She ran.

'Wretched little thief!' For a moment the peasant-woman pursued her, then fell back, muttering.

The Vaga-brat had vanished.

Cata crouched behind a snow-drift. She shivered. Papa said that each season had a part to play, but how the girl hated the Season of Koros! She clawed at her furs. They were itching again, as if her very flesh refused to wear them. In the cold seasons, Papa wore the garb of a bear, and Cata of rabbits and hares. She called it her coat of death, and sometimes she could hardly endure it. But always, if she attempted to discard the coat, the cold would drive her back into its bristly embrace. To the child, wearing the coat was like an act of treachery, and in the brittle black-and-whiteness that held the world in its grip, she felt as if already she were paying the price. In the warm seasons, Cata might have been the princess of the Wildwood; but in the cold, the princess became a slave. For long days, Papa would refuse to let her venture forth. How Cata longed to roam wild and free! They concealed themselves in their cave until the Koros-season passed. Huddled in their furs, even by the fire-pit, the old man and his daughter would eke out their tubers and dried fruits; and when the snow relented, Papa would send the girl out only as if, in truth and not just in spirit, he held her on a tight rein. *Child, do not go far*, he would instruct her, or *Child, come back soon*, as she set out in mittens and moccasined feet, in search of more chill-moss or Koros-berries, and fallen branches for the fire.

She did not tell him that she raided the yards of the villagers.

Cata looked up at the sky. It was ominous. Fresh snow would soon fall, and she had lost the day's wood. She had collected nothing else except a pocketful of black, bitter seeds. She scrambled up, scudding miserably along the scraggy edges of the wood.

All at once she stopped still. She dropped down.

Voices.

'No, Polty, not again!'

'Come on, Bean! Catch!'

'I can't!'

'Here he comes! Flying flop-ears!'

'Urgh!'

Thud.

'You're such a girl, Bean!'

Cata peered through a mesh of barren branches. Returning from the icy depths of the Wildwood, the children were advancing towards her slowly, lingering and doubling back as they absorbed themselves in some curious, raucous game. Their breath turned to clouds and their voices rang hollowly on the thin, chill air. Cata's lips tightened. Intently, from her concealment, she looked back and forth between them. Something was odd: it was a moment before the girl realized that it was their number. They were fewer. Until now, they had

138

been the number of the fingers of a hand; there had been one
for each finger. Now, one of them was missing. Which one?
In their thick coats, she could distinguish only the fat one
and the tall one. The other two hung back, huddled together.
Something had happened.

But they acted the same.

'Come on, Bean! Your throw!'

'Not again, Polty!'

'Yes, again!'

The boys were tossing a flopping, heavy object back and
forth between them. Only now, as the boy called Bean leaned
down, retrieving it, did Cata see what it was. Flakes of snow
were swirling down already and the air was a blurring haze.
But she should have seen the red, spattered trail that wound
back behind the little party. She should have seen the long,
knotty stick that the children in the rear bore between them.

The stick was hung with distended corpses.

Bean held up a rabbit by its ears. Blood dripped redly,
steadily, into the snow. He flung back his arm, and the
rabbit's long hind legs swung back, thumping, over the boy's
shoulder.

'You throw like a girl, Bean!' Polty laughed.

'Shut up, Polty!'

But the throw went awry.

It was Cata's chance. She burst forward, grabbing the
bleeding rabbit.

'Hey! Get her!'

The fat boy flailed forward, but was too slow. Padded
thickly in his coat and mittens, Polty seemed twice his normal
size. The clattering jumble that hung from his shoulders –
traps and slingshots and sharpened sticks – weighed him
down further; but the wild girl, even in her furs, was nimble.
Her moccasins slapped rapidly over the squelching snow.

She vanished again.

'Wretched little thief!'

Polty turned back, red-faced beneath his furry hat. He was
about to ask his companions why none of them had joined

the pursuit; but then, he thought, if he couldn't catch the Vaga-brat, then they couldn't either. Of course they couldn't.

'She's probably starving, Polty,' Bean offered weakly. He was only glad that the game was over. None of Polty's games seemed like fun now, since things had changed. Something was wrong, since The Five had become Four.

'Starving?' The fat boy flamed out. 'Well you can starve now, Master Charity-of-Agonis. Because whose rabbit was that you just gave to the Vaga-brat, Bean, hm?'

'What?' The thin boy's face was blue with cold.

'Your rabbit! Do you hear?'

'That's not fair!'

Polty stood still for a moment, breathing deeply, then trudged laboriously towards his thin friend. Sighing, as if at some tedious duty, he raised his mittened hands and shoved Bean in the chest, quick and hard. The thin boy did not even cry out as he collapsed on to his back.

'Come on!' called Polty to the two lingerers. 'Come on!'

Bean lay miserably, staring upwards, as their companions trudged past him. The sky was blurring from dirty-white to grey. Soon the snow would be falling more thickly. It was time for the children to go indoors.

Cata was concealed.

Deep in the Wildwood, the girl sat slumped, trembling, amidst the falling snow. Cradled in her arms was the bleeding rabbit. She had thought she was saving him from The Five, who were no longer Five; but she knew now that he could not be saved. She focused her mind on the mind of the rabbit and nothing came back to her in return. Only blankness. The rabbit had passed into the place of the fallen ones. It was a place Cata did not understand. It puzzled her, because the fallen were in two places at once. Their bodies remained; yet the essence of them was elsewhere.

Did they ever come back?

Slowly the girl lowered the rabbit to the snow. It was time

to return to Papa; but if she took the carcass, she knew, Papa would say that it was an offering. He would say that it must be used. They would take the fur and flesh; but if the rabbit came back, thought Cata, what would he do? She brushed a light covering of snow over the carcass, then got up and shambled, hunch-shouldered, away.

Poor rabbit! Tomorrow she would come back and see if she could find him. Perhaps he would be alive again, and then they could be friends.

She did not tell Papa. He could not see the blood that had soaked into her furs, staining them first red, then purple-black; and when, sensing something, he asked her what was wrong, the girl's only reply was *Nothing. Nothing.*

But Cata could not come back the next day. That night the snow fell so heavily that even the entrance of the cave was concealed, and many days passed when the girl and her Papa could barely move beyond their mean, rocky home, and the whitened glade outside.

After a few days, Cata started awake to a sharp sound of violence from the glade outside. Her gaze snapped back and forth in the gloom. Papa was gone! But when she scrambled to the mouth of the cave, the girl saw him, and was startled again. His cowl flapping back about his head, Papa was hacking at a tree with an axe.

'Papa! What are you doing?'

Cata had seen the axe before, but until now she had never understood its use. Then she regretted that she had lost their firewood, on the last day she could venture out.

The time of thickest snow was long; but all through it, Cata remembered the rabbit she had left out in the woods. When the snow retreated, she went in search of him. Of course, it was useless. The snow had obscured so many landmarks that even Cata could not find the place again; and slowly the thought came to her that she had been foolish. The rabbit was not coming back. He was never coming back. But it was while she was looking for the little dun-coloured carcass that Cata found something else.

Something extraordinary.

It was by the frozen river, in a clump of trees barricaded by stiff bracken and heavy, curtaining vines, that Cata came upon the strange grove. Protected by her furs, the girl pushed through the dark vegetation that was too thick to wither and fall even in the depths of the Season of Koros. What confronted her was a curious sight. At first she thought the grove was shrouded deep in snow, like all the world outside. But already the fragrance was filling her nostrils, and the unaccustomed warmth was playing against her chapped, reddened face. Cata looked up. Suddenly she had forgotten the lost rabbit that had occupied her thoughts for so many days. Sunlight was streaming through the treetops, bright and warm. But how could this be? It was as if the Season of Theron had returned. Cata parted the dark vines again and outside the snow and cold possessed the world.

The girl turned back to the mysterious grove, stumbling into the centre. She sank to her knees on the fragrant floor. It was covered in petals. White, soft petals. All around her, in the interior of the grove, white flowers writhed up the trunks of ancient elms. Cata clawed at the fastenings of her coat, gazing up in astonished reverence into the streaming warmth of the sun.

What was this place? Cata did not know. But already she knew that this was a special place, and knew that when she slept it would fill her dreams.

From now on, she knew, she would come here each day.

Cata had not told her Papa about the rabbit; now she did not tell him about the special place she had found. Sometimes, dimly, she was aware of a welling of sadness, as if a gap were opening slowly, slowly, between her Papa and herself. Yet how was there a gap? She loved Papa; she loved him with a fierce intensity. But somehow, when she thought of the grove, the girl felt herself gripped by a strange shyness. The secret circle was a place to be alone. There, Cata would strip off her hated furs and lie naked in the centre of the bower, as the fragrance enveloped her and the mysterious warmth coursed benevolently down through the trees.

It was on the fifth day that she saw the snow-tern.

'Ghost-bird,' Cata whispered. It was the name that some gave to the small white bird, for only the most eager, the most intent, could see the bird as it moved on its background of white. The snow-tern was in the centre of the circle, quick and silent and wholly self-absorbed as it picked about amongst the soft petals. How had it strayed here? Cata had seen a snow-tern only once before; but the bird, she knew, was accustomed more to the chill whiteness outside than to the warm fragrance of the secret circle. The white petals must have deceived it.

Cata tuned her mind to the mind of the bird; but it registered no puzzlement. No distress. Only a calm acceptance. She sensed the long journey the bird had taken, coursing through the air on the curving currents that brought it, each year, from the mountains to the valleys. She sensed a blue profusion, an immensity of space; and always, in the bird's inner eye, the vastness of the mountains to which it would return. When the Season of Viana came, thought Cata, the snow-tern would be gone.

The stripy coat descended suddenly. It scythed across the scene like a gash.

'Wood-tiger!'

Cata cried out; then the wood-tiger was gone.

Startled, it had left the snow-tern.

Cata sank to her knees beside it. One of the bird's wings was torn away and the white feathers were dark with blood. Lop-sidedly, its heart pulsing hard, the bird tried to drag itself across the white petals.

Cata had no thought of concealing this from Papa. Numb with sorrow, she carried the snow-tern back to the cave in careful, cupped hands. Papa had taken his staff and was roaming the wood. He had not yet returned. While he was away, Cata made up the fire again and squatted before it, tending to the bird. She bathed away the blood. She made a little nest in a box filled with straw. The bird lay palpitating, its pinprick eyes fixed coldly.

But the bird was not dying. Cata saw the future with a calm, clear certainty. The bird would live with her in its box and she would bring it crumbs and seeds. She would gather beetles from the bark; worms from the earth. She would sing to the bird and stroke its pulsing neck; and when the warm days returned, they would sit in the glade outside the cave and the bird might sing to her. It would peck from her hand. One day she would take it to the edge of the Wildwood and show it the mountains, to remind it of its home.

Cata was happy. But when she told Papa of her plan, the old man was sombre. Tenderly his fingers felt for the bird. He picked it up, stroked it, brought it to his lips; then his hands closed about its neck and twisted.

There was a sudden, sharp crack.

'Papa!'

'It could not fulfil its nature, child.' The old man turned from her. 'The bird is made to sport and swoop in the air. It is made to venture across the vastness of the sky. Shall you carry this bird back to the mountains, when the Season of Viana comes? It is a bird without a wing: what can it do but pine away?'

Cata was sobbing, but then her tears ceased; with the deep knowledge of a child of the Wildwood, she knew that Papa was right. He had taught her a lesson; and it had been a lesson she had to learn.

Later, they would bury the snow-tern under the tree where its death, its real death, had come.

'Papa, you know this place?' Cata breathed, as the old man parted the curtaining vines. Carrying the bird carefully in a shroud of white cloth, the girl had merely followed in her

144

Papa's footsteps. She had barely noticed where his footsteps were leading.

'Child, this is called the Circle of Knowing. It is a sacred place, and known only to us.'

Cata gazed at her Papa in astonishment. Then it came to her that she had learnt another lesson. For a moment she was about to ask Papa whether he had known that she came here; but then she did not need to ask.

He had known; of course he had known.

'Papa, why don't we live here?' said Cata, after a moment.

It was an offering. An atonement.

'Why don't we live here when the cold seasons come?'

'Child, you must know that this is not that kind of place. The Circle is a place not wholly of this world. We can come here. But we cannot stay.'

Cata looked about her wonderingly. Her brow furrowed. Then she looked down at the dead bird again. She opened the white cloth and stroked his chill neck.

In the centre of the circle, the old man knelt stiffly, setting down his staff on the petals beside him. With his gnarled hands he cleared away a patch of the fragrant white flakes, digging a shallow pit in the crumbly earth beneath. When he was finished, Cata placed the bird carefully into the pit and Papa mumbled out a soft chant as the girl replaced the warm, rich soil.

'Goodbye, ghost-bird,' she said softly.

There was doubt in her voice, as well as sadness. The bird had died a long way from home, and Cata was worried that his body should lie here. But Papa's chant, and the warmth of the Circle of Knowing, lulled away her fears.

It was only as they were standing on the brink of the circle, wrapping themselves warmly in their furs again before they stepped outside, that something happened that filled Cata with a sharper, stronger fear.

Lingeringly, she gazed at the place where they had replaced the petals. There was no stone, not even a pebble, to mark the place where the snow-tern had been buried; and for

145

a moment Cata wondered if this was right. Mama had a slab. The tombyard was filled with slabs.

Then it happened. In a shaft of light that fell with a sudden new intensity into the centre of the circle, Cata saw the white petals gathering themselves into the pale form of a bird. The petal-bird fluttered slowly up from the ground and spiralled into the treetops on spread, white wings, vanishing into the radiant brightness from above.

It was the snow-tern. He was going home.

But this was not what frightened Cata.

'Papa!' she whispered.

'What is it, my child?'

Cata was silent. She could not speak, and only gazed, astonished, into the old man's empty eyes. Something was wrong. It was then that the thought came to her that filled her with fear.

He cannot sense it. He cannot sense that the bird has risen.

The curtaining vines swung back into place as they returned once more to the world of snow and ice. Cata had sought to keep things from her Papa. She regretted it; but more than this, she regretted the awareness that there were things he did not know. Could his powers be failing? Taking the old man's hand as they made their way back to the cave, sometimes she would sense that he was losing his way.

Only once did the girl look back regretfully at the dark curtain of vines.

It is over, thought Cata. *I shall not come back.*

Chapter 18

BIRD-BOY

'What is that bird?'

It was the strangest thing.

'Master Jem, that's a man, can't you see? A man with wings.'

The book was so tattered that it might at any moment have dissolved into dust. The leather spine had flaked away; dark stains spread across crinkled pages and the small sharp teeth of rats had gnawed the corners. It was a big book, and weighed heavily on Jem's knees; the smell that rose from it was a curious incense, redolent at once of promise and decay. Pages tore and crumbled as he carefully turned them.

Nirry looked on while Barnabas played.

The bird-man was one of many odd pictures that alternated with pages of heavy-lettered script. There was a pig in armour, bearing a lance; there was a man bedecked with flowers, riding a cow; there was a boy with fish where his eyes should be and a dog with the face of a man. There was a barefoot girl, walking through a field of flame; there was a glowing figure robed in white, pressing to his lips a black horn. There were villagers fleeing a visitation of the mis-shapen Creatures of Evil.

Turning the pages, Jem often laughed. Sometimes he was frightened. Sometimes he felt only a dreamy wonderment.

'What is that arrow, coming out of the sky?'

In the picture the bird-man, who wore no clothes, was leaping into the air from the top of a tower. It was a dark, stormy night and a bolt of lightning, scything from the clouds, enveloped the bird-man in a dazzling light.

'Oh, Master Jem! Haven't you heard of Nova-Riel?'

As they turned the pages, the maid had exclaimed many times over the figures in the pictures. The pig, she declared, was the Swine-Warrior of Swale, who defended Swale from a giant when all the men of the village were too cowardly to fight. As his reward, from one of the great coins in the giant's purse the women of the village had fashioned for the Swine-Warrior a golden trough for his swill; and when it came his time to be butchered, he was eaten in a special banquet in his honour.

The barefoot girl was the Princess Alamane, who had been shipwrecked and forced to live amongst simple fisherfolk. When Prince Yon, her betrothed, had found that she was alive, he refused to believe that she had kept her purity; but when an enchanter made a fire, and said that the princess, if pure, could walk across the fire, she had done so without demur. So it was that the prince was contrite, and never, after the wedding, would doubt his wife.

Nirry seemed to know all the stories. 'Have you read the book before, Nirry?' Jem had asked.

Nirry only laughed. Read!

The book was *The Mytholegicon*.

'Who is Nova-Riel, Nirry?' Jem pursued now.

Nirry looked down; and something, a cloud, seemed to pass across her face. 'I'm sure you could read it, Master Jem.' She moved away, and took up her work again.

Jem sat wonderingly in the firelight and the lamplight, gazing down at the picture of the bird-man.

But it was not a man.

It was a boy.

The print was thick and ornate and old and close together and difficult, too difficult, for a small boy who had only just learnt his letters. Jem bit his lip, running his finger beneath the lines. It was only with the effort of several nights, and at the price of several headaches, that he puzzled out the story of Nova-Riel. Afterwards he would read it again and again.

This is what he read:

1

Know that of the heroes of Ejland, there was none greater than Riel, afterwards called Nova-Riel; for he it was who drove the last of the Creatures of Evil from this land.

For in the time when Ejland first rose to become a great land among the lands of this world, there yet flourished amidst the rich valleys to the north those Creatures of Evil, called the Tarn, who refused to be driven back into the Realm of Unbeing.

So it was that the great warrior Ixiter-Irion, though weary from war against the hosts of Zenzau, said to his king, who was Aon the Ironhand, 'Sire, your kingdom shall have no ease while the Creatures of Evil yet remain in this world. Let me take me to the Valleys of the Tarn, where the great white sheet of the Kolkos Aros mocks the brief passing of the days of this world. There let me build a great fortress, that I may repel the misshapen ones.'

His lord gave consent; and so it was that in the Valleys of the Tarn the warrior Ixiter-Irion raised his great fortress, and gathered about him his men, and did battle with the misshapen ones. There were hornèd bears; there were suction-lions; there were apes with the ravening jaws of wolves. There were river-hawks. There were flame-bats. There were spiders wide as carriage-wheels. There were animal-women and animal-men and those, yet worse, who concealed their vileness beneath a cloak of beauty. All were terrifying, and all were destroyed.

At last, only one remained. This was the flying serpent Sassoroch. Massive in size and strength, yet possessed of mysterious powers of concealment, the glittering-scaled serpent was a formidable opponent; and yet, after seasons had passed, he too was slain, routed and brought low by hail after hail of poison-tipped spears. When he fell, the warrior's men hacked the vast corpse into many pieces.

Then the warrior Ixiter-Irion sent jubilant word to Aon the Ironhand, declaring that the forces of Ejland had triumphed. So it was that the king came to him, and said, 'Warrior, you have repelled the Creatures of Evil?' And the warrior said to the king, 'Sire, they languish in the Realm of Unbeing.'

Then the king said that this was good, and decreed that the warrior should make this place his seat, and that all men should call him Archduke of Irion. And there was much rejoicing in the fortress, and a great banquet was held; but on the day that followed, as a party of the king's men were hunting in the valley, it happened that they were set upon and slain, rent limb from limb. The only survivor was a terrified servant, who told of a golden, wingèd serpent that had descended from the skies, breathing fire.

2

Then there was great confusion in the fortress, and the king called the Archduke to him and thundered: 'Deceiver! You said that you had destroyed the Creatures of Evil, yet still they lurk in the valley below.'

And the Archduke said to the king, 'Sire, I am no deceiver; rather, I have been deceived. I thought I had destroyed the serpent Sassoroch, last and most terrifying of the evil ones; I see now that even should he lie slain on the ground, rent apart as he has rent your men, the hideous thing yet can knit his substance together once more. Sire, I killed him; but he has returned to life.'

And the Archduke decreed he would set all the valleys ablaze, that the serpent Sassoroch should have no place to hide; but the king said, 'My lord, you are fool as well as deceiver. Would you destroy my kingdom, then call my kingdom free? I see now you are impure in heart, and the reward you would have taken from me was unearned.

'Know this, unworthy Archduke: I shall not leave this fortress while the serpent goes free; and for so long as I must remain here, so shall your dishonour grow. Know, too, that he who delivers these valleys from their bondage shall have all the rewards my reign can bestow.'

And Aon the Ironhand, who was old and wearied from wars,

sank to his knees in prayer. 'Sacred one, may there come to this place a warrior true of heart who shall end my captivity.'

Then it was that many seasons passed, and the king lived on in the fortress; but though the fortress swelled in strength as in size, turning from timber outpost to massy edifice of stone, still the valleys trembled beneath the yoke of Sassoroch.

And warriors from all through the kingdom, and from far kingdoms too, when they heard of the reward the king had offered, would brave the valleys to do battle with the serpent; yet even the greatest warriors would fall, or retire, bloodied, from the fray. For Sassoroch was the last of the Creatures of Evil; and the evil one, desperate as he was devious, was determined that nothing should drive him back into the horror of the Realm of Unbeing.

Again and again the serpent attacked; again and again he was slain and cut to pieces. Yet each time he was slain, he would return stronger than before; for when he had been slain once, he returned twice as strong and was doubled in size; and when he had been slain twice, his strength and size were threefold.

So it was that the fortress must be builded ever stronger and become a great castle; and yet its strength remained the same. So it was that the evil Sassoroch was first two, then three, then four times the monster he had been.

3

Now it happened that there lived in the castle a kitchen-boy, mean and dirty, whose fate it would be to achieve what none of the warriors had achieved. His name was Riel; and in the courtyard one day, when he was small, Riel had fallen beneath a moving carriage, crushing his legs beneath the rolling wheels. The cook, who had charge of him, would have had him slain, for the child could no longer do his work; but Naya, the kindly consort of the king, who was barren and had no child of her own, took pity on the kitchen-boy. She took him to sit with her, and would have no harm come to him. And the child was happy in Queen Naya's care, and knew none of the sorrow he had known when he was whole.

Now there was much fear and trembling in the castle as the tenth return of the monster drew nigh. Though many brave warriors had assembled to try their strength, there were those who said that this time the castle could not survive. Some deserted its massy walls, preferring the dangers of the wild, wooded valleys. Some remained, and gave themselves to prayer. The generality resigned themselves to merriment. The halls rang to the jokes of jesters, to the merry melodies of lutes and viols.

So it was that Queen Naya was troubled; and she called to her the king's soothsayer, and demanded of him: 'Soothsayer, what will the future hold? My women tremble; there are omens in the air; the king, cloaked in pride, will not leave this place. Is the castle to fall? Soothsayer, tell me.'

And the soothsayer, blind and in rags, cast up his unseeing eyes to the air, and turned about before the queen and her women; and when he ceased his revolutions, said: 'Queen, there are those who say that when Sassoroch comes again, he will be so great that with one mighty puff his flame-breath will set the castle ablaze. At the mere beating of his wing, some say, the walls of the castle shall fall. And yet, the future is a forking path. It may be that Sassoroch achieves his end, and brings about our destruction; it may be, too, that he does not.'

At this, the queen's women were enraged. One cried: 'Faugh! He is a mountebank! For what has he told us, that we could not know ourselves?' One cried: 'Would he mock his queen? Shame!' Another: 'Send him to the dungeons!' But the queen only smiled, and bade the soothsayer continue.

'Queen, this we may know: that no sword, no arrow, no lance can defeat Sassoroch. Yet there is another way that he may be undone. For he is a creature of the Realm of Unbeing; and though it may seem that his strength is great, yet his tenure in this world is frail. Always he must look before him, not behind him; for to look behind him is to see the way back into the Unbeing from whence he came.

'This I declare: should it come to pass that the monster is made to turn about in a circle, ten times, one time for each of the times he has lived again, then it shall be that his power shall leave him, and he shall lose his grip on this world.'

At this, the women laughed uproariously, and would have the man drawn and quartered for a knave; but Queen Naya only remained troubled in heart, and dismissed the women from her. Then it was that she turned back to the soothsayer, and called him close to her, and addressed him thus:

'Soothsayer, I am sure that what you say is true. Warrior after warrior has failed to defeat the monster, and now the time of reckoning is at hand. But know this: should there be a spell that might make the monster turn, I should use it, though I might lose my life. For I am a barren queen, and have no value; yet I should give myself to save the castle.'

Then it was that the soothsayer's blind eyes seemed to look, as if with a strange vision, first into the queen's eyes, then down, at what she embraced; for through all this, circled in the queen's arm, had been the boy Riel, whom she would not dismiss from her side. The boy was weeping, for the queen had spoken of her death; but it would soon be the queen's turn to weep.

For the soothsayer said: 'Queen, I see a way. But it is a hard way, and one in which your woman's heart may fail you.'

'There is no such way!' cried the emboldened queen; yet knew that she was wrong when the soothsayer said now:

'Queen, it is the boy who shall save the castle. On the night after next, there shall come a great storm. About this rock, all the winds from the white mountains shall sweep down, shrieking; thunder and lightnings shall shake the castle walls. Then, when the storm is at its height, from out of the wild darkness there shall come the monster Sassoroch, ready to destroy us.

'Queen, what you must do is this: when the storm is at its height, you must bear the boy with you to the topmost tower. On the tower, there is a platform that may be approached in secrecy, and there you may go unobserved by guards. There you must strip the boy's raiment from him, and lay him on the battlements, his face against the stone, and leave him there exposed to the hostile elements.'

153

At this, the queen turned pale, and cried out, but the sooth-sayer said only that there was no other way. 'What shall become of the boy?' the queen demanded. 'Would you have him die?'

But all the soothsayer said in reply was that he spoke with a wisdom greater than the world's; and that was when the boy looked up to the queen and said: 'Madam, know that I am not afraid. For as you have been a mother to me, so I have learnt your noble ways; and weak though I am, I know that fear is a feeling to be despised. I am content to die, as you are, if in my dying the castle should be saved.' At this the queen hugged the boy to her, and embraced him; and, sorrowing, declared that the soothsayer's plan must come to pass.

And it happened that the storm came, as the soothsayer had said; and the winds from the white mountains swept down, shrieking, and thunder and lightnings shook the castle walls. So it was that after much fervent prayer, Queen Naya bore the crippled boy in secret to the tower. The tower was a howling place of horror, jutting into an empire of wind and rain; and though the weak woman in her would have snatched the boy back, yet it was that her queenly heart found strength. There she laid the boy, divested of his raiment, face down on the battlements in the howling storm. And Queen Naya embraced him, and called him her son, and withdrew, weeping, to await the sequel.

4

Now among the jesters who congregated in the castle, there was a little man called Motley, who often would be called before the queen. Motley had no jokes, and only one trick; but it was a trick so curious that all were diverted by it. If what he did were real, or illusion, none could decide; for it was given to him to leap up and somersault in the air, not once, not twice, but time and again; perhaps so many times as ten. Often had the boy Riel laughed at the jester's antics; and later, he would say, as he lay exposed on the battlements, he would think only of Motley, twirling on the air once, twice, then again and again.

The air around Riel was wild with rain, that lashed like a

whip against his naked back. The vault of the skies was deafening with thunder, and blinding with flash after lightning flash. The cripple gripped hard at the stone of the battlements, that he might not be swept away; but there came a great gust that tore his fingers free, and his frail form was hurled into the maw of the storm.

There was a cry from below; it was the queen, who looked on in secret to see the boy's fate. The guards looked up, and the waiting warriors; and warriors, guards, and queen alike saw the boy's body buffeted on the wind. He hovered above the tower. In the next moment he would be dashed to the ground.

Then it happened: for the storm was at its height, and what was ordained now came to pass. A crack of lightning fizzed from the air, brighter than any the watchers had seen before; and just as the boy was about to fall, instead he was consumed in the blinding light. The queen screamed. The watchers bowed their heads; but then, when the next dazzling flash lit the air, from a single upturned face came the cry: 'Look!'

For fluttering defiantly above the tower was the boy; but the boy transformed to a wingèd creature, and beating wildly like a moth against the storm. The queen clutched her hands together tight and gasped for joy; but her joy turned to terror when all at once, from the swirling clouds, there burst forth the monster Sassoroch!

Massive as a great ship, sailing on the skies, the monster surged forward, beating back the storm with vast wings. Golden-scaled, glowing with its own luminescence, the monster bore down with its fiery, wild eyes, its huge fangs and claws; and the queen started to see the watchers on the lower tower – guards, warriors alike – casting down their weapons. Some fled in terror, crying that all was lost; some abased themselves there on the tower, dropping to their knees and shrieking into the storm: 'O mighty Sassoroch, spare us! Spare us!' But all that Queen Naya could see was the boy, his tiny form a fluttering insect shape against the monster's glowing immensity.

That was when the boy made his first move, swooping in a desperate arc past the monster's eyes. The hovering creature reared up. A scorching gust burst from its nostrils, enveloping the tower in a ball of flame. The battle, it was certain, was already over; but the boy Riel was not consumed, and flitted for a second time past the glowing eyes. There came a hideous roar, louder than thunder; a snaking of the many-scaled, serpentine head; then the creature's jaws snapped shut. The boy had vanished!

5

The creature hovered like a huge bird of prey above the imploring guards, the prostrated warriors. Only the queen refused to bow down; and though her eyes were streaked with tears she determined to die, if die she must, staring defiantly into the face of the evil one. The thing reared back its head with a mighty snort; but at the moment when the monster might have struck, hurling forth sheet after sheet of flame, there came again the tiny, fluttering presence of the boy. The creature swished around, enraged, discharging on to the air the flaming burden that might instead have roared, unrelenting, through the castle.

Then it was that the flying boy made a yet more daring pass, again so that the monster might almost have devoured him; but at the moment when it seemed that doom had come to him, the boy instead darted up higher, higher, into the enveloping wildness of the storm.

By this time the prostrated figures on the towers had risen up, and in the courtyards below all the denizens of the castle had come forth, heedless of the pelting rain. All watched in astonishment and awe as the vast serpent, high above their heads, turned and turned on the air with beating wings.

The queen counted, holding her breath. Once, twice, three times the creature turned, chasing the tiny thing it could neither catch nor kill. Four times, five times, six. And as the creature turned, and its rage grew greater, so did its fiery scales grow brighter, ever brighter, so that all the wild sky was ablaze with golden light. It turned a seventh time, an eighth, a ninth.

It hovered, uncertain. For a moment it seemed the great creature might lurch suddenly down, crashing into the battlements, scattering towers with its lashing tail, tearing apart the fabric of the castle with its claws. The queen's breath at any moment would burst from her lungs; her eyes strained at the swirling air. She could not see the boy. There were screams, scatterings, from the watchers below. The monster's light was fading.

It happenened all at once: the fangs parting again in an agonized wail; the scales glowing suddenly brighter than before. In a last wild paroxysm of fury, determined this time to destroy the enraging insect, the creature darted round.

But this time was the tenth time, and in the moment of the creature's turning, the raging storm was suddenly gone from the air. The air all at once was a vortex of light. And in the centre of the whirling light was darkness; and the monster Sassoroch was sucked, spinning, into the darkness at the heart of the light. Then all became as it had been before; but for the storm, which had abated; and for the darkness, for daybreak had come.

The queen collapsed, spent, to the storm-battered stones; and the watchers, as if released from enchantment, looked around them and above them, wonderingly. Then slowly, on that rain-slick morning, did the cry go up. It was a cry of joy; for fluttering down from the great vault of the sky came the wingèd boy who had saved the castle. He floated down on to the tower beside the queen, who first hugged the boy to her, then held him up to the crowd, declaring to a chorus of enraptured cheers that this, their saviour, was her son.

And seeing this, the king could not demur; for though he was proud, he was just; and he had promised the greatest of his rewards to the warrior who would release him from his bondage in the castle. So it was that it was a small, crippled boy, and none of the finest warriors of the world, who defeated the last and most evil of those creatures which inhabited the kingdom in the days of its birth. So it was that the kitchen-boy Riel was dubbed Nova-Riel, and became a noble prince; and when in time the king died, became king in his place, and founded a great dynasty.

For Nova-Riel was known by all to be rightful king of Ejland.

Chapter 19

GREEN GARTERS

'Who am I?'

The girl lolled back lasciviously against a barrel, her lips pursed as if for an exaggerated kiss. Her coat slipped from her shoulders. With a teasing hand, she rucked up her skirt about her thighs.

'The Great Harlot of Wrax!' said Polty.

'Ha-ha!' the girl flung back. The name was a rude one the Agonists gave to the goddess of the Zenzans.

It was not the right answer.

'Mistress Rench,' said Bean. 'From the castle.'

This time Leny did not laugh. No one laughed at the things Bean said; perhaps that was why he had such a hangdog look.

'The Lady Imagenta?' he tried again; and ducked as Polty aimed a lazy cuff at his head.

'Blasphemer!'

'As if you cared!'

It was Vel, the blacksmith's son, who got the right answer. 'Green Garters!'

'Yes!' Leny leapt up. Vel caught her in his arms and whirled her about, her dress spiralling high about her thighs. They fell down, laughing, into the snow.

Polty and his friends were growing older.

'Oh, shut your row!' Polty mooched away from the barn door, scuffing his shoes in the slush. His plump hands were sunk deep in his pockets; he kicked at the tussocky grass. These games were no good. No good any more. He was angry, and angrier still when Vel and Leny kept rolling back and forth together in the snow, the girl without her coat, giggling and squealing, oblivious to the cold, the boy whooping, gasping. Did they not even notice he was gone? It was all wrong! He was their leader!

After a moment, Bean slipped into step beside him. 'Everything's changing,' the thin boy muttered. How could it happen? The seasons had passed; yet life until now had seemed strangely timeless. But then Tyl had gone away, departing with her mother to a new life in the south. That was what had changed things. The Valleys of the Tarn, said Tyl's mother, were dying. 'Dying!' Polty had snorted his ridicule; and ridicule swiftly turned to contempt. To the carrot-haired boy, it was soon clear that he had never liked Tyl; none of them, he was certain, had liked Tyl. 'Good riddance!' he had even declared, when Tyl, in tears, had announced that she was going.

Bean pretended that he felt the same. But in secret, beneath the blankets in his bed at night, Bean had shed his own tears; and now, with a terrible ache, he missed the waif-like Tyl.

How he wished she were back!

How he wished he had said goodbye!

Poor Bean! Once, it seemed to him, he had been a happy, simple lad; the tow-headed, cheery son of Goody Throsh from the Lazy Tiger. Everyone could see that he was different now. It was all that growing, his mother said; and indeed her son was growing at an alarming rate. He had always been a lanky boy, but now his long limbs seemed to become longer with every moonlife that passed. Already his height had long surpassed Polty's. Walking with his plump friend, Bean was obliged to stoop as never before. His shoulders were becoming round as wheels. Soon his knuckles would rasp the ground!

For as long as he could remember, Bean had been Polty's follower, beside him through all the golden days of The Five, when together they had come to know every cornfield and orchard that surrounded the village, every burst of birdsong, every tinkling cowbell that sounded on the air. They had flung snowballs in the Season of Koros; in the Season of Theron, they had fished in the river. There had always been the five of them and they had each known their place. And

Polty had always been the leader. Before, at least, Bean had felt this to be true; but now he felt that things were not quite right, and the worst thing, he thought, was that Polty knew. Polty could tell.

Without Tyl, the balance had shifted. Was that why things were changing? Leny was acting strangely; her manner disturbed Bean more and more. And now things were happening between Leny and Vel that Bean did not understand. He only knew that he did not like them.

Polty turned to him suddenly. 'Nothing's changing!' he burst out. His face was reddened and his voice cracked. He punched Bean's arm. 'Nothing!'

'Ouch! That hurt, Polty!' Startled, Bean rubbed the top of his stick-insect arm. Polty punched so hard! There would be a bruise.

But Bean's friend had already darted ahead. A little way along the track that wound back towards the village from the abandoned barn, his fat form twirled round, and he called back, 'I'll race you to the green!'

Bean started after him, kicking up mud on the rutted track. They plunged beneath the icy lattice of a tree-lined lane. It was downhill all the way.

'Can't catch me!' Polty flung back over his shoulder.

It was a lie; of course the lanky boy could catch him.

But did not.

With his long legs, Bean could have won the race easily, but as usual he pretended to be puffed too quickly, clutching a stitch in his side with stylized agonizings as his friend, with a whoop of triumph, forged ahead.

Then, when Polty had a far enough lead, Bean straightened up and stood looking for a moment after the labouring, wobbling form, puffing steamy clouds behind him on to the air. At any moment, Polty seemed likely to slip over in the mud; yet he did not.

How Bean loved him!

Later, Polty and his gang were gathered again in the hayloft at the Lazy Tiger. Outside, evening was drawing in already; inside, only an orange lamp glowed. Delicate smoke curled on the air; the children passed a stolen Jarvel-pipe from hand to hand. Below, the horses were settling into their stalls and Bean's drunken father, Old Ebenezer, was stumbling about in the midst of his chores. Sometimes he sang to himself, snatches of old songs; sometimes he flung out shards of speech that meant nothing to anyone other than himself; that meant nothing, perhaps, even in his own addled brain. He did not know that the children were there, concealed in their secret kingdom at the top of the rickety ladder.

This was Bean's favourite of the many places they met. Warm in his coat of skins, he snuggled into the straw. How sleepy he was! The softness of the straw seemed to mingle in his awareness with the delicate shadowy light in the loft and the warm pungency of the horses from below, and his awareness of the white, soft snow that covered the ground outside. It had begun to fall at the end of the race, as if to mark the moment of Polty's victory.

'Green Garters,' Polty announced, exhaling the smoke from the stolen pipe.

That was when Bean was suddenly awake. Warm in his favourite place, he had tried to think the changes could not really be happening. Everything was as it had been before; the four of them were there, and he could pretend that Tyl would be coming later, or that Tyl could not come away today.

But just today.

Where was she now?

> They say the king had cracked his head,
> They say the king is dead—
> Long, long live the king!

the old man below cackled, half-singing.

'Green Garters,' Polty said again, musingly this time. There was a smile on his face, a smirk; and something was working behind that smirk. He had passed the pipe to Leny, who passed it to Vel. The girl was huddled sleepily against the blacksmith's son.

Bean glanced at her. Leny, Polty had confided to him, was a slut. *A slut*. That was the name for a girl like her; and Bean, considering this, was filled with a terrible sadness. It was not that he thought the accusation false; it was not that he thought it was true. It was just that, considering the big, blowzy girl Leny had become, and trying to connect her to their companion of earlier days, he could not. It was as if Leny had gone away when no one was looking, to be replaced by this creature with too-plump thighs and embarrassing, burgeoning breasts. Her mother, a soldier's woman, was known through all the village as *a slut*. Leny was becoming her mother, but younger.

She was becoming ugly.

She and Vel were huddled together in the shadows beneath the slope of the stable roof. Polty gazed at them, his green eyes flashing. 'I had one of those garters. Did you know that, Vel?'

Bean was sitting up now, his stomach churning. It was absurd. What was this? He reached out, taking the pipe from Vel's hand. Before the changes, Bean knew, Polty would never have said these foolish things; before the changes, Leny would not have started it, offering up, as she had done that afternoon, her taunting, flagrant impression.

'Garters?' Vel's reply came slowly, his voice thick. 'What do you mean, you had one?'

Bean sucked deeply from the Jarvel-pipe; then surrendered it before he quite wished to do so. Polty reached for it, almost blindly.

'I meant what I said,' the fat boy was saying. 'I went to Agondon. You all thought I had to stay indoors, remember? When I had my bad fever. Remember? But I don't get bad fevers, do I, Bean? Eh? Stringbean?'

Bean did not reply; his head was suddenly spinning from the Jarvel-smoke.

So was Polty's, Bean could tell.

'I was in Agondon,' Polty said. 'There were things I had to learn. Can't just watch the animals! She gave me a garter. A green garter.'

Bean thought distantly: why was Polty saying this? When Polty had his fever and could not come out, Bean had climbed up the wall to his friend's room. He had been there many times before; that time, he had seen Polty lying prostrate on his bed. He had stood there while the sweating plump boy mumbled disconnectedly from the illusion-world of his sickness. Of heat and bright coals. Of strange music that would not leave his head. Afterwards, Polty had remembered nothing; he had not even known that Bean was there. 'You were so sick, Polty!' Bean exclaimed, almost admiringly. Polty shook his head. 'There was nothing wrong with me! It was nothing,' he snapped. But this was not true; just as it was untrue that he had been to Agondon. He had never been there; none of them had been there.

Except Tyl, who was there now.

There was a liquid rumble as the drunkard below, his duties forgotten, pissed long and noisily against the stable wall. He sang,

> Prr-prr, pusscat sitting in the tree,
> What can he see? What can he see?
> Does he see me coming? Can he see me?
> What can he see? What can he see?

The slurring voice faded as the old man shambled away; then there was only the pungent silence.

'You're lying, Polty.' It was Leny who said it.

Polty toyed with the long-stemmed pipe. For a moment Bean thought his friend might fling it, with sudden violence, at the girl's head. Instead he passed the pipe to her lethargically, and lay back in the straw.

'Of course I'm lying,' Polty said. 'But what if I weren't? Have you thought about that, Vel?'

Leny had drawn no smoke from the pipe this time. The

bowl lay unregarded, loose in her hand. She had flushed scarlet. 'Don't listen to him, Vel.'

But now the blacksmith's son was sitting upright, his dark eyes intent. Vel was a taut-muscled boy with a heavy cascade of oily curls. A thick moustache sprouted already above the sharp curve of his upper lip. Of late, Polty had begun hissing behind his hand to Bean that Vel, their old friend Vel, was not really one of them.

Look at that swarthy skin! Polty would say. *Have you ever really thought about it, Bean? Zenzau-blood! He's a half-breed. He must be!*

At once Bean had looked with new eyes on their old friend, because he looked with new eyes on their old friend's skin. You could tell a lot from skin, Polty had whispered; in fact, you could tell everything. Bean revolved this revelation in his head.

It was amazing.

Polty said:

'We've all heard of Green Garters, haven't we?'

The children nodded. All children in Ejland knew the name of Green Garters; it was a name that seemed to come to them from earliest life, unbidden from the air. At first only a name, a jingling alliteration from old rhymes and sayings, in time it attached itself to the image of a woman, a bulky woman lifting up her skirt to reveal the bright garters that secured her stockings. Her face was painted and she wore a frizzy wig. When a neighbour's house was disorderly, the women of the village whispered, *Green Garters is coming to tea; You're a daughter of Green Garters, not of mine,* they cried angrily to recalcitrant daughters.

It was a potent insult. If the goddess of the Zenzans was the whore of the world, Green Garters was the whore of Ejland. They all knew her story. A woman of good family who had fallen into turpitude, the harlot lived in a filthy back lane by the market-place in Agondon, scavenging her dinner from the market refuse, from lettuce-leaves and squashed tomatoes on piss-spattered cobblestones, from scraps of meat flung out for cats and dogs. Gold and silver glittered frequently in her palm; but the harlot flung away all her earnings on powder and paint and strong spirits. She stank abominably. A gentleman would shrink, nauseous, from her touch; yet there was something in the harlot that enslaved the passions even of men of breeding. They wanted her; they would go back to her again and again. Every so often, when a youth ran wild, women would say of him: *He's after Green Garters.* With vicious delight, they would hiss the harlot's name when new marriages palled and young wives were caught sobbing in the mornings. It was cruel; but later, as fat housewives, the young women themselves would be beyond concealment, beyond illusion, shrieking execrations for all to hear as they beat their husbands about the head with brooms, dancing absurdly round and round the green. *Green Garters! Green Garters!* the children had once squealed, delighted, when they were small, skipping after the victim until they grew tired, or until another victim took his place.

Now the gang looked expectantly at Polty.

'I've decided,' he said simply. 'I shall go to see her.'

'What?' Bean said hazily. 'How?'

Polty laughed. 'Come on, Stringbean, you should know! Here we are behind the Lazy Tiger. Every moonlife there's a coach that goes to Agondon, isn't there? Isn't there?'

Bean hung his head. 'Yes,' he muttered. Of course there was a coach. They called it Boneshaker; Tyl and her mother had been inside it one windswept morning at the end of the Season of Javander. Now, each time the coach came back, Bean thought that Tyl might be inside it again, but she was not, and as the coach drew away he imagined her waif-like face at the window, that last windswept day.

How his head span! He hated himself.

'The coachman is here now, isn't he? Carousing at the Tiger? He's leaving in the morning. And who do you think will be in that coach? Eh, Beanpole?' Polty lay back luxuriously in the straw. 'Who do you think? And who do you think will be on it when it comes back? With a green garter tied around his wrist?'

'No,' Bean murmured. 'No, no.'

He might have added, but did not: *Your pa won't let you.* It would have been true, but Bean said nothing. He could only sit shaking his bleary head. The little scene was unfolding, it seemed to him, at a great distance.

Now there were slappings, punchings.

Now the straw was flying in all directions.

'You wouldn't dare!' Vel had burst out.

'Wouldn't I?' cried Polty; then Polty's body was pinning down Vel's; Polty's fists were pounding Vel's head.

'Stop it!' cried Leny, and launched herself at Polty. There was spitting. There was a tearing of hair.

'Slut!' Polty was crying. 'Zenzau-blood!'

He was saying aloud the things he should not have said, the things he had said only to Bean.

'Fat pig!' Leny spat in Polty's face.

Vel's thick boots kicked him in the ribs.

'You're finished!' yelled the blacksmith's boy.

It was true. It ended with the fat boy overpowered and breathless, cursing, half-sobbing, as Vel and Leny, laughing contemptuously, clattered down the ladder from the loft to freedom.

It was the end of something.

Polty scrambled up, gasping after them, 'You'll be sorry!' He would have kicked the ladder away from the loft, sending the girl and boy crashing to the ground, but thick ropes tethered it in place.

Chapter 20

THE AMETHYST RING

It would be late that night before Polty returned to the Waxwell house. There were more Jarvel-pipes, while the weed lasted; there was the ale that Bean tapped from the barrels in the Tiger, filling a cracked jug. Polty needed to recover himself after the humiliations of the scene that had passed. Now he had only Bean.

'Aron! Aron!'

Sometimes Bean's mother called him, wanting her son for this or that chore; the boy only yelled back wordlessly, then ignored her. The carousing from the tavern was too loud; they couldn't hear her, could they?

'Where is that boy? Damn him!' Goody Throsh would curse from time to time. He was a useless boy. Still, she was used to him. She was used to everything.

Later, when the revellers had spilt out into the night, yelling and singing, the tavern-woman gazed for a moment from her window before falling into bed beside her insensible husband. In the centre of the moonlit snowy green, she glimpsed her thin son and his fat friend stumbling drunkenly in their thick coats, supporting each other, then falling over, then helping each other up.

Were they laughing?

Perhaps they were.

'Oh, Aron!' she sighed.

But the boys were not laughing.

'Polty, you can't really mean it,' Bean slurred.

'I can!'

'How could you go?'

'I only need the silver!'

167

'You've got no silver.'

'Ah!' A jabbing finger would have bored into Bean's ribs, but Bean lurched to one side and Polty fell over. He plunged face-first into a high drift of snow.

Time elapsed.

Polty rolled on to his back.

Bean bestrode him.

'I'm not!'

Polty held up his hand. He wore no gloves and the fingers were blue.

'Not what?'

Bean screwed up his face. It must have been the ale; he must have been mad. At any other time, he would have been frightened. A stick-insect even in his coat of fur, he leaned over, coming close to Polty's fat red face.

It was purple in the moonlight.

'I know what you meant,' Bean whispered hoarsely; it was rather as if the next thing he might do would be to raise his boot and stamp on Polty's stomach.

He would not have the chance.

'But Bean,' said Polty, in an intimate whisper, 'you know I've been thinking about your old ma. You know your old ma?'

Bean said he did.

'Dear Goody Throsh! Your ma, you know, Bean, is a lovely lady. Lovely. But you know as well as I do, Bean, let's face it, that your ma is also a drunken old slag, and I was think-ing . . .'

Bean swung back his fist.

'She counts, you know! She can count!'

He would have hit Polty then, incredible as it seemed, but Polty's plump fists had grabbed the lapels of the thin boy's coat. Then it was Bean's turn to lie on his back, as Polty kicked him in the ribs several times, told him how useless he had been in the hayloft, spat on him, said he hated him, and reeled away into the night.

Bean lay in the snow, getting colder and colder, for long moments before he could stir himself. He was looking at the moon. It was three-quarters full. It was the phase of the moonlife called Eastmoon; Hornlight had passed and Blackmoon was returning.

They were on the way down!

Polty stumbled home.

If his steps were unsteady, he did not know it. He seemed to glide across the ground. The pathway unfurled beneath his feet unbidden; the moonlight through the frozen branches lit his way harshly. He could think only of one thing. It was not the fate of his friend, Bean; Polty had kicked him hard, but it served him right. Nor did he think about what would happen when he got home.

What would Waxwell say?

Would Waxwell say anything?

The ale and the Jarvel-weed and Polty's consuming anger pushed these questions from his mind. At first light, from outside the Lazy Tiger, the coach was leaving. 'I'll be on that coach,' Polty said aloud. 'I'll be on that coach!' He shouted it to the moon, several times; then stopped when he saw that already he had come in sight of his father's house.

Polty had never quite understood his father. In the case of his mother, there was nothing to understand; she was a sickly, drab woman whose principal interest in life was to display the fact of her sickness. She bored him. She was thin and pale and showed him no affection. She had no interest in him, only a distaste she scarcely veiled; sometimes Polty thought his father felt the same. Again and again the boy would slip away from the house. Sometimes he would be gone for days, and the Waxwells, as he thought of them, seemed neither to notice nor to care. Then Waxwell, as if a switch had clicked in his brain, would be seized suddenly in the grip of his peculiar mania, his obsessive desire that all, even his lumpish boy, be saved in the love of the Lord Agonis.

It drove Polty mad. He knew it was nonsense; but there was something in the force of Waxwell's obsession that even Polty could not resist.

The beatings were the worst thing. First would be prayers, when Polty was forced to kneel on the floor beside Waxwell; then the boy had to lean across the bench in the chill attic room where the physician carried out his operations and held his horrible meetings. *Take them down!* the physician would bark; and if Polty did not pull down his breeches, Waxwell would tug them down for him. *Thwack! Thwack!* came the strokes of the lash; Polty, his fat face grimacing against the tears, could only look up blankly at the iron Circle of Agonis that impended massively on the wall behind the bench. It was like a curse. It was a promise of evil. *Feel it in your heart, boy! Can you feel it? Can you feel the love of the Lord Agonis?*

Polty could not. Now the boy gazed up through the branches at the moon. Suddenly he thought: *I shall not come back.* Why had the thought not come to him before? Suddenly, quite suddenly, it seemed natural as breathing. In a flash Polty saw the folly of his Green Garters plan. Could Green Garters be a real person? Dimly, even earlier than this, it had occurred to the boy that perhaps she was not; but what overwhelmed him now was the folly not of his quest for the harlot, but of his desire to return with a token of its success.

What did he care for Vel, for Leny?

For Bean?

Nothing!

He would be on that coach to Agondon. Silver coins, in the early morning light, would glint as he counted them into the driver's hand. *When do you come back?* the driver might say. And Polty would smile. He would not come back.

The moon shimmered in the boy's dazzled eyes. The force of the new idea was like a blow; but this was a blow he welcomed. He stumbled into the embrace of a sturdy elm, clutching for support at the chill trunk.

'Yes,' he burst out in an excited whisper. 'Yes.'

Something was happening.

Slowly the swirling in his head became still. He closed his eyes; and when, after a moment, he opened them, he raised his gaze slowly to the sky again. The Eastmoon shone clearly, unjuddering, in the cloudless chill air. Now Polty was calm and clear, too.

Polty always approached the Waxwell house from the back. Across a snowy field, that shone silver-purple in the eerie moonlight, he saw it now, the thatch of the gabled roof standing out, pointy, above the little barn and the barren apple trees and the hedgerows that made thick ridges in the snow. Neat white twists of smoke rose from the chimneys, but no lamplight shone in the windows.

The house was sleeping.

Polty hissed.

He knew what he must do. In Waxwell's study there was a sturdy desk; in the top drawer of that desk was a metal box, and in that box, Polty knew, Waxwell kept a cache of silver coins, bright and gleaming. Soon, they would be the foundation of his son's new life.

His son?

Polty spat.

'He's not my father,' he said aloud.

Quietly, carefully, the fat boy made his way across the white field. Waxwell's study was on the ground floor. Polty edged his way to the front of the house.

There was only darkness.

There was only silence.

His heart exulted and he pressed his face against a pane of the window, looking into the empty room.

Yes. It was going to happen.

The window was a sash-window, the sort that slid up and down. For a long time, Polty knew, the catch had been broken on the bottom frame. Palms upward, he pushed against the beams that divided the little squares of glass. The window slid up easily.

Polty stood in the darkened study. It was almost warm. The fire had been left to burn down in the grate and its purplish glow shone from behind the high, hunched back of a sofa that was turned away from the room. Polty slipped off his heavy coat. He cast it across the back of the sofa.

He must work quickly.

Quietly.

The rays of the Eastmoon shone across the desk. There was just enough light. He felt along the mantelpiece for the familiar key. He was shivering, but with excitement, not fear. Time and again he had toyed with the metal box, opening it, gazing on its gleaming contents, picking up the coins in his hands and feeling them lovingly. But only one, only two. Never had he plunged his hands deeply into the box. Now, all mere play was over. He stood on the brink; at that moment Polty's heart pounded so loudly that he wondered that Waxwell did not burst in, confronting him.

With excruciating slowness he slid open the drawer. In the slant of moonlight he could just make out the ornate lid of the box. The key was in his hand. He thrust it into the keyhole and the lid opened easily. *Yes*. The silver sparkled. Suddenly eager, Polty plunged in his hands. *Yes*.

'Yes!' he cried out.

'I don't think so,' the voice came dryly.

Polty's hands, deep in the box, clutched convulsively; he snatched them out. They were rigid fists. Coins scattered into the darkness in all directions. Fixed suddenly in a rictus of fear, Polty did not even register the square of folded paper that he had scooped from beneath the coins in his greedy haste.

Polty was aware of the sound of a ticking clock.

'I don't sleep with Goody Waxwell. I haven't slept with her since you were born,' said the physician, rising from beneath a blanket on the sofa by the fire. 'I thought you would have known that, Tissy.'

'Stop calling me that.'

'Tissy. Miss Tissy.'

The physician made his crabwise way towards the boy. He was wearing only a nightshirt; he was without his wig; his livery purple lips were twitching convulsively. In his hand he held a thick leather strap.

The attack came suddenly.

'Wicked child!' Waxwell roared. 'I'll bring you to the love of the Lord Agonis!'

The enraged physician seized Polty's hair, flinging the fat body across the oaken desk.

'Take them down!'

A hand tore at the fastenings of the boy's breeches; the leather strap whizzed back through the air. Still Polty's hands were clenched in tight fists. *The coins,* was all he could think. *Hold on to the coins.* The stroke of the lash seared his flesh.

He cried out. He swung round. The tight fists struck.

Waxwell staggered back.

Then Polty was scrambling desperately out of the window, his hands like fused bone, his breeches round his ankles; then he was in the snow outside the window, on his back, on his front, and the physician was upon him again.

Thwack! Thwack! The lash descended.

Polty rolled.

He kicked.

He bucked.

It was over.

Somehow the boy was alone again, back in the field behind the house where the snow was silver-purple in the eerie moonlight. His fingernails dug deep into his palms.

The coins.

He was shivering. He had lost his boots and breeches and his shirt was torn.

I shan't go back. He's not my father.

That was what Polty said to himself then, as he lay naked

173

and bleeding in the snow; that was what he said again, a little later, chanting it like a mantra through chattering teeth, as Bean, awakened by a stone against his window, helped his shivering friend up the stairs of the Lazy Tiger.

'Oh, the poor lad!' exclaimed Goody Throsh, when she saw him. 'Who ever has done this? He should have gone straight home!'

Not until Polty was sleeping at last did Bean manage to prise his friend's fingers apart. The treasure he had kept there, clenched so tightly, was hardly the riches Polty had sought. A few coins of little value, that was all, and the folded paper, crushed to a tight ball, that Polty had not even intended to take. Bean thought: *This paper must be important*, and uncrumpled it carefully; only the gentlest touch could prevent it from flaking into a thousand ragged little bits.

He worked slowly, sitting in his moonlit high window, glancing from time to time at the mound of his sleeping friend. It was some time before he could make out the angular writing in the letter; some time, too, before he stopped staring at the silver ring he had found wrapped inside it. The ring was inset with an amethyst stone.

Beneath the warm covers, Polty's breath rose and fell. Dawn was breaking. In the yard, the coachman was harnessing his horse, ready for the first stage of the long Agondon route.

Chapter 21

THE MAGNIFICENT STICKS

'I wish I could fly,' said Jem one day, as the chair skidded to a halt at the end of the Long Gallery. His eyes juddered open and he gazed, as into the unknown, into the stairwell that rose and fell darkly into mysterious reaches of the castle.

Some years had passed. The boy's arms had become taut and wiry; the heels of his hands had grown hard. But still he was aware of his weakness. Now, even here in his special world, Jem would find himself besieged by sadness. He felt trapped. Imprisoned. Up and down, up and down, he would spin along the gallery, but he travelled only on this narrow track. Even the stairway at the end would defeat him. Elsewhere his progress was a laborious trundling; without Barnabas, he could barely turn the chair.

He closed his eyes again, and sighed. 'Barnabas?'

There was silence. Jem was puzzled; always the dwarf would come scuttling behind him.

The silence persisted. Jem heard the callings of birds from beyond the windows. He heard the wind. The weather was warm; life would be burgeoning. White clouds would billow over the sky like sails.

A loud clattering echoed down the stairway.

'Barnabas!' Jem's sorrow turned to surprise. With heavy puffings, the dwarf was descending towards him. Carefully, one little sturdy leg, then the other, strained downwards to each of the worn, steep steps. The dwarf was dragging something heavy behind him.

It was a long piece of wood.

Two pieces of wood.

'I don't understand,' Jem said.

That was before Barnabas held the crutches upright. They were carved and polished, thick and ornate; they were, in a curious way, magnificent. Though they were too big for the little man, he demonstrated their use in dumb-show to his friend. There was earnestness in the dwarf's eyes; perhaps sadness, too. His crippled friend was bigger now, he seemed to say, and stronger. The time had come.

Jem understood. When he was smaller, again and again he had attempted to stand; when his twisted legs had buckled beneath him, he had not known why. *It is the will of the Lord Agonis*, his aunt would say; but the boy was never quite sure what that might mean. He had been like an injured bird, uselessly attempting to flutter its broken wings; and later, though he knew his efforts would be unyielding, still he cursed his confinement and longed for liberty.

He jammed the padded rests of the crutches beneath his arms. 'Barnabas, I don't know,' he said; but he was not quite sure what it was he did not know. Jem breathed deeply and held his breath. He dug his hands hard into the wooden holds.

Yes!

'No!' His breath burst from him.

Struggling up from the chair, the boy felt as if a dark flame were searing up his arms, across his shoulders, down his spine. He lurched back, defeated. He gasped for air. His incapacity was a fact solid as stone. To his mother, the boy knew, his twisted legs bespoke only the unhappiness that had engulfed her young life; she flinched from the sight of them as if with pain. To his aunt they were irredeemable and that was all. This was the way in the kingdom of Ejland; cripples were cripples as the blind were the blind. Had Jem been a peasant-child, he might have been drowned.

But it was only the beginning.

Each day, Jem would try again.

It was useless.

Jem was trying again and each time he tried, he tottered for a few faltering steps before the crutches slipped, or he overbalanced, or his strength gave out and he sprawled to the floor.

Exhausted, Jem collapsed back into his chair. He could not walk. He would never be able to walk. Criss-crossed, the crutches lay beside him where they had fallen. *Clatter, clatter*: it was all they could do. He turned his chair from them, wrenching at the wheels. His arms strained and the chair rocked dangerously. Pain shot sharply up and down his spine.

'Barnabas?'

But the boy had asked the dwarf to leave him.

'Barnabas?'

How could the little man help him to stand?

Jem gulped air, gazing down the gallery. It was empty. Fireplaces and tall windows lined its length evenly, the fireplaces black, the windows bright, hovering high over an inner courtyard. The bright light seemed merely to make darker the gaping hearths, the wainscoting, the scored, glassy floor. The effect was of an alternation of radiance and gloom, vanishing into haze. The portraits could barely be seen.

'Barnabas!' Jem shouted.

The dwarf's name bounded and rebounded down the gallery.

Silence.

Where was Barnabas?

A hot, sudden anger welled in the boy and he longed to run wildly, shrieking, through the castle. A sob caught in his throat and he braced his arms above his wheels, his elbows jutting back. He would not close his eyes. He would drive through the haze. With a cry he launched himself forward.

Jem's cry became a scream.

'Young master!' a voice cried.

Jem could not swerve. From out of the haze the figure, dark and hulking, had stepped into his path. A big hand

177

grabbed at the arm of his chair. The chair swivelled, flinging Jem to the floor.

'Stephel!'

There was a guttural laugh; a glug-glug of swallowing. In one hand the old steward gripped a sloshing bottle; staggering, he extended his free hand to Jem. The boy took it resentfully and held his breath as the servant raised him up.

Stephel stank. He might have slept in a dunghill. His ragged tunic was crusted thick with vomit; burrs and strands of straw stuck to the straggling, dirty-white hair. Clutching Jem by the shoulders, so that Jem seemed to stand, the servant's red-rimmed eyes gazed, barely focusing, into the boy's stricken face.

'You wouldn't kill me, young master?'

Jem's breath burst unwillingly from him:

'Stephel, put me back in my chair!'

The servant ignored the command. Swigging again from the dark bottle, he began instead to stagger up and down before the line of portraits, crushing the boy tight against his side.

Jem's legs dragged behind him on the floor.

'Stephel! Stop it!'

Stephel did not. 'I've been watching you, boy. You and your friend. A dwarf is lucky, don't you know? They used to have a dwarf at the king's court. That was in the old king's time, of course. The dwarf could say anything, anything at all! I should like to be a dwarf, wouldn't you? But you are, I suppose. You've got no legs! Eh?'

The drunkard laughed again and the boy began to slip from his circling arm, his legs splaying.

Stephel yanked him up.

Jem was almost sobbing. The shoe had twisted from his buckled leg and his shirt was rucked high, rasping, against his shoulder-blades.

Stephel had been bad before, but not this bad.

'Look!' He swung Jem to face the portraits. 'The Archdukes of Irion, for a thousand cycles. Is it a thousand? Ten thousand? For ten thousand cycles, for a hundred hundred thousand, they have commanded the Rock of Ixiter. And who holds the Rock holds the Tarn! You know that, boy, don't you? You must have known that.'

Now Stephel was dragging Jem along the line of portraits, his pace growing faster as his speech grew louder, wilder. The old man was raving now, spluttering senselessly. There was something about the Archduke. There was something about the king. There was something about a message that the old man had to carry.

The portraits swelled into Jem's gaze.

On and on the line extended, father following son. Jem had passed the portraits time and again. When he was slow, they had hovered dimly; when he was fast, they had flickered and flashed; but never had they surged out at him as they did now. Some showed men who were young, some showed men who were old; some of the men were bearded and some shaven smooth. There were flowing wigs, fluttering plumes; there were floppy hats and pointy helmets; there were stiff white ruffles and puffed, embroidered sleeves. There was ermine. There was armour. In some hands were parchments and in some were swords; yet in each man's portrait the darkened oils disclosed on the right hand, always in view, the flashing ring that betokened his rank. Each man's hand was long like his limbs and in each man's eyes and in the angle of his cheekbones the lineaments of the Archdukes of Irion could be traced. They were the lineaments of Tor.

Stephel crushed Jem close to him.

'A noble line! A valiant line! Loyal to the crown for a million million cycles! You know that, boy? Look at them! And I have served them! And my father served them. And my father's father. And my father's father's father . . .' For a moment the old servant seemed to sag, reeling; he might have been about to crash to the floor, pinning the boy beneath him.

He rallied; he rolled back his head. He swooped close to Jem's face, his coarse voice suddenly a hideous caress, hissing foully through brown stubs of teeth, 'Do you know who your father is, boy?'

Jem screamed. Uselessly he tried to swing back his arms. Stephel held him, manipulated him like a puppet. 'Let me go, let me go!' He wanted to punch the drunkard, but his arms were held tight.

The old man guzzled back the last of his wine. He was too hasty: it ran down his chin, his hands; it spluttered from his lips. He cried out, suddenly enraged, flinging back his hand to hurl the bottle.

Jem shut his eyes. Twisting his face away, in imagination he heard the bottle shatter, exploding against the wainscot into a thousand glittering shards.

There was a different sound. 'Father!'

The old man started. His hand dropped; the bottle clinked to the floor and rolled away. Then the gripping arm slackened, too.

Jem crumpled. He sprawled heavily. For moments he lay, a twisted heap of limbs, a cheek and ear pressed into the caking dust of the floor; then, thudding over on to his belly, painfully the boy tried to grovel back to his chair.

It was too far. Jem sobbed, cursing his weakness.

'Oh, Father!' Nirry kept repeating, distracted. The drunken old man was shuffling senselessly in a circle, resisting the pluckings of his daughter's hands. Only when he stilled himself and merely stood staring, drivelling, did the maid add at last, 'Master Jem, are you all right?'

Hot and helpless, the boy said nothing as Nirry heaved him back, like a sack, into his chair. Tears blurred his eyes and a wild, humiliated anger burst inside him. Could he have struck Stephel dead at that moment, Jem would have done so.

Now Nirry's hands plucked at him, too. She adjusted his legs. She tugged at his shirt. She flicked the dust from his face and hair.

Angrily he tossed her hand away.

'Forgive him, Master Jem.' The hand kept returning. 'It's

the day. He always marks the day. The Archduke made him carry the message, you see. To the Bluejackets. Two cycles ago – today. Oh, I must keep him out of sight of the Mistress! You won't say anything, Master Jem, will you?' The voice was soft and kind. 'Come on, Father.'

Meekly, subdued now, the shambling old man followed his daughter from the gallery.

Jem was alone. Where was Barnabas?

Sadly Jem gazed into the sunshine and shadows. He stared down at the black floor that was scored repeatedly by his spinning wheels; he scuffed at the wheels with the heels of his hands. He stared up at the low, plaster ceiling. It was a spider's web of cracks. Chasm after chasm webbed the moulded pattern and the thought came to Jem that one day the ornate, heavy ceiling would crash to the floor. Dust would hover endlessly in the pale, bright air.

Jem reached for his crutches.

He was going to walk.

'One.' He counted his steps aloud. 'Two . . .'

The boy reached nine, nearly ten, before he sank forward, gasping. It had been so slow! It had been so hard! He closed his eyes and imagined himself soaring, soaring as a bird flies, towards the horizon where the pale highway travelled.

Applause echoed behind him.

It was Barnabas.

Chapter 22

THE KEY TO UMBECCA

If there was a key to the character of Umbecca Rench, it lay in her relations with her sister, Ruanna. Ruanna, of course, was dead now and had been dead for many cycles, but still she dominated her sister's thoughts. Of the two girls, Umbecca had been the elder by a year, or two, or three; but once they had attained a modicum of maturity the gap between them had generally been thought to be much larger. From her earliest womanhood, it seemed to Umbecca, she had been regarded as an old maid; while Ruanna, in her sixth cycle and still unwed, would seem, in the event, a desirable match. In the Rench sisters, it seemed, nature had provided one of those cruel but not infrequent test-cases of beauty and ugliness, designed to show how each shall fare in the world. When they were children, the plump Umbecca had loved her pretty sister; but as they grew older, the tendrils of resentment had first insinuated themselves, strand by strand, into her heart; then twined and twisted ever more tightly until all other feeling was choked off and killed.

But there was more to their situation than this. The girls were distant cousins of Lady Lolenda, wife of the former and mother to the present Archduke of Irion. But their own situation was by no means so desirable. The Rench family was of the middle station; or rather, would have been, had not the father of the two girls, a spice-merchant, suffered over a cycle or so a series of reversals in the fortunes of his trade with the colony of Tiralos. When the girls were young, the family had kept up a fine house in Ollon-Quintal, the most desirable of Agondon's new 'merchant precincts'. By the time they had entered upon the age of reason, their windows would look on to the rather more equivocal charms of the Bolbarr Road. Theirs was that unenviable position in which one neither languishes in outright poverty, nor feels secure in the possession of even moderate affluence; to the Rench girls, life would present itself as an unending, quietly desperate struggle to keep up certain appearances, when for all the world it was clear that such appearances were false. They were adepts in the saving of scraps of fabric and string.

From the responses of the two girls to their situation, one might have divined much. Ruanna was possessed of a wisdom beyond her age and could not view the family's fate without a certain admixture of irony; left to her own devices, one might surmise, Ruanna could well have been contented in a station lower than that to which the family had aspired. She might have opened a little haberdasher's on the Bolbarr Road, and done well. She was a cheerful girl. Umbecca, on the other hand, burned with ambition; she saw in the reversals of the family's fortunes a personal affront, a slight for which atonement must ardently be sought. In this, she was the ally of her mother.

Umbecca was just entering upon her Fifth when her father died. Torby Rench had never quite recovered from his crash. His attempts over two cycles to rebuild his business had all come to nothing, and this, combined with the ill-concealed contempt of his wife and elder daughter, had, one could be certain, hastened him to his grave. He left his family in considerable debt.

It was at this point that Ruanna, who had until now been so meek and quiet, stepped in with some stern advice for her mother. The family's pretences of gentility, Ruanna pointed out, had proved nothing but ruinous. A little shop was available for lease in the Bolbarr Road. It was their destiny. The family must sell all their remaining fine things; they must accept their true station.

Nothing could describe the horror which greeted this plan. Goody Rench was appalled, and chastised her daughter roundly; Umbecca supported their mother. 'If you had any gumption, girl, *you* could fix our fortunes!' Goody Rench cried, in her anger. Ruanna did not know what she meant; but would find out, soon enough.

Goody Rench had devised her own, more precarious plan.

In their genteel poverty, both Goody Rench and her elder daughter had been much given to the reading of novels, which it was Ruanna's duty to bring to them, in teetering piles, from the circulating library at the top of the Bolbarr Road. To Ruanna's bemusement, it was often the case that Umbecca and her mother would spend entire days lying on the sofa with one volume, then another, of *Love in Several Guises* or *Marella's Brilliant Marriage* or other such frivolous reading-matter. Inert in their shabby little sitting-room, the two women filled their mouths with tea and cake and their heads with romantic dreams of balls and parties and the swooning moments in which a heroine would accept the hand of this or that splendid lord or marquis or duke.

Now it happened that very often, in such works, the heroine began her adventures in humble circumstances; more humble, in some cases, than those in which the family of Rench now found itself. To Goody Rench, the way was clear. Her younger daughter was a beauty.

Ruanna must make a splendid match.

So it was that the resources of the little family were dedicated, from this time on, to providing Ruanna with the frippery and finery which would enable her to make her appearance in society.

Umbecca was at once excited and appalled by her mother's determination: excited, that the family fortunes might be restored; appalled, that this restoration should come about through the agency of Ruanna. Ruanna, for her part, was simply appalled; but her mother had in her a force that was difficult to resist. While her sister looked on enviously, soon the Season was upon them, and Ruanna was part of its glittering round.

Ruanna until this time had been almost the family servant; from now on, she was treated like a queen. But this did not have the effect upon the younger sister that it might have had upon the elder. Ruanna had, in truth, a keen sense of irony. She saw, and saw clearly, the absurdity of her new life. She had no hopes of the splendid marriage; she was, she could see, just one of any number of girls who clung, as her family had long clung, to the fringes of polite society. Her mother, too, was so vauntingly ambitious as to defeat her own object, if her object were indeed simply to redeem the family from its present desperate pass. When a handsome young spice-merchant called for Ruanna, Goody Rench was disgusted. His fine suit and his equipage were to no avail. A spice-merchant! Her sights were set upon a baronet, at least!

But when no baronet presented himself, Goody Rench was not dissuaded. Ruanna had hoped her mother would tire of her plan in time, and come to see the wisdom of the little shop; instead, when Agondon provided no baronet, Goody Rench decided that it was Agondon's fault. Thereafter, the family would repair between the Seasons of Viana and Javander to the spa-town of Varby, where – if truth were to be told – they could with rather more ease maintain the illusion of gentility.

By this time, Ruanna was growing more than a little bored; only her love for her mother prevented her from throwing in the foolish scheme. But there was something else, too: as she observed the follies of fashionable life, Ruanna had begun to pen little notes, sketches, scraps of verse, at first for her own amusement – nothing more.

Then, slowly, they became more. At night, while her mother and sister slept, Ruanna began work in secret on a story.

A novel.

When the novel was finished, Ruanna sought the advice of the young gentleman behind the counter in the circulating library, of whom, as it happened, she had grown rather fond. He knew what to do, and a moonlife later, the three volumes of Ruanna's novel appeared on his shelves. Ruanna, with a smile for the young gentleman, could not resist taking them for the two ardent novel-readers in the shabby sitting-room above the Bolbarr Road. What would they make of them? Ruanna had not, of course, used her own name; the novel appeared as the work of a 'Miss R——'. Mother and Becca would have no idea; they would simply have no idea!

That afternoon, 'Miss R——' hugged herself, restraining her secret laughter, as sister Becca lay so absorbed in the pages of *Becca's First Ball* – Ruanna had been a little mischievous in the choice of her heroine's name – that she forgot to devour more than half of the cream-cakes that her sister had heaped obligingly before her.

To Ruanna, it all seemed an enormous joke. What she could never have anticipated was that all Ejlander society would feel about *Becca's First Ball* precisely as her sister had done. The book was a sensation. Written in a series of letters from a young girl, supposedly making her first appearance in Agondon society, the novel was at once ironic and moving, satirical and sentimental, funny and sad. Without quite intending it, 'Miss R——' had combined, and combined brilliantly, the romantic absurdities of the novels from the circulating library with a sharp and distinctive quality of real observation. The result was enthralling. Soon all the fine ladies of Ejland, and many of the gentlemen too, were alternately swooning and laughing over the experiences of Becca, and speculating earnestly on the identity of 'Miss R——'.

They were never to find it out.

Had Ruanna revealed herself to the world, in those first heady days of her success, there could be little doubt that she might at once have contracted the splendid marriage of which her mother had dreamed. But Ruanna had other plans. She would save the family fortunes by more dignified means. Still working in secret, over the cycle that followed 'Miss R——' produced in rapid succession three further novels. *A Lady's Maid? A Lady!* was the second production of her pen; then came *Marital and Martial* and *The Prickly Path to Wedlock*. If none of these quite recaptured the freshness of *Becca's First Ball* – Ruanna was, in truth, drawing rather more heavily by now on the devices in the books from the circulating library – each nonetheless enjoyed a considerable success. Eagerly Ruanna looked forward to the day when she could pay off the family's debts and set them up in independent comfort. She had no thought of the little shop now; her mother and sister, she admitted to herself, were simply too lazy.

Now Ruanna was no longer in the first flush of youth; but nonetheless she began to receive attentions from an unexpected quarter. Her cousin Jorvel Ixiter, heir of Irion, was at this time stationed in Agondon with his fashionable and expensive regiment.

He came to call upon her.

Jorvel was a cycle or so younger than his cousin, but at once found himself captivated by her charms. This surprised him for Jorvel, though he had barely crossed the threshold of manhood, was already a sated voluptuary. He had thought himself tired of women. To choose a wife – a *wife!* – seemed an impossible task, a matter only for despairing drolleries; but his cousin Ruanna had about her a wit, a fire, a charm that was wholly individual.

He declared his passion.

It was a splendid declaration; one which, indeed, Ruanna was to record *verbatim* in *The Prickly Path to Wedlock*. The Rench family had harboured no expectations from this particular connection; but here at last, it seemed, quite unexpectedly, was the match of which Goody Rench had dreamed.

There was only one obstacle to its success: Ruanna despised her cousin. She thought him a callow egotist and a bore, and refused him.

Jorvel was crushed; but each morning, the young man would call again on Miss Ruanna, hoping that the elapsing of another day might have softened her refusal. He could not believe that she could mean what she said. Ruanna merely received him politely, and after a time bade him good-day. Outrageously, she did not seem disturbed at all by the turmoil she was causing. She simply did not care, it seemed, that she was responsible – entirely, personally responsible – for the unhappiness of three people.

For Goody Rench was distraught too, and so was Umbecca. Goody Rench took to her bed, and announced that she was dying. As for Umbecca, she could seldom remain in *her* bed. She slept badly. Her nerves were frayed. She even cut down on her insistent eating.

The source of Umbecca's emotion was not quite the same as her mother's. It was a long time before she could admit it even to herself: she loved Jorvel. He was the most beautiful young man she had ever seen, a vision of perfection in his splendid red uniform. She worshipped him; but he had eyes only for the *hard-hearted* Ruanna.

Another girl might have ended by despising so blind a suitor. Umbecca found that it was her loathing for Ruanna that now increased to intolerable proportions. She might have believed, absurdly, that if Ruanna did not exist, Jorvel would have loved her; she might have believed, still more absurdly, that could she but punish Ruanna, Jorvel must look on her with favour.

❋   ❋

It was at about this time that Umbecca found the manuscript lying on the bureau in Ruanna's room. Ruanna had become careless; and as her sister read what she found there, a horrible suspicion crept over her.

Could it be?

She rifled the desk; she turned out the cupboards. What she found, in a box in the back of Ruanna's wardrobe, made Umbecca turn pale.

It was true!

Ruanna was 'Miss R——'!

This discovery was one of peculiar horror for Umbecca Rench; later, indeed, she would look back on it as the single worst moment of her life. The horror lay in this: that the revelation did not destroy, but massively *increased* her sister's charms. To what heights might Jorvel's love not rise, if he knew that his beloved was also Ejland's most celebrated lady novelist? He must not know!

But Umbecca was divided. To be in possession of such intelligence, and yet unable to divulge it, was to be at a sorry pass; and though she had intended to tell no one – she certainly could never have told Jorvel – she could not resist dropping certain bitter hints to her mother. Mother, after all, would not unnaturally be furious to know that her daughter, for whom she had sacrificed so much, had all this time harboured such a secret.

The bitter hints rapidly became more.

'She's "Miss R——"!' Umbecca was shouting, by the end of the exchange. 'Don't you see it, Mother? Anna is "Miss R——"!'

It was then that the cruellest development in this story took place. Umbecca's mother had announced that she was dying; but no one had expected that this could be true.

Suddenly, it was.

Goody Rench had never been strong. All at once, her being rebelled against the endless, fretting torments of absurd emotion to which she had subjected it for so many cycles. This last revelation was too much; but whether too much anger or too much joy, Umbecca was never to know. A mighty haemorrhage burst from her mother's mouth and the old woman fell back, dead, on bloody sheets.

Telling Ruanna was the worst part.

Ruanna was distraught; and when she found out the nature

of the revelation which had killed their mother, her distress grew still greater.

Umbecca was abashed. Bitterly, she accused her sister of hypocrisy. What she could never understand was that Ruanna had loved their mother, loved her more truly, more deeply than Umbecca could ever have done. To some, the guilt that consumed Ruanna then would have seemed absurd, as absurd as the ambition which had so fretted her mother, and the envy and spite which had filled her sister. On the day after their mother's funeral, Ruanna accepted Jorvel's hand.

It was a brilliant match; or at least, so it seemed in the eyes of the world. Shortly afterwards, Jorvel's father died, and he returned to Irion to take up his title. Umbecca of course accompanied the couple, to assume the role of her sister's companion and then, when the children came, of maiden aunt.

As for Ruanna, she may not have loved her husband, but she loved her two children, and was kind – consistently kind – to her sister. 'Miss R——', the mysterious authoress, was to produce only one further novel, a cycle or so later, called *A Beauty of the Valleys*; but the work was thought to mark a falling-off, and 'Miss R——' wrote no more.

This at least should have given Umbecca satisfaction. It did not; and nor did the knowledge that Ruanna's marriage was evidently unhappy. For after all, even in making a sacrifice, Ruanna had taken the one thing her sister truly wanted. It was not to be forgiven. Four cycles had passed since Ruanna's death; and Umbecca still thought of her every day.

She did not read novels any more.

Chapter 23

THE VISION

It was the beginning of an enchanted period.

At first, it seemed merely an awkward one; Jem's nine steps might have been but a taunting machination of chance. Days were to pass until the exhausted boy could raise himself up again, and many more until he could plant the crutches confidently, launching himself along the smooth passage of the gallery. But he knew, soon enough, that it could be done. His bowed leg, Jem discovered, was stronger than he had thought; for a moment it could bear his weight as he swung the crutches forward. This was the hardest part, angling his torso for the forward lurch. As he braced himself, the burning in his arms and back would return, but less sharply.

Slowly, through the cold season of another year, Jem mastered the long, flowing strides he would need. How he missed the easy, rolling motion of the chair! But then it came to him, almost with a sense of sadness, that the chair was no longer the friend it had been at first. Waiting at the end of the gallery, ready to receive him again, the chair was now a symbol not of victory, but of defeat. At the end of each session on the crutches, slumping exhausted into the creaking wickerwork, Jem would long only to rise again. He was deformed: he knew that; but if he could stand and walk, not roll on wheels, then to stand and walk was what he must do.

The buckled leg caused untold trouble. Unwilling to flow forward with the arc of his body, again and again its twisted foot would catch on the calf of the bowed leg. It slid sideways; it obstructed the crutches. How adept Barnabas became at running behind his friend, ready to grab at the recalcitrant foot! It was dangerous. They were both a mass of bruises. Time and again Jem fell, usually on top of Barnabas.

Often they laughed.

Sometimes they cried.

Now and then, when he had fallen too many times, when he could not even drag himself back to the chair, Jem was ready to give up. More than once, he wailed, 'It's no good! It's no good!' Again the crutches clattered to the floor; again Jem's anguish echoed down the cold, hard passage. Then Barnabas would look at him with imploring, tearful eyes; and Jem's despair would vanish as the snow would vanish in the warm gusts of the Season of Viana. Then Jem laughed, and cried, 'Oh Barnabas, I'm a fool!'

It was true. From the time he took his first faltering steps, Jem had known that his life would change. That year, as the Season of Viana returned in reality to the valleys, Jem and his little friend began a great, secret adventure.

Until now, it had been only the gallery that had been the object of their afternoon expeditions. Now, as Jem walked with ever more confidence, he decided that the time had come to venture further afield. Barnabas, with beaming eyes, agreed. For two cycles the boy had lived within the vast labyrinth of the castle, yet he had known almost nothing of it but for a few familiar chambers. Now the dwarf would lead him to the mysterious treasure-troves, the sources of the candlesticks, the goblets, the shields.

In the warm days that followed, as sunlight sluiced goldenly over the ivy-covered walls, the two friends set out to explore the castle. It was a journey that proceeded in fits and starts, returning again and again to the place from which it began; it was a mission undertaken while Jem's mother was sleeping, and his aunt, who would not approve, was not to be seen. If it were a quest, it was a quest only for wonderment, and one in which the hero would always be home for tea.

It was besieged by awkwardness. The dwarf with his short legs puffed and panted; the cripple with his crutches stumbled on the stairs. Every day a little crisis came. But Jem would forget these, as he forgot the fits and starts. The adventure was a trail that could not be abandoned, a skein to be followed irresistibly, inevitably, until its end was reached. In memory, Jem saw himself proceeding like a wraith through room after room of the ancient edifice.

This is what he saw:

The Great Hall, once centre of the life of the castle, lay torn open to the sky. Ferns and flowers caroused over overturned benches and decaying collapsed beams; ivy swung pendulously from the minstrels' gallery while rooks wheeled and cawed in the raw, exposed air.

He saw the dim library, draped thickly with cobwebs, heady with the pungency of rotting books; he saw the chapel, burnt black by flames, where powdery ash still rose up and fluttered when footsteps, or crutches, disturbed the floor.

The armoury was stripped, but for scattered remnants. There were broken-handled axes; there were tattered standards; and standing as sentinel was a rusted suit of armour.

Jem saw the Archduke's apartment and the apartment where the king had stayed. The rooms, once resplendent, now stood ruinous. There were bowed ceilings and floors; there were cracking wainscots. There were tattered hangings and sagging sofas and beds where black mould sprawled cancerously over the covers.

Everywhere, vermin squealed and scurried. There were rats, spiders, beetles, slithering worms. Walls dripped and oozed; pools of standing water seethed with slime. Stinking holes plunged beneath filthy garderobes.

But Jem, through it all, was entranced by the journey.

He ascended to an attic heaped with bric-à-brac. There were hunched chests and piles of parchment; there were pictures and rolled maps and moth-eaten clothes.

'Oh, Barnabas!' Jem breathed, lowering himself slowly to the dusty floor. A long, low chord came in reply as the boy, awkwardly but eagerly, arranged his stiff legs on a scrap of carpet, pungent with mould. Shafts of light shone through the gaps in the roof above, slipping warmly between the cracked tiles and cobwebbed beams. The sunlight ignited the warmth of the fabrics and sparked off innumerable soft glints and gleams from the hard, tarnished objects that crouched amongst the clutter.

Jem sighed. For long seasons he had dreamed that he, too, could go exploring as Barnabas did; he had dreamed that he, too, could bring back splendid things. Bounty! Plunder! Already, in the places they had been, Jem had found a little wooden soldier, his uniform painted in chipped scarlet; he had found a medallion stamped with the seal of the Archduke and collected innumerable red and blue arrowheads and, one day, a pocketful of musket balls. Each new possession had been borne back to the alcove in triumph. There was a book of silhouettes, a deck of cards; even a magnificent dead crow that had perched on the hearth, fixed-eyed and staring, until Nirry, with a shriek, had flung it into the fire.

But here were untold treasures. Jem did not know where to begin. Sitting on the soft carpet, the boy reached first to a painted wooden crown. A shower of gilding flaked away as he placed the crown on his head and turned, smiling, to Barnabas. Barnabas began a tune on the hurdy-gurdy. It was one that Jem had heard before, but he could not say when. Always, the strange music seemed to evaporate into the air, escaping from memory, at the very moment it had issued forth.

Next, Jem reached for a roll of parchment. It was an ancient map, revealing the contours of a kingdom of islands. The parchment was cracking and the ink was fading, and though Jem had learnt his letters he could not make out the words that were written against the jagged masses of land. A ship and a spouting whale were drawn in the sea, and in the corner of the map was a spiky compass, tilted on to its side in the direction of north.

The map intrigued Jem; but after a moment he put it aside. He pulled at a tasselled cord, setting off a tiny, dusty landslide from the top of a heavy box. A scarf threaded with strands of spun gold tumbled across his legs. It was strangely heavy as Jem pulled it towards him. It was a splendid scarf; but only concealed something stranger, more wonderful. There was something wrapped inside.

It was a small silver box, which shone out brilliantly as Jem raised it up. Little claw-like legs were fashioned at each corner and the lid and the sides were tooled richly with ornate, swirling patterns. They might have been the hieroglyphs of a forgotten language. The lid was shut fast. What could be inside? In the front of the box was a keyhole; but running the scarf through his hands again, then scrambling about amongst the bric-à-brac, Jem could find no key.

He set the box before him on the carpet. He turned again, appealing, to Barnabas. The dwarf only played on, his expression unaltered; but later Jem would think it was then that the tune had changed, subtly but decisively, as if leading him through the dim corridors of the spirit to a place he had never been. The music prickled at the surface of his skin, and a desire overcame Jem to touch the box again. This time he attempted no force, but ran his fingers gently, delicately, over the intricacies of the silverwork. It was when he probed beneath the ridge of the carved lid that Jem knew, as if by instinct, how to find what he had sought. The box had no key, but there was a catch. A secret catch. The lid juddered open, just a little, and it was only with a slow, deliberate reverence that Jem, reaching forward with the fingers of both hands, opened the lid just a little wider. Wider.

The box was empty. Inside there was only darkness: a lining of soft, black felt.

Jem's spirits sank. He looked up. Now the light was shining almost with a painful sharpness into the musty, abandoned world, and the boy screwed up his eyes. It was when he looked down at the box again that he saw that perhaps it was not empty. But was this an illusion? For it seemed to Jem that the black felt lining was beginning to vibrate, then to give off a purplish, unearthly glow; as he watched, it seemed to him that the bright shafts of light and all the rich colours of the attic around him had vanished, faded away. Then even Barnabas and his music had faded, leaving the boy alone.

Now the glow gathered into a shape, a form; Jem, to his astonishment, saw that the black interior of the box now contained a purplish, glowing key.

He gasped. He reached for it. His hand hovered above it.

A voice. 'Jem.'

The boy looked up. Glowing with the same empurpled aura that filled the box, the figure loomed above him, tall and lean, dressed in the motley of a harlequin. A silver mask concealed the harlequin's face.

'Tor!'

But was it Tor? Jem would never know, for in the moment when he said Tor's name, his hand plunged irresistibly into the silver box. He would have seized the key, and with a triumph he could not explain, he would have offered it to the harlequin.

He could not; for in the moment when he touched it, the key was gone.

So was the harlequin.

It was as if a shutter had been open for a moment, then closed again; and everything was as it had been before.

❊ ❊

Only one thing was different, though it took Jem a moment to realize it. It was Barnabas. The dwarf had stopped playing and when Jem looked around he smiled to see that his friend was sleeping, his head slumped over the hurdy-gurdy, his toothless mouth hanging slackly open.

Jem rubbed his eyes. Had he been sleeping, too? He must have been dreaming. But what a strange dream! It left him feeling alarmed and strangely restless.

Curiously Jem gazed at the empty box. When they left the attic, he would leave behind the other things he had found. But he would take the box, and in the alcove that night he would find a special place for it in a gap, a nook, where a brick had come loose above the fireplace.

'What a lovely Jarvel-box,' said Nirry that night.

'Jarvel-box?' said Jem.

'Quality-folk keep their Jarvel-leaves in them. For smoking. I say,' the maid giggled, 'I don't suppose there's any in there now?'

She would have reached for the box, but for some reason she seemed to think better of it and stopped. But often Jem would bring the box forth and gaze into its emptiness; sometimes, when he woke in the middle of the night, he would lie watching the rays of the moon as they gleamed and glimmered on the old, rich silver. A strange, sad apprehension filled him then, and he thought back to his dream of the glowing purple key.

It must have been a message. A sign.

But what could it mean?

❁   ❁

The quest was almost over.

The next day, Barnabas led Jem down and down. At the bottom of slippery stairs he saw dripping cellars. In the light of a flaming torch, he made out rows of metal-banded barrels and dark bottles crusted thick with dust. Deepest of all, through trapdoors too perilous for the friends to pass through, Jem saw narrow cells with heavy barred doors; he saw a low chamber filled with spiky racks and mysterious rods and levers and wheels.

'Barnabas, what is this place?'

The dwarf, who could not answer, offered only a melancholy chord. That was when Jem felt a strange oppression. It was a sense of evil; and sadly, he wondered if this was how their expedition ended.

It was not. The dungeon was only a stage upon the way.

The next afternoon, Barnabas indicated that now they must undertake the most arduous part of their quest. They had been to the castle's depths; what must come now was an ascent higher than any they had attempted before.

Even in memory, this would not seem easy. The journey was a relentless upwards spiral. Staircase followed staircase; the steps grew ever more narrow and dark. Round and round they wound between cylindrical walls.

Jem's muscles strained. 'Barnabas, how much longer?'

They rested; Barnabas played the hurdy-gurdy.

They began again.

They rested again.

'Barnabas, I can't go on!'

Jem fought back the pain. He bit at his lips and at the linings of his cheeks.

'Light! At last!'

He flung forward his crutches. Agonized, he crawled from the deep well of the stairway. The pain in his back had never been so strong. His breath tore from him in anguished gasps.

But Jem's agony would turn to joy.

'Oh, Barnabas!'

The sun poured like balm over his prostrate form. Warm winds turned and twisted on the air and when Jem at last raised himself up, he gasped, this time not with agony but with astonishment.

In the days of the castle's glory, four towers had soared imperiously above the keep. One corresponded to each point of the compass. Now, three lay in ruins: the north, the east, the west. The dwarf had led him to the top of the south tower.

Was this, Jem wondered, where Nova-Riel came?

Standing at the highest point of the castle, Jem realized, he stood at that moment higher than any other human in all the Valleys of the Tarn.

Perhaps in all Ejland.

Enraptured, the boy gazed from the crumbling battlements. Rising behind the castle, like a dazzling sheet of crystal, was the icy immensity of the Kolkos Aros. A sense of awe rushed over Jem. Gazing at the white mountains, he could have cast down his crutches before him, sinking helplessly into a willing submission. White clouds rolled hugely overhead.

Jem turned at last. Stretching before the castle, supine beneath its raised rocky platform, were the lush pastures and woodlands of the valleys. They were so far below. From the tower, even the lesser heights of the castle seemed small. Marvelling, he stared down, as if at some battered model, at the tumbledown outhouses, the crushed curtain wall, the drawbridge that spanned the quagmire of the moat. The village beneath was laid out as if on a map: the green in the centre; the temple and the tombyard; and stretching beyond them, the straggling houses, the patchwork fields of farms.

For a long, lingering while they gazed.

Jem, forgetting his crutches, leaned forward eagerly from one stony embrasure of the battlements; Barnabas scrambled up and sat cross-legged in the next, coaxing a mysterious, ethereal music from the heavy box on his chest. There they remained, lost in reverie, until the warm wind flickered with evening chill.

One thing stood out.

Scanning the patchwork of the valleys, Jem noticed a roadway, dusty-white in the seasons of heat, that wound away from the village to the south. He followed it with his eyes. Over high hills it travelled, and through deep stretches of forest, turning and twisting with the contours of the earth, and as he followed it to the distant horizon, it came to Jem that this was the roadway in his picture. It was the roadway he would follow into his dreams, skimming impossibly over the pale surface, while Barnabas played as he played now. Where it led Jem did not know; he knew only that Tor, and adventure, were awaiting him:

Come on, Jem! Jem, come on!

After that day, Jem would never be the same. Something

in him had changed. Something had been revealed to him; but just what that was, he could not say.

It was Jem's most glorious day.

But it would not end gloriously.

Chapter 24

A DISCOVERY

Click-click. Click-click.

They were the faintest of clicks. Umbecca had fallen into a light trance. The clockwork motion of her hands and the click of her needles and the torpor of the warm day had her almost sleeping, as her niece slept, breathing in slow rhythm in the canopied bed. Replete before the remnants of her solitary tea, the fat woman sat on the sofa by a hearth swept clean of ashes, unpiled with logs. Her eyes, from time to time, drifted shut in the thick warmth; the Season of Viana was swelling again into the fiery Season of Theron. How warm it was! But it would not last. The click-click of Umbecca's needles bespoke her preparations for the cold months that would return, soon enough. She was knitting a scarf.

Click-click. Click-click.

Umbecca smiled, starting another line. But there was a hollowness behind her smile. Later, before dinner, she would retire to her cell, returning only after she had recited the litany she now repeated five times daily. It was a promise and a penance. Mumbling the long, rhythmic lines of words, Umbecca renewed, again and again, her vow to be ever more fervent in her faith.

Lord Agonis, tomorrow I shall serve you more truly:
I shall look for you with eye-globes so eager that my eye-
*   globes shall crack, bursting bloody;*
I shall work for you with hand-flesh so ardent that my hand-
*   flesh shall swell, bursting bloody;*
I shall hold you so hard to my heart that my heart shall split
*   open, bursting bloody:*
Lord Agonis, tomorrow I shall serve you more truly . . .

On and on the litany continued, unravelling through many meandering ways; yet always it came back to tomorrow. Tomorrow. Did the past not matter? It could stain and spoil for ever; but virtue, unlike vice, could not be fixed indelibly. In the eyes of her god, Umbecca believed, her niece's yesterdays would ever be present; but her own, she was certain, had blown away like chaff. In her heart she came to her god each day as if she had never come to him before. She promised to be ever more fervent in her faith; she offered penance not for the failings of the past, but in anticipation of the failings of the future. How great would these be? Umbecca was frightened. Her knees would burn with pain when she rose at last from the floor; her little eyes would be red-raw with tears. Her piety had always been her pride, her joy. Now it had become her prop and stay. She was unhappy; unhappy in a manner she could barely understand.

Often now Umbecca was aware of an ache, thudding hard inside her ample, soft chest. *Thud, thud*, like a companion heartbeat, it was always present and would not leave her, booming into the quiet of the night as she lay unsleeping on her hard bed; pulsing like a presence in her cell behind her as the whispered litany rose to its culmination. Sometimes she would forget it, and the thudding, unheeded, would mingle into the sounds of rain and chinking teacups and fluttering birds and the hundred unregarded sounds of dissolution as it inched its way through the ruins of the castle. Then she became aware of the thudding again, and knew with a strange dread that it had never gone away. She became aware of it now; *click-click, click-click*. It came in time to the rhythm of the needles.

She looked across to her sleeping niece. How lightly Ela's breath rose and fell! Lulled by the ichor of the black bottle, the invalid would sleep as she had slept as an infant, long and peacefully and through many hours of daylight. Uneasily, with the thudding at her heart and temples, Umbecca thought back to when Ela was really an infant, pink-cheeked, not pallid, and sleeping purely. How beautiful she had been!

In those days, Umbecca had been the age that Ela was now; there had been no thudding then.

'My poor niece,' she said aloud; Ela, of course, would never understand that her aunt had always wanted for her only what was best. But what could she do, when Ela had cast herself beyond the reach of redemption?

Ela stirred, exhaling deeply. Later, her aunt knew, as the afternoon declined, the sleeper would wake; and through an evening of murmurous remarks, of vacant-eyed noddings and dulled traces of memory, would sit propped at the table by the casement, pushing her boiled mutton and boiled potatoes about her plate until the food had stirred into a shapeless lump and Nirry came at last to take it away.

'You must eat, niece,' her aunt would say; but like a cloud, unvoiced but impending, the question hovered above them: *Why?*

On every other evening the boy would eat with them, rolling back and forth from the table in his chair; but now the mother was barely conscious of the son she had loved so ardently. *Jem, tell me . . .* she would begin, or *Jem, where . . .?* But the questions trailed off, or Umbecca would say, as the boy too hastily grabbed his knife and fork, *Jem, remember our benediction*, or, *Come, niece, time for your medicine*, and the invalid's eyes would wander, unseeing, away from the gaze of her son.

It was the best way, Umbecca would once have thought, considering that the boy could barely live for long. This seemed certain: her god had judged against him. Yet undeniably, with each month that passed, the child was growing taller, stronger; and a day would come, Umbecca feared, when her compassion for him would collapse like a house of cards. The invalid-chair troubled her; and once or twice, she knew, the child had even attempted, pathetically, to walk on sticks. Sticks, made to relieve a temporary injury! It alarmed her. Often now she would look at the boy and sense the whirring thoughts behind his eyes and feel only a strange repulsion and dread. Had she done wrong, leaving him to the dwarf? She was aware of the question; but stronger than this question in Umbecca's mind was the one word, *irredeemable*. Was anything redeemable? Umbecca knew, with a rush of anguish, that she longed only to escape, rattling away in the carriage to the Waxwells; and yet, fanning the dark flame of her anguish, came the knowledge that her escapings, for all their frequency, had brought her none of the contentment she had wanted. Sometimes she wished she could cry out in pain.

Thud.

Thud.

It was growing louder.

She threw down her work.

The skein of wool seemed suddenly contemptible. Bright-dyed, it lay against the dull fabric of the sofa like an accusation. It was scarlet. Like a harlot's lips. What had she been thinking of? She had dyed the wool with her own plump hands. Scarlet! It was an obscenity.

A droning disturbed her. In the shaft of light through the open casement, a fly buzzed and looped, homing in lethargically on the debris of the tea with its abundant sweet crumbs, its streaks of cream and sticky jam. With a swiftness that belied her bulk, Umbecca leapt up. Snatching her knitting, as if it were a weapon, she beat back and forth at the air until the fly, confused and angered, blundered back through the casement. Umbecca sighed and let the knitting fall. She rubbed her eyes with her hands; she leaned, suddenly tearful, on the wide window-ledge.

The bright world outside the window was a blur. Hotly the latticework of an open panel pressed at her arm through the fabric of her sleeve; shards of sunlight glittered up jaggedly from the golden circle that rested on her breasts.

'Oh . . .' Umbecca let out a soft lowing. On impulse she pulled the pendant over her head, letting it lie beside her in a line of pale shadow. She was sleepy, so very sleepy; yet still she was aware of the thudding, softer now but still insistent, insistent. How she longed to ease her laboured heart! The sunlight poured scaldingly on to her heavy black breasts, and all at once, clutching at her tight collar, Umbecca began to unbutton her bodice. The rustling fabric was like the plumage of some huge, flightless bird; but now it was parting, peeling back, a darkness giving way to blazing white. It was a hot day; Umbecca wore nothing beneath her black gown.

'Oh . . .' she lowed again, scooping her fleshy abundance rapturously into her hands. Painfully in the brightness, the flesh shone, creamy but for the purple nipples with their huge puckered aureoles. Absurdly, in Umbecca's reverie, it was as if she had exposed something never seen before. She had discovered a new land; all at once, with a sudden hot shuddering, Umbecca was aware of the vast reaches of flesh, the rolling hills and dales of it, that strained beneath her gown, squashed like dough: the huge hanging upper arms and ponderous belly, the cushioning pleated immensities of buttock and thigh and calf.

It was all so soft.

It was all so soft . . .

Umbecca rested her cheek against the hot mullions of the window. Hot, salt tears fell from her eyes; and in her reverie she did not hear the click-clicking door, opening behind her, as she had not heard the hooves and the rumbling wheels as the carriage rolled into the courtyard below. The droning fly had wheeled back towards the casement, settling unhindered on the creamy, sticky breasts.

'Ma'am?'

Umbecca started. 'Nirry!'

Chapter 25

UMBECCA'S BUTTONS

'Ma'am, Goodman Waxwell . . . '

Quickly Umbecca drew her bodice together. 'What, girl?' The fat woman did not turn. Her voice was unnaturally loud. 'Yes, Nirry, take the tea things. It's about time! How many times do I have to . . .?'

Had the girl seen? Could the girl know? Umbecca thought, *I have only to stand here, my back to the room, until she goes. Until she clears the tea things.*

But there was no clatter of tea things; Nirry's footsteps only came nearer. 'Ma'am,' snuffled the maid, 'Goodman Waxwell's here . . .'

'What? Here, girl?'

It was almost a shriek. Umbecca almost turned. Wildly she gazed to the courtyard below.

The carriage!

Horror overcame her.

Then came the voice, 'Mistress Rench? Mistress Rench?' The physician had followed the maid up the stairs. 'Pardon this intrusion, my good woman, but I have been in the village . . .' Had he seen? Had he looked up at the window? Frantically Umbecca was buttoning, buttoning. Could he know? Could he tell?

He was almost beside her. He had said nothing.

The knitting!

She clutched it to her breast. She swivelled round, shrieking, 'My dear Goodman Waxwell! Yes – do, do come in. Such a pleasant day, I was just—'

Umbecca gasped. If her plump face, already bright as the wool, could have coloured over again with a second bursting infusion of shame, it would have done so. The physician could only look on, startled, as she tore at the scarlet wool, dragging it savagely from the needles with a screech of laughter. 'No, no, Goodman Waxwell! You don't imagine? Really! It's just some trash I was looking over for Nirry. For the maid! Really it won't do, Nirry, it won't do!' she cried, flinging the desecrated knitting, needles and all, from the casement.

'Ma'am?' Nirry faltered, hovering. She was confused, almost ready to turn and go when the fat woman charged suddenly towards her, grabbing her arm and propelling her to the tea-table.

'Look at this slovenliness, girl! Really! Here's Goodman Waxwell, come for tea, and yesterday's rubbish—'

'Ma'am? This was today's—'

It was. The fat woman had eaten four gooseberry tarts, three slices of seed cake and six scones, all with cream. And all only a few fives earlier.

If that.

Umbecca's shout rode over the maid's snufflings, 'And yesterday's rubbish not cleared away! Oh, Goodman Waxwell, what *ever* must you think?'

This last was flung back over her fat shoulder. She was standing over the maid, pointing and prodding, a bustling, scarlet-faced ball of exasperation.

Was it the heat?

Perhaps, thought Nirry, it was the fly: glancing up, as she heaped the tea-tray, the maid was astonished to see a big, juicy black one come floundering from a gap in the buttons of the fat woman's bodice. Zig-zagging on the air, it hovered for a moment over the denuded tea-table, before lurching on to the topmost of the sticky, heaped plates. Unwisely, Nirry attempted to shake the tray; the topmost plate almost crashed to the floor.

'Stupid girl!' Umbecca rolled her eyes. 'The fly will follow you out. Leave it. Bring us our tea. Hm? Girl?' The fat woman turned back expectantly to the physician. 'Goodman Wax-well!' she laughed. 'Oh dear! Servants!'

There was no reply.

Nirry, in the doorway, looked back uncertainly. Should she tell the mistress about the undone buttons? No. It would never do.

It was the heat. It had to be the heat.

But there was something else.

❋   ❋

Nirry had been having a bad day. It had begun, in truth, in the middle of the night, when she awoke to a muffled commotion in the courtyard. Suddenly fearful, the maid crawled from the cubby-hole where she slept, darting to the kitchen window. There in the little square she saw a rickety cart, and in the cart were two burly men, cursing as they pushed a third, senseless man sprawling on to the cobble stones. Nirry rushed out as the cart drove away, the men laughing and gesturing obscenely. She knew them well enough: revellers from the Lazy Tiger. She could only hope they had not awoken the mistress.

What happened next was an anxious night of nursing. 'Oh Father, Father!' Nirry sighed. It was the third time in as many phases; this time his dirty-white hair was red with blood.

A miserable, exhausted day succeeded the unhappy night, and now something else, something more alarming, had happened. Should she say?

Nirry bit her lip.

'So, tell me, Goodman Waxwell,' the mistress was attempt-ing, her shriek at last subsiding a little, 'and what pleasant purpose has brought you to us today?'

She smiled. She patted the place beside her on the sofa.

But Goodman Waxwell did not join her.

'Ma'am—' Nirry attempted. 'There's something else—'

The smile dropped from the fat face, but Nirry shambled back nonetheless, the tea-tray clinking. There were dangerous shiftings in the porcelain pile as she leaned confidentially over the back of the sofa. 'It's Master Jem. He hasn't come back.'

'What, girl?' Umbecca hissed.

Nirry was concerned. Master Jem had been colder to her since the bad day with her father, but she still joined the boy and the dwarf each day for tea. What else could she do? She loved her father. She loved the boy. She loved the dwarf. Life was confusing!

'He goes off with Barnabas. In the afternoons.' The maid was whispering; she was not sure why. 'They haven't come back yet—'

'Nonsense, girl!'

Nonsense? The fat woman looked at her as if she were mad. *Go, go*, said the look in her eyes.

Nirry coloured. With a snort she swung the tray back towards the door. The top plate fell and rolled across the carpet.

'Buttons!' said Nirry, loud enough to be heard, as she kicked the door shut behind her with her foot.

But Umbecca was not in a mood to notice buttons.

Nor was the physician.

Growing calmer, for the first time Umbecca registered the disorder of her visitor's dress. Goodman Waxwell was not wearing his wig. The sparse hairs which covered his bald, peeling pate were standing up at angles. He was not wearing his jacket. His shirt, crumpled and soiled, was pulled out over his breeches. He was not smiling.

Was it the heat?

The smooth confidence of his manner was gone; back and forth, back and forth, he was pacing the carpet, in a strange sidelong motion with his crabwise steps. Umbecca's fears of moments earlier were gone, forgotten. A sudden, sickening exhilaration swept through her heart.

Could it be?

'And Goodman, what brings you to us, this fine day?' she attempted again, levelly.

He stopped, staring at her.

'Sometimes, it is the only way.'

Umbecca blanched. What could he mean? There were dark stains down the front of his crumpled shirt. Suddenly, Umbecca saw that they were blood.

'The boil must be lanced.'

'Goodman?'

Chapter 26

WAXWELL SEES THE DARKNESS

'A boy rode to my house this morning.' The Goodman's voice was flat. 'That lanky, gormless one from the Lazy Tiger. He asked, Would I come? There'd been an accident at the Tiger. You may imagine, my good woman, that I was hardly eager to ply my trade within the portals of that sty.'

'Goodman, indeed!' Umbecca had divined, of late, that Goodman Waxwell's boy had gone to the bad, spending his days in the tavern and refusing to return home. How tragic for the poor gentleman! It was so unjust! Children, it was clear, were nothing but a trial.

The pacing began again. 'It seems one of the revellers in that den of iniquity had fallen down a flight of steps, twisting his foot. The old man was dying, the boy said. Would I come? "Boy," I said dryly, "are you asking for me in my role as physician? Or do you seek me in some spiritual capacity?" The boy had nothing to say. He stood blinking. Disgust surged in me. I said, "Boy, on a prospect of payment that is most uncertain, am I to embark on the journey into the village so as to poke and prod at a drunkard's foot? Your request is denied. It is also absurd. I imagine the patient shall be well enough, when the effects of his last night's debauch wear off."

'But the fool began to plead; not so much, I suspected, from concern for the patient, as from certainty that the mistress of the Lazy Tiger would beat him if he returned without me. Only later did I learn that the drunkard was the boy's father. I would have turned the boy out of doors; but, as it happened, my wife's soft heart dissuaded me. "Go with him,

Nathanian," she said quietly. Dear Goody Waxwell! She is such a good woman.'

'Dear Goody Waxwell,' Umbecca mouthed. The excitement of moments ago was subsiding ever deeper. She looked down sadly.

Buttons.

With slow, efficient fingers she fastened them again. There was no need to fear. Her visitor was not watching.

'The scene at the tavern was one of chaos. Tables were upended and chairs smashed. Broken glass glittered on the floor; everywhere the evidence of debauchery betrayed itself. But the place was empty and silent in the morning. I stayed my nostrils against the sour ale and the – ah – *urine* and the lingering reek of smoke. Quickly the boy led me through the low-raftered front chamber to an apartment at the back.

' "He's here? He's here?" The tavern-woman burst forward, blocking my path. She was shrieking and shrilling. Her clothes were dishevelled and caking, tear-tracked paint was cracking from her cheeks like plaster. She was wearing a red wig. "Oh, Goodman Waxwell, you'll save him, won't you? My poor Ebby! Poor, poor Ebby! He's been a good man! He's lived a good life! His only failing was to like his little drop . . ."

' "For the sake of Our Lord, woman!" I pushed past the harlot.

'The dingy little room had a dirt floor, and in a narrow aisle between a clutter of barrels and bottles and other paraphernalia of the tavern's trade, the patient lay on a makeshift stretcher. The boy had tried to carry him upstairs, it seemed, but the old man had cried out, refusing to move.

'I approached the stricken form.

'Reeking like garbage, dressed only in a ragged jerkin, Ebenezer Throsh lay lolling, his toothless mouth open. They had removed his breeches and stockings and I could see that his right ankle was empurpled and swollen massively. Shaky on his feet, the old man had fallen as he ran for cover from the tavern fight. I prodded at the swelling. The drunkard stirred, moaning. I listened to his breathing and the slow throb of his heart. The harlot, twisting her hands, was standing by, whimpering. I turned to her sternly and informed her that her husband was facing the time of reckoning. Though he had only twisted his ankle, the shock of the accident had vanquished, at last, his much-abused frame. The burnt-out drunkard was, indeed, hovering close to death.

'The woman's whimpering became a wild, despairing cry. "Oh Goodman Waxwell, save my poor husband!" She sank to the floor. She clutched my knees, blubbering absurdly that her husband had been the most true, the most good, the most virtuous of men. "Foolish woman, speak not to me of virtue!" I thundered. "Look rather on this hulk of humanity and consider the lesson that is laid out for you here! Here is an emblem of this cursed village and its fate!" I gestured sweepingly.

'But the piteous cries became only worse, and it came to me that the woman, though she barely knew it, was pleading not that I patch and caulk the worthless hulk but redeem, rather, the degenerated Essence that should soon be plunged into the Realm of Unbeing. Even in so vile a creature as this painted harlot, I saw, there yet remained a glimmering of the faith of her childhood. For all the long course of her debaucheries, she remained aware of their inevitable, agonizing terminus.

'I turned back to the patient, thinking only to administer a draught that would speed his passage to his deserved, final judgement.

'That was when I saw that a way was open, for so dingy was the squalid room, so bleak and dark, and so bloated had the foot become, so monstrous and inflamed, that at first I had failed to register the most shocking fact about it: that squashed across its spatulate tip were not five, but *seven* toes. An icy horror gripped my heart. Still the woman was wailing.

'I shook her. I slapped her face. "Woman, would you have me lance the boil of his vileness now, while yet he clings to a torn skein of life?" She gazed up at me, uncomprehending. I swivelled back, grabbing at the seven-toed foot. The old man roared in agony, but I shouted over his cries: "Woman, there is a way!"'

※　※

'I dispatched the boy to bring me what I needed. "Quiet, woman!" The harlot was gibbering in the corner now, her peeling face a mask of fear. "If you must speak, remember your litany! Or has your long course of debauchery shaken even that most primary knowledge from your heart?"

'At last the boy, ashen-faced and stumbling, returned with the boiling water, the towels, the lamp. I rummaged in my bag. First must come the lancing, to drain off the fluid; I took out my long, round-eyed spike. Then the more radical course of treatment. Ah yes, my little sharp-toothed saw would be sufficient for such soft flesh, such weakened, brittle bones. I stripped off my jacket and rolled up my sleeves.

'In the lamplight the little room was weirdly lurid, its dinginess become instead a backdrop of evil glitterings, reflected in the curves of dark bottles, playing on the panes of the tiny, dusty window. "Hang the lamp from the ceiling, boy!" I urged. In the jaundiced light the travesty of nature stood out yet more hideously, an enormous blackish-purple blood-pudding of flesh so variegated, so distended, so engorged that nothing could appear more nauseous.

'I made my preparations, seeking the place to administer the lancing. Back and forth, back and forth, I traced the point of my spike across the flesh. As I did so, the whimperings of the woman were joined by new, rising sounds from the drunkard's lips. At first, they seemed merely the gibberish of a man in pain. Had a man of virtue been so afflicted, I might have held a beaker of brandy to his lips, to give him ease. But Ebenezer Throsh was no such man, and the gibberish, I soon realized, was a tide of the vilest blasphemies, the foulest obscenities.

'"Hold him down, boy. Hold him tight." I plunged the spike into the ballooning flesh. A wild cry rent the air and a rush of gore exploded from the foot, spurting forth like a pent-up geyser, breaking free at last. The vileness splattered every corner of the room.

' "No! No! Ebby! Ebby!" The harlot was on her feet at once, clawing and clutching at my shoulder. I flung her off. The drunkard, in agony, was bucking, twisting. "Hold him, boy, hold him! We must work quickly if his Essence is to be saved." The spike fell from my hand; I seized the saw. Black gore and yellow pus dripped from the ceiling and the swaying lamp. Faintly, with rapid precision, I drew the blade across the ankle; beads of blood would be my marker. There was no time to lose. I gripped the handle hard and dug down, ripping through the flesh.

' "No!" It was the harlot. She had grabbed the spike. She hurled herself at me, crazed with grief. The boy started forward. "Leave her, boy! Hold the old man!" I struck the spike from the harlot's hand; then I struck her face, back and forth, back and forth. "Foolish woman, do you think I act on anything other than the command of the Lord Agonis? Submit, woman, and pray!" I seized the saw-handle in my fist again and with three swift strokes severed the old man's foot.

'Gout after gout of blood gushed forth. "Did you heat the poker, boy? Quick, quick!" The boy blundered back to the kitchen fire; but before I could cauterize the spurting stump, the wretched old man had risen up, shrieked the name of the deposed king, and fallen back, inert. I grabbed his wrist, just in time to feel the last departing throbs of life.

'I turned tenderly to the weeping harlot. "He is dead, Goody Throsh; and I am bound to tell you that in his last moment your husband cried out a name which to all worshippers of the true god must for ever be consigned to execration and shame. Yet truth, I have always felt, must be tempered with compassion; and perhaps, poor woman, all was not lost. I made the severance in the moment before his death; your husband's cry may have been merely the last departing shriek, just in time, of the evil which had so

215

corrupted his being. Learn from his fate, and dedicate your-self to the worship of the Lord Agonis."

'The woman gave forth no more wild bewailings, only nodding and sobbing quietly now, and when the boy appeared in the doorway, the glowing-tipped poker descended in his hand, and slowly cooled, as he saw through brimming eyes that all was over. My hands and my garments were soaked with the blood which, as you see, still stains me.'

Chapter 27

WAXWELL SEES THE LIGHT

Umbecca was trembling.

In the course of his narrative Goodman Waxwell had paced up and down before her many times; crabwise here, crabwise there, he had paused before the window and before the faded tapestry and by the bed where Ela lay sleeping; but his narrative had been addressed neither to the window, to the tapestry, to the insensible form on the bed; nor, it seemed, had it been addressed to Umbecca. Throughout his story, the dishevelled physician had seemed only to stare ahead with fixed, unseeing eyes. Now, alighting on the sofa beside Umbecca, he turned to her, suddenly ardent. The fat woman, on the brink of offering *Goodman, how shocking. What a dreadful experience for you*, or *Goodman, what sin exists in this world*, instead gasped, and coloured again as he seized her hand.

'Dear lady, it has all been revealed to me now! I feel as if I am one who has wandered, life-long, through a labyrinth of darkness, only now to find himself, suddenly and after all, a child of light.'

Umbecca's heart beat hard; the thud-thud of the companion beat was harder, louder, too.

'It had to be done, don't you see? And it must be done again. I have been a dupe! I have been a fool! All this time I have been the merest stooge of vanity, arrogant in imagining that my Essence shall pass unhindered into The Vast. I see now that it has deserved only to be rent and flung with bitter scorn into the abyss!'

What could he mean? The grip of the hand grew tighter and the Goodman's eyes, staring into Umbecca's, glowed as if with fire.

'Ah, my good woman, the sanctuary to which we aspire is like a shining citadel, to be reached only at the end of a long, winding road. From that road there branch many byways, false turns and dead ends and deceiving loops; and many of its ways are mysterious, dusty and dark. The journey we must make is a treacherous one. Yet, when we stagger at last to its end, wretched in spirit as in body, ragged and longing only to cast aside the tattered garments of this world, is it to be granted that he who has stridden proudly, certain of his way, looking neither to his left nor to his right as his sisters and brothers stumble, or are irresolute, or are lured into the byways – is it to be granted that he who has fixed his eyes firmly forward, pausing not to assist those who stagger blindly – is it to be granted that the gates of that citadel shall be flung gladly open for this man, or that he shall not rather be turned back with execration and loathing? For has that man not betrayed, in his pride and presumption, a sacred trust that was vouchsafed to him? I say yes! I say he has! And I say, my good woman, that I am that man.'

'Goodman, I don't understand!'

Now Umbecca was frightened. The physician leapt up and began to pace again, excitedly this time, his burning eyes fixed on her face all the time.

'You don't see? My good woman, what happened to me today was a test. A sign. These last years have been years of horror for the followers of our faith. Must not the Lord Agonis have wept, have sobbed and wailed for our ravaged land? But there is talk now from the dark kingdom of Zenzau; it is said that our triumph is certain, and the destiny of our race shall come to pass. We shall carry all before us in the holy war! For the tide of our faith, long at its ebb, is returning now in a great gathering wave. And as that wave washes over us, my good woman, as it crashes and cascades and froths and foams, are we to forget the most sacred words of our litany? *I shall hold you so hard to my heart—*'

'*That my heart shall split open, bursting bloody.*' Umbecca's little pink lips whispered the words, and her little eyes gazed almost tearfully at the Goodman. A profound sadness was filling her slowly and the thudding had travelled decisively to her head, pounding at her temples like a drumbeat.

Nirry came in with the tea.

❄ ❄

In the time since her last exit, the maid had ventured tentatively down certain dark passages. Fearfully she had pushed open certain creaking doors. Quietly at first, then loudly, she had called up one, then another, winding stairway, 'Master Jem? Master Jem?'

But only her own echoes came in reply.

She set down the replenished tray. 'Excuse me, ma'am—'

Goodman Waxwell looked at her sharply, but the mistress seemed to notice her not at all, to be roused neither to ardour at the second enormous tea, nor to protest at the maid's undeniable delay. Both responses might have been expected. Unpiling the tray, ruefully setting out the cakes and sweetmeats she had made for Master Jem and Barnabas, Nirry attempted again, 'Ma'am, Master Jem—'

The fat woman's gaze snapped suddenly towards her. 'Go, girl!'

'Ma'am?'

'Go!'

Nirry flushed, and was about to flee, but Goodman Waxwell caught her wrist. 'My good woman, let her stay,' he said to the mistress. 'Stay, child, and hear wisdom!' he said to the maid. 'No barriers shall divide us when we come to face the judgement of the Lord Agonis.'

Uncertainly Nirry, directed by the physician, lowered herself to the very edge of the sofa. The mistress did not look at her, nor did she touch the tea. Incongruously side by side they sat, the fat woman and the thin girl, as Goodman Waxwell resumed his address.

'Consider the dead man, Ebenezer Throsh—'

'D-Dead?' Nirry faltered.

'Hush, girl!'

The physician did not pause. 'The dead man, Ebenezer Throsh, was a traveller who had lost his way.' The pacing began again; the words swelled like music. 'But why, I ask, had this fate befallen him?

'There are some who are enmired in a darkness that ascends, like sputum or like bile, from the blackness of their hearts. These are the most culpable in their sinful ways, for there is blackness in the hearts of all women and men, and it is our sacred trust to halt its insidious dark rising.

'Those who fail are the weak of this world. What is to be done with them? First, we must condemn them; then, as we condemn them, hope that perhaps their hearts may break; and, in breaking, become open to the love of the Lord Agonis.

'The dark-hearted appear fair, but in truth are rotten with corruption. But there are those, too, who display outwardly the misshapen attributes of the creatures of evil. Of all the travellers on the dusty, winding way, it is these who are most shunned; and rightly, for what they bear is the badge of a corruption that shall, in time, consume them. Yet, if this badge is to be rent from them, what then? Could it be, I ask myself, that the old man, Ebenezer Throsh, his deformity cut from him, is even now proceeding through the portals of The Vast? Oh, my good women, I must believe it is so!'

The physician sank to his knees, trembling. He raised his hands to the air, the fingers splayed. 'I must believe that I have redeemed my wayward brother, and scourged, in redeeming him, my own proud heart!'

He snatched back his outstretched hands, clutching them together in fervent prayer.

'Praise the Lord Agonis!' Umbecca cried suddenly. In the course of the physician's monologue, as if hauled by invisible hands, she had seemed to swell forward from the depths of the sofa until she merely perched, intent and massive, on the edge of her shabby cushion; now, all at once, her cry ascending, she blundered forward, upending the tea-table, sending the laden tray crashing to the floor.

Nirry screamed. She jumped to her feet.

Oblivious, Umbecca sank beside the physician. He was reciting the litany now, and the fat woman's little mouth, through the crackings of sobs, struggled to follow him as he formed the sacred words.

❉ ❉

Nirry looked about her helplessly. The tea things, flung from the overturned table, lay before her like the ruins of a tiny city.

'Oh no, no!' She scrambled amongst the devastation. The little cakes and tarts that had been meant for Master Jem and Barnabas were sinking, melting into a spreading lake of tea. Quickly, the maid set the teapot upright again, but a lesser stream still ran from a crack in the side.

'Oh, no!' It was the best porcelain! Cursing, she plucked the upended plates from the hot lake.

Some were chipped.

'Join us, girl.' A plump fist groped, grabbing Nirry's skirt. The maid was about to rise; she gasped as she was dragged instead into the little enclosed world of the litany. She wanted to break away, running from the apartment.

She moved her lips soundlessly. The litany was muffled, uttered quickly into tightly knotted hands. What did it mean? To Nirry, nothing; or rather, only dim memories of her girlhood, before the Siege. It was a matter of cold knees on stone-flagged floors; of half-understood words sometimes muttered, sometimes declaimed; of solemn, heavy songs that would weigh her spirits down. It was chill mornings before the sun was up in the chapel where the servants gathered for prayers; and on each Blackmoon and Canonday, and at the Festival of Agonis and on Atonement Day, and Foretelling, and the other special days, the servants, in a long crocodile, forbidden to talk or laugh, would file down the path to the temple in the village where the mutterings would be softer and the declamations louder and the songs would go on as if they would never stop.

She had forgotten it all since Mother died.

Lord Agonis, tomorrow I shall seek you more truly:
I shall call for you with voice-cords so tautened that my voice-
cords shall snap, bursting bloody;
I shall crawl for you across fields of briars until my knees and
hands tear open, bursting bloody . . .

Nirry's knees were in the cream and cakes; her skirt was in
the tea. Slowly the spilt, scalding liquid was creeping through
the fabric of her uniform.

Lord Agonis, tomorrow I shall serve you more truly . . .

Nirry leapt up with a scream, 'I'm burnt to death!'
'Girl!' Umbecca grabbed her.

But in the same instant the physician suddenly snapped
out of prayer, his eyes springing open. He seized the fat
woman by the shoulders. 'Mistress Rench! Where is the
Vexing?'

Umbecca cried out.

The maid was leaping up and down, flapping her skirt.
She gasped:

'I tried to tell her! I tried—'

The physician did not hear. 'Where is the Vexing?'

Nirry stopped. She stared ahead. Raw, hot pain was travelling up her legs. In that moment, several awarenesses
rushed upon the maid. She sensed that the flappings of her
skirt were to no avail: her knees were burnt with boiling tea;
she saw that the fat woman's bodice had burst open, exposing
a huge, ugly breast; she registered, really registered for the
first time, just what it was that had happened in the tavern;
and in the same moment a terrible meaning attached itself to
the physician's repeated, shouted question:

'Where is the Vexing?'

Umbecca was moaning. Waxwell shook her. Had she heard
his question? Did she understand?

'Oh Goodman, Goodman!'

Sobbing, the fat woman fell forward, into the physician's
unwilling arms. Her huge bulk listed massively over his
slight, twisted frame, surging at once with shame and joy.

Her blood coursed through her veins like fire. How close had evil come to her today, whispering with its hot breath into her ear, running its burning fingers down her neck! With a heave of horror, the incident at the casement came back to her. Now Goodman Waxwell had shown her the way; now her faith came rolling back to her, crashing over her vastness like waves.

Umbecca was oblivious of her exposed breast, rubbing and squashing against the physician's bloody shirt.

With a sharp shove the twisted little man extricated himself from beneath her. Like a great stricken animal the abandoned Umbecca pitched slowly to the floor.

Her sobs came harder, faster.

On the bed, Ela was stirring.

The abused young woman struggled to reclaim herself. For so long, too long, she had lain enmired in treacly oblivion. Dimly she knew that something had been done to her, that a great wrong had been committed against her. Now, slowly, it sank into her awareness that another great wrong was about to be enacted within the walls of the castle, and that the wrong, this time, was to be done to her son.

She almost cried out, but could not.

Not yet.

Goodman Waxwell blundered from the room. 'Vexing! Vexing!' he was shrieking. 'Where are you, Vexing?'

Outrage surged in Ela's drugged veins and with a last effort she forced herself to the surface.

No one looked at her. No one saw.

She clenched her fists.

Chapter 28

THE ABOMINATION

'Vexing! Vexing!'

Waxwell's cries rang wildly through the castle.

The evening was drawing in and the corridors were darkening; the descending sun glowed redly at the windows, but here, away from the courtyard, windows were few. Only one narrow slit, high in the vast solidity of the outer wall, would cast its burnishing illumination on the scene that was shortly to be played out, the final act of Waxwell's visit that day.

Scuttling in his hideous crabwise motion, the physician had soon passed the few apartments he knew.

'Vexing?' he cried again.

Vexing.

Vexing.

His voice echoed back to him.

He looked around him. He looked up. Draping cobwebs hung, pendulous, from the ceiling. In the far corner a stony archway disclosed the presence of dark, winding stairs.

'Vexing?' Waxwell whispered this time. Why was he whispering? There was a scuttling of rats. Where, he tried to remember, did they keep the Vexing? The physician imagined a dingy cupboard, where the Vexing lay unmoving, enmired in his deformity. Had it been like that? Oh, surely, surely. Tragic, of course. But the Vexing's tragedy would come to an end.

The whisper again:

'Vexing?'

The physician was turning, turning, his eyes darting this way and that. Years had passed since he had treated the Vexing; years, he saw now, of foolish neglect. He had seen the Vexing as a hopeless case. *Irredeemable*. He had thought it. He had said it. But such was human vanity! There was so much one could do, so much to be done, if one opened one's heart to the Lord Agonis! The knowledge vouchsafed by Him could lead us all to redemption.

Even cripples.

Even bastards.

'Vexing?' The voice was sterner now, louder. The physician did not mind the echoes. Why should he mind? Ah, but a gnawing, nagging anger was rising in his breast. Had he not always had the Vexing's welfare at heart? *And how is the Vexing?* he had asked the fat woman, asked her many times; he had expressed, indeed, an admirable concern. *How is the Vexing?* Had it not always been his first question? His last? His only real question?

'Vexing?'

That was when Waxwell heard the strange sound, a high, undulating wailing that might have been the music of another world. His moist lips twisting, the hunched figure was suddenly aware of the ruined immensity of the castle, its darkening vastness, as it pressed mysteriously all around him. The sound came from the stony archway, the archway that led into the winding staircase.

It stopped.

Then a swinging lamp came into view, filling the archway with a haze of golden light.

Then the voice:

'Barnabas! I can't go on!'

The Vexing! But who was Barnabas?

Goodman Waxwell concealed himself behind a pillar. The lamplight in the archway grew brighter and a creature, not the Vexing but just as misshapen, emerged into the corridor. Waddling laboriously, the thing was like some grotesque cross between an infant and an old man, with a big, wizened head and tiny arms and legs.

Waxwell watched, trembling with disgust, as the abomination first extinguished the light, then carefully set down the lamp upon the floor. The thing looked up appreciatively, with a toothless smile, at the narrow slit that let the light through the wall; then, flexing its pudgy little fingers, set them to work on the polished box that was strapped across its chest. The weird music rang out again, like the wordless evil spell of some strange puppet-master, as the exhausted Vexing hauled himself on sticks down the last remaining stairs.

The dwarf ceased his playing and applauded, just at the moment when the sticks slid, clattering, from beneath the Vexing's arms.

'Barnabas! We did it!' Jem collapsed, gasping.

'Vexing!' Goodman Waxwell burst forth.

The voice was a wild, imperious screech. Jem looked up first in astonishment, then in terror, as the enraged physician bore down upon him. Waxwell seized him, shaking him, shrieking between foaming lips of the divine plan and the accursed of the earth and the eternity of horror that was the Realm of Unbeing.

'Would you mock your deformity, Vexing? Would you defy the will of the Lord Agonis? What would you be? Would you be Nova-Riel?'

'Let me go! Let me go!'

Jem writhed. His crippled legs could not kick, and Goodman Waxwell was holding his hands.

'Oh, but the infection has spread already! You are possessed by evil, Vexing! Your heart is rotten!'

The dwarf's tongueless mouth was shrieking without sound and tuneless wheezings juddered from the hurdy-gurdy as the little man leapt and lunged ineptly at the attacker.

He darted in, clawing at Waxwell's thighs.

Once.

He leapt back.

Twice.

Waxwell struck out. He flung the dwarf to the floor. There was a heavy discord from the hurdy-gurdy.

Three times.

'Abomination, go from me!'

This time, the physician sprang from the Vexing. He seized the fallen crutches and advanced on the dwarf.

'Master Jem! Master Jem!' a voice was calling.

But Waxwell did not hear. He was undaunted, and Jem could only sprawl helplessly on the floor, too spent even to cry out, as the physician, bellowing about the evil one, and the disguises he wore, and his insidious devices, dashed the crutches down once, twice, then again and again, on the scurrying, then prostrate, form of the dwarf.

'Stop!'

Nirry rushed forward.

The physician span round.

But it was not for the maid that he dropped the crutches, letting them clatter again to the floor. It was for the figure in white behind her, that the maid had left leaning, almost sinking, against the wall. Wasted and pale, but suddenly formidable, Lady Ela rose up, stepping forward, and the voice that came from her colourless lips was a judgement and a curse.

It echoed.

'Vile, deceiving man! Go from this place, and never return! Go from this place. Go. Go.'

And as he slid away, the physician only spat back, with eyes of flame, 'What could I do? Would your bastard-boy defy his god? Would he be Nova-Riel, of whom the heathen legends tell?'

'Mother!' Jem gasped, as Ela sank beside him. He buried his face against her breast. His eyes were shut tight; it was over; but all Jem could see, and he would see it again and again, was the heavy double thickness of the crutches, swishing high above the physician's head, then smashing down.

Once.

Twice.

How many times?

The shadow of the crutches swept massively across the wall, in the lurid crimson of the sunset light. First there was the sound of splintering wood; then the crunch of bone.

END OF PART TWO

PART THREE

The Approach

Chapter 29

THE QUILTED COACH

Almost three cycles had passed since the Siege.

Deep in the valley beneath the Rock of Ixiter, the village of Irion decayed slowly. In the bitter Seasons of Koros, when night lingered impatiently at the edges of the day, only the straggling smoke from a chimney or the thin glow of a candle in a window would testify that this little tumbledown cottage, or that, with its peeling whitewash and tattered thatch, was still a place where life went on. Headstones in the tombyard pitched sideways and cracked; the temple seemed about to do the same. With each new fall of heaping snow, the great stone triangle of the pediment sagged more heavily; only delaying teasingly, it seemed, the day when it would crash to the portico below.

Poverty lay across the village like a shadow. Crops failed in the disordered seasons. This was a place where scrawny chickens scratched disconsolately in unyielding yards; where goats gave only a thin, drizzling milk and ribs showed sharply in the sides of the oxen that were driven reluctantly back and forth across the fields.

The Season of Theron was brief but treacherous. Then, the Wildwood edged jealously closer, pushing bricks from the tombyard wall with thick roots and entangling branches. Spores hovered thickly over the village green, cast on to the air from a thousand illicit flowers, and all the little orchards that surrounded the cottages hung heavy with apples and peaches and pears that fell unripely and rotted quickly in the long grass that soon would be frozen, snapping stalks.

The faces of the villagers were etched deep with sorrow. Life for them had become merely a bitter, dull round. With each passing cycle, more would depart, setting out along the shabby lane, the thin beginning of the pale highway, that wound away southwards from their blighted fields and houses. There they would go, sons with sad but determined eyes, taking their leave of weeping mothers; sometimes fathers, proud but humbled, bearing their gaunt wives and dirty, barefoot children, would heap their few things on to rickety carts, to be pulled away by a donkey or a skinny, weak mare.

Those that remained were sunk deep in dejection, and often deeper still in the raw potations that issued unceasingly from the house where the tiger sprawled sleepily on the sign above the door. For long intervals there was no sound of hammering from the wheelwright's shop or the cooper's; the blacksmith's forge was cold and the miller, downstream, kept his sluice-gate shut.

But change was approaching.

'Chaplain?'

'Sir?'

'You're not dozing again?'

The chaplain had been doing no such thing. Surreptitiously he had raised a corner of the curtain; one did rather miss the sight of the world. The sun was bright today. Thick woodland, he knew, lined the road on each side; but looking down, he saw streaks of dappled gold, passing – alas, not rapidly – on the road beneath them. How long would it take to reach Irion now? A moonlife? Two?

'You're looking out, aren't you?'

The chaplain denied it suavely; he went so far as to permit himself a little, airy laugh. Others would never have been so bold. 'You forget, sir,' he said gently, 'that I am a Received man. There are times when I must consecrate my thoughts to the love and infinite mercy of the Lord Agonis.'

'I do not forget that you are a smooth-tongued, sly hypocrite.'

The barb stung. The chaplain was a man of deep sincerity; he had always found it the best way. There were times when it seemed to him that the eyes behind the visor were possessed of a vision that seared like fire through the thick, embroidered fabric.

Absurd, of course. The explosion in Zenzau had ruined the commander's eyes; that was why he must spend much of each day gazing, if he were to gaze at all, only into the darkness of his visor. How unfortunate that he also insisted on keeping the curtains closed! The old man was becoming more and more eccentric. The explosion in Zenzau had disordered his body; might it not also have disordered his mind? The chaplain thought it likely.

The little clock, set in the wall by the commander's head, chimed the fifteenth. 'Time for our prayer,' the chaplain said pleasantly. He reached for the commander's hands and pressed them, seeking his theme. The rocking of the coach gave him his clue.

Travel.

Lord Agonis.

Quest for the Lady.

He mumbled out some litany-lines, and proceeded, 'Liege of Light, hear our prayer. Look on us now from the Place of Indwelling and pity, we implore you, your humble servants. Grievously have we strayed from the path of righteousness. Miserably have we stumbled; contemptibly have we fallen . . .'

The coach jolted hugely on the rutted road. The bloated form of the commander lurched dangerously.

The chaplain did not falter. '. . . And rolled where we have fallen like beasts in a sty.'

Yes, this was good.

'All-merciful one, from the fastness of your concealment, gaze upon us now with eyes wet with sorrow, that we might struggle to find in ourselves the goodness which in time shall . . . *infuse* the world.'

The Zenzan tea-infuser, set in a corner of the coach, was the source of this last inspiration.

'Look on us, Lord, in the hope that we may find you. For the Lord and the Lady, all praise be.'

'For the Lord and the Lady, all praise be.'

Sitting back, the chaplain studied his commander, but not ardently. Olivan Tharley Veeldrop had been a man infamous, even to many on his own side, for the ruthlessness with which he had prosecuted his career. To present this career as a catalogue of murderous cruelty would hardly be difficult. Redjacket propaganda had depicted the commander as a ravening beast, jaws dripping in their lust for prey. It was a diverting image; but hardly to be believed of this gentle old man in the quilted coach. A pair of magnificent, curling moustaches were, perhaps, the only remnant of his former glory.

The commander remained slumped behind his visor, as if in the grip of religious emotion. During their journey, he had taken to marking the passing of each fifteenth with prayer. It was a little wearing, the chaplain thought. As a duty, the practice was enjoined only on the Enclosed, and seemed hardly appropriate for a military man. But the chaplain knew where the idea had come from. In *Marital and Martial* by 'Miss R——' (second volume; the celebrated 'cavalry letters'), much was made of the fact that, even on the battlefield, the hero would not fail to observe the strictest devotions. Some might say that such a man would swiftly have lost his life; some might say that he should have done so, being a prig of the first water. To 'Miss R——', it seemed, the noble Bevine's actions were wholly admirable; but one specimen, indeed, of the exemplary conduct by which he had at last won the hand of the fair Alrissa.

Or Evelissa.

Or Meroline.

The chaplain should know by now; a shelf set into the quilting of the coach, between the curly-spouted tea-infuser and the bejewelled looking-glass, contained the full 'Agondon

Edition' of the novels of 'Miss R——'. He had spent much of the journey in reading them aloud to the commander. How the old man loved them! From the ceiling of the coach swayed a golden, ornate lamp, which, for the purpose of the readings only, the commander would permit the chaplain to light.

Soon it would be time.

Today they were starting *Becca's First Ball* again.

Behind his visor, the commander's eyes were open. In his darkness, he thought of their destination.

Irion.

Yes.

He would complete the circle. When he had learnt he was to be sent to the Tarn, the commander had been outraged. It was a slight. A dishonour. He had teetered on the brink of refusing the appointment; but then, the old man had changed his mind. The Tarn, after all, had been the scene of his greatest glory; there was, besides, a certain something that he had kept in the Tarn. A certain little thing; he must mention it to the chaplain. Perhaps it would not be impossible, after all, to restore the glory of the name of Veeldrop!

But bitterness swiftly replaced these pleasing thoughts, and the commander thought again of what had happened in Zenzau. To think, he had been about to cap his glory, to achieve his last and greatest victory! Then, everything had crashed down around him. Again and again he had cursed his fate.

No, not fate.

The Red Avenger.

Chapter 30

THE BLEEDING

'Papa!'

Cata woke with a gasp.

She blinked. She rubbed her eyes. Spots of sunlight were glowing, greenish-gold, through the foliage at the cave-mouth. Dimly the interior of the cave assembled around her, with its rough walls and floor and jagged, low ceiling.

It had only been a dream.

She was sitting up on her narrow couch, her blanket pushed back. On the other side of the fire-pit Papa lay sleeping, his breath slowly rising, slowly falling, beneath the fabric of his dun-coloured robes. The hammering of Cata's heart subsided.

In her dream she had been deep in the Wildwood, wandering as she had wandered a thousand times before, bare-legged through a sea of brackens and ferns. But something was wrong; her instincts seemed dulled, and the wood around her had grown strangely silent. There was no sound of wind, no rustling of leaves; there was no cheep of birds or tickering of tiny things, concealed in a richness of leaves and bark. She had felt that her senses were thickening, coarsening; and as she pushed deeper into the ferns and brackens, it seemed as if she could no longer feel their catchings, their scrapings, their spikings at her skin. The air was growing chill and the shafts of light that poured down through the treetops were dimming, darkening. Snow began to fall.

That was when the alarm, hard and urgent, gripped Cata's heart; all at once she was aware that she was lost. Here in this wood that was traced on her senses like the veins on a leaf, Cata could not find her way back to the cave.

Papa! Papa!

But he would not hear her, and it seemed to her that he would never hear her again. Then the snow was falling more thickly, and the light through the trees, then the brackens and ferns, then the trees themselves had given way to a world of featureless, heaping snow.

Papa!

It was a dream she had dreamt before.

Cata scrambled up, straightening her shift. She pushed back her tangled hair and wiped her nose, but silently, on the back of her hand. Cautiously, her eyes straining in the greenish dim light, the girl leaned over her Papa's sleeping form.

His cowl had slipped back from his face in the night, exposing the seared pits where his eyes had been. They were doomed to remain fixed for ever open; and Cata, as always, felt a stab of sorrow. Only dimly could the girl imagine the terrible things that had happened to her Papa; but she knew that he had been hurt, cruelly hurt, and felt for him the pain that she had felt for the bloodied bird, sprawled on the white petals, or the rabbit that she had saved, but saved too late, from the cruel games of the village children.

It was the greatest pain she could feel.

She wanted to embrace her Papa, tenderly but hard; instead, quickly, lightly, Cata kissed his forehead, drew his cowl forward and twisted away, skipping down the shelf of rock to the cave-mouth. The old man had not stirred. Cata pushed through the concealing leaves and passed, with one backward look, into the bright morning.

The dappled enfoldings of the Wildwood surrounded her, insinuating deeply into the ragged glade. Cata's heart surged. She stretched her limbs, luxuriant in the warmth; and ignoring the smoking heap of the charcoal-pile and the squirrel that sat, munching at an acorn, on the stump beside the cave-mouth, she launched joyously on to the familiar, tangled path to the river.

The dream, with its strange forebodings, was forgotten.

237

Cata hunched low, slithering through the greenness.

The way, where it had become an entangling tunnel, had grown harder for her now. Almost three cycles had passed since her birth, and though the girl remained as she had always been, a feral urchin in rags, her brown limbs had become longer, firmer, just as her snubby, gamine face was turning lean and angular.

Sometimes, in the evenings before they slept, Papa would pass his fingers tenderly over her cheekbones. *Ah yes, child*, he would sigh, *you shall have your mother's beauty*. And Cata, as she lay down to sleep, would be puzzled, for she could not understand how it might be that she should possess anything of Mama's, while her Mama lay unmoving in the earth.

The swift-flowing river sparkled in the sunshine, burbling and dancing over rocks and reeds as it wound its way through the tall, thick pines. With a single lithe motion Cata twirled on a hump of rock, arms upstretched, then cast aside her shift and plunged into the rippling, liquid silver.

Afterwards, as she lay in the embrace of soft, tall reeds, Cata felt the contentment she always felt in the brief seasons of heat. The sun caressed her torso and limbs, licking at the glittering moist beads that slipped and trailed across her brown skin.

How she wished all her days could begin like this one! Cata stretched, rolling in the reeds. Later she would wander through the woods, brushing between the ferns and long grasses, chattering to the squirrels that scurried through the undergrowth and the birds that fluttered down from the trees. Casually, as if it were a game, she would gather nuts and berries and the secret, whiskery roots that she would boil in the evenings in the black cauldron. The tough flesh melted into crumbly, sweet chunks. Papa called it wood-meat. They ate it with a tart, dry fruit that they plucked from the vines that grew about the cave-mouth.

Then the evening would wane and Papa would sit, pipe in mouth, on the stump beside the cave; and Cata would sit at his feet, nuzzled against him. *Papa, tell me about Mama*, she would say, or, *Papa, tell me about when you were small.* But what she wanted were not the stories that she had heard a hundred times but only the gentle sound of the old man's voice, sadly lilting in the little glade. Warm breezes played gently about them, fragrant from all the fruits that would fall too quickly, and a hundred briefly blossoming flowers.

The river burbled. Clear-winged insects skimmed above the water; fish flickered beneath. But Cata did not see them. Lying on the bank, she had first stared upwards, into the golden-greenness that poured down through the trees; then she had shut her eyes and the spaces behind her eyes became crimson, mysterious caverns; in the caverns strange shapes unfurled and danced slowly, as if to a music that was not the music of the river but of something deeper, darker, concealed inside the world.

Cata sighed. She drew a hand across her drying skin, her fingertips passing first idly upwards and downwards between her bare thighs and her lean throat; then pausing, as they had paused before, first at the swelling tenderness at her chest, then at the soft mound between her parted thighs. Her fingers loitered, lingered.

There was a swishing in the undergrowth.

Cata started, springing up in time to see the flicker of bright stripes, disappearing back into the concealing green. Wood-tiger! She had thought he was gone, far away. Cata did not stop to slip back into her shift. All at once she was crashing after him, clumsily now, calling his name, 'Wood-tiger! Wood-tiger!'

She plummeted on. Golden flecks of light skittered across her skin, slipping and catching like the scrapes and scratches that she did not, could not feel. Immensely the greenness of the forest rose around her. But Cata did not see. Cata did not know.

She was only rushing wildly.

239

She stopped.

Where was she?

Her nostrils twitched and her ears and eyes were suddenly keen as thorns. She turned. A curtain of vines hung before her. That was when her forgotten dream came niggling, nudging at the edges of her awareness. There was a strange foreboding, like a presence in the air. Why had she come blundering like this, so foolishly? Cata could stalk through the undergrowth like a hunter. Cata could talk to the trees and the swallows.

'Wood-tiger?'

The girl knew only that she wanted to find him; the one thing she could not explain was why.

'Wood-tiger?' Cata whispered again now, gazing, almost sightlessly, into the thick curtain of vines. The river seemed far away now and the green shadows of the Wildwood surrounded the girl on all sides, deep and dark. Only the tiniest dapples of sunlight shifted across her skin as she moved. There was an incense of flowers.

Then she knew.

Cata parted the curtain of vines and stepped into the secret place. It had been a place that had frightened her when she was small. She had not come here since the day they buried the snow-tern, so many seasons before.

The girl sank to her knees amongst the petals. She closed her eyes again, then opened them. It did not matter. In the warm season, the Circle of Knowing was dim. In the perfumed shadows, she could barely see.

She breathed deeply. Drifting through her mind, like a soft call from afar, came the vision of the ghost-bird rising, spiralling upwards, from the place where she now knelt. Yet, Cata knew, the body was still beneath her, tunnelled through by worms and crumbled away into the rich, dark grains of the earth.

Cata felt a sadness. But it was a warm, gentle sadness.

There were no birds in the Circle today. Had there been birds by the river? When Cata was younger, birds would flap down to twitter beside her, water-voles, too, and squirrels from the trees, and her old friend the otter would gather around her like shy, proud sentinels. A sleek salmon might nuzzle at one hand and, stretching the other to a robin or curling worm, the wild girl would feel herself enfolded into a quiet, but rapturous communion.

It had not happened today. It happened less often now; and with a deeper sadness Cata realized that her old friends were dying or going away. The seasons were defeating them. Something had gone wrong; for even as she looked back over her short life, Cata knew that the chill from the Kolkos Aros had not always descended over the valleys for as long as it descended now. With each cycle of the seasons it remained for longer, too long, for life after life of the hanging moon.

Cata was squatting in the centre of the grove, concealed on all sides by the curtaining vines.

She said aloud, 'Something has gone wrong.'

The girl scooped up a handful of scattered petals; she held them aloft and let them flutter from her fingers. In the gloom, she gazed down at her parted thighs. For a moment she seemed disconnected from herself, floating high and ethereally in the pungent branches above her.

But she was aware of a presence, close by.

'Ghost-bird?'

The girl swayed, rocking on her haunches. The tenderness in her new swellings had returned, coursing in soft downward pulses to her thighs.

That was when she felt the sudden, liquid movement inside her. She moaned, but without pain, and doubled over. Her hands were first locked, as if protectively, about the moist centre of the spasms; then the viscous, hot fluid filled her cupping palms, then spilt through her fingers to the scattered petals beneath her. She knew what was happening, with an access first of shame, then of a calm, proud knowledge.

She gazed up. Someone was looking down at her. A white, ethereal form. It was the vision of a woman.

A beautiful woman.

'Mama!' Cata would have gasped, but could make no sound.

Still the blood ran from her.

Then it was over and the girl subsided on to her side, marvelling, sinking into the heat and the moistness she had made. Later, when she rose at last from the grove, her torso would be stuck thick with bloodied, stiffened petals.

The ghost-Mama was gone.

But lying there, her eyes flickering dreamily, in a glimmer of fugitive light Cata saw that the curtain of vines was parted, just a little; and the slitted eyes of the wood-tiger watched her for a moment, deep and intent. First they were black; then they flashed gold.

Chapter 31

DREAM OF BARNABAS

'No! Nirry, no!'

'I'm sorry, Master Jem.'

Jem was dreaming.

The day that Barnabas had gone away had been the bleakest of the boy's young life. In sleep, he lived through it again and again. Over and over he made his way laboriously down to the kitchens where the maid, her sleeves rolled back loosely, was hacking with a blunt knife at pink-red offal. It was the guts of a pig killed the day before. Nirry had held it while her father stuck the knife. She flung the hackings into a bubbling stew-pot.

'But how could he go?' Jem pursued. He could not support himself and was leaning, almost sprawling, across the scored, greasy benchtop, his face close to a disarray of radishes and turnips and ragged, whiskery parsnips. There was a pungency of onions.

'He can walk.'

'But not far!'

'He walked away.' Nirry's voice was flat. 'On the Agondon Road, I dare say. Where the stage-coach runs. He had a little bag of coins. Oh, I don't know. A dwarf can disappear. Easily. Easily.'

At this point in his dream, Jem sometimes wept. Sometimes he shouted. In real life he had only looked at Nirry wonderingly. She seemed not to care; nor to care for him. His crutches had slipped to the floor beside him and in a moment he would have to say, but did not want to say, 'Nirry, help me up.'

Jem was weak. It was the first day he had walked on his

243

crutches since the day on the tower. Since then, the moon had passed through all five of its phases.

His gaze drifted from Nirry's pinched face. The kitchens, sunken beneath the level of the courtyard, were lit by windows high in the wall, emitting streaky light. The cobblestones in the courtyard were wet with rain.

That morning, Jem had woken early. It was as if he had known that something had happened.

That something was wrong.

Then he was aware of the unaccustomed silence, filling his little chamber like a tangible thing. The stertorous rhythm of the crack-ribbed breath was gone; then he looked down and the little mat that had stretched beside his bed had gone, too.

'Barnabas?'

It was a moment before Jem had seen the other things: that the clutter of objects in the alcove had been ordered, set neatly against the walls; that the emptied floor had been swept clean; that his chair had been moved away from his bed and that leaning against the wall by his bed were the crutches, carved and polished, thick and ornate, that he had sought not to hold, nor even to touch, since the maddened physician had cast them down.

He reached for them.

'Barnabas?'

He had known even then.

After the beating, nothing had been the same. The dwarf, who had scuttled merrily about, who had hauled himself vigorously up the stairs, had been left weak and slow. His ribs were cracked, his limbs black with bruises. For a time he could take only the briefest steps before he would slump down, inert with pain.

Only slowly did strength return to him. But it was a lesser, damaged strength.

They had kept the smashed pieces of the hurdy-gurdy, the splintered wood, the keys of yellowed bone, the mysterious interior drone-strings. But when the dwarf had first come back to consciousness, floundering up from his abyss of shock, his wizened face had only looked at the remnants sadly.

Jem said uselessly, 'Can it be repaired?'

They would hold a ceremony in the alcove some nights later. The fire would be lit and leaping bright; Barnabas would spread the pieces neatly on the hearth; then, one by one, would feed them to the flames as Jem and Nirry solemnly watched.

One day the maid would bring the dwarf an old lute, but it was missing three strings and besides, his little hands could not stretch to play it. Without the hurdy-gurdy, he was lost.

Later, after Barnabas had gone, often Jem would sit alone in the alcove, hunched and unmoving in the wickerwork chair. Then he would think back to the strangeness of the dwarf, knowing that he had understood so little about him, but marvelling that he could ever have had such a friend. Already Barnabas seemed to belong to some half-forgotten, childhood land.

It was Jem's first lesson in the transience of things.

Only the objects were left behind. Glinting palely in sunlight, richly in lamplight, they jutted and arced and tilted around him, the tarnished candlesticks, the dented goblets, the shield emblazoned with the Redjacket arms. There were the books and rich garments and crouching animals, a piglet stuffed with straw and a little wooden horse. There were tattered standards and the bejewelled scabbard and the slate on which the dwarf had shown Jem his letters. There was the kaleidoscope, left beneath the window; there was the Jarvel-box, silver and ornate.

There was the picture of the pale winding road; gazing on it, sometimes Jem tried to imagine Barnabas passing over that road, with his little bundle slung back over his shoulder and his little purse hidden in a pocket of his waistcoat. Where, Jem wondered, could Barnabas have gone, stealing away on that rain-slick morning? He tried to imagine the dwarf passing sadly, or perhaps joyously, into some new scene of life.

He could not.

To Jem, it was as if Barnabas had vanished from the world.

'Damn.'

The knife slipped, slicing Nirry's thumb. She gouged her nails suddenly into the guts, tearing at the fibres of yellow, moist fat.

'Oh, damn.'

She turned away, snuffling, wiping her nose on the back of her wrist.

'Nirry?' Jem was trying to stand, pushing himself up from the crowded benchtop.

She turned back.

'He was losing his magic,' was all she said. 'He would have died if he stayed.'

Jem's face was ashen. 'But he didn't say goodbye!'

'Didn't he?'

Nirry came to him. She was about to embrace him, perhaps to sob, but she laughed instead, exasperated, holding up her bloodied hands. She wiped them on her apron and bent swiftly, retrieving Jem's crutches.

'I didn't want to touch them,' he said.

'I know.'

The kitchens were cavernous, chill in the morning, stretching back through cave-like archways into ghostly regions that once had rung with perpetual bustle. Here, the air had been always a fug of smoke and steam, clashing and colliding with a hundred aromas; sharp hooks had hung heavily with game and every spit had been always turning. Blood had run in rivulets across the floor.

'Nirry?' Jem turned back on the first step of the stairs. 'What did you mean, he was losing his magic?'

'Your crutches, Master Jem. Look at your crutches. You're

bigger. But so are your crutches. Dwarves are magical. Didn't you know?'

Jem gazed down at his crutches, thoughtful and sad. Then he looked up. As if it were an echo, he could not say from where, he imagined at that moment that he heard the hurdy-gurdy. There it was again, the strange music that had wound like smoke, or like a highway, through his dreams. On the night when they had burnt what remained of the polished box, the rich wood had rung and juddered strangely in the fire; then came a crack and the flames unlocked, briefly but headily, an intense, sour-sweet perfume.

Chapter 32

MARK OF THE VAGA

'Koros of the Rock, hear your child. He knows that the end of The Atonement shall come, at last, in his time. And he is ready to play his part. Koros of the Rock, hear your child.'

Silas Wolveron had woken from his own troubled dreams and made his way, slowly and laboriously, to the tombyard. He felt himself weakening; he must make the Avowal. Once again he had repaired to Yane's slab. Once again he had felt for the mechanism, clearing away the moss and weeds. The tomb-slab opened, silently, swiftly. Standing, gripping tightly to his staff, the old man chanted the prayer that his half-sister, Xal, had taught him.

'Koros of the Rock, hear your child. He knows that the Evil One shall return, at last, in his time. And he is ready to play his part. Koros of the Rock, hear your child.'

Sometimes the old man would reflect on the irony that Umbecca Rench had paid for this slab. Had it not been for her cousin, Yane would have no memorial; or rather, no memorial that the Agonists could understand. Yane had become a creature of the Wildwood. Her real memorial was of a different kind. But the slab had come in useful, nonetheless. It had worked its way into the Destiny of Koros. Umbecca had not known that the craftsman was a Vaga – Xal's son. The Rapture was strong in the boy, and had told him what to do.

'Koros of the Rock, hear your child. He knows that the Key to the Orokon shall come at last, in his time. And all that is foretold in The Burning Verses shall come, at last, in his time. Koros of the Rock, hear your child.'

With his head bowed, the blind man might almost have

had eyes to see, and been looking into the open grave. But even his night-vision was failing him now. There were times, more and more, when he felt the power slipping, and felt himself slipping, slowly but inexorably, into the abyss of his final darkness. The girl could sense it, he knew. But he did not think she understood. Not now. Not yet. His heart ached when he thought of the suffering she would feel.

When he turned away from the slab, the old man stumbled and almost fell. He breathed a dry, choked sob; he knew he could not come here many more times. He had promised Xal that he would keep this ritual; but soon it would be a promise that he must break. The Avowal could help him no longer. He must conserve his failing powers, waiting for his destiny. Soon would come the time when he must play his part.

The old man breathed deeply, steadying himself.

He must not weaken.

He must not fail.

But as his destiny approached, Silas Wolveron found himself thinking more and more on the past. He would tell beguiling stories to the girl, but in the darkness of his mind he thought of different, terrible things.

THE FALL OF SILAS WOLVERON

1

Often, Silas Wolveron would think of his father's face. By the end of his life it had fallen naturally into seams like the scars his son bore now.

Eliak Wolveron had been a hopeless drunkard. Gamekeeper to the Archduke – the old Archduke – Eliak had been the child of pious, upright parents, but some urge to destruction, lodged deep in his breast, had seen him tumble from their staunch Agonist ways. His brother was his opposite. Uncle Olion became Lector of the temple. He looked on the gamekeeper with a tight-lipped disdain.

Eliak's boy grew up in two worlds: first, there was the

world of the Wildwood, deep and soft, where the rustlings of leaves were like mantras on the air and the boy ran barefoot through a kingdom of green. As his daughter did now, Silas had known the ways of the wood and all its creatures; and if he had known ugliness too, and pain, the Wildwood had filled him with a sense of a world beyond, more wonderful and mysterious than his father could know.

It was a kind of victory.

Then there was his uncle's world. For a long time, Uncle Olion sought to take Silas from his father; but Eliak clung to his son with an angry, blind insistence. 'I'll die before you have him!' the drunkard once shouted, bursting into the temple during the canonical. His brother descended from the lectern in wrath, his voice filling the temple like thunder as he commanded the impious wretch to go. But Eliak only spat in his face, 'I'll die, do you hear?'

And he had.

Eliak Wolveron had at last gone too far. The Archduke had no choice but to dismiss him from his post. It was the Season of Koros. The days were bitter as Eliak's heart, and one night, reeling senselessly across the village green, the drunkard had collapsed and passed out in the snow. He was dead before morning.

From then, Silas was the ward of his uncle, and it became the pious duty of Uncle Olion to obliterate from the boy all memory of his past. When they had found his father in the snow, Silas had been a bedraggled waif of almost two cycles, filthy and barely able to speak in human language. By the time he had reached the brink of manhood, he was a model of the aspirant to Agonist grace, as radiant in his cleanliness as in his moral purity. He would stand before his uncle's visitors like an exhibit, flawlessly returning the answers to the Chain Prayer. Each Canonday, his piping voice led the Canticles; solemnly he read the Orations from the Commentaries. At the end, he held the salver to collect the coins. The childless Uncle Olion looked on him as a son, and gazing on the boy in a transport of piety would congratulate himself on the success of his campaign.

His victory over the evil Eliak was complete.

The boy, for his part, was filled with a passionate sincerity. The love of Agonis possessed his heart. To the villagers, his piety became a thing of awe; men would bow to him and women bob respectfully on the rare occasions when he would walk forth amongst them. The knowledge that when the time came he would be Received in his uncle's place was a source to them of deep joy, a comfort for the future; but joy turned to sorrow when the wife of the Archduke, a woman of deep faith, decreed that such a boy should not hide his light in the provinces. He should be sent to Agondon. Master Silas could become one of the great men of the faith – one of the Elect; perhaps, in time, an Inner of the Ascendancy! From afar, the glory he would reflect on his humble home would be all the greater. It was destiny. A party of Elders was summoned to the village. Only the most pure could be chosen for Temple College, and when the boy learned that the Elders had chosen him, he sank to his knees in an ecstasy of prayer. He sobbed.

He was at the end of his Fourth when they sent him to the city. Mounting the cart that last morning, his heart almost burst as he looked back at the Lectory, its high windows golden in the rising sun. His uncle clutched his neck. The boy clung to him. His love of the Lord Agonis and his love of his uncle were twined together in his heart like vines. He had forgotten his first days in the Lectory: the cold baths and the beatings; the long days spent locked in the cellar, screaming until he could scream no more. It had all been for his good. Uncle Olion loved him.

Silas never saw his uncle again. For a time, long letters would arrive at Temple College, filled with affection and pious exhortation. Silas, in his cell, would fall upon them eagerly, and sometimes, as his knowledge grew, would smile at the simplicity of his uncle's faith.

Then the letters trailed away.

It was at about this time that the young man became prey to troubling dreams. In the dreams, the new life that lay so vividly about him, the riches and incense within the school walls and the bustling life of the city without, seemed to have flickered from existence like an illusion. The last seasons of his life might not have passed at all. He had returned to the village; at last, as if the past were clawing him ever backwards, he was again the child of the Wildwood, Unclaimed by the Lord Agonis and barely possessed of human language.

It was a long time since Silas had dreamt like this; not since his early days in Uncle Olion's house. The beginnings of that first new life had been filled with mad desires. Painfully he had longed to tear off the shoes that crushed his feet and the collar that circled his neck like a chain. Later, after many beatings and prayers, the sharp desires passed. Only sometimes, as he lay on the brink of sleep, the lessons and sacred songs and Chain Prayers of the daylight world would peel back from the boy's tired mind like a skin, and there, beneath, lay the recollections of the Wildwood. He sank into them as into soft grass; and next day, a dull shame beat mutely at his temples. He prayed fervently.

With time, he thought he had crushed all remnants of his Unclaimed self; yet even then the remnants, like crushed glass, still glittered intensely. As birds wheeled high in the Season of Javander, ready to vanish as the snows impended, or when the green shoots of the Season of Viana forced themselves at last from the frozen ground, the recollection of the days before his Claiming would creep back inexorably into the boy's mind; then he would be filled with a longing, like an ache, as if a secret had been vouchsafed to him in a language he could no longer understand.

Now a sharper pain began in Silas. Some mischievous imp, buried deep in his mind, seemed determined to destroy his repose. Each night, as he lay in his narrow cell, the visions of the Wildwood were growing more intense. Meanwhile, his uncle's letters, having first grown briefer, then less frequent, had now stopped entirely; in the fog of his panic it seemed to the young man that these things were connected. For two cycles, in Uncle Olion's house, he had felt himself bound to his uncle as if by an invisible chain; now, the thought came to him that the chain had never been broken. Nothing need be said: for all the leagues that divided them and all the time that had passed, Silas might still have been the shivering boy who stood before his uncle while his uncle flexed a whip. *I can see into your heart, Silas,* the old man would whisper, *and I can see that your heart is impure. Come, Silas. I must purify you.* And in the early days the boy had screamed and kicked and cried; later, he would bow with reverence in readiness for the lash. It was right. It was good. But now his uncle, it seemed to Silas, had abandoned him. In despair he imagined himself standing again before the old man, and his uncle turning from him in disgust, the whip cast down in a gesture of futility, as if a rotten wall, plastered uselessly afresh for season on season, had given way at last to irretrievable decay.

Shame possessed Silas; yet outwardly, his studies proceeded apace. To his preceptors, he was all that he should have been; which was, perhaps, because they paid him little attention. To his fellow collegians he seemed, when they considered him at all, to be a strange, lonely figure. He spoke to them seldom; they thought of him as a provincial, just a provincial. None saw the turmoil that seethed inside him.

3

Once in each phase, on the day after Canonday, the students were permitted to venture into the city. The day of liberty was known as 'Wall'. To the wealthy young noblemen of the college, of whom there seemed to be many, 'Wall' marked a return to the indulgences of their former lives. At curfew, they would reel back into college on unsteady feet; then, between hilarities of shushings and stumblings, the cloisters would ring with their drunken voices. There were bawdy songs and jests. Silas, stirred from sleep, would cover his ears. He burned with shame.

After the first such evening, it seemed to him that the outrage must surely be punished. As the perpetrators shuffled blearily to Canonical next morning, a righteous outrage filled the young provincial. Retribution must swiftly follow! Yet when the Maximate stood at the podium, nothing was said. The service proceeded as if all were in order. Silas was shocked, confused. Later, at breakfast, he could not eat, and only glared when one of the drunkards, in a soft, concerned voice, thought to ask him if he were unwell. Poor Silas! He knew so little. Later, he would come to a wry knowledge of the wealthy and their depravities. A corrupt world permitted them to flourish, even in the strongholds of the Lord Agonis. Silas, his despair turning to zeal, dreamed for a time that he would be a great reformer, reclaiming the lost capital of Ejland from iniquity. But now this dream was over. *Inside*, thought Silas, *I am a hollow, echoing drum. I am helpless to alleviate even my own vileness.*

One day, in the midst of his despair, Silas was told that he had a visitor. His heart leapt. Uncle Olion had come to him! He rushed to the Portal Room, relieved and eager; but his relief soon turned to disappointment.

There was surely some mistake. It was a bleak day in the Season of Koros; the light in the Portal Room was dim; but as Silas stared through the latticed screen he could see at once that the visitor was a woman. Erect and slender, she turned to him, her face concealed in a veil.

'I'm sorry, I—'

'Silas! Don't you know me?' The veil fluttered as the woman laughed, a light, airy laugh like a tinkling of chimes. With a swift grace she plucked away the veil. Shame fought in Silas with astonishment. It was Lady Lolenda, wife of the Archduke – but how strangely altered! Gone was the black-garbed figure he had known, who sat in stately devotion in the simple village temple; in her place was a sparkling, bejewelled creature in patterned silks, her powdered hair heaped high beneath an elaborate hat. 'I see you're surprised, Silas. But Agondon, after all, is not Irion. And Irion' – her smile was wry – 'is not Agondon. You do know what I mean?'

It appeared that political duties had called the Archduke to court, and of course his wife must come to the capital, too. Silas was only a little surprised at the lady's apparent eagerness. Impatiently, the young man sought news of his uncle. It was then that the lady became suddenly earnest.

'Oh Silas, your uncle has been very ill—'

'No!' Silas almost cried out. His heart was clutched as if by an icy hand. He had thought of his uncle's silence as a judgement upon himself, reverberating wordlessly along the invisible chain; all at once he was aware of his callow self-absorption. He was mortified. He had not written to Uncle Olion since the Season of Theron; now, the snows of the Season of Koros were thick on the streets outside. He sat dumbly as Lady Lolenda told him of his uncle's long agonies.

'But he's better now?' Silas urged. 'He's well again?'

'Silas, shh.' The lady's fingers slipped beneath the grille. She had removed her glove. Her touch was cool, but soft. 'I have some papers. Books. He wanted you to have them. Come to me at "Wall".'

And in his mortification Silas could barely consider what the lady's words might mean; he felt only a dull wonderment that a fine lady should know of the custom of 'Wall'. She left him a small, stiff card, printed with an address.

4

Some afternoons later, a nervous Silas found himself standing before the tall, polished doors of a house in the most fashionable district of Agondon. He was about to knock when he noticed the bell.

In his year at college the young man had availed himself only twice of the liberty of 'Wall'. The first time, he had proceeded for perhaps a matter of lengths up the crowded thoroughfare that ran past the portal. The city, as he had seen it when he arrived, was an alien blur of clip-clopping hooves and jostling crowds and vast, overmastering houses. Fear possessed him. He turned and rushed back through the arched gates.

The second time, he went further afield. Silas still shuddered when he thought of that day. What filth he had seen, what degradation! That was three Canondays after his arrival. After that, he had not gone out again. Solitary and silent, he remained in his cell through the unwanted liberty of 'Wall', his head bent earnestly to his studies.

Now, a footman in a powdered wig led Silas through long apartments, lavish with gold and marble. There were rich tapestries and huge, extravagant paintings. Bright threads glittered in the swirls of patterned carpets. Naked statues cavorted on fluted columns. The young provincial, prim in the black trappings of his faith, could not but gaze about him, at once appalled and marvelling. He had never been in a house like this before. The footman, with a wry smile, left him at the door of a luxurious chamber. Silas entered uncertainly. Heavy curtains concealed the windows and only a soft glimmering of candles gave light to the perfumed darkness.

Later, Silas would regard what followed as the decisive moment of his life. It was here that his destiny was resolved; here, nowhere else, that the burden of unworthiness that had hovered above him now descended with its soft, unconscionable weight. How long had it taken?

'Oh Silas, I marked you out from the first. Silly boy! Didn't you know? Didn't you guess?'

In the darkened room she had floated towards him like a mysterious, beautiful spirit, a Lady Lolenda different again from the cool woman of fashion who had faced him through the screen of the Portal Room. Her hair was undone and her voice was playful; and though Silas knew that the afternoon had been long – though he recalled the ceremonies of tea and conversation and the awkwardness when he rose, stammering, to go – afterwards, in his dreams, it would all happen in a single, irresistible motion, the footman's wry smile and the closing door giving way inevitably to the stroking hand, and the arms that drew him into a shuddering, soft embrace.

'Hush, hush.' She smoothed his hair.

5

That was the beginning of his life of impurity. It was rather as if, having for so long been gnawed inside by guilt, he had been compelled in the end to give his guilt an outward, fleshly form. When it was over, she told him that she would expect him again, on the next day of 'Wall'. He could not speak and his eyes were cast down. She laughed and twisted his hair. Unbidden, the footman returned and led him back through the long, lavish apartments; then Silas was standing outside the polished door again, at the top of the tall steps from the street. Fresh snow had fallen and the sky was empurpled with evening.

He would not go back. This first time, he vowed, would be the only time; his ruined life must be consecrated now to penance. Perhaps, after a scourging of many seasons, he might at last propitiate the wrath of the Lord Agonis. He prayed. He wept. That night he lay not on his thin mattress but on the stone floor of his cell, naked and shivering. In the days that followed he bathed again and again; his arms ached from pumping the icy water. He would not go back.

Canonday came and went; then it was 'Wall'. It was no good. In the night, even as he lay unsleeping and cold, the dreams had hovered in wait for him, shifting, shuffling ever closer through the darkness.

It was the Wildwood, come to claim him.

That was when he knew he would never be free. The cycles since his father's collapse in the snow had gone for nothing. They had blown away like chaff. And when sleep came at last and he sank into the wood, now it was not the tender green softness he had known but a steaming sinister jungle of cacklings and cawings. It was inside him. Again and again, that Season of Koros, he would return to the Lady Lolenda.

It was always the same; and when it was over, she would whisper with a smile that she would be waiting for him on the next day of 'Wall'. Every 'Wall', she would be there. It might have been a bondage that would last for all his life; it might have been a sickness and he might have been dying. Lust, in the interludes between the days of its discharging, mounted in the young man like pus inside a boil. By Canonday, it was intolerable. As he passed through the loved, familiar rituals of the canonical, in his mind he enacted a different, secret ritual. Already he had returned to the perfumed dark room. Soon, the most sacred songs and stories, the most holy symbols of faith, were intertwined for Silas with his longing for depravity. The Maximate led the chanting of the Litanies of Agonis. Silas heard the litanies of his own lust. He thudded with desire. He saw himself rutting and grunting like a beast. The censer, like a pendulum, swung in the Maximate's hand, indicative of worldly time that so swiftly passes. In imagination, Silas felt Lolenda's supple hands. He bit hard on the aureoles of her breasts.

'When's your Immersion?' she asked one afternoon, as they lay, spent, on her silken sheets.

Silas started. He had not thought she could know of this. He disentangled himself from her limbs. He reached hastily, almost angrily, for his breeches.

'Silas?'

How could he explain? Seasons had passed since he had first come to this room; yet all this time, as he had wallowed secretly in vice, in the outward world he had remained the earnest youth whose piety, back in Irion, had seemed a thing of awe. Now he was to be Received into full fellowship of the college. In a moonlife more, in a ceremony in the presence of the Archmaximate, Silas would descend naked into the Pool of Purity. Years of study yet remained to him, but from now on Silas would be one of the Elect, destined for high rank in the Order of Agonis. Some had been collegians for four years, or for a full cycle, before they were called at last for Immersion; Silas, it seemed, had been marked out as a youth of special promise.

He looked back at the bed. The room, as always, was close and hot, the curtains drawn, the fire flickering high; there was no other light but from perfumed candles. In the dim haze, Lolenda's limbs were sleek, golden. Silas felt a heavy, dull thud of horror.

It had to end.

It all must end.

With an access of shame the young man knew that his piety had become the merest by-blow of guilt. Sinning, he had assumed a mask of sinlessness; impure himself, he seemed radiantly pure. Poor Silas! He was very young then; he had not understood how common was his lot.

He fled.

'Silas? I'll be waiting!' Lolenda called after him. She rolled sensually over the stained sheets, laughing.

7

The moonlife that followed was an agony for Silas. He had known, of course he had known, that he must break it off with Lolenda. On Immersion Day, in the most sacred rite of the faith, he would consecrate himself to a lifetime's purity. He would forswear the desires of the flesh for ever. Again and again, in that painful moonlife, Silas hovered at the foot of the staircase that led to the Head Preceptor's room. He would cast himself at the old man's feet and beg forgiveness. He would pour his unworthiness from his breast like blood.

But he did not.

One evening, as Immersion Day drew near, the Head Preceptor called Silas to him. Trembling, Silas ascended the staircase at last.

It was over.

It had to be.

The turbulence of his heart, the young man thought, had burst unbidden on to the very air; there was nothing he would have to say. The Head Preceptor, knowing all, would look at him gravely; then, with a sorrowing heart, dismiss him. There would be no Immersion. There would be nothing. Silas Wolveron would be going home.

'Ah, Wolveron.' The Head Preceptor smiled. 'We thought it was time you met the Archmaximate. Archmaximate, our most promising pupil . . .'

Silas almost broke down. Tears blurred his eyes. Trembling, he sank to his knees to kiss the hand, plump and circled with rings, that extended towards him from beneath lavish robes.

But later, he impressed the Archmaximate with all the evidence of earnest piety. He spoke with confidence on the great questions of the day; he descended adroitly to the finest points of theology. At the end of the evening, he joined the two Elders in prayers. The young man from the provinces had made a brilliant impression.

He left, choked with emotion. Though Silas despised the blackness that festered inside him, his way was clear to him now. He could never leave this life; he loved it too much; never could he betray the trust that had been placed in him. He must go to Lolenda. He must tell her it was over. But to the Head Preceptor, he would say nothing. There was nothing to say. The piety of his future life would atone for the sins of the past.

8

Silas would never forget his last visit to Lolenda's house. It was two days before his Immersion and he should not have left the college; he was 'breaching Wall'.

It had to be done.

On the steps before the polished door he turned anxiously, looking behind him. The first time he had come here, snow had lain thickly along the quiet street; it was heaped heavily on the bare branches of the trees that were now in riotous blossom. Birds sang. It was early in the morning.

'I'm sorry, her Ladyship—'

Silas pushed past the footman. He knew the way and he

strode defiantly through the echoing, empty apartments. He had no courage; twice, in the last weeks, he had come at 'Wall', resolved each time that this time was the last; twice, the delicious rituals of lust had overpowered him.

But not this time. Not this time.

'Silas!'

The brightness dazzled his eyes. The curtains were flung back and morning flooded the room. Tall windows opened on to a stately garden, and before the vista, at a table laden with breakfast-things, Lolenda sat alone in a trailing night-gown, reading a novel. She cast it down.

'Silas, are you mad? The Archduke does like one to amuse oneself, but—'

'It's over, Lolenda.'

'What?'

'I've come to tell you it's over. It can't go on.'

'Silas, what can you mean?' She rushed to him, caught him in her arms.

He was impassive. He was not even trembling. Sobbing, Lolenda turned her face up to his. He looked down at her. It was a shock. For so long, for too long, he had known Lolenda only as the diaphanous, sensual wraith of a perfumed dark-ness; he had succumbed to her illusion of beauty. Now, in the harsh morning light, he saw the illusion stripped cruelly from her: he saw the deep wrinkles round her mouth and eyes, and the sallow, coarsening skin at her neck.

Silas remembered the day of 'Wall' when he had wandered alone about the city. How long ago it was! Numb with misery, he had barely looked about him as he ploughed ever onwards, seeking only to exhaust himself. *Anna Javander!* came a drunken cry; it was a blasphemy pertaining to the goddess of water. Silas leapt back as the contents of a chamber-pot sloshed from a window to the ground at his feet. Panic assailed him. He had blundered into a region of dingy alleys. Filthy hovels were crammed meanly together; above, their teetering eaves were almost touching. The stench was intolerable. Ragged children gazed at him incuriously.

Then, Silas felt the hand on his arm. He turned, and in the dim light saw the face of a woman, pitted and seamed beneath a thick layer of paint. She smiled in hideous, unmistakable invitation. Silas shuddered and hurried on his way.

How often had he thought of that invitation: that broken-toothed smile; that cracking, pallid paint. Always, he could think, there had been one depravity he had shunned. There was a depth to which he would not sink. Now he saw that this was not so. What difference would it have made? The old harlot, rotten with pox, might as well have been Lolenda.

She might have been Lolenda.

His face registered only a flicker of disgust.

'How old are you, Lolenda?'

'Oh, Silas!' She broke from him. She strode across the room. She wrung her hands. She swivelled back to him. 'Who is she, Silas? Who's the little harlot?'

'It's not like that, Lolenda.' He spoke through clenched teeth. 'I have a duty. A trust. I must make a vow—'

'You fool!' At first, her face was incredulous. Then she laughed; flung back her head and bellowed. She collapsed on to the bed. She rolled from side to side.

'I have to go,' Silas said coldly. He didn't understand her. He would never understand her.

'You mean you didn't know?' Lolenda flung after him. She was wiping her eyes. He turned back. Her expression was almost a leer, hideous in the worn, shabby face. 'Poor Silas. You're so green. But then I suppose that's why I like you. I've always liked temple-boys. They have so much to give.' She stretched out her arms to him. 'Poor, poor baby. Come back to Mama. Come on.'

'I don't understand.' Silas did not move.

'I've made you.' Lolenda stretched, luxuriating. 'I have power, Silas. What were you? A pious provincial. Common, common, common! Do you think you'd have had a future without me? The Archmaximate and I are old – well, *friends*. Let's say I've put in a word for the boy from Irion.'

'No! You're lying!'

But Silas knew she was not. His legs gave way beneath him.

He collapsed.

Yes, it was true.

She had destroyed him. She had destroyed everything. His success, like his piety, was a hollow sham. He had wanted to be a beacon of faith, burning bright. Now he was the merest, guttering candle. How his pride was humbled! He was an abject, grovelling thing.

She came to him. Her nightgown engulfed his curled, convulsing form.

'Silas, Silas.'

She was standing astride him. She slithered down, her legs splitting wide. Her fingers, through the fabric, pulled at his hair, plucked at his blubbering lips, his cheeks. She dragged him upwards. He was shuddering, gasping.

'No. No.'

But it was no good. His tongue drivelled. She arced back, moaning. There was only the heady, moist reek of lust. He flung her away. He shrugged off his coat. She circled him, leering; he grabbed her.

'No!'

'Yes!'

He thrust her on to the bed. He tore at her gown. Then he was ripping at his own shirt, his breeches. She rolled away from him. He clawed at her. She scratched him; she was laughing, laughing.

Then it happened. She screamed.

9

That morning, the light had no pity. Its brilliancy divulged Lolenda's withered dugs as it disclosed the scattered flecks of ash on the hearth and the dust that floated unendingly on the air. It glinted in the greasy smearings of the breakfast plates and brought to light the chamber-pot that peeped from beneath the bed. Pitiless, it exposed the naked youth, hollow-chested with jutting ribs; it exhibited his scrawny arms and the bandy sticks of his shanks. It painted its pallor over his hairless flesh, and against the pallor made manifest all the more the red, mysterious mark that spread like a stain along the inner softness of his thigh.

Lolenda's face was like a mask. She pointed. Her finger trembled, and when her voice came, it was a whisper, hoarse with horror.

'The mark of the Vaga!'

Her collapse came slowly, inexorably as night.

'Oh, what have I done? Go from me, go—'

Silas dressed slowly, numb with shock; he might have had no nerves in his hands, his limbs. Had he known? Had his uncle known? The boy was told only that his mother was dead, and once, when he had asked if she had been a villager, Uncle Olion, his eyes cast down, had said that she was not. Had the old man known that she was a Vaga-whore? But no; he could never have known. For if he had, wouldn't it all have been futile, the chainings, the gaggings, the baths in icy water – all the long passages of the boy's Claiming?

'Lolenda?' Silas turned back in the doorway. 'You said you had some letters. From Uncle Olion.'

Lolenda was sobbing. She looked up through her tears. 'Your uncle is dead, Silas. He died – oh, seasons ago. You didn't care. That's why I thought—'

'Lolenda—' He moved towards her. He wanted, one last time, to sink into her arms.

She shrank from him. 'No. No.' Her voice had gone flat. 'Dirty Vaga. Dirty!'

Silas could only leave and, afterwards, wonder again, then again, if he had known. All these seasons, as he had come into his manhood, the stain had been growing, spreading. Didn't he think? Didn't he guess? They called it First Blood; it was the mark borne by Vaga-men where Theron, god of fire, had stabbed his brother, the Vaga-god Koros. It was the punishment of lust; dirty Vaga-lust.

There could be no question of Immersion now.

It was a day later when Silas stood, grim-faced, before the Archmaximate. Outside, the air was bright; in the old man's study, the curtains were drawn. A fire leapt in the grate. 'One does get so cold,' the Archmaximate said kindly, and was about to invite Silas to sit with him by the fire when the declaration, so unexpected and shocking, spluttered suddenly from the young man's lips.

'Wolveron, why? Why?'

There was much more that Silas might have said; but did not. The Archmaximate leant forward; he caught the young man's hands in his. 'My son, your gifts are great. Don't throw them away for – what? A momentary fear? In time, you will be one of the great men of the Order. Oh, Wolveron, we are all of us unworthy in our hearts—'

A strange fear possessed the Archmaximate. The interview was a customary thing, expected to proceed in a customary way; never before had an Appellant of Immersion announced, at this late pass, that he was leaving the college. There was almost pleading in the old man's voice: to no avail.

Silas stood untrembling, eyes downcast. His decision was made, and if he had decided not to reveal all, who could blame him? Lolenda would hardly confess her degradation. It was too much. Silas bit his lip.

There would always be a secret he must keep.

'There's nothing I can do for you, my son? Nothing you need?'

Again, Silas found himself turning back in a doorway. He knew what he wanted. The Archmaximate was a kindly man. Silas did not think his request would be greeted with scorn.

It was not.

'Irion?'

'In the Valleys of the Tarn, Archmaximate. An obscure living, but my home. Where I belong.'

There was a silence. The fire crackled in the grate. 'Very well, Wolveron. I'll see what I can do.'

The old man sighed.

It was absurd. There were some who must be given to a simple piety, it was clear; that had always been the way. But Wolveron? It was as if the young man were suffering from a disease.

'You are a strange fellow, Wolveron. In a space of moments, you have thrown away your life. Your entire future life.'

'Is that so strange, Archmaximate?'

But the interview was over.

The door clicked shut. The Archmaximate returned to his soft chair by the fire. He warmed his hands. He sighed again. Poor Lolenda! She had liked this one.

❊ ❊ ❊

Old Wolveron made his way back through the woods, placing his staff before him slowly and carefully. Was he sure of his direction? He did not quite know. He had immersed himself, for too long, in bitter reverie. If tears could come to his eyes he would have cried. But what would be the use? It did no good to think on the wasted years.

'Papa?' His child appeared before him on the path. Her voice was subdued as she took his arm. 'Papa, it's this way back to the cave.'

The sun poured down through the trees, green and golden; but their destiny hovered above them like an impending cloud.

Chapter 33

THE NOVA-RIEL ROOM

'Ale!'

'Coming, Master Polty!'

It happened innumerable times each day. First the thunderous command, echoing through the tavern; then the woman's heavy boots, clumping loudly on the narrow, twisting stairs. Polty, on the soft bed of the best chamber, rolled lazily on to his side. He rucked up his nightshirt, taking aim at the chamber-pot. The acrid spurtings missed their target, spreading instead in a steaming pool across the patterned rug. The fat boy gave a satisfied smile. He lolled back.

'Ooh, I'm quite puffed!' Goody Throsh bobbed girlishly through the door, a spread hand against her heaving bosom. With a theatrical curtsey she set down the tankard on the mahogany inlaid table by the bed; then, smoothing her apron, perched carefully on the bed beside Polty. It was something she did each day. 'Are you feeling any better, Master Polty?' she would ask.

'A little,' he would say. 'Thanks to you, Wynda.' She insisted that he call her by her familiar name. When Bean tried the same thing, she had boxed his ears.

'Master Polty!' she would say. 'You'll make me blush.'

But she did not. The widow looked sadly, fondly, about the chamber, with its musty hangings, its dark, polished furniture and the many pictures, foxed and faded now, that she had chosen so eagerly at the outset of her marriage. What quality-folk had slept here in the early days! The chamber was called the Nova-Riel Room, and was a testimony to the splendours of the Tiger, in the days when it had been more than an alehouse for Vulgarians. The bed alone was magnificent. A heavy four-poster with brocaded velvet curtains, it was a big bed for one boy, even a big boy; but after all, Master Polty was quality, too. Best quality in the house since the Siege! Besides, her son now slept here too, though too often, she was aware, Aron slept instead in a chair by the window, or outside in the hayloft, after he had quarrelled with Master Polty. Really, she wished her son had more respect!

A swampy stench was rising from the rug.

'Wynda, I've been thinking,' said Polty, sipping his ale. 'Has Vel been coming into the Tiger of late?'

'The blacksmith's boy? Ay, he's been in many a time, Master Polty. Always with that tarty young girl.' Goody Throsh pursed her lips in disapproval. 'Can't think what she's called.'

'Leny,' replied Polty, a little too quickly.

'Leny, that's right. Blowzy little trollop. If there's one thing I can't stand, it's a loose woman. Now you, Master Polty, I'm sure you'll be finding yourself a much nicer girl.' She gazed admiringly at the boy's girth. In the seasons that had passed since he came to the Tiger, the young man had ballooned to a bulk much larger than he had ever attained before. Wobbling white flesh enveloped him like a cushioning element of his own.

His bursting cheeks registered a blush. 'Oh, Wynda!'

'No, don't you "Oh Wynda" me! You're quality, you are, and I know you shall be a great man one day. You just need to get up and around again, that's all. When you start to feel a little better.' She fluffed shyly at his carroty curls. 'You know I've nearly finished embroidering your waistcoat.'

'Wynda?' said Polty, a moment later, as the landlady retreated, pink-cheeked, to the doorway. 'When the blacksmith's boy comes again, will you tell me?'

Goody Throsh said she would. Her life had become a round of tending to the boy; there was nothing he could ask that she would refuse or question. Sometimes, when he was sleeping in the afternoons, she would sit and stroke him, only breaking off, a little guiltily, at the sound of Aron's footsteps on the stairs. She could not help herself. Master Polty was her consolation. He had been sent to her, she knew, as recompense for her husband's death and for the renewed, sturdy faith that had grown in her heart since then.

Poor Ebby lay in the tombyard now, beneath a stoneless mound in a weedy corner. One day she would have a huge slab of rock carved in memoriam; as her own time of dying drew nearer she would sit beside it and talk to him, wondering fondly if there was ale enough for his dry throat in the realms of The Vast, and how he was managing to hobble about on only one foot. *Ebby?* she would whisper. *It's Wynda. Wynda with the golden curls.* But now she would spread her goodness in the world where it was needed; it was what was demanded of her. There were some who said she was a bad woman. They said she kept a disorderly house. They would look on her and whisper, *Green Garters.*

It was a lie! She had never worn garters under her skirts.

Leaving Master Polty that afternoon, Goody Throsh paused on the stairs. With a furtive hand she delved into the pocket of her apron. Ah. Yes. She liked to make sure that it was still there. She had thought she might give it to Master Polty this afternoon, but it was pleasant to savour the waiting.

Just a little longer.

Fondly she drew forth the amethyst ring. For a time, that wretched boy Aron had tried to conceal it from her. From his mother! When Goody Throsh found out, she had taken it from him indignantly. Had the boy been trying to steal from his poor, sick friend? But Aron was too much of a fool to be a thief. His guilt glowed in his face at once. Try as she might, Goody Throsh could muster no affection for her son. He was a colourless, weak boy. Ebby had been an old rogue, but at least he had fire. Life. What did Aron have? Nothing!

The amethyst ring glinted in the light from the landing-window. Wynda Throsh gazed on it, and brought it to her lips. She forgot her inadequate son. Aron! What did he matter? From the moment she had seen the ring, she had known where her true affection lay. She thought back to the time of the Siege, and all the busy trade she had plied with the Bluejacket soldiers. She smiled indulgently.

She had seen a ring like this before.

❊ ❊ ❊

'Bean,' Polty said that night, 'I've been thinking.'

'Mm?' Exhausted from the chores of the day, the lanky boy nuzzled deeper into his pillow. Lying with Polty in the big bed, he was accustomed by now to his friend's drunken murmurings. They were merely a sound that filled the silence after the revellers left the tavern, a little more intrusive than the rustling trees outside or the mournful hootings of the damask owl. He wrapped the blanket more tightly around him. There was a hint of chill in the room tonight. Polty had been far gone enough not to protest when Bean had dared to open a window. The sour reek of the fat boy was dispersing mercifully.

Polty tugged sharply at the blankets. 'Bean!'

'Wh-what is it?'

'It's Leny.'

'Leny?' Bean hardly thought about Leny now. They had all grown older. The childhood world of The Five was long past, long gone.

'You know I've been very sick, Bean.'

'I know,' said Bean. It was true; Polty had been very sick, some seasons earlier. Since then, he had been lying in a drunken stupor while Bean's mother waited on him, hand and foot.

'Bean? I think I'm well again.'

'What?'

It was astonishing, if true.

Bean struggled upright.

The springs squeaked as Polty's bulk rolled towards his

friend. A pudgy paw gripped Bean's shoulder. 'Have you really thought about Leny, Bean?'

Bean was not quite sure what Polty meant.

'She's a very pretty girl, is Leny.'

'I suppose. You said she was a slut.'

'That too. But you haven't really thought about Leny, have you, Bean? Oh, don't worry. It doesn't surprise me. I'm the one for the thinking, after all. But it's all her fault, you see. Leny. It's all her fault.' The fat boy eased himself just a little upright, the better to permit the escape of a windy blast from his bowels.

❄ ❄ ❄

That night, as Polty slept at last, Bean felt troubled again by the fear of change. He had begun to think of it as the 'shifting-sense'. When his father died, Bean had known a sudden, sharp horror. This was a different feeling, slow and creeping, but just as frightening. It was a feeling that things that should have been solid were moving, shifting beneath his feet. Bean did not like it.

When, Bean wondered, had Polty last spoken of Leny and Vel, and the break-up of The Five? That night was the first time for a long time.

It would not be the last.

It was Leny, Polty would say, who had destroyed their little kingdom. With her harlot's lust she had captivated Vel; because Vel had fallen, the boys had been divided. Had they not been divided, should Polty have dreamed of going to Green Garters? Then Polty should not have had to steal the silver, and Waxwell would not have been turned, as he had been turned, into a monster of rage and vengeance. Why else had he cut off old Ebenezer's foot?

It was Leny's fault. All Leny's fault.

As Bean revolved the chain of reasoning in his mind, he had to admit that it had in it something convincing. It was, in a sense, true; and though Bean could see that perhaps it had just been time, and growing up, that had wrecked Polty's

271

kingdom, he could see too that Polty did not want to consider this.

There had to be someone he could blame.

With blame would come vengeance.

It was some evenings later in the smoky bar-room when Bean, rushing between tables with a brace of foaming tankards, suddenly saw Polty in a shadowy corner. Bean's grip on the tankards slackened.

'Hey!'

Ale slopped down the back of a collar; a sunburnt neck twisted angrily.

'Sorry. Sorry.'

Bean slammed down the tankards, retreating to a chorus of familiar curses. His mother, in a red wig, her face caked in paint, was leaning lasciviously across the bar, listening with delight to the vulgar jokes of a fat horse-trader from the next village. Bean dug an elbow into her side.

'Ma, why is Polty here? Ma?'

'Boy! More ale!' came a cry, through clouds of smoke.

'What is it, Aron?' Goody Throsh snapped. 'Can't you hear the gentleman? Go, go!'

Bean bit his knuckles. He had just come in from tending to the horses; how long had Polty been in the corner? Was it Polty? Who was he with? The lean boy strained his eyes through the smoke. He saw the familiar blaze of orange curls; he saw the fat rolls of neck, arched back and guzzling. That was a sight he knew well enough, but his friend had not been downstairs for many moonlives. That was when the thought came to Bean:

It has started.

'Polty! You're down!'

It was some moments later. Bean wiped a cloth energetically over the table where Polty sat, dressed in his new embroidered waistcoat; sat, as Bean now saw, with Leny and Vel.

'Down?' Polty looked up, smiling, at Bean.

Was he drunk?

The blacksmith's boy was drunk. Bean looked at him; it had been so long since he had really looked at Vel. The boy's moustache, that had sprouted early, had grown to its full, dark luxuriance. Vel was bigger, stronger, too; the muscles of a blacksmith rippled under his shirt. His hands were huge. He gripped Bean's stick-insect arm and twisted. 'Where's our ale, boy? We called for more ale!'

'Oh, Vel!' Leny giggled. 'It's Bean, remember? Bean!'

Leny's breasts had grown enormous, and seemed to threaten to burst from her blouse. Her blonde hair was curled into long, cascading ringlets. She leaned confidentially across the table to Bean, a hand cupped protectively about her dainty glass of spirits.

'Vel and I are going to be married, Bean. Isn't it marvellous? Our old friend Polty is the first to know.'

'Married?' Bean said foolishly. It was all he could say. The dark crack between Leny's breasts disturbed him, as did Polty's hearty, congratulating smile.

Was Polty drunk?

Bean was not sure. But later, when Polty went up to bed, Bean saw that his friend took the steep stairs with confidence. 'This room really does stink something shocking,' he declared, flinging open a window as Bean closed the door. 'I'm surprised you haven't noticed, Bean. Still, I suppose you were never much of a one for hygiene.'

'I suppose not,' Bean said glumly. He set down the candle. Polty turned back from the window, and for the first time Bean took in properly the waistcoat his mother had embroidered for his friend. From a dark background, threads of all colours burst out profusely like an overgrown garden, with flowers of all sorts in promiscuous riot.

'It's magnificent,' said Bean.

He was not even envious. Bean had never had an embroidered waistcoat. His breeches were ragged and poorly patched, and for many moonlives his shirt and coat had been too short, far too short, for his lengthening limbs. But he was accustomed to it. That his mother should spend her mornings making clothes for Polty, while her own son went in rags, seemed to be merely in the order of things. There was something special about Polty, Bean knew. Something imposing. It had something to do, of course, with his friend's huge girth. Now, the rich embroiderings that rioted over that girth made Polty more imposing still.

For a moment Bean was glad; then alarmed again. Between a plump thumb and forefinger Polty plucked a hair from the front of the waistcoat. The hair was a frizzy, corn-yellow strand; but what alarmed Bean was not the hair. It was, rather, the silver ring that flashed on Polty's finger as he raised his hand. There was a glitter of amethyst from the inlaid stone.

'Where did you get that ring?'

'Your ma, friend. Wynda said she was keeping it for me. Isn't it marvellous what she does for me?' The fat boy slipped off the magnificent waistcoat, laying it carefully over the back of a chair. 'A wonderful evening!' he smiled. 'And tomorrow shall be more wonderful still! Oh, cheer up, Stringbean! You look so glum!'

Bean wondered again:

Is Polty drunk?

The fat face beamed with pleasure and pride.

❄ ❄ ❄

In bed, when they had snuffed out the candle, Bean attempted, 'But it was yours.'

Polty, settling beneath the blankets, gave a satisfied sigh. 'Hm?' The casement rattled in a stirring breeze. The stench was dispersing.

'It was yours,' said Bean. 'The ring. It was in your hand.'

'Hm? I must sleep, friend. I really must sleep. Tomorrow, I'm going to see my father.'

'Your father?' Bean's heart thumped hard. All through that night, Polty slumbered peacefully, but his thin friend beside him barely slept at all. *I'm going to see my father*. What could Polty mean? It was not until his friend set out in the morning, his pursed lips whistling a merry tune, that Bean saw that Polty meant to visit Goodman Waxwell.

❄　❄　❄

'Polty!'

Polty turned back, his waistcoat glowing brightly. Sunshine poured benevolently about him. Across the green, his friend came running after him, gawky limbs flailing.

'Friend?'

'You're coming back, Polty?'

'What? Of course I'm coming back! You're odd, friend, do you know? You're really odd.' Polty shook his head.

The gawky boy flailed to the edge of the green again, but turned back just in time to watch Polty disappear into the warren of lanes, overhung with elms, that wound away to Goodman Waxwell's house.

Only then did a curious thought occur to Bean. *He's not my father*, Polty had said; but could it be that the fat boy had now simply forgotten the truth? Had something crucial slipped out of his mind, vanished from his awareness as he lay sick in bed? Bean had heard stories of such things; this must be what had happened to his friend. Polty, Bean was sure, had not known that the amethyst ring was his own; and if this was forgotten, perhaps forgotten too might be the paper, crushed for too long in Polty's plump hand, that Bean had uncrumpled so carefully, so slowly, on the night his friend had come. Afterwards, he had slept, overwhelmed at last with weariness. When he jerked awake to sudden footsteps on the stairs, the clumsy gesture of his hand as he tried to sweep up his treasures had left only powder where the letter had been. His mother's eyes had darted to the ring.

'It's his,' said Bean.

'Of course it's his. He's quality, he is.'

'I think his pa thrashed him.'

'His father? Nonsense!'

And of course it was nonsense. Bean's brain revolved the phrases he remembered from the letter. *I trust my boy into your care*, that was one. *This ring is my token*, that was another. Another, *When he comes of age*.

His father?

Nonsense!

Bean had been getting confused, that was all.

And now Bean was running over the green again, plunging into the warren of the overhung lanes. 'Polty! Polty!' he called, suddenly alarmed. He had to catch him; it was imperative. Did Polty think he was returning to his father?

But then Bean was lost in the green depths of the lanes, and which way the physician's cottage lay, he did not know. He had taken the wrong turning; he could not find the right one, and now, could think only of some terrible violence that might at any moment be unfolding in the neat, clean rooms of the physician's cottage. A thick vein hammered in his forehead and the dapples of the sun through the leaves were dazzling. He traced back his steps.

Which was the way? The lane branched this way; the lane branched that.

'Hello, friend.'

It was Polty, smiling.

'Polty, don't go there.' Bean's long fingers clutched his friend's arm.

'Friend, what are you talking about now?' And Polty, whistling, bent his casual steps back towards the village. The fork in the lane was left behind.

'You're not going there?'

'Going where? I've been to see my father. Dear Father! He gave me a little gift.' The fat boy seemed so happy.

'Gift?' said Bean. 'What gift?'

Polty almost laughed at him. Into the pocket of the magnificent waistcoat the plump thumb and forefinger dived for an instant; for an instant Polty held the gift before his friend's eyes. Then it was gone.

Bean did not understand. It was nothing! It was just a little bottle filled with black, viscous liquid.

'It's ink!'

Now Polty did laugh. 'It's medicine, friend. Something to make us feel very much better.'

Chapter 34

THE FORETELLING

'Mistress—'

'Thank you, Stephel.'

Umbecca was wearing her best bonnet, and carried a basket in one hand. Permitting the old man to help her down from the cart, she might have imagined herself a woman of more grace, ready for a rather more graceful occasion. The shabby servant with his grizzled beard might have been an elegant footman instead, and the ramshackle cart a shiny coach.

'Stephel,' she called behind the retreating cart, sweetly, 'you won't go near the Lazy Tiger?'

'Gee-up!' the old man grunted to his mare.

'Hmph!' But Umbecca only smiled.

Jem was excited. He had clambered down from the cart by himself, and now, steadying himself on his crutches, was looking curiously down the shadowed lane. Empty in the hot afternoon, between overhanging elms it wound away from the green, towards the place his aunt called the Lectory. That was where they would go today.

'Aunt,' said the boy, as their walk began, 'what is the Lectory?'

It was a question he had asked before.

His aunt smiled again. 'A big house.'

'As big as the castle?'

'The biggest in the village.'

'But why?'

It was a game.

'Because it is an important place,' Umbecca said sagely. Then she corrected herself. 'Because it once was.'

Sunlight shone brightly between the shadows of the elms.

The lane was rough and dusty. Pits and ruts marred its pale surface and tufty weeds pushed up thickly between scattered, sharp stones.

'It's not too much for you, Jem?'

'Oh, no!' the boy gasped.

He had almost fallen.

The walks had been Ela's idea, and it was to have been Ela who would be Jem's partner in them. They had made a start: in the long Season of Koros, rucked heavily in their coats, the boy and his mother had passed back and forth through the corridors of the keep; as the chill relented and the snow melted they would have ventured out, too, into the cobbled passages and courtyards of the bailey. But by then, it was Aunt Umbecca who had to be Jem's companion, as it was Umbecca who accompanied him now, in swelling heat, in this latest, most ambitious walk.

'Jem! We shall be stronger,' Ela had said; and she had smiled, gripping her son's hand.

But it was no good. She was still too weak.

'When will Mother be better?' Jem asked now, planting his crutches carefully between the pits.

Umbecca, as always, assumed a solemn air.

And a vague one.

'Ah, Jem, who can say?'

'Can nobody say?'

A pause. 'Goodman Waxwell—'

Jem swivelled round, suddenly defiant. 'You don't believe him!'

'Oh no, Jem!' The plump face looked almost shocked. 'Once, once . . . but let us not speak of that unhappy man. It's a fine day, Jem, is it not?'

'A fine day. If Mother were with us . . .'

Jem did not go on.

'Poor Jem,' his aunt said a little later, as the boy paused to gather his strength. Her plump hand stroked his hair. 'Mother is as well as she can be, I know.'

'I know,' Jem echoed. 'I know.'

Ela had tried so hard. On the night of Goodman Waxwell's madness, when at last the maid had helped her back to her bed, it had seemed that the pale young woman might collapse and never rise again. But in the moment before she sank back, spent, Ela's last action had been unexpected and wild.

'Lady Ela, your medicine!'

The black bottle had whizzed through the air, shattering in the fireplace into a thousand fragments.

That night, and through the day that followed, Ela had slept without stirring. It would be the last quiet night she would know for many phases. Afterwards, for night after night, she lay awake, gasping and sweating, staring into a blackness of churning phantoms. How she longed for oblivion to enfold her again! The daylight hours were possessed of a brittle brightness, like ice that at any moment seemed about to crack. 'Warmer today, don't you think?' Umbecca would say. But Ela shivered and could not speak. Haggard and drawn, she huddled by the fire, twisting her hands, toying with her hair; and every so often, involuntarily, a leg would jerk, an arm would twitch.

Click-clack, click-clack, went her aunt's needles.

'Do have something, niece. Those tarts are delicious.'

But nor could Ela eat.

'I shall send for Goodman Waxwell!' her aunt burst out one day, when Ela had fallen to the floor and could not rise.

'No,' Ela whispered.

Goodman Waxwell? Through the churning darkness of her mind, the wretched young woman saw again the naked purple lips of the physician, baring back as he jammed the stopper from the sticky black bottle between his teeth, then pulled it forth. *Pop!* Even in memory, the cheerful, silly sound would batter back and forth in Ela's mind, *pop-pop-pop*, until it swelled into a sinister, booming echo. It was the echo of her doom, and though there were times when Ela could know nothing but the fact of her sickness, of her craving, now the awareness flashed on her with a harsh, pained intensity: *They tried to kill me*. Yes. Perhaps they had not tried to kill her body. But they had tried to kill her mind. Ela clenched and unclenched her hands. A wave of wild craving swept over her again. How she longed to sink into the dark, sweet oblivion! In the world of the treacle, there would be nothing to trouble her. In the treacle-world, everything would be sweet and warm. But it was only a sweet, warm death. Ela thought of the treacle and she saw Waxwell's face, leering at her. Laughing. She would not give in, she would not!

I'll send for Goodman Waxwell. Her aunt's words echoed in Ela's skull. She clawed at the carpet. She tore the scream from the depths of her being, *'No!'*

And there was something in her passion that stilled even Umbecca. The fat woman stepped back, her heart pounding. She spread her hand across her black bodice and closed her eyes, sighing bitterly. Her niece craved the treacle; but there was a pride in Ela, her aunt saw, that was stronger. That would conquer the craving.

Through the days that followed, Ela would struggle hard, determined to be free at last from the treacle's sticky grip.

Umbecca picked up the bell.

'Nirry, help Lady Ela up.'

Nirry did so. 'Ma'am?'

'What is it, girl?'

'Will there be anything else?'

Umbecca sighed again. 'No.'

No. She would not send for Goodman Waxwell. There was no question of it. The threat had been a lapse, that was all.

'Is this the place, Aunt?'

'Yes, Jem. The Lectory.'

Jem peered curiously through the rusted gates. Surrounded by a high wall, the house was big and dark and almost smothered by the overgrown garden. Ancient hinges creaked in protest and Umbecca smiled sadly as the boy, a little tentatively, pushed the gates open.

Hanging branches hindered them as they made their way round a crunching cinder-path.

'Why do they call it the Lectory, Aunt?'

'Oh, Jem!' This was a question he had not asked before. 'The Lectory! Where the Lector lived.'

'But who was the Lector?'

'The most important man in the village.'

'More important than the lord?'

The fat woman's crunching footsteps stopped. 'You speak of the lord of the castle, Jem. I speak of the lord of the temple.'

Jem turned back. 'The Lord Agonis lived here?'

His aunt had fallen behind, burdened, perhaps, by her heavy basket. Her answer came from a swathe of green obstruction. Just for an instant, her voice was strained. 'Oh, Jem! No, no. His intermediary. His mediator. His minister. The Lector.'

None of this meant very much to the boy.

'It's all to do with the old days, then? When they believed? When they *all* believed, I mean.'

The boy gazed towards the derelict house, and for a moment felt strangely troubled. Along the length of one wall was a curious edifice which appeared to be made of glass.

'Yes, Jem. The old days,' came the fat woman's voice, no longer strained; and her footsteps came crunching forward again.

She had changed as much as her niece. There was a calm, a benevolence in her now that had come only since the night of the physician's madness. It was as if something in her had snapped; as if she were no longer quite what she had been.

There had been no more visits to the Waxwell house, and around her neck she no longer wore the glittering, golden Circle of Agonis.

'Are we there yet, Aunt?' Jem said.

'Soon.'

'How soon?'

His aunt had gone on ahead now, and turned back. 'Poor Jem! Is the cinder-path hard for you?'

'Oh no!' Jem's chest heaved. 'It's just that I'm hungry, that's all.'

It was true. The sun had passed the midway point in the sky and still they had not reached their destination. Red-cheeked, Jem hung from his crutches, gazing after his aunt's waddling bulk. They had moved to the back of the big house; then through a stretch of garden that hid the house completely; then through a second, smaller gate that led into an orchard.

'When we were young,' Umbecca was saying, 'Ruanna and I used to come here each Canonday. How happily we used to file along the lane, chattering and giggling, in our girlish muslin! Twirl, twirl, went our parasols!

'The Lector always held a reception after Temple. Oh, only for the quality-folk, of course! Deadly dull. But Ruanna and I would slip away to the orchard. How we loved it here! What dreams we both had then! We gazed up at the Foretelling and wondered what would become of us. That was before the Duke had chosen my poor sister, of course. Oh, it took him a long time to choose her!'

The air was heavy with a ripeness of apples.

'Here, Jem,' said Umbecca, a moment later.

'Aunt, what is it?'

Their destination had appeared suddenly, coming into view round a screen of entangled branches. It was a mossy edifice made entirely of marble. Two steps led up to a round platform, banded in a semicircle by a low bench. In the centre of the platform, on a high plinth, was a vast ornate bowl; raised above the bowl, as if suspended in the air, were two figures, large as life, a man and a woman. They were naked, holding hands, and looked down, as if benevolently, on those who would sit, gazing up at them, from the marble bench.

'She was a lady he sought. And lost,' said Jem's aunt. Her voice was distant. 'They say one day they will be reunited. It is the Lord Agonis, Jem. The Lord Agonis and the Lady Imagenta.'

Jem did not reply. He was not sure what to say. Instead, moving carefully round the cracking platform, he paused, gazing first upwards at the chill white bodies, then downwards into the bowl. The bodies, he saw, were of surpassing beauty, though streaked and stained and furred with moss. The bowl beneath was evil-smelling and ugly, sloping encrustedly to a shallow, festering pool.

'It was called a Foretelling, a fountain like this. It showed what had not yet come to pass. The image shimmered in the water, like a dream.'

With a satisfied sigh, Umbecca removed the chequered cloth from the top of her basket. She spread the cloth and smoothed it on the bench between them; she popped the cork from a bottle of cider. Then came the loaf, the ham, the tongue. Then the seed-cake, the buns, the tarts. 'I think we've earned ourselves a little something, don't you, Jem?'

'I think so!' Jem had to laugh.

They fell to greedily, munching and passing the bottle back and forth between them, in the intense shadows of the overgrown, rotting orchard. As the sun began to descend, a golden shaft of light pushed insistently through the tangled leaves, strangely illuminating the figures on the fountain.

'Wave away those flies, Jem, there's a good boy.'

Afterwards, replete, they gazed up at the statues. The golden light was falling more intensely.

'Are they what you'd call a legend, Aunt?'

'Mm?'

A light breeze rustled at the branches behind them, and a tiny crash marked the fall of another apple. The basket beside them was entirely empty. Before they left, they would fill it with fruit.

'They're a legend, aren't they? Like Nova-Riel.'

His aunt looked at him, almost sharply. 'You know about Nova-Riel?'

'Barnabas—'

'Oh. Yes. You know, Jem, that lightning never strikes twice?'

She said no more.

Chapter 35

THE TEMPLE IN RUINS

'You enjoyed your walk, Jem?'

'Oh, yes!'

'Of course you did.' Ela hugged the boy. 'I declare, your cheeks are red!'

The pale young woman was lying on the sofa. A blanket covered her from the waist down and a volume of a novel lay open on her lap. It was a silly book, some old nonsense she had found amongst Mother's things, but vivid enough! Her afternoon had been spent in Agondon, in a world of gaming-tables and society balls. Poor Ela! Her adventures would be only mental ones now. For a moment a sadness came into her eyes. Then she checked herself. She smiled and fluffed her son's blond hair. How tall he was becoming! How strong! Every day he looked more and more like Tor.

'Oh, Jem, if only I could come with you! But never mind, Aunt shall take you out again. While the weather lasts. You will, Aunt, won't you?'

'Niece, really! Of course I shall.'

It was settled. That day's expedition was to be only the first of many. Each morning, through that brief, hot season, Stephel would harness up the old mare for the drive down the road from the Rock. Below, on the flatter, shaded reaches, while the old man repaired to the Lazy Tiger, the sturdy boy would strike out on his crutches, his aunt waddling uncomplainingly beside him, or ahead, or often, increasingly, behind. Each day there swung, from her plump hand, a basket filled to the brim with tongue or ham or salt beef or chicken and Nirry's best cakes and tarts and pastries, concealed beneath the chequered cloth.

They ranged far and wide. Twice they went back to the overgrown orchard, which seemed to hold a strange fascination for them both. They looked up again at the figures on the fountain, and saw that the figures seemed to shift in shape, perhaps in attitude, with the play of light through the tangled branches. As his aunt dozed, Jem explored the pathways of the orchard, and found that the wall that marked its far limit divided the grounds of the Lectory from the tombyard. For a long moment he peered over the tombyard wall. The grave-slabs lay impassively in the hot sun. They disturbed him a little. He was not sure why.

A second walk was to a far outlying field, on the first slow risings of the uplands above the village. In the middle of the field stood a big wooden barn, empty and silent beneath the dark heights of the castle and the dizzying pallor of the mountains behind. Their hearts lifted as they sat, guzzling cider, in the middle of the open space. After their picnic, Jem explored the gloomy barn and happily prodded, with the end of one crutch, the tinder-dry ruins of a marvellous hay-stack. It was filled with rats!

A third walk led them by the bank of the river, along the tow-path to a place of rapidly gushing waters that Jem's aunt called the mill-race. They stared across the bank at the hunched edifice of the mill, with its huge, slowly turning wheel. That afternoon the miller was standing, leaning on a railing, on a ramshackly wooden platform above the water. Umbecca hailed him, a little awkwardly. He did not hail them back. He had plucked a long straw from his raggedy hat and was gnawing at it contentedly.

They avoided the villagers, in so far as they could. In their walks they circled about the village, keeping to the sleepy back lanes. To Umbecca, as to Jem, almost by instinct, the central cluster about the village green was an unwelcoming place, much as was the thick, mysterious wood that pressed against the village on the southern side. Sometimes, looking at the distant villagers, Jem was filled with a sudden fear.

He was not sure why.

But there was one place his aunt could not resist.

Jem was drawn to it, too.

It was deep in the recesses of a sleepy afternoon when they stepped through the crumbling arch of the gate. Midges and dragonflies skittered lazily through the grass that grew profuse as reeds at the river, overwhelming alike the crumbling slabs of graves and the path that wound between them. The brightness of the sun, where it shone, was intense; the blackness of the shadows was in sharp-edged distinction. In the air there was something impending, as if here, in a place where nothing could happen, some event was yet always on the brink of being.

Jem said, 'Is it true, Aunt, that the dead linger here?'

On some days, Umbecca might have admonished the boy, lamenting that he should have heard such Vaga-superstitions. Today, her voice came quietly, thoughtfully, 'Some say they do. I've never quite known. When we die, we pass to The Vast, unless we have been wicked and are consigned to Unbeing. But it is said that there are wicked ones who will not leave this world, though death has claimed them. They remain in this world, but are not of this world. They linger in these places of the dark god Koros.' Umbecca's eyes grew big and she loomed comically towards her nephew, her hands held up with the fingers writhing.

Jem squealed, delighted, and swung himself away.

'So the tombyard is a place of the dark god, Aunt?' he resumed, after a moment.

'Jem, of course. That is why the temple must be built in the tombyard. Or the tombyard around the temple. Otherwise, the dark god would gain too great a purchase. That is why the dead must lie only before the dwelling-place of the Lord Agonis.'

Jem was confused.

'Is this a place of Agonis, then, or Koros?'

'Oh, Jem! Agonis, of course! The temple is ... *was* his dwelling-place, and he would suffer his dark brother to commit no evil in its surrounds. In the early days, Jem, they built tunnels under the temples, that ran from beneath the altar to the tombyard walls. The tunnel ran in five directions, from a point beneath the altar. They called them cross-tunnels. The idea was that the good influence of the Lord Agonis had to extend to the very boundaries of the tombyard, so as to keep the evil Koros at bay.'

'Would there be a cross-tunnel under here, then, Aunt?'

'No, no, Jem. This was in the early days.' Umbecca smiled. Sometimes the boy could be so simple!

Their gaze turned to the dark vines that swathed the temple portico. A mysterious awe gripped Jem's heart as they made their way up the steps. Umbecca held apart the draping vines and her nephew passed through. It was as though they had entered a dark cave.

Jem gazed silently at the barricaded portals. The paving beneath his crutches was buckled and cracked and strewn thickly with leaves. There was an old rocking-chair, rotten with age, a dead bird, a half-unravelled coil of rope. To turn, and look out at the bright world through the vines, was to feel oneself to be inside a green, cool prison.

That was when Jem recalled the small girl – the girl on the path, turning back, taunting him, and for a moment, through the mesh of the vines, he seemed to see her standing there again, as she had been.

A ghostly form, defiant.

That was the first day he had tried to stand.

'We never came back here, did we, Aunt?'

'Jem?'

'I remember we came here. When I was small. Then we never came back.'

'No, Jem. We didn't.'

Umbecca had turned her back to the boy and was standing

uncertainly at the barricaded doors. Her voice was wistful. 'It was the day of the Vaga-fair, Jem. It was our duty to keep the vigil in the temple portico. To make sure the Vagas didn't desecrate the temple. Well, that was the idea. Do you know, I think it was the last time the Vagas came? It must have been the only time after the Siege.'

Umbecca had placed her hand on a rusted chain. Sadly she reflected that in the end it had been time, quite without the aid of the Vagas, that had desecrated the Temple of Irion.

Time; and a war, long ago.

The rusted chain slipped from its place. Jem's aunt gave a little gasp. The barricades had decayed and there was a mournful creak. A door swung open; slowly, reverently, the boy and his aunt entered the greater cavern of the temple. Its interior was almost wholly dark, illumined only by the pastel shafts of light that still were able to insist through the thick foliage and cobwebs that curtained the cracked panes of the stained-glass windows. From the high pillars and the arched vault of the ceiling, enormous cobwebs hung like tattered flags. The air was foul.

'I haven't been in here for two cycles. Three,' Umbecca breathed, oblivious.

Jem made his way slowly forward. Underfoot, the cool tiles of the floor were a crunching, arrested miasma of dust-whorls and bird-droppings and powdery chunks of plaster and dull, unglittering glass. Rats scurried from the path of his crutches.

Jem passed between the long lines of ornate, carved pews. At the head of the aisle, he looked up to the altar, where a great mahogany Circle of Agonis had fallen from the wall and lay, listing. His eyes roved over the podium of stone where the rotting remnants of a huge book were secured by a thick iron chain to the lectern.

Jem wandered down by a side-wall. Intrigued, he gazed at the monuments to the illustrious dead: the scroll-like tablets fixed into the wall; the inscribed stones in the floor; the tombs on which recumbent statues lay. A knight in armour rested beside his lady, their hands clasped in a stony, cold death. It was the Fourth Archduke of Irion; for here were the memorials to all the Archdukes, stretching back for endless epicycles of time. The thought came to Jem that all the faces in the Long Gallery were here to be found, rotted to skulls, secreted in these walls and beneath these floors.

It was a strange, sad thought, and he wanted to tell his aunt.

'Aunt?'

They had not spoken since they entered the ruined temple. As the boy made his way down the aisle and round the walls, Umbecca had sat in silence, alone and unmoving, in a back pew that was free of debris.

'Aunt?'

She did not reply, and when he approached her, Jem saw that she was crying.

Chapter 36

THE MOST UNPLEASANT THING

Only one of their walks was a failure. It was marred by what Jem's aunt later described as a *most unpleasant thing*.

They had struck out in a new path, following Tombyard Lane not in the direction that led to the Lectory, but the opposite way, towards a place on the fringes of the wood that Umbecca called Blossom Cottage. It had been the home of an old maid, she said, and explained that she and her sister had often come this way during the course of their charitable rounds.

But as they progressed ever further from the village and took first one, then another fork in the way, Jem began to wonder where Blossom Cottage could be. His aunt, carried along on a tide of reminiscence, had no thought that they might be lost. She was speaking of her sister's marriage to the Archduke, and the great rejoicing there had been in the valleys.

'They all said it would be one of the Rench sisters. Umbecca or Ruanna. Do you know, there were bets in the Lazy Tiger? Imagine! There was no choosing between us, of course. Really, none at all.'

'But you're glad you weren't chosen, Aunt? Aren't you?' It was the first thing Jem had said for some time.

'Hm?'

'He was a traitor. The Archduke.'

Umbecca's bright flow of words ceased. She smiled weakly, and Jem reflected, not for the first time, that his aunt looked strangely naked, strangely bereft, without the glittering golden Circle of Agonis she had always worn around her neck.

He took advantage of the lull. 'Aunt, are we lost?'

They were, of course; but that was not the *most unpleasant thing*.

'Oh dear!' Umbecca was suddenly contrite. 'I was so sure I knew the way. But after all, it has been ... oh, a good four cycles!' She paused, and seemed deep in thought; then breathed deeply and said, 'I think, my dear, we had better find our way back. Hm?'

Jem was shivering. Through the canopy of elms that rose above their heads he could see that the sun was going in, and the wind that had begun to stir about them was no warm breeze but a chill squall. Some moments later, rain began to fall. It pelted through the branches. They were not only lost, but wet, too.

But that was not the *most unpleasant thing*, either.

The *most unpleasant thing* took place when the sudden shower had passed, and they had almost, as it turned out, found their way back to the village.

'Really, my dear, I was sure I knew the way! We were always assiduous in our charitable visits, Ruanna and I. Assiduous! After all, we knew what it was to have no prospects in this world. "Girls," our mother used to say to us, "it is your fate to be persons of quality but in *name*. Only through your beauty shall you advance in this world." Well, never was a truer word spoken, I dare say!'

'Aunt!'

It was Jem who cried out first; later, he would be a little ashamed of the cracking squeak that had issued, unbidden, from his constricting throat.

But Umbecca's voice was cracking, too. 'Jem! Oh, for the love of the Lord Agonis!'

They huddled together; for standing before them in the wet road, staring up at them curiously, was a large cat-like creature with a coat of stripy fur.

'Aunt, is it the tiger?'

'It is the tiger, Jem. I heard tell of him in the old days. I never thought he was real ... Oh dear, I think he's going to pounce. Do you think so, Jem?'

She babbled on. But Jem only stared into the golden, intense eyes, and as the mysterious slits gazed back at him, the boy felt possessed of a strange calm. He did not believe the tiger would hurt them.

Quiet surrounded them, but for the dripping branches, until all at once, slithering over the quiet like quicksilver, came a low, steady ululation that was not quite a howling, not quite a hum, but something somewhere between the two. It was a sound of singular purity.

The tiger's eyes flared with bright interior flame; then, bowing its head, the creature turned swiftly and vanished into the trees. Only then, when the tiger had gone, did Jem see the stranger who had made the sound. The tall, cowled figure was standing in the shadows, almost obscured, at the side of the narrow, muddy lane.

Jem's heart pounded. Now he was afraid.

But he saw that his aunt was not afraid at all.

'Silas.' She spat out the word like something bad.

'My dear Umbecca! No, don't thank me,' the old man said. His tone was wry, almost amused.

'Silas, we're lost. Which way is the village? You'll tell us that, won't you?' she snapped, for all the world as if the old man had been withholding the information for some considerable time.

'Oh, Umbecca! Just don't pretend you'd do the same for me!' The old man chuckled; then he pointed with his staff, and turned away.

In a moment he, too, had vanished amongst the trees. The meeting was over. It was what Umbecca would call the *most unpleasant thing*.

'Aunt, who was that man?' Jem said, astonished.

But the violence of the answer astonished him still more.

'A wicked man!' Umbecca burst out. 'A wicked, wicked man!'

The village soon came back into view, around the next turning of the muddy lane.

Chapter 37

KILLING ROCK

'It's been such a long time!'

'Hasn't it?'

'I've missed it.'

'I know.'

Bean, almost a child again, scampered ahead clumsily. Soft ferns swished about his thighs; the canopy of the Wildwood rose above him, huge and radiant. *Green, green grows the Wildwood*, he sang, his voice tuneless and cracking; swallows scattered from nearby branches.

'Polty, come on!' Bean called back happily. The hot days of the Season of Theron seemed to be stretching interminably this time, and with each that passed, Bean's happiness grew. The alarm that he had felt before was gone. Polty had changed. With his waistcoat and his ring, he was a different boy. Sometimes it was almost as if the past had returned. Such a time was now, the first in many seasons that the boys had gone together to bathe in the river. They carried rough blankets over their shoulders.

'Polty,' said Bean, when they were deeper in the woods, 'what is the *secret* you're not going to tell me?'

Polty had to laugh. It was a foolish question, but Bean, in his happiness, could think it might be answered. 'Why do you think I have a *secret*, friend?'

'I know you do, Polty. You always had *secrets*.'

'That's not true. I had *ideas*. I *have* ideas,' he corrected himself.

Bean pursued, after a moment, 'What *idea* do you have now, Polty?'

The river came into view, distantly through the trees. Polty aimed a punch at his friend's spindly arm. 'To race you to the river!'

He lurched ahead.

This was a game that Bean knew well enough. But something had changed. It was different this time. Polty hung back before the end of the race.

'I'm puffed! I can't!'

'Polty?'

He was leaning against a tree. Plump hands waved Bean away, urging the lanky boy to push ahead. 'Go, friend, go! I'm just puffed. Go.' For a moment, Bean lingered. Then he flailed away.

And away.

He was gathering speed. Suddenly Bean was running as fast as he could, lunging and pelting through the encompassing richness, vaulting the fallen trunks of trees, crashing triumphantly through constraining undergrowth.

He flung back his head.

He laughed with glee.

Bean's limbs were useless. Bean thought so; everybody else thought so, too. But now the limbs that were stupidly long, that he could not tell to go where he wanted, were all at once possessed of a keen, commanding power. The river surged out brilliantly from the screening verdour; Bean careered on, thrashingly, almost into the water.

He teetered on the bank, his long arms wheeling.

'I won!' he called back, absurdly, through the trees. 'Polty, I won!'

The splendour of the river filled his eyes and ears and Bean's boots pressed into the soggy bank.

He ripped them off.

The river, in the bright season, was a cascade of energy, roaring triumphantly over its stony bed, slipping and sliding through the green peaks of the Wildwood to the precipitous, quickening drop of the mill-race downstream. Bean cleaved the water with steely arms, kicking back against the surging current.

But later, Bean's glee would turn to alarm.

'Polty?' he called. 'Polty?'

Bean lay on the bank, spent.

For wild moments he had not thought of Polty at all. Now he wondered if Polty had ever appeared through the screening trees. Had Polty finished the race?

Bean scrambled up.

That was when he saw the flash of colours in the grass. *Polty's waistcoat.* He swept it into his grasp. Bean span around.

Water.

Boulders.

Polty's bright head was not to be seen.

Then Bean was scudding along the side of the squelching bank, first slowly, then faster, chasing the current to the bend in the river.

'Polty!' he cried out. 'Polty!' The voluminous waistcoat trailed from his hand, catching on reeds, smearing in mud. The harsh sparklings of the water dazzled his eyes. Bean's breath came in bitter, hot gasps. All he could think was that something had happened, but quite what had happened, he could not be sure. He could not think. The scene awaited him; that was all he knew.

Downstream.

It was not until later that a feeling began in Bean that was to stay with him, and grow, through all the long course of that strange afternoon. It was a feeling that someone was watching him.

Someone secret.

Someone hidden.

In the place where the river bent away from the Wildwood, just before the dangerous quickening of the mill-race, was a ledge of rock jutting over the water that was known to the villagers as Killing Rock. In earliest times, in the days of the First Kingdoms, it had been the primitive justice of the Tarn chieftains to cast their enemies from the ledge, bound hand and foot. Rapidly the bodies were borne away, tossing and twisting in the turning waters to the place where the climactic cascades tore sharply downwards, foaming over boulders. He who survived, it was decreed, should go free.

Few did.

Later, in times of strictest purity, it had been the custom of those who had Fallen to offer themselves to the justice of the mill-race. The Fallen, for the most part, were unwed girls, seeking in death an escape from shame.

Children were told not to play at Killing Rock.

But did.

Bean hurried to the Rock. In the days that had gone, The Five had played there. Many times the strongest swimmers, Polty and the blacksmith's boy, had dared each other into the dangerous waters, vying to see who could venture closest to the mill-race, holding back against the tug of the current. Of course, they knew who the winner would be.

You tire too soon, Vel. That's your trouble.

I don't have your blubber!

You tire too soon.

Bean burst upon the scene.

'What happened?'

But he knew at once. On the bank beneath the ledge of Killing Rock crouched Leny, in a thin shift, and Vel, without his shirt. Together, anxious and dripping water, they were leaning over a supine Polty.

'Is he dead?' Bean's voice rose cracklingly, absurdly.

'Polty! Polty!' Leny slapped the plump cheeks.

'Hello.' The eyes sprang open. 'Bean, there you are.' The fat boy gave a few little coughs and struggled upright, the white naked mound of his torso creasing into huge hanging rolls of fat. Red whorls of hair were flattened between his pendulous, feminine breasts; wet breeches clung to his enormous thighs. 'Some friend he is!' He grinned at Leny.

'Bean?'

'He knows I've been sick. Does he look out for me? No. He leaves the current to carry me away. Still, what could a stick-insect do? Leny, I think you made the best choice of our two friends.' A plump hand squeezed Vel's arm. Hard as rock! 'You saved my life, friend.'

The blacksmith's boy grinned.

'You're a hero, Vel. Do you know that?'

Bean looked on miserably. Blundering on to the scene after everything was over, he could only feel like a clumsy fool. The surging strength of moments before had drained from his limbs like water through a hole. Could he have saved Polty from the current? In the days of The Five, he had always known he was the weakest of their number; now, part of the remaining four, he knew that this would still be so. He offered pathetically, 'I brought your waistcoat, Polty,' holding the muddied garment aloft. Had his friend responded by hitting him, Bean would have thought he had deserved it entirely. Instead, Polty merely took the waistcoat calmly, slipping it round his shivering girth.

'We're having a picnic,' said Leny, linking an arm in Polty's. 'But we told you, didn't we?'

'I don't think so,' said Polty. 'Bean and I just thought we'd come down to the river, that's all. What a lucky coincidence! Well, we'll be off. Leave the lovebirds to it!'

'Polty, don't be silly! Come on, you must join us now.'

The fat boy had no choice but to relent.

The little party made their way up to the rock, where Leny, on a chequered rug, had set out a lavish spread: pies, cold chicken and custard tarts. Bottles of ale and bottles of wine were arranged in neat rows.

'Are you all right, Polty?' Leny asked, as the guest of honour settled himself on a corner of the rug; or rather, on much of it. She shifted the hamper.

The fat boy looked a little pale again, it was true. Poor Polty! Was he about to have a turn?

'The tiniest sip, that's all,' he said.

'Hm?' said Leny. 'A drink? I'll get you a drink!'

It was not what Polty meant. He rummaged deeply into the interior of his waistcoat.

'Ah! At least he didn't lose this!' he said, relieved, and shooting a glance at Bean, the fat boy drew forth the little black bottle that his friend had seen only once before.

Pop! He pulled out the stopper; and just for an instant, the merest instant, brought the neck of the bottle to his lips.

'Ah . . .' Polty leaned back with a satisfied sigh; then, fixing the stopper in place again, returned the bottle to the interior of his waistcoat. 'My medicine,' he murmured. 'The tiniest sip. That's all you need.'

But several times, as the afternoon wore on, Polty brought forth the bottle again.

The picnic was splendid.

Sullenly, on the fringe of the group, the disgraced Bean was permitted to join in, and watched as his companions sloshed back gallons of wine and ale and gorged themselves on the chickens and pies and custard tarts. Bean had little, but no one noticed. By now, the curious, disturbing awareness had begun in him: that they were not alone. That they were being watched. He might have said something, but he felt he could not speak. For the rest of them, Bean felt, he barely existed.

Poor Bean!

The sun poured richly over the high, smooth rock.

'Isn't this just like old times?' said Leny, packing a Jarvel-pipe. She was thinking back fondly to the days of The Five; and indeed the long afternoon bore some resemblance to *some* of their childhood. How happy they had been! Naked and brown, after long days on the river, The Five would gather on the golden heat of the rock. The heat would caress them; they would plunge into the water; they would swim a few strokes and clamber out, cool again, then climb back to the rock. The currents could not catch them; they were young, lithe animals.

Now they were older.

Polty rummaged in his waistcoat for his medicine. 'What is that?' Leny said idly, eyeing the little black stoppered bottle. In the days of The Five, the friends had often tried curious potions and powders, procured by their plump leader. *Father's*, he would laugh. *He'll never know.* Thus the little group had been initiated early into the properties of these strange mixtures, realizing that medicines made to cure the sick could often make the well feel still better.

Or worse.

'Try.' Polty held out the bottle to Leny.

'Mm! It's delicious, isn't it? Like treacle.'

'Only a little, that's all you need.'

'Whew! Cool again,' said a dripping Vel, casting himself down beside Leny again. She prodded the little black bottle at his lips.

'Vel. Try.'

Vel tried. 'Mm. It's good.' He had peeled off his breeches and he lay on his back, his neck arching, the apple in his throat jutting sharply out. Glittering, clear droplets rolled across his skin. 'Where's that treacle?' he murmured, a little later.

'Mm, yes. The treacle,' Leny said.

Plump fingers held the bottle out again. 'A little, just a little. That's all you need.' But several times more the bottle passed forward, though only to Vel and his intended bride. Bean was left to look on, but not enviously.

Not quite.

Something was stirring in the lean boy's brain.

'A dot on the tongue. The merest dab,' said Polty, interrupting a story he was telling. He would never return to it. It did not matter; it was only some fragment of childhood memory, and was borne away as if by the current below.

Vel was rubbing his eye.

'There's something in your eye?' Polty leaned over the

supine boy. 'Let me.' He peeled back the skin of the lid, peering inside with a scientific air, as if indeed he were the physician's son. 'No. I don't think so.' The skin snapped back. Leny and Vel were almost sleeping; Leny stretched on her side against Vel, her breasts spilling hugely from the neck of her shift. Around them, bones and bottles littered the rock; the rug beneath them was rumpled into chequered mountains and valleys.

'Something in my eye,' Vel said wearily.

'No, there's not. There wasn't.'

'Polty, what are you doing?'

The question was Bean's. There was no reply; the fat boy had eased his bulk beside the blacksmith's boy, lying full length on the other side from Leny.

Moments passed.

'Vel?'

'Mm?'

'Vel?' Polty's voice was soft. 'I didn't mean it, you know. What I said. When I said you were a Zenzau-blood. I wanted to tell you that, Vel. I mean, that I didn't mean it. I meant to say that before.'

'Mm. Mm.'

'What are you doing, Polty?' Bean had twisted his forehead tight. He felt as if something might snap in his brain. That was when he wanted to cry out suddenly:

Polty! Someone's watching!

But somehow he could not.

Or did not.

Polty's hand ran across Vel's upturned body. He felt the muscles of the chest, the thighs. 'Ah, Vel, You're so strong! And I'm so weak. Pink, ugly blubber. And sick, too! There's no contest between us now, is there? You've established your superiority, Vel. You're better. Best. First of The Five! The current could never catch you now, could it?'

As the fat boy whispered these words, he had traced a finger in a light, wavering line from the base of Vel's abdomen to the jutting, hard apple just beneath his jaw; it was the finger that was circled with the amethyst ring. He lifted up his hand, repeating, 'The current could never catch you now, could it?'

He snapped his fingers in Vel's face.

That was when something snapped in Bean's brain. *Polty's secret!* Now he knew it. A rush of admiration for his friend's genius fought in him suddenly with a surge of horror.

'Polty! No!'

But Vel was standing already. He was staggering forward; Bean's clutching hands grabbed, absurdly, for Polty. He was crying out, but his cries only vanished impotently on the air. It was as if the lean boy had no volition of his own; as if only Polty could act to save their friend.

'Bean, don't be a fool!' Polty flung him away. 'Don't you understand? This will bind you to me for ever!'

'Polty, there's someone watching!'

But Polty wasn't listening.

'Polty, can't you feel it?'

But Polty could not.

'What's happening?' It was Leny. Wretchedly, bleary-eyed, the girl was rising, floundering to the surface of her trance just in time to see Vel diving, as he had dived before.

And before.

She had heard what Polty said. Vel's superiority had been established. Yes. But what was happening? The golden light swirled before her eyes in strange patterns.

A voice came, 'Dear Leny.'

Vel? Back so soon? Leny swayed forward; but the arms that caught her were not Vel's arms. They were arms like white dough, soggy and heavy with hanging fat. A tide of vomit swelled in Leny's throat. Her knees gave way.

'Leny, Leny. Dear Leny . . .'

'Polty!' Bean scrambled to his feet. He had hit his head when his friend flung him down. He staggered. His gaze swivelled wildly.

The rock, the river.
The river, the rock.

'Pretty, pretty Leny . . . '

Rough hands ripped her dress. She was naked underneath.

Vel's head bobbed above the churning water.

Bean lurched forward.

'Lovely Leny,' Polty breathed. He pushed her, unresisting, on to the chequered blanket.

Bean leapt.

The rock.

The river.

Polty's breath came in hot gasps.

First there was the shock of the violent cascade. Then came the panic. All control was lost to him.

Bean's limbs wheeled.

Afterwards, he would think: *I tried to save him.* He would think: *There was nothing anyone could do.*

There was an instant of grace when the current slackened in the pull of a fallen branch.

Bean grabbed the branch.

He flailed towards the shore.

He lay, breathing heavily, in the mud of the bank. The river filled him, possessed him. All the world was a silvery cascade, rushing towards the violence of the mill-race.

He scrambled up.

There's no contest between us now, is there?

Bean was scudding along the squelching bank.

You've established your superiority, Vel.

Scudding, scudding, down towards the mill-race.

First of The Five.

Bean arrived just in time to see the broken body lifted into the air on the miller's wheel.

He cried out.

He sank to his knees on the marshy bank and closed his eyes. When he opened them – it might have been an aeon later – he would see, gazing at him from the opposite bank, the small, ragged figure that had been watching them all through the long, bitter course of that hot afternoon. The dark eyes above the high, slanted cheekbones stared impassively into Bean's stricken face. The girl's long hair billowed darkly behind her.

It was Cata.

Cata knew.

Chapter 38

BLUEJACKETS, BLUEJACKETS

The coach appeared to be turning a corner.

Pitched just a little against the quilted wall, the chaplain took the liberty of lifting the curtain. The corner was on a hilltop. Looking down, the chaplain saw, as in a panorama, the vast convoy of which they were the head. It was, he had to admit, an impressive sight. Stuck in the darkened coach, day after day, one did rather forget the extent and, indeed, magnificence of all that came behind them.

The chaplain saw the long lines of blue-painted wagons, trailing into the invisibility of the next valley; closer, the massed blue ranks of infantry, marching in formation; closer still, just behind them, the blue cavalry mounted on their blue-draped steeds. The impression was of an immense blue crocodile, writhing slowly, hugely, over the curves of the pale highway. He saw the blue flutterings of the banners and flags. Raised bayonets spiked the blue air. The chaplain registered the *thud! thud!* of drumbeats, and realized that he had heard this sound perpetually beating, beating, through all his long days in the quilted coach.

Bluejackets, Bluejackets, heading for Irion.

Soon it would stop. Soon they would be close.

They would not go in at once. The commander had ordered a full reconnaissance; and now, though he had always known of this plan, the chaplain began to consider its implications. They alarmed him. Just a little.

There were two possible ways to imagine the Valleys of the Tarn; or so the chaplain had thought until now. One was to think of a pleasant, pastoral image: amorous swains and milkmaids, a windmill, a burbling stream. Love-notes nailed to trees in a wood. The second way was rather less attractive, involving cow-dung, dinner-tables made of rough planks, no proper crockery, and peasants with malodorous stumps of teeth.

The chaplain had never left Agondon before, but was sufficiently versed in the ways of the world to expect the second image to be the true one. One thought of a Tarn-dweller, said the chaplain to himself, and one thought of a creature that was shambling. Hulking. One had not thought, until now, of a creature that was dangerous. The chaplain gazed solemnly at the moving army. Had he been told, a year or so ago, that he would now be part of this convoy, he would certainly have laughed.

The commander stirred. 'Chaplain?'

'Sir?'

'I know what you're doing.'

But letting the curtain fall again, the chaplain reflected that perhaps his life, from a certain point of view, had come full circle.

The old man reminded him of his mother.

The chaplain's name was Eay Feval.

As a young man, he had been possessed of that supremely bland species of handsomeness, at once wholly perfect and wholly without interest, which suggests that only through bitter trials shall its owner acquire some redeeming leavening of character. It is in the nature of life that it provides such trials; but not always. Not inevitably. The dashing of a hope, the love affair gone sour, might never happen; might not even be missed. So had things been with Eay Feval. He was not without wisdom. But he was, in certain things, without experience.

In youth, he had cared for his mother, who was ill, but not interestingly. He had loved her dutifully and read to her in the afternoons. She was sometimes amusing. She was on close terms with the Archmaximate, and when she died this prominent connection enabled the young man to receive, with few preliminaries, his anointment into the Order. Conveniently, at about that time, a Canon Lectoracy in the Great Temple became vacant. Eay Feval succeeded to it.

His, some would think, was an enviable life. He lived in a luxury which he was able to take for granted; there was nothing likely to impede his progress in the world, and nothing had. Of course, it might have been said that he could, by now, have risen to great prominence in the Order of Agonis. It might have been said; but seldom was. Failure exists only where an attempt has been made. Eay Feval had no desire to be one of the world's 'great men'.

As he grew older he retained his looks, in a form only a little more faded than before. From a distance, he was still a handsome young man. He was the sort of man that many a woman might wish to marry, until she thought better of it. The black garb of his faith suited him well. His Circle of Agonis was always gleaming; at all times he wore immaculate white gloves. The gloves hid no mystery. There was nothing to conceal in the appearance of his hands; but there was nothing in the world that he wished to touch.

The affairs of the kingdom disturbed him but little. His sinecure in the Great Temple had afforded him introductions to the best families of Agondon, and by middle life he was long settled into a pleasurable round of tea-parties, card-parties, dinners and balls. He was one of life's courtiers. To many great ladies he was a valued confidant. Nothing shocked him and his advice was always good. The ladies, of course, were deeply pious, allotting much of their days to their devotions. So it was that their spiritual adviser, as they would call Eay Feval, was permitted to visit them on terms which might, to some, have seemed alarmingly intimate.

But scandal never tainted the name of Eay Feval. No one disliked him; no one, besides, thought him capable. A wag once came up with a useful formulation. Many a man, he said, had entered the bedchambers of Ladies A—, B—, and C—; Eay Feval was the one man who had entered *only* the bedchambers. It was true; which might have made it seem all the more unjust that Eay Feval had now been plucked suddenly from his fashionable, pleasant round.

Talk of the Great Revival had been heard for some time in the drawing-rooms of Agondon. Now it was one of Eay Feval's admirable characteristics that, as well as listening attentively to others when required, he was also able to expatiate at length, in a manner utterly convincing to his hearers, on any topic on which he might be required to have a view. He was not a bore. On the contrary; he would speak only when required, and cease when others ceased to be entertained; or rather, a few moments before. It was an instinct he had.

At about the time that Revival talk was afoot, Eay Feval happened to attend a reception at the house of Lady Cham-Charing, a woman a little out of his regular circle. Lady Cham-Charing, as all knew, was much exercised by the impiety of the provinces. Inevitably, conversation turned to the moral wrack and ruin which, by all accounts, had utterly overwhelmed the northern regions; inevitably, Eay Feval offered a compelling address on the subject. Taking the example of the Valleys of the Tarn (he plucked the name from the air at random, meaning by it merely *a benighted province*), he advocated a Revival that would burn away sin like a forest fire, raging unchecked over hill and dale; a Revival that would scour the heart with flame; a Revival that was, as he memorably put it, *incessant, incendiary,* and *incandescent*. It was one of his best speeches. Revival, it was clear, was the fashion this season; and so for a time, until the fashion had passed, Eay Feval would be its avatar. It would do his diary of engagements no harm.

Thus things would normally have proceeded, but for two considerations. The first was the Archmaximate. He had not been present at Lady Cham-Charing's; but the good woman was an intimate of his, and relayed to him in rapturous terms the substance of Eay Feval's address.

The second thing was the times – the age, the era; though

if there were a third thing, it might perhaps have concerned certain intimate matters, pertaining to a particular friend of Lady Cham-Charing's, which Eay Feval was believed to have spread abroad. The confidant, perhaps, had become a little careless.

The Archmaximate summoned him.

'Ah, Eay, my boy! Dear Eay,' he began, but his manner soon assumed a solemn formality. 'Eay, I have returned this day from an audience with His Imperial Agonist Majesty,' he went on; this, as Eay Feval well knew, meant an audience with the First Minister. 'For a cycle, His Majesty has expended his efforts on the conquest of the heathen Zenzans. That conquest is accomplished. Now we must turn our attention to the moral and spiritual reform of the lands which are in our care. His Majesty has decreed that each of the Nine Provinces, and our territories in Zenzau, are to be placed under the direct rule of a military governor.

'These men have been selected from the noblest heroes of the wars of the last cycles. Lord Baral, who crushed the Redjackets in the southlands, shall become Supreme Commander of Varby and Holluch. Midlexion shall be the Earl of Tonion's. Lord Michan, Liberator of Wrax, shall return to the Zenzan capital. Prince-Elector Jarel, Great-Admiral Lord Cral, General Lord Gorgol shall be similarly rewarded; and, ah, Olivan' – here the Archmaximate faltered just a little – 'Olivan Tharley Veeldrop, hero of the Siege of Irion, shall return to the province to which his name shall be bound for eternity in bonds of glory. What do you know of Commander Veeldrop, Eay?'

The question was hardly difficult; everyone in Agondon was well aware of the hero of the Siege of Irion who had now fallen so disastrously from favour. Eay Feval's fervent execration of Veeldrop had come in useful at a number of gatherings, successfully filling those rather dull Tiralos-drinking stretches when he was obliged to remain with the gentlemen after dinner. They always concluded that he was a good sort. But Eay Feval was no fool. The Archmaximate had spoken of a 'hero'. He had used the word 'glory'.

This was evidently some sort of test.

'Olivan Tharley Veeldrop is a great man,' said Eay Feval. 'I should say, indeed, that he is one of the greatest men our Agonist lands have produced. From humble origins, he has risen, hawk-like, to become the fiercest warrior our generation has known. Without him, could the blasphemies of the Redjacket reign have been driven from our realms? No. Without him, could we have crushed at last the foul impieties of the Vianans? The thought is laughable. Our race is indebted deeply to Olivan Tharley Veeldrop. He is old now, and there are some who would condemn him for the failings which are inevitable in any long career. But I am convinced he still has much to give, and equally – yes, equally – there is much he should be given.'

The Archmaximate beamed with pleasure.

'And I think you're the man to give it to him, Eay.'

Eay Feval smiled back politely.

'Archmaximate?'

❋   ❋   ❋

The chaplain, far from Agondon now, rummaged beside him for the tinder-box. It was time to light the lamp again, and read again from *A Lady's Maid? A Lady!*

There were some, the chaplain was thinking, who would be plunged into despair by a banishment like his.

But this was not Eay Feval's way.

The wick flared. As the lamp began to glow, the golden spines of the 'Agondon Edition' shone out brightly on their little inset shelf. That was when Eay Feval recalled a story he had heard, long ago, about the identity of the mysterious 'Miss R——'.

Of course, it was only a rumour.

Chapter 39

BLOSSOM COTTAGE

'A wrong turning. That's what happened last time. Quite simple, really. Left-hand, not right-hand. Or was it right-hand, not left?'

Jem paused in the shadowy lane.

'Aunt! You do know, don't you?'

'Jem, of course!' The fat woman laughed. 'Oh, how could I have forgotten the way to Blossom Cottage?'

Some days had passed, and with them, it seemed, had passed the threat that the warm season was over. Bright sunlight dappled the lane; Umbecca's basket swung from her hand. Everything was as it had been before, and they had set out a second time in search of Blossom Cottage.

They came to a turning: left-hand, not right.

'The tiger . . .' Jem ventured.

Umbecca no longer seemed concerned. 'In the old days . . .' she began airily.

'When you were young, Aunt?'

'No, my dear, before my time – in the time of the old king's father. Then, wood-tigers roamed freely through the valleys, and were a great danger to the villages.'

'Like the serpent Sassoroch?'

'Perhaps not so dangerous as Sassoroch! But they would kill the goats and chickens in the farmyards, and little children who wandered into the wood.'

Jem shuddered.

'But what happened to the wood-tigers, Aunt?'

It was their new game. His aunt turned to him and her little eyes widened. They blazed like coals, and her voice was thick.

'The Great Hunt!'

She swooped close to the boy. He almost squealed.

'The old duke, he was the present duke's father, swore to rid the valleys of the "striped fiend". Hunters gathered from all through the Tarn. For all the seasons of one cycle the hunt went on. Relentless!'

The thought filled Jem with a strange feeling, at once of excitement and appalled horror. Poor wood-tiger! He imagined the yelpings of a thousand hounds. He imagined the hammerings of a hundred horses' hooves, crashing through the woodland.

His aunt's voice became distant.

'Yet always there was talk that one tiger lived on – and lived on and lived on, and would not die. We heard the stories when we were – oh, mere girls, Ruanna and I . . . '

Then all at once Umbecca laughed sharply, and said something she had not said before:

'Silly talk!'

Jem was confused. This was not part of the game.

'The old man—' said the boy after a moment.

What should have followed was a tale of lurid wickedness, of a madman who tore the livers out of children and cooked them in the charcoal he burnt, deep in the forest. *Tap-tap! tap-tap!* would come the old man's fingers, rapping at the windows when the children were in bed.

But Jem almost knew it could not be true.

Umbecca was silent.

'The wicked old man—' Jem's voice was louder.

'Wicked, Jem?' His aunt's was soft. The light fell through the trees with a peculiar sharpness, imprinting a dark lattice on the pale surface of the lane. 'A rude man. A foolish man. He is only an old hermit. Once he lived in the village. Then he took himself into the woods. I shouldn't bother about him, really I shouldn't.'

'Aunt, but you said—'

They came to a second turning, right-hand, not left; and as Jem gazed after his aunt's waddling bulk, that was proceeding a little hurriedly, just a little ahead of him, he suddenly saw that there was not, after all, any heavy basket, swinging leadenly from her plump hand.

Everything was not as it had been before.

❊ ❊ ❊

'Aunt—'

'Look, Jem! Here we are!'

Blossom Cottage appeared before them suddenly, manifesting itself as if by magic from amongst the foliage of the deep lane.

It was a surprise in other ways, too. Jem had expected the cottage to be tiny, a single-storeyed hovel of rough clay bricks, tangled in the tendrils of draping vines. In truth, it was a substantial, gabled edifice, with twin dormer windows perched in the heights of half-timbered walls.

Nor was it a ruin.

A neat picket fence marked the boundary of a clipped lawn, lined at the edges with immaculate shrubs. A crunching drive led to a door with a shiny brass knocker. Obedient honeysuckle twined above the lintel; from the chimney wound a neat curlicue of smoke.

Jem's aunt rapped at the shiny knocker.

'Aunt—' the boy began again.

He was hanging back on the drive, peering curiously up at the house. In the bright sunlight it bore a strange resemblance to a cake, elaborately iced.

The dark-garbed figure that opened the door might have been waiting on the other side in readiness. The figure bobbed respectfully and Jem, coming forward, saw it to be that of an elderly woman, bow-backed and wizened, in the uniform of a maid.

She was much neater than Nirry.

The wizened face crumpled into what was almost a smile as Jem, uncertainly, his brow furrowing, followed his aunt into a tidy hallway. The old maid scurried forward, politely indicating an interior door.

She stepped in ahead of them and cleared her throat.

'Mistress Rench, Mum. And Master Jemany.'

Everything in the little drawing-room might have been contrived to make Jem feel awkward – the floral wallpaper and chintz chairs, the ornamental plates in a glass-fronted cabinet, and sitting stiffly upright by the window, the pale, thin woman in black who inclined her head in greeting to his aunt.

'My dear, you look well!' Umbecca sailed forward. The thin woman did not rise, only turning her cheek slightly to receive the embrace.

Umbecca was unabashed.

'Jem! Come on! He's shy,' she added, with an abrupt laugh, perhaps too abrupt.

There was no answering smile on the thin woman's face. Her forearms were folded neatly in her lap and a glittering, golden Circle of Agonis hung at the front of her tight bodice.

When she spoke, her voice was distant, without expression. 'My husband will be joining us shortly,' was all she said as Jem lowered himself gracelessly into one of the stiff, high-backed chairs.

Tea was laid already on a low marquetry table.

In the hallway, a clock ticked loudly. In here, its sound could still be heard; but the sharp, precise *tick! tick!* seemed only to make more evident, as Umbecca's laugh had done, the thick, muffling silence that filled the room.

'Jem! Don't slouch so,' the boy's aunt hissed.

But the high-backed chair was hard and slippery. How did the thin woman sit so upright? Jem gazed about him, suddenly miserable.

Deeply miserable.

There was a carpet on the floor with a brown-red, swirling pattern; there were cut flowers in vases on little round tables; there were stiff, embroidered antimacassars on the backs of the chintz chairs. Dainty figurines lined the mantelpiece: a fat farmer with a grinning red face; a milkmaid with plaited butter-yellow hair.

Jem gazed into the thin woman's face. It was impassive; yet he perceived in her all at once, like a fact in a book, a bitter spoiling sourness, a welling loathing, that threatened to spill over like milk on Nirry's stove.

He was frightened.

'Aunt—'

The door flew open.

'Ah, my good woman! And our young friend, I see!'

Jem gasped. He swivelled round.

'You had a pleasant walk, I take it? Yes, the weather is so much nicer! Goody Waxwell has been entertaining you, I trust?' The jovial, unctuous words boomed in Jem's ears like shots; the twisted figure came crabwise across the carpet, rubbing its hands together and smiling eagerly.

Umbecca was standing, beaming and expectant.

Then Jem was struggling to stand, too, clutching at the slippery polished arms of his chair.

'No, no, young man, don't trouble yourself, please!' The physician wore an immaculate new wig. A stiff white handkerchief burgeoned from the pocket of his jacket. 'Goody Waxwell and I are not offended! We understand, we understand everything! – Mistress Rench, how lovely to see you . . .'

Smack!

Smack!

A kissing of cheeks.

'My good woman! We knew you would not desert us.'

Jem had fallen back into the slippery chair.

'Now, I'm sure this young man would like a little something . . .' Hovering over the marquetry table, the physician lifted the dome-shaped cover from a salver which, Jem now saw, was heaped high with cream-cakes. 'A little something, young man? Hm?' A hand with dark whorls of hair on the back extended the generous offering to the boy, and for a moment the hand was all that Jem could see: the hand and what it contained, enormous, rich and oozing.

A creamy gob spattered his thigh.

'Aunt!' he cried out. 'Aunt! Aunt!'

But the fat woman had only turned away. The tears burst suddenly, hotly from her eyes.

'Oh, Jem! Jem!' She covered her face.

Goodman Waxwell, taking no notice, was saying only, 'So, the Vexing shall give us trouble, shall he?'

The hairy face had replaced the hand, swooping in close. A sickening stench, as of something rotten, reeked from the neat, clean costume.

Jem was slipping, slipping down the chair.

He bucked sideways. He was sprawling on the floor. He scrambled for his crutches; he raised himself up. He lurched to the door.

'Ugh!' spat the thin woman, unexpectedly. 'His legs!'

Her husband laughed.

But did not move.

The old maid appeared, blocking the way. She was so small! So weak!

But Jem was a cripple.

He turned back to his sobbing aunt. 'Aunt!' His voice cracked. 'How could you? How could you bring me here?'

She did not reply: she could not.

There was a shift in the light; a cloud, perhaps, had obscured the sun. But it was in that moment of darkening that Jem saw, as by an interior light, much that he had failed to see before. He saw the awkwardness, the uncertainty at the edge of his aunt's manner, that had persisted through all their happy days together; he saw the fugitive look, the downcast eyes, when certain things had been said, or recalled. He remembered when she had stopped to speak to a village woman, an elderly woman, and now he knew that this had been the old maid.

Of course.

And more than once there had been letters his aunt was reading, letters that she crumpled swiftly away, when the boy, or his mother, had looked at her quizzically.

His aunt had lied; she had lied about everything.

Jem gazed at her and his eyes filled with tears. She was turned half away from him in the stiff chair. In her grief, a button at her breast had opened. There was a glint of gold and Jem saw that she still wore, concealed beneath her garments, the chill, glittering circle of her Agonist faith.

The scene ended quickly.

'Aunt!' Jem wailed, and for a moment Goodman Waxwell watched him, bemused; then in one swift, sharp motion strode forward, knocked the crutches from beneath the boy's arms and sent him sprawling.

He barked to the maid, 'Take these vile sticks and burn them! They are implements of the evil one.'

With a flourish, the physician pulled the handkerchief from his pocket. He might have been about to wipe his hands on it. Instead, he looked down at the startled, gasping cripple, who was attempting ineptly to crawl away. He sighed and bent over, as if to some irksome but necessary duty.

Some duty of his profession.

'So, the Vexing does not want to eat our cakes!' he mused. 'A pity, it would have been so much more pleasant for him. But we have other ways.'

He cradled the boy's head in his hand, as if with tenderness. The handkerchief descended and the sickening stench Jem had smelt before now overwhelmed his nostrils, suddenly hot, suddenly burning.

If he tried to avert his face, it was to no avail.

As the caustic odour filled him, Jem heard, tolling in his awareness like a bell, the *tick! tick!* of the clock in the hallway, unrelenting; he heard the gluggings and gurglings of his aunt's snivellings; he heard the reedy, oblivious tones of the thin woman as she leaned forward stiffly above the marquetry table, 'Shall I pour, Nathanian?'

Then came oblivion.

Chapter 40

A TICKING CLOCK

Tick! Tick!

The first thing that came back was the clock. In each of the neat rooms of Blossom Cottage, the heavy clunkings of the mechanism could be heard, counting out precisely the units of the day. To Goody Waxwell as she sat stiffly in her drawing room, to the physician in his study, to the old maid as she polished and dusted, the clock counted out the heartbeat of the cottage, uniting them in the element of time. Often they were barely aware of the tickings, or the mournful *bong!* which sounded on each fifteenth, and each five within it. But the clock was always with them, and within the clock, they knew, was the secret spring that uncoiled across each moonlife with so scrupulous a deliberation, as if in the impetus behind each tiny *tick!* was the infinite restraint of a power that could easily have burst forth in wrath. It was like the power of the Lord Agonis, that pulsed in each moment of the life of the world.

Tick! Tick!

Then came the voices.

'Liege of Light, hear our prayer. Look on us now from the Place of Indwelling and pity, we implore you, this tormented child. Aid us, O Liege, as we take the evil from him, and bring him, as a postulant humble and weak, to cower in submission at the place of your judgement. Abet us, O Liege, to be strong in our faith, as we ready ourselves now to do your divine work. To the Lord and the Lady, all praise be!'

'To the Lord and the Lady, all praise be!'

The first voice was Waxwell's, sonorous and low; the voices of the women were a devout chorus.

319

Jem was awake now, but his eyes were shut tightly. There was a weight at the lids; they might have been pressed down with heavy coins. His mouth was parched and he was aware that it was stuffed with some rough, bulky substance.

Where was he?

Then he remembered. Fear stabbed through the boy like a knife. He would have cried out, but could not. He would have leapt up, but could not. Something held him down. Dimly, from the first swirlings of oblivion, the memory came to him of a flight of narrow stairs; of a sparse white room. He knew now that he was blindfold and gagged, bound to a hard table. He felt the tight heat of the leather straps. Gooseflesh rippled his skin; the air was chill. Then he recalled the rough hands that had torn quickly, contemptuously, at his clothes.

They had stripped him.

'The boy wakes, Nathanian,' came the voice of the thin woman. It was distant and unconcerned.

'Hm. Yes.'

Jem felt the physician's coarse hands, prodding sharply at his shins and thighs.

There was a sigh. 'It is worse than I thought. The sap of evil has spread far already. I fear that to cut below the knee may not avail—'

'Goodman, no!' Umbecca's voice wavered.

'Fear not, my good woman. The pain shall be brief. After the cauterizing, there shall be soothing creams . . . and think of the devout life he shall live hereafter!'

A cry broke through Jem's gag.

'Hold your noise, spawn of darkness!' Jem felt the hand suddenly strike his face. He could not flinch. Even his forehead was secured by a strap.

Then came the smack of the physician's moist lips, hissing close to his ear. Now the tone was soft with mercy.

'You are becoming a man, Jemany Vexing. But what sort of man shall you be? From the sites of your deformity, the sap of evil is spreading already through your frame. Consuming you. Oh, child, we have seen the signs! Your love for the impious ones: for the traitor Torvester! For the heathen dwarf! Your foul implements of unnatural walking, as if you would defy the will of the Lord Agonis! Even now you show yourself, by your resistance, to be gripped inextricably in the hold of evil! Only if we take the evil from you shall you know the compassion of the Liege of Light . . .'

Jem was struggling, but his bonds were too strong.

'Oh no, Vexing. Oh no. I think another little sleep is in order.' Waxwell laughed coldly, and Jem, for a second time, smelt the hot reek of the handkerchief as it descended over his nostrils.

'No!' he tried to cry. 'No! No!'

But his dry, stuffed mouth could form no sound other than a muffled, animal wail. This time, as his consciousness swam, he felt first the droplets of a chill liquid, sprinkling across his skin; then heard the physician turning back to the women and remarking in a clear, calm voice, 'Come, good women, we shall leave him now. The unguent of purification must first do its work. For one so young, he is mired deep in wickedness – even now, on the brink of his new life, the evil in him would struggle against our goodness! Let him lie here for the course of this night. At first light, the time shall be nigh. Good maid, where is my whetstone? The blade must be keen.'

The blade must be keen.

Jem's body had become a feelingless mound beneath the straps that held it down. Now a violent shiver shook his frame, and all at once a sweat broke through his skin, pained and chill, like a million million pinpricks of colourless blood.

A door swung shut.

He was alone.

His senses blurred and shifted, but this time a heavy, drugged sleep did not claim him. Perhaps his fear had made him resist; perhaps this time he had inhaled less of the handkerchief's caustic perfume. Obliquely he drifted through the plains of consciousness, aware of the chill in his naked flesh; aware, too, of the alien droplets that slithered like snails across his torso, his limbs. The *unguent of purification*, Waxwell had called it. Slowly, as the ticking clock boomed in the darkness, as an owl hooted in the trees outside, Jem felt the liquid begin to itch.

To burn.

How he wished he could move his arms!

The clock offered up its mournful *bong!*, marking the passing of another five in the slow but inevitable journey to the daylight. The sounds came to Jem horribly loud, booming in his skull as in a vast, echoing cavern. Sometimes he surrendered to them, swirling downwards with the echoes; sometimes he tensed himself, struggling to the surface.

He tried to think.

But what could he think?

At first light, the time shall be nigh.

And Jem would not even see the light!

He strained, listening for voices from below. For a time there had been murmurings, perhaps of prayers; and once – suddenly, sharply – a burst of tears.

Now they were silent. Were they sleeping?

A sly wind whistled about the gables. Softly it rattled at the catch of the window, then insinuated itself into the room, coiling like a snake round Jem's naked limbs.

He shivered.

Tick.

Tick.

For a time he must have lapsed into oblivion again; for the next thing he was aware of was the soft touch of a hand, smoothing his hair.

Gently.

Very gently.

His body jerked. Was it time? Was it time?

'Shh. Jem, Jem.'

It was Aunt Umbecca's voice.

'Oh Jem, let me look at you. I must look at you.'

A hand pulled at the blindfold, and when it came away the boy was gazing up into the earnest face of his aunt, illuminated in the light of a single candle. The room around her was still deep in darkness. Had she come to her senses? Had she come to release him? Jem forced a sound from his parched throat; but his aunt made no move to untie his gag.

'Shh,' she repeated, and smoothed his hair again. 'Shh, shh. Are you frightened, my darling? Don't worry, it shall soon be over.' The voice, filled with kindness, was a soft coo. 'When I was a little girl, I had a dreadful pain. Worse than yours, Jem. Mine was right inside me! In my belly. The physician said he would have to operate. How frightened I was! Mother was alive then and, oh, how I pleaded with her! *Please, please, Mama*, I cried, *don't let the man cut me open!*'

These last words were spoken in an imitation baby-talk. The fat woman laughed fondly at the childish memory; then shook her head.

'What a silly girl I was! And all the time I had – oh, such a pain. In my belly! But do you know, Jem, after my operation that pain had gone for good. It was all for the best, don't you see? That's what you'll feel like, my darling. Soon.'

Jem's eyes were a dumb-show of horror.

But his aunt did not see. Trailing her fingers across his shivering limbs, she was pacing slowly round and round the table; and now as she spoke she seemed to be speaking more to herself than to him.

'You see, my darling, there can be no other way. It's because of what you are, Jem. Haven't you wondered just what you are? Other children have a father and mother. Did you know that? Did you wonder why you had no father, Jem?

'"Jem Vexing", that's your name. But that just means you're a bastard, Jem. Do you know what "bastard" means? It means your mother is a whore. A harlot. A filthy harlot!'

The voice was suddenly loud. Umbecca shook with rage. Wax spilt from the candle in her hand and Jem flinched as the droplets splattered his leg. The buckled limb was alive, leaping with feeling.

But then it had always been alive. Only buckled.

Jem's eyes filled with tears. He fought them back, scanning the shadowy forms disclosed by the shifting candle. He glimpsed a sloping ceiling, a dormer window; he glimpsed a huge iron Circle of Agonis hanging imposingly, high above him, in the gable-end wall.

An altar.

Now Umbecca had turned from the boy and her voice, though soft again, seemed to rise like bile from black pits of bitterness.

'It was in the time of the Siege. The harlot gave herself away to a common soldier. A common soldier! That is why you are as you are, Jem. Your twisted legs are the badge of your bastardy. When you were born, Jem, a seed was planted in you. It was a seed of evil. That seed must be rooted out and destroyed.'

She turned back to him, her fat face puckered with emotion, and Jem tensed, horrified, as she caressed him again, more ardently this time, running her fingers up and down his twisted legs, his thighs, and the parts that lay between.

The boy shuddered violently.

He wanted to be sick.

'You are growing to manhood, Jem. Ahead can lie only a mire of turpitude. But soon all shall be well! Soon the evil one shall be banished from your heart! Then you shall sit in your chair beside me, as you did when you were small. Remember the day of our vigil at the temple, Jem? How happy we were then? We shall be happy again! Together we shall live a life of quiet devotion. In time, perhaps, you shall become a beacon of goodness in this evil village. Oh, it must come to pass! Oh, Jem, Jem!'

Umbecca's bulk, sobbing and moaning, collapsed across the thin defenceless body of the boy. Jem could barely breathe, and in his aunt's sprawled state, the candle in her hand tilted dangerously above his forehead. He shut his eyes tightly.

How he hated his aunt! He had believed her lies and, believing her, had come to love her. What a fool he had been! Could the boy have burst from his bonds at that moment, he would have lashed out, striking Umbecca, and if he had killed her, would not have cared. All his life since Barnabas had gone now seemed to him nothing but chaff, dry and brittle and blown away on the wind.

There was a quiet click as the door opened. A dark figure slid gently forward.

'Umbecca!' Waxwell's voice was tender. 'You know we must leave the boy to be purified. Come away. Come. The night's darkness is still deep around us. Leave him to his last sleep of sin. Leave him . . .'

'Oh Nathanian, are we doing the right thing?'

'My good woman! Shh! Shh!'

Umbecca permitted him to take her in his arms and they lingered thus at their altar, for a little too long, before the physician led her meekly from the room.

Jem was alone again.

He breathed deeply. They had forgotten his blindfold, but without the candle the room was in any case enmired in a deep darkness. It was the night called Blackmoon. Not the merest glimmering at the dormer window relieved the chill oppression of the dark.

Bong!

The clock in the hall marked another five. The soft, low sound was like a harbinger of doom. How many more times would it sound, Jem wondered, before the light came to leaven the darkness? The tears that he had tried to hold back now ran freely down the boy's face.

This was the bleakest point of his despair. The entrapment he now felt, he saw, was but the beginning of a life that would be like this, always. He had believed he was not just a cripple; now he would be a cripple, just a cripple, for ever.

It was over.

It was all over.

Could Jem have willed himself to die, then and there, he would have done so. Anything not to live as Umbecca would have him live, mutilated and useless, unable even to walk on the 'vile sticks' that Waxwell had ordered the old maid to burn.

In the delirium of the night, his tormented body alternately shuddered with cold, then burnt with fever. He lay counting the strikings of the clock; or beginning to count them, then losing count.

Then trying again.

Useless.

It was always useless. Was time not passing? But after a long time, Jem began to think that the dark element that enveloped him had grown a little lighter. It was only a suspicion, but at once a renewed stab of fear assailed him.

Then came the creak of a footstep on the stairs.

It was the lightest step, and at first Jem told himself he had not heard it at all. It was only the desultory *creak*, the random *crack!* of shifting timbers in a house at night.

Then the door opened.

Jem started. For a long time, though he had barely sensed it, a taut, familiar pressure had jabbed insistently at the base of his abdomen. Now the pressure was suddenly released; the scalding liquid spurted over his thighs. He tried to stop it but could not; then he didn't care. He lay back, sobbing.

The time had come.

But it had not.

The figure that loomed over Jem this time carried no candle; only in the dark grey that had replaced the black could the boy even make out its dimensions.

What happened now should have happened quickly;

instead, it was an affair of infinite languor, crawling to its conclusion as the impending light crawled, a little less slowly, into the murk of the dark grey. Only with a succession of weak, awkward tuggings did Goody Waxwell release Jem's bonds. She shuffled about the table as if in her sleep; yet at each creak of the floorboards she stopped, standing still as a statue. At these times she seemed barely to breathe, and sometimes Jem wondered if she would ever move again. He watched her intently; and if the thought came to him that this release, perhaps, were no release at all, but only some new preparation for the morning, it did not linger. When the bonds that held down his hands were released, he reached up stiffly for the gag across his mouth. Tugging it free, he might have blurted some ill-formed question, 'Why? Why are you doing this?'

But his tongue and lips were dry and swollen: he could not speak.

Then he understood.

When the last strap was free, Goody Waxwell crept carefully back to the doorway. It was as she turned back in the last lingering moment, gazing on him forlornly, that Jem in the gloom of incipient dawn saw something he had failed to see in the afternoon light. She must have meant him to see it; it was something she had learnt to keep concealed. Goody Waxwell raised her arms. At the end of the left was the small, pale hand that had tugged so weakly at the boy's bonds.

At the end of the right was a stump.

She was gone.

Jem fell back, astonished, on the cold, wet table.

It was only for a moment. He raised himself up. He rubbed his limbs. He was free; yet not free at all. He could not walk, he had no crutches, and was lying on a table in the high attic room of a house far from home. Desperately he looked towards the dormer window.

At first light, the time shall be nigh.

The time was nigh.

It had to be.

His gaze swivelled from the window to the door. At any moment, surely at any moment, would come a confident *clump! clump!* of footsteps on the stairs. For this time the one who came would be Goodman Waxwell, and this time Waxwell would be bearing an axe.

It would not happen, it would not!

Afterwards Jem could barely remember how he had dragged himself from the table to the window. He was without thought, a mere mechanism of tautened, straining muscles; but if what he wanted was instant death, or some wild chance of escape, he could not say.

He pushed the window open and hauled himself through.

Chapter 41

NIGHT-WATCH

'What's that sound?'

Morven sighed. 'Nothing. An owl.'

'An owl is not nothing.'

'An owl is nothing.'

Pause.

Morven was waiting. He could count the instants. Yes! He was right.

'But how?' Crum whined. 'An owl—'

Morven hissed, '*Who!*'

A splendid joke.

Could Crum understand? Of course not. 'An owl has wings,' he pursued. 'It can fly—'

'It can frighten Recruit Crum,' murmured Morven.

'I wasn't frightened—'

'But is it of interest to Sergeant Bunch? No. Will you rush to him to report your owl? No. Will he repair at once to the commander's tent, burning with the force of the revelation? I don't think so, do you? Are we watchers of nature? We are sentries. That, my dear Crum, is why an owl is nothing.'

Morven permitted himself a satisfied smirk. *Upon such small victories,* he thought wryly, *the health of my spirit must now depend.*

Tragic!

A scrawny, bespectacled young man, Plaise Morven had been a student at the University of Agondon before the outbreak of the last Zenzan war, but as he was a student of nothing useful, only Juvescials, he was obliged to go for a soldier; to put down his books, as they said, for his musket.

To forgo his gown for his jacket.

To bear his burden for country and king.

It was too absurd. Still, it was a source of drollery; Morven had composed, indeed, a number of brilliantly witty letters, exercises in an irony sufficiently refined to slip like sand, he had no doubt, through the coarse intellectual grasp of Sergeant Bunch, who was, he had ascertained, the commander's censor. Bunch! A bullying, bawling imbecile. Ugh! The knowledge, which was inescapable, that he was the intellectual superior of every person he met was, at least, a source of some comfort to the young man.

Only his glimpses of Commander Veeldrop disturbed Morven's complacency a little. Now there was a fellow he should not like to cross! *Power corrupts.* Undoubtedly it was true. This was the burden of The Jelandros, third of the Theatricals of Thell, the great masterpiece of the Early Post-Juvescian Age, or Age of Thell.

Shifting the weight of his poised musket, Morven meditated for a moment on the genius of Thell, who had taken the Agonist hexameter to heights never since surpassed. How appalled Morven had been when Professor Mercol, turning back from the window one day in Javander Term, Tiralos-glass in hand, had sighed as if he were bored and described the Great Caesura of the fifteenth canto as 'obvious'. Fatuous old fool! The dried-up pedant wouldn't recognize genius if he were in the same room with it.

Crum had embarked on another narrative of his childhood, this one evidently involving owls; Morven felt no obligation to listen.

'Morven?' Crum attempted after a moment. 'Are you listening?'

No reply.

Crum set his mouth glumly and stared into the night. The country road wound away, black and empty, before them. Their solitary lamp was a mere flickering candle in the vast extent of darkness.

He had been trying to tell Morven what owls meant; Morven, of course, never listened. An owl's hooting at Blackmoon was an omen. It meant that there was enchantment in the air. Well, it could. It depended; but everyone knew that.

Poor Morven! Sometimes, Crum felt sorry for him. He knew nothing!

Crum yawned.

In the clearing behind them, the camp was quiet. They were all asleep. Even Commander Veeldrop was probably, at this moment, sleeping.

Oh, to sleep! When Crum was a little boy, he had been so excited when the soldiers came through. He would have joined them then and he would have been proud. He didn't know then what he knew now. Slog, slog, day after day, then sentry-duty at night! And they didn't even get to wear those bright red jackets.

He stamped the ground.

So cold!

And this the Season of Theron!

The thick-set peasant lad was from Varl, southernmost colony of the Agonist Deliverance. It had been a miserable day in his little village when the Seeker Squad arrived, demanding volunteers; and one just as miserable, Crum saw now, when they read out his name for a posting to the Tarn. That was where they were going now, wherever that was. All he knew was that they were going there ... and they were going there ... and they were going there.

One day they would be there.

Yes, and he would be an old man with a beard down to his boots!

Recruit Olch, who could wiggle his ears while keeping the rest of his head completely still, had said the ground underfoot would all be made of ice. Soldier Rotts, who was mean because he wouldn't give Crum a puff of Jarvel-pipe, said there would be white mountains in the sky. Crum didn't know which to believe; he could imagine neither of these things. It was just getting colder, that was all he knew; and the more they marched, the colder it got.

'I wish I were back in my bed in Varl,' he said.

Morven winced. Varl! The appalling accent told its own story. He considered making some disparaging reference to the culture of the colony, but as, to his knowledge, there was no such thing, he contented himself instead with, 'Tucked in by Mother and wrapped up warm?'

He could have done better; still, it was late.

Or rather, early.

Crum's lip trembled. 'I meant, I wish I were in bed with a whore,' he blurted.

Ah! Now this was the opening Morven needed. 'In bed!' he snorted. 'Your sort of whore would have you against a wall.'

He was proud of this particular sally; he had used it, indeed, several times before. *Your sort of whore.* Yes, he rather liked that. Raffish. Man-of-the-world. That he was yet without experience of whores, or women generally, was beside the point.

So was his companion; of that much he was sure.

'I'm on the same pay as you. Aren't I?' Crum returned, after a moment.

Dear me. He was like a little terrier, coming back time after tedious time to the pacification of an old shoe. 'Well, I don't think I've been docked, have I?' Morven said tartly. 'Disgracing myself on my first taste of strong liquor. Hm?'

Crum sniffed resentfully. 'It wasn't my first!'

'No?'

'No!' Crum was becoming a little boisterous.

'Don't push me!' Morven deplored violence.

But Crum broke off suddenly. 'Did you hear that?'

'What?' Morven smoothed his jacket. 'I heard nothing except an ignorant lump of peasant who has no sensibility for *irony*—'

'Shh! There was a sound.'

'Your pet owl again?'

'No.'

Behind a line of elms on the other side of the road was one of the fields where they were keeping the horses. Every so often during the night a snort or a low whinny would emanate through the screening foliage; but these were sounds, like those of the owls, which for purposes of the watch would not count. They were *nothing*.

But Crum had heard something.

Someone.

'Morven?' Crum whispered.

Morven had been slouching. His back stiffened and he stared ahead. 'Hm?'

'Do you think we should have a look? I mean, should one of us—'

'Mm.' Morven waved dismissively in the direction of the trees. The little flicking of his fingers was a most accomplished gesture. It had in it the manner of an intellectual superior, condescending to some tiresomely lowbrow companion; in it, Morven managed to suggest that, should Crum insist upon the proposed course of action, of course he, Morven, would not stand in his way . . . but that he, Morven, was for his part taking very seriously indeed his responsibility of standing stock-still, keeping his eyes peeled, as the sergeant enjoined, which one of them, at least, should continue to do . . . and, given that the activity was demanding and complex in ways which Crum could not *possibly* hope to understand, there could hardly be doubt as to which that *one* should be. Let Crum indulge his whims as he would, the flicking fingers seemed to say, Morven simply could *not* be disturbed . . .

Crum sniffed; then stopped himself.

Go, said the fingers.

Crum looked round furtively, screwing up his eyes. Had the dark of the night grown deeper? He reached for the lantern. He hunched low and tipped back the brim of his hat. With a careful, long stride, Crum stepped into the road, his bent ankle hovering, trembling, in the air for long moments as he failed signally to bring it down before him.

It was a stony road; his boot was sure to make a dreadful crunch . . .

333

Whoo-oo!

It was the owl.

'Ouch!' Crum fell into a heap.

'Crum!'

'Oh! I think I've twisted my ankle.'

Morven sighed and strode into the road.

'Morven!'

Morven looked down. Crum's grip was tight.

'Take your hand off *my* ankle,' Morven whispered.

Crum was snivelling. 'There's an owl.'

'I heard. Now let go.'

'Morven? It's hooted three times.'

'Oh?'

'What if there's a Weird?'

'What?' Morven burst out.

'Shh!'

Morven wrenched away his ankle. He pulled back the catch of his flintlock loudly. 'Who goes there?' he demanded into the darkness, in his most imperious university voice.

There was a sudden high shriek and a huge pale form crashed into the road through the screen of trees.

Crum cried out. Morven fired wildly.

There was a thump.

It was over.

Or almost. The white stallion thundered into the night. Rearing, it had cast its rider into the road.

'You killed him!' There was fear in Crum's voice. He was on his feet now, his ankle forgotten. They rushed towards the body of the thief.

The figure lay face down, a dark heap.

'What shall we do?'

'I don't know!' Absurdly, Morven thought of the Great Caesura.

'You men! What's going on here?' It was Sergeant Bunch. With one hand he was stuffing his shirt-tails into his breeches; in the other, he held aloft a lantern. Woken from a dream about a certain lady in the spa-town of Varby (who kept a *most* pleasant establishment), the fat sergeant was in no mood for nonsense. This had better not be *nothing*, or these men would be on a charge.

The sergeant took in the situation at once.

'After that horse!' He cuffed Crum. 'You! Here!' He shoved Morven back. 'Keep him covered. He may be armed.'

'I think he's d-dead, sergeant.'

'Shut up.'

The lamp hovered over the prostrate form. The thief was long and lean, dressed in a floppy hat and the ragged, dirty robes of a beggar, but as the sergeant's rough hands turned the figure over, the front of the costume fell open to reveal a glimpse of a bright, particoloured costume.

'A harlequin!' Morven mouthed.

Had he killed him?

Then it happened.

The sergeant pushed away the hat which had fallen down over the harlequin's eyes. There was the unexpected glimpse of a young, but wasted face; then the strange sensation that the face was shimmering, dissolving beneath the flickering lamplight. The bright diamonds of the suit of motley flamed out; then, in an instant, the figure was gone, and all that was left lying in the roadway was a hat, with a hole from a musket-ball in the brim, and the empty robes.

Morven gasped. 'That can't happen.'

Sergeant Bunch looked up sharply. 'What are you gawping at, man? Get back to your watch!'

Sergeant Bunch attempted, unsuccessfully, to return to his pleasant dream. It was to no avail. After some fives of tossing and turning, the fat sergeant lit his lamp again and turned his attention, idly, to the beggar's hat and robes that he had retrieved from the roadway. They were tattered and filthy. He thought he might as well fling them on the fire, but some impulse made him examine them.

He turned out the pockets and found only two things. One

335

was a green reed, a sort of whistle. He brought it to his lips and made a high, sharp toot; then he snapped the reed and tossed aside the pieces. Vaga-rubbish! The other thing was a scrap of paper, torn from a book. It was rich, creamy paper, and was carefully folded. Sergeant Bunch unfolded it. A message? There were only four words, penned in an elegant, curving hand. A lady's writing.

Tor, I love you.

The sergeant arched an eyebrow, and wondered if the commander would be interested in this.

Chapter 42

KEY TO THE OROKON

'Am I dying?'

But it was different this time. This time, dying was something gentle, a dreamy, sweet sleep. Jem's eyes flickered open on to a blur of brown-green; then closed again. He might have been floating. The strength that had propelled him from the dormer window seemed only the most distant of memories now; the vertiginous moment before he fell only some old, untroubling pang.

'No, child, you shall not die.'

Jem was not startled to hear the voice. It fluttered into his awareness as a dry leaf, detaching itself from a branch, descends to the rippling surface of a stream. The voice was rich and low; it was weary and wise. In that voice, all the sufferings of the world might have been collected; they might, too, have been redeemed.

It was a voice Jem had heard before.

'Who are you?' he murmured, into the brown-green blur.

'Hush, child. You are not yet strong.'

Jem drifted back into something that was almost, but not quite, sleep. Dimly he recalled himself falling through the air, and the soft, spiky pungency that had broken his fall. He had barely made a sound.

But he was not lying in the hay-stack any more.

Jem stirred.

This time when he opened his eyes they focused. First he saw the rocky contours of the cave, shadowy in the irregular light; then the smoky fire in the centre of the cave; then the dark-robed figure at the fire. The figure turned to him, bearing a chalice. Steam rose from the aromatic liquid.

'Child, drink this.'

Jem drank. The liquid, though bitter, was strangely comforting. Then the image came back to the boy of the laden tea-table at Blossom Cottage.

Shall I pour, Nathanian?

He looked at his hands. His nails were broken and his wrists circled with scratches. He was beginning to shake. He gazed up, and tried to gaze steadily, at the tall, bent figure that loomed over him.

A wicked man. A wicked, wicked man.

And then Jem glimpsed, beneath the old man's cowl, the scar-seamed face with its empty eye-sockets.

'Ugh!'

The gasps of shock, and of pain, came together. Jem jerked upright, suddenly tensed, and at once was aware of a sharp, spreading soreness. He was stinging all over.

Gently the old man took the chalice from his hands.

'Child, be careful. Your wounds are still raw.'

'Wounds?' whispered Jem. For a moment he sank back, blackly despairing, thinking only of Goodman Waxwell's axe. He lifted his head. He looked down, far down, struggling to see. He was lying on some low, crude arrangement of matting. The bottom of the little bed was deep in shadow; but in the shadow Jem could just see, jutting up at angles beneath the blanket, the familiar contours of his feet.

His tension relaxed.

❄ ❄ ❄

Later, Jem would recall his escape from Blossom Cottage.

First he had crawled into the cover of the trees, then deeper into the woods. There, sometimes he had grabbed on to low branches, able to haul himself almost upright; more often he clawed his way forward on his belly, dragging his crippled legs behind him. Sometimes, deep amongst the burrs and briars, he lay exhausted for long minutes, naked, cold and bleeding. Might he have died? There had come a time when he was aware of nothing but pain, and then of nothing; except, in what had seemed a last access of clarity, the contours of the face that had hovered over him, startled and intrigued. By then, the morning glimmered greenly through the leaves, and the face had seemed almost a part of the foliage.

It was not the old man's face.

'I am Catayane.'

It was evening, some days later, when the girl's blurred form at last assumed definition for Jem. Until now she had only lingered in the background of the cowled old man, her father; and yet Jem knew it had been the girl's face that had appeared to him in what had seemed the moment of his death. He was sitting up in his rough bed now, contemplating the bowl of crumbly, sweet chunks that the girl had shyly brought to him.

He looked up.

'Catayane.' He repeated the name slowly; he was shy, too. The girl looked at him. The face beneath the tangle of dark hair was broad, with high cheekbones and deep, intent eyes. Jem gazed into them.

She had saved his life.

Did the boy think then of the dirty little child, years earlier, who had taunted him because he could not walk? Perhaps; but he thought more of himself as he had been then, biting his lip, gripping hard to a frond of trailing ivy, as he held extended, in the palm of his free hand, a glittering golden coin.

You dropped this.

'Do you still have the coin?'

The girl only laughed. That first time, she turned, flitting away. But later, she stayed by his side for longer; and reaching for the boy's fingers she had him feel for a hard

339

circle at the edge of her sackcloth shift. She had sewn the harlequin's gold into the hem.

'I shall always have it,' she said.

Jem, hearing this, felt a strange joy and wonderment; often, when she was beside him, he would feel for the gold.

The days passed.

As Jem's strength returned, Cata would help him, bearing his weight, as he moved from the cave into the glade. There they would sit in the dappled afternoons and into the long evenings, sometimes with the old man, sometimes alone.

Jem marvelled at the strange girl's ways. Sometimes birds or beasts would come to her, a nervous squirrel or robin; once, even a blazing-tailed fox. When Jem asked the girl about her powers, she only shrugged. She seemed barely to understand his amazement.

Indeed there was much she seemed not to understand. Sometimes she would say, 'When you are well, I shall take you to the river,' or, 'When you are well, we shall go deep into the woods. We shall seek Wood-tiger and find his lair.'

Jem would only smile and shake his head. 'I shan't get better, Cata.'

The girl was scornful.

'Your scratches shall vanish, your bruises shall fade. You shall get better. Your legs shall untwist.'

'Cata, I'm a cripple. You know I'm a cripple.'

'It's not true! Papa would break your neck!'

It must have been a game the girl was playing.

❉   ❉   ❉

'Papa,' the boy said later that day, for he had adopted the girl's name for the old man, 'is it your intention to break my neck?'

'You're not frightened of me, are you, child?'

'Frightened?' Jem could only smile. But the thought came to him, as if from another life: 'Aunt Umbecca says you're evil.'

The old man looked solemn. 'In her eyes, I am. There are

340

those who would have us play a part, though it is not our part to play. There are those who would not have us live at all, if we are to live in the same world with them. Umbecca Rench is one such. In your fever, child, you spoke of many things. Terrible things. Poor Umbecca!'

'Papa,' Cata broke in, 'Jem shall walk, shan't he?'

The old man was smoking his pipe, sitting on the stump by the entrance to the cave. He heard the fear in his daughter's voice and drew her to him. 'Child,' he said gently, 'you are thinking of the snow-tern. It could not fulfil its nature. But what of this boy? Shall he fulfil his?'

'Papa, I don't understand!'

Above the high lattice of leaves, the evening edged closer to another darkness. Time was passing, but to Jem, these days he spent in the Wildwood were enchanted, unconnected to the ordinary flow of life.

Only sometimes did the thought come to him that his concealment here could not last. Then he thought with a pang of his mother and Nirry, and it came to him that perhaps they, unlike him, were living through these days in ordinary time.

Did they think he had died?

How much time had passed?

The days of his recovery had drifted by now into a languorous, eternal present.

But these thoughts troubled Jem only as he lay on the brink of sleep; as time kept passing they troubled him less. At night, very lightly, as his wounds faded, the girl would come and lie by him, turning on her side, curling a protective arm across his chest. Serenity possessed them. From deep in the woods, they heard the hooting of the wise damask owl.

Their breath rose and fell softly in unison.

When the last day came, it did not at once announce itself as different from the days that had gone before. There was no chill in the air; no wind rustled the leaves. It did not seem to

Jem that the birds had gone quiet, though later he would reflect that perhaps they had. Perhaps the sun, too, poured more goldenly into the glade, assuming the sickly richness of the Season of Javander; perhaps the leaves were already falling, falling thickly, on to the forest floor.

Yes, the signs were everywhere that day, after all.

'Child, you have resumed the condition in which you set out, that day your aunt led you to the evil cottage. But is this your nature?' the old man asked.

Though the question was a curious one, Jem knew at once what it meant. He found himself trembling; then he became aware of the deep silence that prevailed in the glade. It was some moments before the old man spoke again, and when he did, his voice seemed to come from a distant place.

'There is one more remedy I may try.'

He retreated into the cave, and when he returned, he bore in his hand a small cheesecloth bag. His fingers undid the string that tied its mouth and he poured a little of the contents into his palm. He bent towards the children and they looked on, awed and silent. The sand shimmered dazzlingly in the richness of the sunlight.

'Has the time come, I wonder? I had believed that these grains were for myself, to halt the fading of my damaged senses. But I am old. Soon . . .'

'Papa?'

He was sagging forward. Blunderingly, as if for support, his hand sought for Jem. It was the hand that held the sand. Opening his palm, the blind old man let the grains fall into Jem's hair, over his face and flickering eyelids.

Cata, kneeling beside the boy, drew in her breath.

'If I am right,' her Papa said, 'this child has appeared to us not as he should be, but in the most imperfect mimicry of his nature. This child is one whose appearance in this world is only the merest shadow of the truth of his being.'

Now the old man turned to his daughter.

'My child, gather for me many handfuls of the earth of the Wildwood floor. The richest earth, plenteous with spores and crumbled leaves and the ordure of owls and the dry discarded carapaces of beetle-wings. Collect me fresh, chill water from the river. These elements we shall mix into a lush viscidity, and into The Viscidity we shall stir the glittering sand. Then, I am certain, its magic shall manifest itself to us.'

These things were done; and when they were done, Jem was made to lie in the centre of the glade, wrapped in his blanket on a carpet of leaves. Close beside him, a fire burnt, and suspended over the fire was the bowl that held The Viscidity.

It was beginning to bubble.

※ ※ ※

The old man knelt by the boy and Cata looked on gravely as her Papa, at first slowly, at first softly, began to chant. It was a mumbled gabbling that hinted at strange dimensions; a wild sound, but not an animal sound. It was the sound of a wild human.

Cata rocked on her haunches. She arched back her throat and the wild sound, unbidden, issued also from her tongue.

The fire crackled.

It was a fire built from special barks and branches, and it burnt with a heavy, sweet-smelling smoke. The smoke became thicker; it rose churningly into the air, meeting and mingling with the falling golden light.

With tender hands, Old Wolveron drew open the blanket that enfolded the boy. For long moments the old man's fingers trailed over the pale skin, from forehead to feet, from feet to forehead. Distantly, as if from a great height, Cata gazed on the boy's nakedness. By now, his many scars had faded to invisibility; he was whole again.

Or almost whole.

The boy's eyes were closed and he was barely breathing, and even this shallow breathing, it seemed, was becoming still. He might have been dying.

Tears began to fall from Cata's eyes.

The old man broke off his chanting suddenly. He seized

343

the bowl from the smoking fire and poured The Viscidity suddenly, brutally, over the boy's flesh. Cata cried out, but her cry was hollow, feelingless, like the random unthinking call of a bird.

'Help me, child. Help me,' her Papa said.

Cata answered with the actions of her hands. In the darkness of The Viscidity were a thousand tiny glitterings; she wanted to touch them.

And she wanted to touch the boy.

Eagerly the girl joined her Papa as he spread The Viscidity over the impassive face, over the torso, over the limbs. They rolled the body over, then over again. They poured The Viscidity into the hair and over the eyelids; they rubbed it into the small, tender parts between the thighs. Then, when The Viscidity wholly covered the body, Old Wolveron took the bowed leg in his hands. He massaged the blackened slipperiness. He tightened his grip.

He cried out.

It was as if he were taking, possessing the boy's pain, forcing it through the conduit of his own tormented being.

There was a sound of snapping.

First the bowed leg.

Then the buckled leg.

Cata felt sick. The smoke billowed more intensely from the fire, burning her throat and her streaming eyes. Her vision blackened. When the blackness passed, she saw that her Papa had retreated from the fire and was standing, turned away from her, leaning on his staff.

'Key to the Orokon,' the old man intoned, 'it may be that my magic is not strong enough. It may be that my own damaged being is too frail to take into itself the burden of your suffering. It may be . . . it may be . . .'

He swayed, as if he might fall.

'Papa,' Cata whispered. Then she shouted. 'Papa!'

For Jem, like a figure in a trance, was rising, staggering like a young faun to his feet in the swirling smoke and the golden light. The trance-like expression faded from his face, to be replaced by a spreading, slow astonishment.

He was standing!

He gasped. He cried out. He might have been in pain.

Cata moved forward. The boy was black all over, black as night, but sparkling with a thousand tiny points of light. She grabbed his hands; she drew him to her, marvelling. Smoke obscured her Papa and for an instant they were together, the girl and boy, in an eternal moment that defied the flow of time.

She whispered his name. 'Jem.'

It was like a magic word.

She pulled away.

'Jem!' Suddenly she had released his hands. Suddenly she was running. She hurtled through the woods. 'Jem! Jem!' She shouted the magic word, cried it to the trees and the earth and the air.

She leapt up.

She whirled about.

Yes, she had known it!

He was running after her.

❄ ❄ ❄

In the glade, leaning on his staff, Old Wolveron was swaying, almost falling. Smoke swirled around him like a foreboding of the blindness that now, he thought, would engulf him, finally and for ever. With his half-sister, at the fair, when the girl was small, Wolveron had known that the rare, glittering sand was somehow to be part of the part he must play. He had not known, then, that this part would not save his night-vision, but deprive him of it. It was right. It was good. But if his ruined eyes had been able to sob, the old man would have sobbed at that moment.

'You have played your part well, half-brother,' came a voice.

'Xal?' Wolveron turned.

'The Rapture is stronger in you than I had believed. You

are more than a half-Vaga, Silas! Yours, I am sure now, is a heart that beats wholly for the all-merciful Koros.'

The old woman stepped into the grove. From behind the trees she had been watching, and had seen all that had passed. Tenderly, she led her half-brother to the stump by the cave-mouth and there she sat beside him, gripping his hands. She pushed back his cowl, running her fingers down his mutilated face, along the tracks where the tears might have fallen.

But now the tears might have been tears of joy.

'But Xal,' the old man said in wonderment, 'how is it that you are here? I did not think you should ever come back!'

'Come, Silas, you must have sensed it. We have been here, all the time, while the Key to the Orokon has been here with you. Oh, we are not as we were before. There are only our ragged survivors now, in a shabby camp on the village outskirts. We ply what trade we can, but the old, grand fairs on the village greens are, alas, a thing of the past.' The old woman looked down sadly. 'Besides, soon enough, there shall be different festivities in store for Irion.'

'Xal?'

'It is as was prophesied. The conquerors have carried all before them; and though they are as nothing compared to the evil which soon shall engulf these realms, yet, to the Children of Koros, they can seem evil enough. Wherever the Bluejackets come, we are reviled. In the last cycle, they have pushed us ever northwards from Harion; and even here, we know, they are following behind.'

'But Xal, why have you not made for Agondon? There, can we not still be licensed entertainers?'

'There are many of us who have travelled down the pale highway. But, half-brother, how could I go to Agondon, when I knew our destiny was unfolding here?'

There was a silence between the half-siblings. In the centre of the grove, the smoke was clearing and the fire was dying down.

'Xal, shall I be blind now?' said the old man at last.

Xal looked closely into the ruined face. 'Not yet, half-brother. What you have done today may have prolonged the moment; or perhaps it is just that the moment is not yet. But, yes, half-brother, in time it shall happen. The threads are unravelling. The end may come slowly; it may come quickly. But it shall come.'

'Yes. It is ordained.'

'My dear brother!' A sob caught in Xal's throat and she embraced the old man. 'The Rapture shows us that all is a pattern, and all our sufferings are part of the pattern. At first, Silas, it shall seem that you have failed. But you have not failed. You have played your part, as the dwarf played his. You have begun the Third Stage.

'It is ordained that five times, and in five ways, the Key to the Orokon shall transcend his crippled being. Each time, the power he gains shall be too weak to aid him in his quest. The first time he shall move, but not with his legs; then the second time, again, he shall move, but not with his legs. The third, he shall walk, but only for moments. The fourth, he shall walk again, but only with another. The fifth time shall be the greatest transcendence of all, and come only when he has found his destiny.

'This last transcendence, too, shall fail, for it shall happen in a dimension not our own; but thereafter the child shall walk, and in his own dimension. Only then shall he be ready for his quest. Then the harlequin must play his part.'

'I have feared for the harlequin,' said the old man. 'Is he safe?'

'He is safe, brother. But he is in waiting. His time has not yet come.'

Then the old man felt sad again, at the thought that his own time had been, and now was gone.

❈　❈　❈

It ended, of course. It ended suddenly.

Jem's legs were straight and strong. He crashed through the undergrowth. He caught Cata. She darted away. He caught her again. They whooped and shrieked. On and on they ran. There were no obstacles; the woods faded around them like a green illusion and they could have been careening through a dimension of their own. They cried out their names.

Then it happened.

A horse.

A rider.

They crashed back at once into the dimension they had left. Jem cried out. So did Cata. The horse, huge and black, was rearing in their path, as if at an apparition in its way.

'*Whoa!*'

The rider struggled to control his mount. In a sharp instant, Jem took him in: the black boots, the white breeches, the blue frock coat with its diagonal, white sash. The three-cornered hat.

Cata spun on her heels.

'Jem, quick!' She grabbed his hand.

'Halt!' cried the Bluejacket.

There was a crashing of hooves. There was another rider behind him.

And another.

Another.

'Ugh!' Jem cried out.

His legs crumpled beneath him. He tried to grab Cata's hand again, but could not.

He tried to scramble to his feet again, but could not.

His legs were buckled. It had all been an illusion! It had been an illusion!

The riders surrounded him.

He screamed Cata's name, but suddenly Cata was an illusion, too.

She had vanished.

He could only lie, helpless, as the Bluejackets dismounted and peered down at him, prodding his muddied form with the blades of their bayonets.

'A Vaga-brat?'

'It's a boy.'

'A pity!'

Laughter.

'What shall we do with it?'

The crippled boy hid his face in his hands. Leaves, brittle and golden, fluttered down from the trees.

ＥＮＤ ＯＦ ＰＡＲＴ ＴＨＲＥＥ

PART FOUR

Gallows on the Green

Chapter 43

CANTICLE OF THE FLAG

'I don't like these britches.'

'What do you mean, you don't like them?'

Crum tugged at his crotch. 'They're too tight. And this tunic is silly! I don't see why we can't wear our uniforms.'

Morven rolled his eyes. 'Sergeant Bunch explained, didn't he? We're supposed to blend in. Two simple peasant lads, visiting the Vagas. Really, Crum, I thought you'd find it easy. You of all people.'

'Hm?'

Morven strode ahead. He puffed, only a little gingerly, on his clay pipe. Yes, he had scored another victory there, he thought. Poor Crum really was hopeless. How droll that he, Morven, a fellow of culture and refinement, should be more impressive in the role of Tarn peasant! Still, all the masters at the Junior Academy had praised his Beggar of Wrax. If there was one requirement for acting, Morven knew, it was imagination.

The Vaga-camp came into view, straggling over a field on the outskirts of the village. For the length of the last moonlife, the United Regiments of the Tarn Mission had secreted themselves in the Dale of Rodek, a deserted, deep valley on the far side of the Wildwood. Scouts, on horse or foot, conducted their furtive sorties into the villages they were shortly to subdue. Morven and Crum had a part to play.

'Why are you walking like that?' Crum caught up with Morven.

'What do you mean? I'm being a peasant. Sort of shambling. Hulking. Lumbering.' Morven considered adding that he had modelled his gait on Crum's, but thought better of it.

'You look like someone stuck a carrot up your arse.'

Morven had been drawing back on his clay pipe, and broke off in a fit of coughing. 'Recruit Crum,' he said, recovering himself, 'has anyone ever said you have a positive talent for vulgarity? I recall Professor Mercol said it of Dronwal, the great chronicler of the Late Horen Dynasty. This in my view is a pernicious misapprehension; however, to you, Crum, I think Mercol's ironic praise might not unarguably be applied with . . .'

But Crum was not listening. He gazed towards the Vaga-camp. Clustered about an old barn, the camp straggled across an outlying field, on the first risings of the uplands above the village. To Crum, it was a magic vision, a tableau of painted vans and stripy booths and ponies, bright against the back-drop of the castle and the mountains. Jangling bells and the scrape of a fiddle drifted along the lane, taking Crum back to the Vaga-fairs of his childhood. That was before everything in Varl had got so bad and the Vagas had gone away. This was not a fair; it was poor and paltry and shabby; but here, now, in the Valleys of the Tarn, it was enough for the homesick young man. Suddenly this awful northern place seemed not so awful after all. The day was even warm.

Crum forgot his ill-fitting disguise and skipped forward impatiently.

'Morvy, come on!'

'Crum, this is not supposed to be fun!'

Morven had to run, just a little, to keep up. He was most annoyed. Shambling and hulking did not go together with running. Besides, they were supposed to keep together! For the thousandth time, Morven wished he were back in Agon-don; he even wished that he were sitting in one of Professor Mercol's lectures! A creeping disgust came over Morven as Crum led him into the Vaga-camp.

In Morven's eyes, the camp was only a mean collection of broken-down vans and faded tents. Smoke drifted up lag-gardly from little, random fires. Skin-and-bones horses wandered where they would, untethered. There were naked, dirty children. Say what one would about the military, at least they kept things in a certain order. The Vaga-camp was nothing but jumble, dirt and noise. There could be no life of the mind in such a place! A woman in a turban and bright robes passed them by, and Morven was appalled to note that she held a sucking infant to her breast. She smiled at Morven; to his greater horror, there even appeared to be something of a certain . . . *invitation* in her eyes.

Morven flushed scarlet.

A group of dark men, with rings in their ears, looked up at the two imitation peasants. In their look was neither suspicion nor hostility, but there was, perhaps, something knowing. Perhaps it was just that the men were intoxicated, thought Morven with distaste. They were passing a large earthenware jug between them and swigging from it fulsomely. One of the men was plucking at a curious stringed instrument. Around his forehead he wore a purple band.

Morven shuddered and pulled Crum away. Crum protested. He had been about to accept a swig from the earthenware jug. The men laughed as the soldiers staggered away.

Crum was unabashed.

'Morvy, look!' The young Varlan pointed to a dark blue curtain, embroidered brightly with stars. 'It's the Woman of Wisdom! Come on, let's see if she's there!'

But this time Morven did not follow his friend. His jaw was set firm, but a faraway look had come into his eyes. He knew what he must do. Mentally, he would compose a description of these degraded people and their camp; he thought that perhaps a certain hint of the versification of Dronwal, suitably modernized, would be exactly what he needed. Yes. His thoughts pushed themselves into ornate couplets. When it was time to give their report, Sergeant Bunch would be staggered by Recruit Morven's powers.

And suddenly Morven was happy.

It was the old maid who had the first apprehension.

One morning in the yard behind Blossom Cottage, as she hung out Goody Waxwell's underpetticoats, the old servant was surprised by the apparition of a crone, more ancient than herself, who hobbled forward, holding aloft a small wicker basket. 'Thimbles, needles or bobbins?' The crone's voice was wavering, but imperceptibly became firmer, fuller, as she enquired as to the darning the old maid might do, and the colour of the costumes she should most like to mend.

Aron Throsh, that is to say Bean, was the next to sense that something odd was about to happen. At the Lazy Tiger, dabbing a moustache of ale-froth from his lips, a neat, precise young man who had ridden up on a roan mare suddenly gripped Bean by the arm and asked if the boy could recite the Chain Prayer. Bean's bowels registered a lurch of fear; his character of late had become furtive, secretive.

'Leave the boy be,' slurred Stephel, deep in his cups.

Later, driving back up the road to the castle, the old man stopped to toss a coin to a beggar. Until now, he had never seen a beggar on this road; but before he could consider this, the ragged figure was sitting on the cart beside him, telling him of his sorrows, inviting Stephel's confidences in return. Next morning in the castle, Nirry had to turn the beggar out. Something about him left her ill at ease. 'Motley! I ask you!' she heard the fellow saying, leaning towards her father with a strange intensity. The beggar was speaking of other members of his profession, expatiating on their oddities. Insinuatingly he mentioned a fellow who wore, concealed beneath his rags, the garb of a harlequin.

'You'd never have seen a fellow like that now, Master Stephel?'

It was all over a few days later.

In the days before the Bluejackets came, shrivelling leaves were detaching themselves from the branches and drifting dryly on to the air. On the last evening, Goody Throsh paused as she donned her red wig and gazed out over the green. 'A change is coming,' she said to herself. Clouds had gathered and the lingering light might have been strained through an unaccustomed filter; the houses on the far side had assumed an air of fantasy, as if they were not wholly tethered to the ground. The old woman rouged her cheeks and went below. A brown leaf fluttered against the window. It caught briefly against a pane, then scurried away.

'And just the other day I thought it was warmer,' Recruit Crum was complaining at that moment. Crum's mouth was full. In the depths of the Dale of Rodek, the young Varlan peasant sat huddled in his greatcoat, glumly spooning up his lumpy rations. He looked accusingly at Recruit Olch. 'You said I'd get used to it, Wiggler!'

'I never. Brr!' Olch mimed an exaggerated shiver. 'You ain't seen the first of it yet, Varly. You know, if I was you, I'd be pissing in me pants from now on.'

'What?'

'It's like me old man used to say, I reckon. *Chilly air, chilly there*. Stands to reason, don't it? I'd watch out, Varly. Certain things might – snap. Know what I mean?'

'No!' Crum's eyes grew wide.

Soldier Rotts laughed, his paunch wobbling. 'Don't worry, lad. Them Tarnies might put a bit of heat under all our arses, come the morning! You're quiet, Professor. What do you reckon, eh?'

Hunched over, Morven tore off another chunk of his bread. The young scholar had been quiet for some days. He was humiliated. He had composed such a brilliant speech about the Vagas. He had thought that Sergeant Bunch might be impressed; perhaps even take him to repeat it before the chaplain. But Sergeant Bunch had only shouted at him and told him to talk properly. Properly! Morven looked up, as if into the distance. All he could see was a line of latrines. Miserably he struggled to answer the question.

'You speak as if we might be in a foreign land, Master Rotts. Yet this is Ejland, is it not? Might one not argue that the Tarn is to be seen not as a part peripheral to the Agonist lands, but as the very element most vital to their identity? Consider, for the sake of argument, the Chronicles of Dronwal . . .'

Pwarrp!

'Aw, Rottsy!'

Soldier Rotts flapped the tail of his coat. 'It's them beans!'

Recruit Olch sniggered, and wiggled his ears, just for the sake of it. Recruit Crum, huddled in his greatcoat, sniffed. The thought of the morning filled him with dread. They would have to march again, and it would be so cold!

❈ ❈ ❈ ❈

Next morning, the change foretold by Goody Throsh had come decisively.

All through the night the leaves had scurried, rat-like, over the green, pursued by sharp, fitful squalls of rain. Now a grey, drizzling mist hung over the village, and Aron Throsh, carefully carrying a cracked earthenware pot, could see only a dim haze through the window on the landing as he descended the stairs from the Nova-Riel Room. Lying in bed, he had listened all night to the scurrying rats. 'What is to happen?' he said aloud, several times, while Polty snored. Their room stank again. For the length of the last moonlives, Polty's stomach, or more precisely his bowels, had experienced a series of violent disturbances.

Bean stepped gratefully into the chill tavern yard. He breathed deeply. It was as he was upending the heavy pot that the boy heard the blast.

Boom!

It was like thunder. Birds wheeled and cried.

In the silence that followed, Bean lowered the chamber-pot slowly to the ground. The latest liquid issue of Polty's bowels formed a dark sludge in the bottom of the sluice-drain. Cautiously, Bean padded back on his bare feet into the tavern. He crossed to the window of the empty bar-room and opened it, peering out. The sound had come from the green.

'Aron! What was it?' His mother's voice floated anxiously down the stairs.

Thud.

Thud.

Then came the drumbeats, and it was the drumbeats, more than the blast, that signalled that the old days in Irion had ended. Something had happened.

It had happened at last.

The villagers gathered slowly on the green. Rain began to fall. Finely it pattered over the brown of the faded grass and the yellow of tiny weeds and the mauve and red and orange of the fallen leaves; steadily it webbed the dun-coloured, huddled shoulders of the peasants and the bright jackets of the soldiers. It slipped around the black, open lips of the cannon; it slithered on the whiteness of the beating drumskins; it sluiced from the brim of the chaplain's hat as he surveyed, doubtfully, the scene before him.

'Do you think they're all here, Sergeant?'

'Not all, sir.'

'Well – there's enough, I dare say.'

The drumbeats ceased, and with a little assistance from the sergeant, the chaplain stood up awkwardly on the barrel that he had commandeered in haste, if with ample apologies, from the boy at the tavern. Imposingly, Eay Feval unrolled a creamy parchment. He cleared his throat.

A horse whinnied.

Laughter.

'Women and men of Irion . . .'

At the edges of the crowd, already some were slipping away. Eay Feval smiled tightly. Something should have been done. But. But. The commander had been precise. Nothing but what was strictly necessary. Surreptitiously, Eay Feval patted his pistol, feeling the satisfying heaviness against his ribs.

'Women and men of Irion . . .'

Plop!

He was holding up the parchment at a high angle, but to no avail. The ink was running. Feval sighed. Never mind. He would improvise. He took a deep breath and the words rolled easily from his lips.

He proclaimed the splendours of the Bluejacket regime; he proclaimed the power and glory of His Imperial Agonist Majesty, the might of his armies and the justice of his laws, his valour and his mercy and his wisdom and his piety; he lauded the great victories in the Zenzan lands and the new glories which now were to descend like gentle rain (there were sniggers in the crowd) to every corner of the blessed and most-favoured kingdom of Ejland.

Irion was to be restored to its former glory.

Irion was to become a garrison town.

'All hail the King!'

'The King!' the soldiers cried; and the wet drums slapped out a rhythm again as the Bluejacket standard was unfurled over the green. Pipes skirled, shrilling out the Canticle of the Flag, last and greatest of the Songs of Prevailing. At this point, the commander had suggested, Eay Feval might lead the villagers in song. The fervour of the anthem would stir their simple hearts.

Cement new loyalties.

Heal old wounds.

Eay Feval, looking at the villagers, could hardly think it a good idea. They had probably forgotten the words.

Chapter 44

THE CHAPLAIN CALLS

Some days later, the chaplain paid two calls. Both were to villagers who had not appeared in response to the summoning drumbeats.

His first visit took him to the castle.

'Captain Feval, ma'am,' sniffed a sullen servant girl, ushering him into a cavernous apartment. How shabby it was! How gloomy! With a fastidious air, the chaplain looked about him. Through the curtains of a big bed, he glimpsed the supine form of an invalid. The fat woman in black, sitting by the fire, made no effort to rise. She did not even look at him. His lips pursed tightly.

'Mistress Rench?'

'Captain? I had been expecting your commander.'

Feval coloured. He had not expected this woman to be difficult. Was she not a sister-by-marriage to the Archduke of Irion? He assumed her to be a loyalist. He hoped he was not about to find himself mistaken.

He bowed low. 'Please, my good woman: do not imagine that it is the intention of my commander to show disrespect. Know that I, Eay Feval, am merely an outrider, an emissary, an ambassador who offers the first distant implication of greeting from one who shall, in time, receive you with the full ceremony to which you are entitled. Might I add, too, that I am, for my sins' – he gave a little laugh – 'not *captain*, but *chaplain*?'

'Chaplain?'

The fat woman had appeared to be sunk deep in some private misery of her own. Sorrow hung over the apartment like a pall. It was a sorrow greater, Eay Feval sensed, than any occasioned by the arrival of the Bluejackets. But now the woman was looking up at him with a flicker of interest. She took in his immaculate black garb. Her hand, trembling just a little, hovered over a bell. 'You'll take tea?'

'Indeed, my good woman.' It might be politic; Feval always wished to do what was politic. Mistress Rench was a woman of some importance, after all.

She rang for the servant.

With an affected polite nonchalance Eay Feval gazed about him, mentally rehearsing the topics of conversation. First, the castle. Yes. Forgiveness was to be sought of the good woman for the disruptions she must suffer as several of the United Regiments took up residence in the bailey. Fulsome assurance must follow that her own apartments were on no account to be disturbed. Yes, that was right; though care should be taken not to imply that her consent or permission was required in the disposal of the castle. It was not. At this point, in order to prompt patriotic feeling, something of the quality and valour of the United Regiments might be established, with particular reference to the Fifth Royal Fusiliers of the Tarn. The chaplain might show the woman his own regimental badge – it *was* rather attractive – and expatiate on the glorious role played by the Fifth in the late Zenzan wars. In the long cycles of their exile, he might say, the regiment had yet retained the Tarn spirit. No need to add that not a single Tarn man was now to be found in any of the old regiments.

Yes, that would do. That would do nicely. The preliminaries over, Eay Feval might then introduce the real topic of his visit.

There was a crash and a high-pitched cry.

It came from below.

'What is it?' The chaplain sprang up. His hand darted for his pistol. The men were below; he was in no danger. But something was wrong.

From the stairs came the slap-slap of hurrying feet.

The maid shrieked for a second time when she barged in to find the chaplain's pistol aimed directly at her face.

'By the Lord Agonis, do shut up!' her mistress demanded. 'What is it, girl?'

The maid caught her breath. 'It's Master Jem, ma'am—'

'What?' The fat woman's face was suddenly pale.

'Them soldier-men downstairs. I saw them. They've got him!' The girl launched herself at Eay Feval, knocking the pistol from his hand. 'Filthy Bluejackets!' She gouged his eyes.

'Nirry!'

It was over in a moment; a sharp slap from the girl's mistress restored calm. The pistol lay gleaming on the worn carpet; Eay Feval returned it swiftly to the interior of his jacket. In its place he brought forth a crisp white handkerchief, dabbing at the skin above his left eye. Really! It was too much. The vulgar little minx had drawn blood.

Mistress Rench retreated to the hearth. She was facing the mantelpiece, her back turned from him, as she offered levelly, 'Chaplain, I trust you will accept my apologies.'

'Indeed, my good woman. But this little misunderstanding perhaps may be turned to good effect, introducing as it does the deeper purpose of my visit.' He crossed to the door and called down to the men. 'Have the boy brought up, Corporal. No need to delay. I think we have established his provenance,' he added, with a tight smile for the maid.

The maid sat snivelling.

'A patrol found the boy in the woods,' the chaplain explained. 'Naked. Covered in mud from head to foot, I ask you! At first we thought he was a Vaga-brat – they lose them sometimes, as they ramble about. Of course we quizzed the boy, but he seemed to remember nothing of his ordeal. It was the local surgeon who informed us that a young cripple had gone missing. Vagas again, I have no doubt. They sell the clothes; it's surprisingly common. Still, I'm glad to report that they left his hair. And teeth.'

'The Lord Agonis be praised!' The fat woman's face, turning back from the fireplace, was a study in emotion. Her expression bespoke the long anguish of one whose child was missing; the sudden rapture of unexpected reunion; the troubled anticipation of the child's continuing distress. 'And you say he remembers nothing?'

'Not a thing.'

'Poor Jem!'

※ ※ ※ ※

The chaplain's second call was to the Lazy Tiger.

Equally formal, it was accomplished more simply. The crone who kept the tavern, hideous with her red wig and bright-painted cheeks, endeavoured a little resistance at the door, until her lanky boy had the sense to intervene.

'The surgeon's boy. Where is he?' Eay Feval snapped.

No pretence of politeness was required this time; his pistol drawn, the chaplain thundered up the stairs to the Nova-Riel Room. It was really rather exciting; besides, Sergeant Bunch's men were behind him, and the chaplain knew there was no real danger. He opened the door and a most unpleasant aroma, like excrement, assailed his nostrils.

It *was* excrement.

'Master Waxwell? Poltiss Waxwell?'

The bloated figure on the bed barely stirred. The chaplain turned awkwardly.

Sergeant Bunch knew what to do.

'Get up, lad. You're under arrest.'

Chapter 45

JEM ON THE SCAFFOLD

The transformation of the village was swift. Waxing had almost declined to black when the Bluejackets arrived; by the next Westmoon, Irion might never have slept, as it had slept, for so many years. The castle was a hubbub of life. Soldiers thronged the ancient courtyards. The 'Blue Ejard' fluttered from the battlements. Convoys of carts, like slithering serpents, wound their way up to the crag.

Below, the village green was all tents, vans, crates, whinnying horses. It was almost as if the Vaga-fair had returned, but in a strange new guise. Gone were the flowing silks and glittering trinkets; in their place were musket-balls and spit-and-polish boots. Bugles and drums and shrill pipes replaced the fiddles and the hurdy-gurdy.

All over the village, barns and stables, houses and fields were pressed into the service of the United Regiments. The castle alone could not accommodate their numbers. 'How many are there?' the villagers asked each other. They could not say; the soldiers on the green, that first morning, seemed but a fraction of the numbers who now appeared. For a time, parties of arriving Bluejackets were seen on the road into the village each day. Some said there were a thousand. Some said ten thousand. The villagers knew only that the Bluejackets now far exceeded them in number.

It was only a short time before the tithes were imposed. The restoration of the village was a vast task, after all, and the villagers must pay their share. Parties of Bluejackets visited every dwelling, demanding payment in coins or kind. Few could afford it; but few would refuse. Those who did were denounced as traitors and bundled away to the castle dungeons. Over the moonlives to come, villagers would resort to desperate measures to pay the tithes. Some would sell all their possessions. Some would be forced to sell themselves. Some would go to the Vaga-camp, seeking loans; but the Vagas had no loans to give.

Vaga-tithes were double.

The Vaga-camp was raided regularly. The Vagas paid their tithes; nonetheless, they were suspected of all manner of crimes. There was a great deal of stealing in the village after the tithes were imposed, and when anything was stolen, the Vagas were blamed. Soon, they were blamed for more things, too; and when it was for things they could not possibly have done, the talk turned darkly to 'Vaga-magic'. The villagers, it seemed, had forgotten all the delight that 'Vaga-magic' once gave them. Now, if milk went sour, it was Vaga-magic. If an apple went rotten, it was Vaga-magic. When the weather was bad, it was Vaga-magic again; and the weather, in the Tarn, was usually bad. How the villagers hated the Vagas! Frequently Vagas were set upon and attacked. Some were killed. But the Vagas never protested; for who, after all, would listen if they did? Not the Bluejackets; and not the villagers, who blamed the Vagas for the miseries of their lot. Though the Bluejackets had begun to punish the Vagas severely, there were many who said they were not severe enough. There was no end to the trouble the Vagas were causing.

It was Vaga-crime, for example, that made the curfew necessary. It did not apply to Bluejackets, of course; only to the villagers, for their own protection, and to the Vagas, to keep them from marauding at night. After the passing of the twelfth fifteenth, no villager and no Vaga was to be seen at large.

Villagers would be taken into custody.

Vagas would be hanged.

Later, Jem would think back with horror to the first time he saw a hanging.

When the Bluejackets had broken up their camp on the green, they had left one thing after them: a gallows. The first victims were villagers who had failed to pay their tithes. Then, after a short time, the victims would be Vagas. Vagas, caught doing this or that. Vagas after curfew. Vagas stealing bread. Vagas abducting babies from their cots.

So many Vagas.

So many hangings.

The hangings would become a regular thing. Once in each phase, on the day before Canonday, the peasants would gather on the village green. Drums would beat when the time drew near, but the excited crowd would need no summoning. The atmosphere was festive. Vendors hawked ale and delicious, rock-hard Tarn-cakes. First would come the declaiming of the Vaga's crime, and the peasants would boo and hiss. Then, when the trapdoor dropped beneath the Vaga's feet, they would cheer. The 'Blue Ejard' would be raised again, and again the band would play the Canticle of the Flag.

It was the chaplain who accompanied Jem to the hanging. Aunt Umbecca declined to attend. She thought that the event, though undoubtedly a good thing, might be a little distressing – but edifying, perhaps, for Jem. They were hanging the Vaga who had kidnapped him.

The chaplain had asked if Jem would be able to stand on his crutches on the scaffold, while the crime was declaimed. In times to come, Jem would regret that he had agreed to this; and regret still more, with a bitter, deep sorrow, the useless and wicked sacrifice that was made before him that day. But it was shortly after Jem's return to the castle, and his mind was still unclear. Everyone had spoken of the evil Vaga, and Jem's narrow escape.

The accused was a man Jem had never seen before. Jem was never even told the man's name; the man was described only as a 'filthy Vaga'. But he was not filthy; he was only dark-skinned. For a Vaga, he looked strangely naked. They had stripped him of his bright costume and his turban and dressed him in a drab grey robe. Afterwards, Jem found out later, they took the robe away to use it again next time. Truly naked, the Vaga was then bundled into a pit on the edge of the village. Heathen Vagas could not be buried in the tomb-yard. The man did not look brave and he did not look strong, but he faced his death with a startling, almost unnerving calmness.

On the scaffold, Jem stood swaying, looking down at the faces that looked up at him. In his confusion, he felt a sense of power; he felt a curious wonderment. Beside him, the chaplain spoke of the evil of the Vagas, who would stoop even to the abduction of a mere cripple. When Aunt Umbecca had told Jem this story, her voice had trembled and she had burst into tears. From the lips of the chaplain, it was a rousing piece of oratory, bursting with righteous indignation. With a sweeping gesture, he flung back his arm, gesturing at the slender, swaying figure of the cripple.

'. . . An innocent walk through a leafy lane! Picture the scene: bright, dappled sunlight shone through the trees! Birds sang! The sky, above the lattice of the branches, was blue! Who could believe that this sweet scene should turn so swiftly into a scene of horror? Picture this poor cripple and his aunt, chattering happily, enjoying the sweetness of nature on a warm day. Then picture the poor woman looking away for the merest moment, delighted at the sight of a butterfly on a leaf. "Here, dear Jemany! Look at the bright butterfly!" she calls, turning back, her face overspread with a smile imbued with all the tenderness of her love for the boy. But lo! the unspeakable horror of that moment; for while the loving aunt has turned, out creeps the wicked Vaga-man from the trees! Has the poor cripple even had time to scream? No! In a flash, the poisonous handkerchief is clapped across his face!'

Jem could barely listen to the chaplain's words. The faces before him shifted and blurred. He was still not well, he was sure of it. He had expected his aunt to call in Goodman Waxwell, but when he had asked if he would have to see the physician, Aunt Umbecca had turned, almost brusquely, and said that he would not. Quite unnecessary! But the poisonous handkerchief, Jem was sure, was still affecting him. He thought of the Vaga-man and felt a surge of anger. What might the Vaga have done to him in the woods? The chaplain had said Jem should consider himself lucky that he still had his teeth.

And his eyes.

Yet how unreal it all seemed! Since the Bluejackets had brought Jem back to the castle, the only things that had seemed real and solid were the crutches on which he was standing now. He remembered the terrible helplessness he had felt, after the soldiers laid him down on the sofa. Then came his aunt sailing blackly towards him, bearing in her hands the magnificent sticks. *I saved them for you, Jem.* Her voice was trembling. *They were lying in the lane when the Vagas took you.* Dear Aunt Umbecca! How grateful Jem had been!

'A mere cripple!' the chaplain cried again. 'And yet, this boy is no *mere* cripple. On the contrary: all of us who live in these valleys owe young Jemany Vexing a debt; for the terrible story of this abject boy may be seen, rather, as a beacon in our path, lighting the way to the truth about the Vagas. For epicycles, we of Ejland have languished under the persecutions of this wicked tribe. Beguiled by their seductive ways, have we not failed to take the true measure of their depravity? Increasingly, their vileness may be seen in all its colours. A Vaga, let us recall, is a follower of Koros; and like his dark god, he is evil! He is dangerous! Women and men of Irion, let us all cheer now as this wicked Vaga meets his deserved death!'

The drumroll sounded.

That day, Jem's eyes filled unaccountably with tears as the trapdoor dropped beneath the evil Vaga-man.

Chapter 46

POLTY IN A BLACK HOLE

Polty knew despair.

He did not know where they had taken him. As they bundled him from the Lazy Tiger, the Bluejacket thugs had not only bound him, hand and foot, but blindfolded him and knocked him on the head for good measure. It was gross injustice; the fat young drunkard had barely been capable of struggling. All he had known was a queasy sensation of jogging, jostling; pushing, pulling. There was a clip-clop of hooves and the rumble of a cart and heavy boots on stone steps. There were coarse voices raised in laughter. Once, suddenly and shockingly, a rough hand grabbed him between the legs. It squeezed. Polty would have cried out, but that was when he realized that they had gagged him, too.

A heavy door squealed back. Then came oblivion.

By now, he did not know how much time had passed. In a damp, stinking cellar, he lay on straw, chained to a wall. There was no light. Sometimes he could hear the guards talking on the other side of the door, but the door was too thick for him to hear what they said.

There were some, it was true, who would have said that Polty's new life scarcely differed from his old one. When he was free, he lived in filth and darkness; now he was in a dungeon, he did the same. When he was free, he lay motionless all day; in the dungeon, he did the same. Had the Bluejackets wished to imprison Polty, it might have been said, they needed merely to place a guard on the door of the Nova-Riel Room.

Or not even that.

But this was not true; and as Polty lay in this new filth and darkness, he was slowly discovering why. It had been his choice to languish, as he had languished, in the Nova-Riel Room. Now, all choice had been taken from him. The difference was fundamental.

There was, besides, another difference; and one which, from Polty's point of view, was equally fundamental.

He had nothing to drink.

And nothing to eat.

'Half-sister! What is it?'

This time, when the wise woman came to Old Wolveron, she did not manifest herself like a wraith from the silence, but blundered into the grove and cast herself before him, her body wracked with sobs.

It startled the old man, for he had never seen his half-sister in such distress. At that moment, he was himself in despair. He had been waiting for her on the stump by the cave-mouth. He had thought she had come in answer to his call; he saw now that she had her own desperate suffering. He struggled for command of himself and gripped Xal's hands. With his weakening powers, only after a time could he understand her pain.

Of course.

The man who had been hanged for the boy's abduction.

It was her son.

Trembling, Xal told of how the Bluejackets had come, bursting into the camp on the morning of the hanging. 'When I heard the drumbeats from the green, I thought my heart would break. I had sensed, as we travelled here from Harion, that my son's death was soon approaching, and he would meet it in the Tarn. But, oh Silas! To meet it like this! I know that the suffering of this time is ordained. I know that these things must come to pass, but now I feel that The Rapture is no aid to me in my agony. Silas, I have cursed! I have cursed The Rapture, and I have cursed our destiny!'

A new flood of tears burst from her eyes, and the blind

man, slipping from the stump to his knees, embraced the old woman, awkwardly but hard. Withered, crisp leaves were falling about them and the air was chill. After a time, when Xal's tears had again subsided, Old Wolveron began a speech he had long meditated.

'Half-sister, you came to watch me as I played my part. Now I have played it. I am an old man, weak and confused. Seldom do I wander the Wildwood now, for I fear that I shall lose my way. Now, I glimpse nothing of The Rapture. I languish here, enveloped in my past—'

The old woman's grip tightened on his hands. 'Silas, there may come a crisis which shall yet propel you forth!'

The old man moaned. 'Tell me not of it, half-sister. I can bear no more. For me, there is nothing beyond this place. But Xal, why do you stay? Why do your people stay?'

'Half-brother, indeed The Rapture has weakened in you! Our destiny here is not complete. I am bound not to go; but Silas, there is more. There are those of my people who have tried to go, rumbling in their vans along the pale highway. But Bluejacket soldiers guard the roads. They turn us back, with curses and threats. They want us here, Silas. They want us to stay.'

Drying her tears, the old woman let her gaze wander now about the grove. That was when she saw that something was wrong. At the mouth of the cave, the curtain of vines had been torn away; inside, Xal could see that her half-brother's few possessions had been overturned.

The cave had been ransacked.

'Oh, Silas! I have been lost in my own distress! What has happened here? What has happened to you?'

The old man sighed. 'They have been here, Xal. I am thankful only that the girl was not here when they came. She might have been driven to some wildness; then, perhaps, they would have taken her, too. Half-sister, they were looking for someone. When they could not find him, they turned their attention to me.'

Xal nodded. 'They were looking for one who wears the

garb of a harlequin. Many times they have sought him in our camp. But Silas, they have not hurt you?'

'Only threats, half-sister. Evil words. I am unhurt by those, after all I have endured. But it seems, Xal, that it avails me not to have in me only *half* the blood of a Child of Koros. In their eyes, I am as much the Vaga as you, and must pay the double tithe. If I do not pay, they shall hang me. Will that be the silence that comes at last upon my senses?'

'Oh, Silas!' The tears came again to Xal's eyes. 'All that I have is yours, but . . . oh, how shall we bear this?'

'Perhaps we shall not. If I were young again, I should hide in the Wildwood where they should never find me. But I am old, and cannot run from them. I think only of my poor child. Xal, what shall become of her? In the next moonlife they shall return for the tithes. When I have nothing to give them, they shall take me. I shall have to tell the girl – soon I must tell her. But I am frightened at what she may do.'

Xal looked down sadly, and thought of the bitterness their fate held in store.

❈   ❈   ❈   ❈

It seemed that an eternity of blackness had passed before the bolts of the dungeon slid back. Polty stirred from a miasma of hunger and fear and craving for drink and mad, vengeful thoughts. Dimly he was aware that he had soiled his breeches, front and back. His stench rose about him like the vile aroma of a sewer.

'Here.'

That was all the guard said as he slammed down a metal tray on the floor. On the tray were three things; the first being a chipped, dirty bowl, containing a lumpy mixture of luke-warm gruel.

Rations!

At last!

Polty was so starving that he fell upon the gruel like a ravening beast, slurping and guzzling and scooping with his hands. He lolled back, almost grateful, only wishing there had been more. For a time, until the foul mixture had worked through his guts, and a fresh load of squelching liquid filled his breeches, Polty might even have said that he enjoyed his meal. But then, he would have guzzled up a trough of pig-swill, had there been one there.

The bowl, licked clean, lay upturned in the straw beside him. Languishing again, only slowly did Polty even consider the two remaining items that had been left for him on the tray. The first was a candle. It was not much of a candle; only the merest stump, already on the verge of slipping, guttering out, in a lake of hot wax. Soon it would die, but to Polty at that moment any light was tantamount to a miracle. Gratitude welled in his heart for this simple kindness; for a moment he almost considered that perhaps he might even venture to thank the guard, next time his rations came.

If they came.

Then he saw the paper. It must have been slipped underneath the bowl; now it was stuck to the bottom. Polty pulled it away and gazed at it in the candlelight, turning it over in his hands. It was a small, folded square.

It was a letter.

In the time – it seemed such a long time – since he had been thrown into the dungeon, Polty had been consumed alternately by hunger, rage and fear. In his madness – for it was, he knew, a madness – he had not tried to think about his imprisonment at all. He had not asked himself why they had locked him up; he had not wondered what would happen to him next. Now, as he opened the letter, Polty's heart bounded, and it seemed to him that these very questions had burned in him all along.

Would the letter offer a clue?

Had Polty considered the matter, he might have expected the letter to be from, say, the Bluejacket commander, setting out the nature and terms of his sentence. Or perhaps, in view of its manner of delivery, he might have expected a secret letter, some comforting assurance of an impending escape-plan, smuggled in by a friendly guard.

It was neither of these things.

The letter was from Leny; but it had not, Polty realized, been addressed to him.

It was a suicide note.

The candle guttered and the cell was dark.

Chapter 47

THE CHAPLAIN CALLS AGAIN

Business was booming at the Lazy Tiger.

Goody Throsh was enthralled; or rather, she would have been enthralled, if one thing had not made her miserable. Late one night, as she was wiping down her tables, the old woman suddenly threw down her cloth.

'What I don't understand,' she burst out, 'is *why*.'

Her son had been bolting the doors, and went to her.

'Oh Aron, you're too young!' she moaned. She was close to tears. 'You don't remember the last time! They don't come to build! They come to destroy.' Her make-up was a moist sludge, oozing down her face; her embrace was tight and clinging.

Clutched for a moment, almost breathless, against his mother, Aron Throsh felt a surge of love, and a terrible regret for all the bitter, spoiling things that had, as he saw it, blighted his life. At that moment he would have liked to sink to the floor with the old woman, sobbing with her endlessly; for a moment it seemed that she wanted this, too. Then his emotion was checked when he heard the glugging words that welled up through his mother's tears:

'Poor, poor Master Polty!'

It was Goody Throsh who broke off the embrace.

When her voice returned, it was suddenly hard. 'Well, it's back to the old days, then!' She wiped her face with the back of her hand and adjusted her red wig.

'Ma?'

'Oh, for the sake of the Lord Agonis, boy! Don't stand there gawping!'

Later, from the window of the room he had shared with Polty, Aron sat staring sleeplessly. His heart was too full to lie on the bed and he kept thinking he would cry again. First he would think of his mother and then he would think of Polty. Round and round it went.

Behind him, the stench of the room was gone. The sheets were clean and he had rolled up the carpets. Before him, the green was quiet at last. Only the murmurings of a pair of sentries drifted up to him on the chill air.

'Wiggler?'

'Hm?'

'Where you from then, eh?'

'Me? Holluch. Holluch-on-the-Hill, they call it.'

'Is it a pretty place?'

'No place like it, Varly.'

Vaguely, Aron imagined a house on a hill. Smoke curled from a chimney and the sun shone. In the sky there were white puffy clouds; in the grass were big, round-faced flowers. Children played. 'They all wiggle, then?'

'What?'

'In the hill place. Do they all wiggle like you?'

'I'll say! *If it's not wiggling, it's wobbling.* That's what they say, home in Holluch. You should see me old dad.'

The soldier called Crum shifted his feet. 'Wiggler?'

'Hm?'

'What they make us come here for, then?'

'What?'

'I mean, what we come all this way for? What for?'

Wiggler sniffed. 'Stands to reason, don't it? War and stuff.'

'Oh.'

Aron closed the casement at last.

❋ ❋ ❋ ❋

In the time since the Bluejackets had come to Irion, the villagers had caught not a single glimpse of the man who had become their new military governor. It was not to be wondered at; the soldiers, in all their long march from the south, had never been addressed by their commander-in-chief. All was relayed through the chaplain. Rumour grew; and when a blue coach was seen passing through the village, heavily guarded and with curtains drawn, rumour flourished. Some said the commander was a sick man and should never have undertaken the long journey. Some said he was deformed, or horribly wounded. Some said he was so unimpressive in person that he preferred not to show himself, but to remain the puppet-master, working behind the scenes.

One day, by the Lectory gates, two small boys glimpsed a grossly fat form being helped from the coach into a sedan chair. Dressed in an ornate elaboration of the Bluejacket uniform, with glittering epaulettes and many medals, the fat man grunted as his men moved him. Loudly he complained of his gout, and several times lashed about him with a bejewelled stick, catching his men several passing blows. It was a blustery afternoon, but the soldiers sweated under their burden as they carried the fat man up the cinder-path.

This was the first inkling the villagers had that their new governor was to reside not in the castle keep, like the departed Archduke, but in the Lectory.

To Umbecca Rench, it was a sacrilege; but only at first. She thought back to the time of the Siege. In the Siege, it was from the Lectory, deserted by then by its rightful incumbent, that the Bluejacket general had directed his assault. Umbecca was divided; if she feared the Bluejackets, at the same time she sensed that their cause was right. Her problem was how to ally herself to it; how to enter adequately into its spirit.

Memories came back to her.

You do see, Becca, don't you?

Her brother-by-marriage had stroked her hair and kissed her eyelids on the night before he gave up the king to Commander Veeldrop.

It has to be the Blues.

Yes. It was right.

Blue is the side of the Lord Agonis now. You do see, Becca, don't you?

Umbecca had wept; but she knew that her brother-by-marriage was right.

These reflections played heavily on her mind the day the chaplain paid his next call.

※ ※ ※ ※

'You will recall, my good woman, that I declared myself to be but an outrider, an emissary, of my commander.'

He bowed low, and with a flourish produced a square of card, fluttering it for a moment on the air before her eyes. He had not endeavoured to remove his dress gloves, Umbecca noticed; the creamy square of card in the white hand was a sight tantalizing to the fat woman.

The chaplain held the card against his chest for a moment, pacing the shabby carpet.

Hm.

His brow furrowed.

Something better might be brought up from supplies.

He looked towards the bed. This time the curtains had not been drawn. The girl was very pale. Beneath her eyes were dark circles; a little black bottle lay beside her on the table. Ah yes. In a flash, Feval saw a memory of his mother, who had lived for six cycles behind drawn blinds in her luxurious town house in Agondon.

He turned, smiling. 'Your niece is improving, I trust?'

'Poor Ela! I am afraid improvement is hardly to be hoped for. She rallied; but my nephew's disappearance was of course a great blow to her.'

It was true. How long, how hard Ela had fought against the sticky grip of the treacle! But when she had thought the boy was gone, Ela's craving had returned in full force. This time it could not be resisted. Poor Ela! Umbecca could not conceal the hint of a smile. Her niece was not so strong as she liked to think. Ela, in fact, was weak. Weak! Umbecca's smile slipped into a firm, hard grimace.

'But the boy?' the chaplain was saying.

'Oh, he's very well!' Umbecca's attention snapped back

into place. 'Mercifully, poor Jem has no memory of those Vagas. Do you know, Chaplain, I wonder that we do not banish those wretched heathens from our realm.'

'Indeed, my good woman! I think perhaps the commander would be in agreement with you. I think you would find you had much in common.'

'Oh?' Umbecca flushed with pleasure; she had glimpsed something of the curly printing on the chaplain's little card. She was sitting on the sofa. All at once the visitor had flitted behind her. 'I would be correct, Chaplain, to assume that you have something to tell me?'

The white glove twisted on the air before her face, the card suspended between two fingers. The chaplain's voice purred in Umbecca's ear. 'And I would be correct, my good woman, to say that you were a person of a station considerably higher than your residence in the village of Irion might lead one to believe? Irion, I mean, as it was. As it has been. The bad years, I mean.'

Umbecca permitted herself a little laugh. 'Chaplain, you know full well, I am sure, that the lord of this castle is my brother-by-marriage. You perhaps even have heard of Miss Ruanna Rench, for a time the most celebrated beauty in all the Nine Provinces? She was my sister, my – my *Twinned*.'

'But of course!' the chaplain said, though whether he meant that of course he knew this, or of course Umbecca was the sister of a great beauty, was hard to say. He let the little card fall from his fingers. 'I think I need only say, my good woman, that your turn has come. You are about to become a leading light in a glittering new world.'

Umbecca seized the card from her lap.

'A ball!' she breathed. She clutched the card against the Circle of Agonis that glittered goldenly on her ample black breast.

Feval smiled again. 'I am glad to see you are a woman of piety. Between you and the commander, I can see, there shall be no barriers.'

'None?'

It was a question that the chaplain did not answer, but one which was to reverberate in Umbecca's mind over the coming moonlife as she prepared for the ball. For the first time, the fat woman found herself turning her attention to the topic that had so engaged the lesser personages of the village: the commander. Could this rumour of the gouty old gentleman be true?

She hoped for someone dashing, like Chaplain Feval.

When Eay Feval arrived back at the Lectory, a young lieutenant of the commander's guard asked to speak to the chaplain urgently. It seemed that the commander was behaving oddly.

Eay Feval pursed his lips. This was not good news. All his plans depended upon the commander. But then, what could it mean that the commander was being *odd*? Since arriving in the Lectory, he had spent his days locked in the apartment that had been hastily prepared for him. The ardent prayers of their days in the coach seemed now a thing of the past, as did their readings from the works of 'Miss R——'. Sunk in reflection, the old man kept his room in darkness, but demanded that the chaplain bring him the ornate golden lamp that had swung above them in the quilted coach. The lamp, said the commander, must be lit at all times. It was not that the commander wanted the light; he would seldom remove his visor. He wanted, rather, the sound that the lamp would make.

A low, insistent, snake-like *hiss*.

In the hall of the Lectory, a group of young recruits were laying new floorboards. More persistent hammerings and sawings echoed from the cavernous drawing-room beyond, where the ball was to be held. Had all the noise upset the commander? Prancing, almost skipping over the holes in the floor, the chaplain was making for the old man's apartment when the lieutenant called, 'Sir! He's this way!'

The chaplain turned back. Astonished, he noted the lieutenant's indicating hand. 'Lieutenant, you don't mean—?'

'He's sitting at the desk. He says he's going to make it his centre of command.'

'But the light!'

'He says he doesn't have to look at it, sir.'

Eay Feval made his way back to the lieutenant. The two men strode rapidly along the shabby corridor that ran down one side of the house. Perhaps it was the fumes, the chaplain was thinking. The air was a toxic swirl of paint and polish and wallpaper-glue. Perhaps the commander just wanted respite.

'He's not raving? Rambling?'

'Oh no, sir, he's very happy. He says he wants you to read to him again.'

'He is mad!' muttered the chaplain. Then, with a smile for his companion, added, 'Lieutenant, you did not of course hear that remark.'

Chapter 48

FIVE CRYSTALS

As I wake, as I sleep, his eyes well to weep
And his heart shall bleed for my sin.
As I work, as I pray, he is looking my way
And his heart shall bleed for my sin . . .

Umbecca's heart swelled on a tide of joy.

Beneath the massed voices surged the hefty, stentorian rumble of the organ. At once pealing yet profound, the sonorous music seemed to well from bottomless depths beneath them, yet to rise and bear their voices upwards on cadences that resounded to The Vast itself.

As she stood, stiff-backed and crisp in her best black, Umbecca held her Cantorate high. She loved the little book, proud of the tooled leather cover on which her initials, like wreathing tendrils, were bonded to the curves of the Circle of Agonis. She barely needed to look down at the pungent, close-printed pages.

He has not left us! He shall return!
Bearing his lady, with love he shall burn!

The words welled back to her from girlhood days, carrying her with them on a tide of memory to a time when she and Ruanna, dressed identically in flummeries of lace, had been those *two peas in a pod*, those *lovely little Rench girls*. How the faith had possessed her then, as she stood in the Great Temple by mother's side, and an enormousness of sound enfolded her spirit, and all the vastness of the temple, into a rich apprehension of the mystery, the glory of the Lord Agonis.

Umbecca gazed up into the window of stained glass that

arched high above the altar before her. She saw the cracked panes, but saw, too, that soon they would not be cracked. Soon they would be whole. Already the Temple of Irion had assumed a measure of its former glory. Her eyes misted over. A pallid brightness of the Season of Agonis fell through the jagged mosaic of light.

Jem, beside his aunt, was swaying a little on his crutches, but he had not wanted to sit when everyone else was standing. The words of the songs were still unfamiliar to him, and sometimes he would lose his place in the Cantorate. Then, as now, he would lapse into a mere opening and shutting of his mouth, while his eyes roved across the interior of the temple.

It was the fifth time he had been here since the Bluejackets came, and still the transformation amazed him. The temple was clean and bright. The vines and the cobwebs had been cleared away and the walls were freshly whitewashed. Thick, vertical logs propped up the ceiling and the portico outside. The best craftsmen from Agondon, his aunt had reported admiringly, were already hard at work.

Jem's eyes roamed across the altar that stretched beneath its heavy, vast Circle of Agonis; across the lectern of stone, raised high above the congregated, where the heavy book lay ready for the chaplain's address; up, up, over the Foretelling of coloured glass to the vaulted heights of the ceiling.

The boy felt a sense of awe. He swayed dangerously.

'Jem!' his aunt hissed.

The last canticle was from the Songs of Prevailing, which expressed not only the ardour of the Agonist faith but the assurance that, in time, it would spread to all the world:

> *And as he walked across the green*
> *The rays of love were brightly seen*
> *Soaring high*
> *In flaming dye*
> *Into the forehead of the sky . . .*

Jem was confused. Had the Lord Agonis walked across the village green? Aunt Umbecca would surely have mentioned it. And what was the 'flaming dye'?

> *And he shall come*
> *And overcome*
> *And we shall come*
> *And overcome*
> *In his name!*
> *In his name!*
> *And one day all the world*
> *Will say the same!*
>> *Praise him, praise him*
>> &c.

The congregated had been led in the sacred songs by a pale, balding young Bluejacket who had taken up the role of Cantor Lector to Eay Feval's Lector. When the canticles were over and the congregated were seated, the chaplain – as it seemed he was destined still to be known – ascended to the lectern. Sky-blue robes with long, loose sleeves covered his customary costume of black. He wore a curious hat.

Before him, the congregated sat in expectant silence, eyes turned upwards. The chaplain looked down over the assembled faces, already familiar to him. In the front rows sat Irion's few glimmerings of quality: Mistress Rench and the cripple-child; assembled officers and their ladies. In the middle were assorted servants and the more respectable people of trade; in the back, and bulking large, the peasants, ragged but cowed, and men of the ranks. Guards stood, bayonets at the ready, at the sides of the altar and the doors at the back.

The commander had not come.

Eay Feval looked down at the El-Orokon, turned a creamy page, and cleared his throat.

He began with his text.

It was one of his favourites.

*For each crystal was a thing of rare beauty; but the
Crystal of Agonis was rarest of all.*

Ork. Juv.II. 36/25–6.

First he said it softly, almost mumbling; then he repeated
it, arching back his throat, with a sonorousness that rose like
the descant of the organ.

Now he would explain what it meant.

'Women and men of Irion,' he offered, 'it is written that
Orok, father of the gods, in the moment of commencement of
the Time of Juvescence, when gods would live among the
races of this world, and this world would not be benighted,
as now it is, as now it must be, in this Time of Atonement,
but bathed in the radiance of a sacred light—'

Eay Feval took a breath.

'It is written that the dying god Orok, in the moments
before his dying into the Rock which was to be the Rock of
his dying, and which was called the Rock of Being and
Unbeing, and was to be the centre of the Vale of Orok, in
which the races of this benighted world were to live, before
they were benighted, in the time that was the Time of
Juvescence—'

Eay Feval took a *deep* breath.

'It is written that the dying god Orok gave to each of his
children *a province*, and *a crystal* which embodied the powers
of that province.'

Eay Feval paused. He might have been considering.

Contemplating.

His eyes scanned the ceiling. A good approach, the chaplain had always found, was to take a particular word in the
text and to interrogate it remorselessly; this was the approach
he would adopt today.

Crystal? Or province?

'*A crystal*,' he said emphatically. 'But what do we mean by
a crystal? This, of course, is one of the many mysteries of the
El-Orokon. It is a mystery on which we must meditate long
and hard.'

To Jem, who thought it quite clear what was meant by *a crystal*, the mystery lay, rather, in why the chaplain should say there was a mystery.

But Jem was only an ignorant boy.

'Now, to you and me' – at this point in Agondon, Eay Feval might have said, *Now, to the vulgar*, but he thought perhaps it was not appropriate today – 'now, to you and me, the word *crystal* suggests, does it not, a certain clear and definite image. What, I wonder, does it suggest to you?

'Perhaps it suggests something in the nature of jewellery.' The chaplain's eyes swept the front pews. 'I am sure one or two of the ladies in our midst, when I said the word *crystal*, might have had just a little vision of, ooh, something in the *crystal brooch* line, something in the *crystal necklace* line, a little *crystal something* to decorate the tender earlobes of the fair sex?'

There were titters.

'I don't think the dying god Orok gave his daughter Javander a nice new sea-green brooch in a silver setting, do you? Perhaps a nice pair of *drop-earrings* in burnished umber for the earthy Viana? Dear, dear me! I don't think so!

'What ever can it mean, then, that he gave them all *a crystal*? To some, perhaps, it suggests a vessel made of glass. Hm? Perhaps some of you of the officer class – I am thinking of a *particular* regiment here, you understand – might be thinking of that magnificent *crystal decanter* I have noted in your mess, graven with the name of one of the great ladies of the Agondon stage?'

There were guffaws.

'I don't think that's *quite* what the dying god Orok gave to his five children, do you? One of those apiece, graven with his name, so they'd remember him? I don't think so!

'Perhaps some of you – yes, some of you up the back; it's our more *rustic* brethren in particular I have in mind – might be thinking of those Vaga-fairs you've all been to – oh, don't deny it, we've all of us slunk along to those heathen little entertainments just once or twice in our lives, haven't we?

Roll up, roll up! Hm? We've all had that little bit of curiosity in us – you know the sort; it's silly and you know it but you *just can't help it* – we've all had that bit of curiosity in us which sends us slinking – slink-slink-slink – along to the tent of that wizened old Woman of Wisdom. Hm? Says she'll tell us our future, doesn't she? A likely story, I should think!

'But where does she see it? Hm? What does she use? She looks into a *crystal ball*, doesn't she? Were you thinking about that, you up the back? I think some of you were, weren't you? You were thinking, *Ooh, that's a nice present he give them, weren't it? I always said I wanted one o' them!*'

Eay Feval nodded fulsomely, his face beaming smiles, as the laughter rippled through the congregated, then subsided.

It was going well.

His smile faded and his expression became stern. 'My friends – my *flock* – let us meditate, let us meditate deeply, on the crystals the dying god gave. For what, after all, did he give his children, but tokens of his love? It was his love that he gave them, was it not? And to whom, I ask you, did he give his greatest love?'

His eyes darted from left to right, looking over the assembled faces as if, perhaps, in expectation of an answer; and indeed, here and there, an involuntary panic passed across the features of a peasant or two. But today there would be no indecorum. After a moonlife or so it was clear, even to this unpolished crowd, that questions from the lectern would be answered from the lectern.

The answer filled the respectful silence.

'It was to Agonis! It was to Agonis that he gave his greatest love! Think well, my friends, on the meaning of this fact. For we are, all of us, the Children of Agonis. No, not the children of his loins, for it is written that we of the earth are creatures of a lesser breed – but children of his care! Children of his mercy! Children of his love! Think well, my friends, on the destiny that this lays before us.'

There was more in this vein, much more; but Jem, by this time, had lost the thread. The boy's brow furrowed. The chaplain seemed to be saying that because the Lord Agonis was the best god, therefore the Agonists were the best people; that they should make sure they all knew it, and that everyone else knew it, too.

But there was more to it.

Or less to it.

Jem could not be sure. He could think only of the crystals; but the chaplain had made even those confusing.

After Litanies and Final Canticles, the congregated as they filed from the temple would shake the chaplain's hand. The lower orders, of course, would pass swiftly by, eyes down and mumbling; but with persons of greater quality it was the custom of the chaplain to exchange a few pleasantries.

'My dear lady!' He gripped Umbecca's hands and retained them in his grip through the dialogue that followed. The fat woman and her young charge were the last worshippers remaining in the temple portico. Jem looked out into the chill tombyard. Eay Feval arched an eyebrow at Umbecca.

'You are looking, if I may say, decidedly enhanced.'

'But Chaplain, of course! Your sermon was a masterpiece. You have lifted me on the love of the Lord Agonis. Seldom, indeed, have I been lifted so high.'

'Dear lady, that would be some feat; but I suspect perhaps there is another reason, lurking in the chambers of your heart, for the enhancement I note? A *prior* reason? A reason, perhaps, a little more *earthly*?'

'You scorn me, Chaplain! What ever could you mean?'

'I was thinking, dear lady, of a certain ball.'

The time of the ball was drawing near.

'Chaplain, really! Eager as I am to fulfil my duties to the society of this province, you may be assured that I fulfil them only in so far as they are, if I may say, *of a piece* with my duties to the Lord Agonis!'

'But dear lady, of course! Had I suggested otherwise?'

The last worshippers had vanished from the tombyard.

'Chaplain,' said Jem, 'where are the crystals?'

'Pardon?'

The chaplain had not expected the cripple-child to speak. The child's forehead was furrowed unattractively as if he had been thinking about something difficult. The question, evidently, had sprung to his lips unbidden.

Always a bad sign.

'The Crystals of Orok,' Jem said. 'Where are they?'

'Oh, Jem!' said Umbecca. 'You haven't understood a word the chaplain said!'

Chapter 49

POLTY IN A GLASS

'Pooh, don't he stink?'

'He's a dirty animal!'

'That caked-on shit! I'm going to throw up!'

'Come on, keep pumping!'

The nauseated taunts of the guards barely registered in Polty's ears. He was blinded by the brightness of daylight; then blinded and deafened by the shock of chill water. Rough hands pushed him and pulled at him, jogged him and jostled him. He was scrubbed and rubbed; he was scraped and scoured.

What were they doing?

Why?

When they held him down and he heard the *strop! strop!* of leather, then saw a razor flash above his eyes, Polty thought they were about to cut his throat. It had all been some game they were playing. Now they were tired of it and it was over. He tried to scream and they shoved a soapy rag into his mouth.

But all they wanted to do was to shave his tangled beard.

Now it was over.

Wrapped in a white sheet, Polty sat in a stiff-backed chair in a large, strange room. The guards had withdrawn and he was alone. Before him, some distance away, was a desk. It was a desk of extraordinary dimensions, far more impressive than Goodman Waxwell's: an enormous rampart of carved mahogany, set squarely on legs that were fashioned like the fluted columns of the temple. It was a desk for an important man, and one might have expected it to be cluttered with the appurtenances of such a man: the official seals; the maps; the documents of state. Instead, the desk was empty but for a set of small books that filled one corner.

The desk sat on a large, lush expanse of carpet, coloured green, rather like swirling, patterned grass. Only two objects filled the expanse: a spindly, curving chair, covered in a fabric of blue chintz, and, more oddly, a slender wooden figure, the height of a tall man. It was a tailor's dummy, and it was dressed in the uniform of a Bluejacket soldier. It was, in fact, a captain's uniform, complete in every detail, even to the braid-brimmed, three-cornered hat that perched atop the mannequin's featureless round head.

Boots, stockings and garters were laid neatly below.

But it was at the edges of the carpet that the true oddity of the room began, for the space surrounding the desk and the grassy-like area before it was filled wholly with plants. All was a riot of teeming leaves, of spiking stalks and green lolling tongues and burgeoning fan-like fronds of ferns. There were twisting tendrils and trailing vines and bright, flaming flowers. A pallid, hot light bathed the room from above. Looking up, Polty saw that the ceiling was made of glass.

For a time he had wondered what the room could be. And where.

Now he knew.

In games of childhood, Polty and his friends had crept through this place when it had still been abandoned, and the riotous greenery had filled it entirely. He had thought they had imprisoned him in the castle; now he knew that it had been in the Lectory. The place where they had brought him now was a long room that ran down the side of the Lectory's outer walls. Polty had heard the Waxwells speak of it, in a curious mixture of wonderment and alarm. They called it the Glass Room. The old Lector, the mad one who had run away to the Wildwood, used to sit in here and write his canonicals.

There was a rustling of leaves.

'Nearly there. Come on,' came a voice. 'You know, sir, it would be easier if we used the bath chair. We could cut a path through the leaves—'

'Don't be absurd, man!' came a blustering voice. 'What would you do, treat me like an invalid?'

'Sir, of course not!'

An irritated 'Hmph!' was the only reply as the leaves parted to reveal the stricken bulk of a gouty old man resplendent in dress uniform, a garish affair of sashes and epaulettes and medals, supported on the arm of a thinner, younger man in black. The old man had magnificent curled moustaches; equally magnificent, covering his eyes, was a capacious visor of thick embroidered cloth.

Polty wondered if the man were blind.

'Is he here? Hm?' the old man asked, as the younger man, with evident relief, relinquished his burden into the groaning green leather of the chair behind the desk.

'He is here, sir.'

The younger man flashed Polty a little smile, and then, to Polty's greater surprise, a conspiratorial wink. With precise movements he perched on the blue chintz chair and crossed his left leg over his right. Then, it seemed, he thought better of this, and crossed his right leg over his left. But he thought better of this too and instead sat with his hands folded neatly in his lap. It was some moments before it came to Polty that this was the man who had come to arrest him. How long ago had it been? He had noted then, as he noted now, that the man wore white gloves.

❋   ❋   ❋   ❋

Some moments passed before Commander Veeldrop pushed back his visor and gazed, blinkingly, on the figure in the white sheet.

All at once Polty was trembling.

What was to become of him?

In the darkness of the Lectory cellar he had thought again

and again on his likely fate. He had cursed Leny; he had reviled her memory; he had even, in fleeting moods, felt tenderly to the girl, and wished only that she had not been driven to do what she had done. He had seen the suicide note only for an instant before the guttering candle had plunged him back into blackness, but the words might as well have been seared on his brain. There they were, every one of the girl's pathetic phrases, scrawled illiterately in a childish hand.

My deer Vel.

My disonner.

Damn the bitch! Her very incoherence was a kind of gruesome clarity, declaring her inability to live any longer after all that her wicked betrayer had done. She would follow her beloved Vel, crashing across the mill-race.

When the guards had taken Polty from his captivity at last, the wretched boy had been convinced that it was to face execution.

The axe?

The noose?

The firing-squad?

Now he was confused.

'Roll, my boy?' the commander asked.

Polty looked at him blankly. He was not sure he had heard correctly. Then he saw that Commander Veeldrop was extending across the desk a brown-leafed, neatly-packed cylinder of Jarvel-weed. Flushing, Polty endeavoured to stand, but it was awkward in the sheet. The chaplain bade him be still and, smiling, bore the Jarvel-roll to Polty's hand. Tinder flared. Polty might have been an honoured guest.

'Poltiss – I may call you "Poltiss"?' the commander began. 'I gather you've been having a little trouble, hm?'

Polty coughed. 'Leny?'

The commander leaned forward, drawing back on his own Jarvel-roll. 'An unpleasant business—'

'Oh, I know, sir—' It had occurred to Polty that he should call this man *sir*.

'A most unpleasant business indeed. Which is why I should like you to know, Poltiss, that I shall have none of it—'

'Indeed, sir!' Polty's head was spinning already. The Jarvel was the finest he had ever smoked. He nodded fulsomely, spluttering, 'But, sir, I can assure you, nothing of that sort shall ever—'

'Of course not! If there is one thing I have always deplored, it is that sort of—'

'Oh, sir, so do I—'

'But Poltiss, put it out of your head! They are gone!'

'Sir?'

'Banished! That is so, isn't it, Chaplain?'

The chaplain smiled assent, and the commander went on, 'To say that I have always deplored such persons would be the grossest of understatements. We don't want such people here. The girl was bad enough. My men found her, in a fine state I assure you, sobbing on some wretched *rock* above the river—'

'Sobbing?' Polty was almost laughing.

'Indeed! Pathetic, isn't it? Seems she had intended to jump, but couldn't. As for that mother of hers – flinging round accusations, waving the girl's "suicide note", demanding what she liked to imagine might be "justice" . . . They disgusted me, the pair of them. I might add that the local blacksmith has no thought in his head, no thought at all, that his boy has been . . . *murdered*. "I always warned that boy about that Rock," he told my men, "and now I sees that I be right."' The commander chortled. 'A good man, I gather. A most reliable workman.'

Polty was leaning forward intently. Dimly, inexplicably, the thought came to him that his life, which he had thought to be over, was instead entering a new phase.

'One might have punished them more severely, of course. The accusations were, to say the least, serious. But' – the commander waved a nonchalant hand – 'justice and mercy.

Justice and mercy, Poltiss. It is the cornerstone of government. Remember that, my boy, and perhaps you may follow in the footsteps of my greatness.'

The commander leaned back, gazing at the ceiling. Pale clouds writhed from the Jarvel-roll in his hand; bigger, paler clouds filled the sky above. He studied them. The two sets of clouds, inside and outside, might at that moment have seemed to mingle.

The old man stirred.

'Hmph! Finest Jarvel, hm? When I smoke this, do you know what I say to myself, my boy? I say, *Where would we be without the Agonist Deliverance?*'

A wheezing laugh followed on this remark. Polty's brow furrowed. He had never quite considered that the Jarvel-weed he smoked came all the way from the colonies in Zenzau. It was a strange thought.

'Of course, the chaplain here does not approve. Do you, Chaplain?'

The chaplain crossed his legs, right over left. 'I said nothing, sir—'

'Feval, I say you are half a man! Not even half!' the old man burst out. He permitted himself a second wheezing laugh; and all at once, Polty was laughing, too.

Half a man.

Not even half.

'Poltiss, take off that sheet.'

'Sir?'

'Chaplain, assist him.'

The chaplain did so; and in a moment Polty was standing naked before the two men, beneath the pale light from the glass-panelled ceiling. The thick, generous Jarvel-roll had vanished from his hand.

The commander's gouty pain was evidently eased on the soothing waves of Jarvel. It was with almost a lightness of step that he emerged from behind the desk, supported now only on a bejewelled stick, to stand close beside the naked young man.

'Poltiss, show me what you're wearing.'

Polty looked up and saw the sky turning, turning.

'I'm naked, sir.'

'Your hand, Poltiss. Show me your hand.'

The chaplain picked up the young man's limp hand, bringing it up to the commander's gaze. The old man looked on the amethyst ring that Polty, all this time, had continued to wear.

'Ah yes,' said the commander. 'Chaplain, the costume.'

And then it was Polty's body that was turning, turning, as carefully, almost tenderly, the chaplain removed the captain's uniform from the figure of the mannequin and placed each item, one by one, upon the young man's form.

No one spoke.

When it was over, the chaplain, still silent, led him by the hand to the edge of the green carpet. He parted a curtain of vines.

Polty's gasp came slowly, but was deep. Behind the vines was a looking-glass. Polty had never liked to look at his reflection; to do so had been to confront the fact of his ugliness.

No longer.

The young man had not yet considered the changes that the last moonlives had wrought in him, for the figure of the captain that he saw now, mirrored before him, was not the monster he might have expected, bursting from the uniform at every seam. Intrigued, Polty ran his fingers down the glass.

Was the vision real?

He looked closer, into the green eyes that gazed at him above jutting cheekbones; he looked closer and saw a sharp jaw; he swallowed and watched the bobbing of the apple in his throat. He reached up, removing his three-cornered hat. Then Polty saw that his carroty hair had grown. Flaming curls cascaded freely round his face.

He was handsome.

He was beautiful.

He was *thin*.

Marvelling, he turned back to the gouty old man, who stood in the centre of the carpet, swaying on his bejewelled stick, watching him intently. The commander extended his hand, perhaps for Polty to kiss.

Polty moved forward; then he saw, in a flash of pale light, that Commander Veeldrop wore a ring just like his own.

The old man staggered forward, falling into his arms.

'My son!' he breathed. 'My son!'

Chapter 50

UMBECCA IN A GLASS

'Tighter!'

'It can't go any tighter, ma'am.'

'Of course it can!' Umbecca took a second deep breath. 'There. Another three fingers or I'll say you're not trying. Pull!'

Nirry pulled. If only she could get a little more leverage! The temptation to jam her foot into the broad backside was strong. Fat-arsed old cow! The maid's muscles juddered like taut wires and the strings were cutting her hands. With a lurch Nirry flung herself forward, tugging the knots tight.

She fell back, gasping. Her back and arms were aching, her hands red-raw. Four times the mistress had donned the new gown; three times she had removed it and demanded alterations.

'That was three fingers, girl?'

'Four!' the maid lied desperately, staggering back to her feet.

'Four?'

The colour played high in Umbecca's plump face. With delicate little dance-steps she swayed before the glass. It had all been worthwhile! The task, or rather tasks, had been the most difficult she could recall. For the length of the last moonlife, Umbecca had dedicated herself to twin goals. One involved her gown; the other, her girth.

Umbecca had been dieting. Rumbling with starvation, the fat woman had paced up and down the length of her niece's chamber, flinging herself on the sofa from time to time in postures of languorous abandon. Like a lovelorn lady in an old tale, she had sat gazing miserably from the casement; like an angered bird of prey, she had hovered over her sleeping, stick-thin niece as if about to shake her, scratch her. Decisively she declared for a nap, a walk, a drive, in each case demanding that her maid should tend to her; with the passing of a moment, the desire was overturned. At meal times, the powers of her nose became acute, able to catch the merest waftings of a roasting chop from below. Insidiously, the aromas crept up from the kitchens. Pork crackling! Oozing, rare steaks! Chicken basted with honey and burnt just a little black, served with fresh peas and potatoes mashed in cream and herb butter! Officers' dinner-time was an exquisite torture. Luscious, smooth gravy seemed to fill Umbecca's mouth.

Sleep brought no relief. At night, beneath the Icon of the Lady on her wall, she would wake suddenly, her senses filled to bursting with the precise sensation, the exact texture and taste of a lattice-topped lemon tart sprinkled liberally with coarse, brown sugar. Or cake: moist, dark plum-cake with finger-thick icing! Scones: plate after plate, crumbly and hot, heaped high with lashings of quince jam and cream!

She would lie back, moaning.

It had all been worthwhile.

All the torture had been worthwhile. Umbecca surveyed herself in the glass with pride.

Not a jot of difference, Nirry thought with pleasure.

Carefully Umbecca's hands smoothed her elaborate bodice. The gown had been the labour of many days and nights. In Ela's wardrobe, Umbecca had found an unworn dress of an exquisite blue silk, like the 'Ejard Blue', but feminine, soft, and silky; from the chaplain she acquired a length of blue curtain-fabric, rich and velvety, which remained from the renovations at the Lectory. The sea of blue formed itself – or rather, was formed by Nirry – into Umbecca's fabulous gown. Swathes of Ela's dress provided a dazzling front-panel. There were high ornate burgeonings at the shoulders; there was intricate beading over the bodice; there was elaborate stitching on the ruffles at the sleeves. The neckline plunged low. There was a huge bustle and a sweeping train.

When the dress was finished, Nirry's labours were not over. A vast-brimmed, veiled hat must complete the ensemble; then had come the embroidering of the many stiff petticoats.

Umbecca demanded perfection. 'Lazy, stupid girl!' she would exclaim, each time she took it into herself to decry her maid's handiwork. More than once she had ripped out Nirry's stitches and flung the fabric to the floor. The leg-o'-mutton sleeves had been particularly trying; they had reminded her, after all, of legs of mutton.

❅ ❅ ❅ ❅

Nirry languished in a torment as great as that of her mistress; but hers was not her own fault.

Relieved of her duties elsewhere in the castle, Nirry was now Umbecca's personal maid. Her lot should have been easier; but how she longed for her cavernous kitchens! They might as well have vanished. Their tranquillity was gone and in their place was an inferno of perpetual heat and steam and noise. Bustle, bustle, all day long.

Meanwhile, Nirry was trapped. So far as she could see, her morose father, drinking himself into a stupor in a corner of the stables, was in no worse a state. She felt like joining him. Her self-pity was boundless. When the fat woman spoke and her back was turned, often the maid would open and shut her mouth in grotesque, silent imitation. She pulled wild faces, twisting her supple features this way and that.

Do this, Nirry.

Nirry, don't do that.

Nirry, don't go down where the soldiers are.

Nirry, come here. Nirry!

Once she caught Lady Ela looking at her from the bed. Nirry flushed scarlet; but then Lady Ela smiled.

Of course!

She wanted to escape, too.

The prospect of a brief respite from the mistress was, when Nirry considered it, the one positive feature of the ball.

Umbecca stepped back.

The dark was drawing in. In the soft glow of the lamplight, and through eyes half-shut, the looking-glass disclosed, she liked to think, the image of a much younger woman. Much younger, and much thinner. For a moment, she saw the image of her sister. *Ah, Ruanna!* How many years was it now since she had died? And then Umbecca felt a surge of satisfaction, simply in knowing that she, unlike her sister, was alive.

'Shall I see to Master Jem now, ma'am?'

'Master Jem?'

Then she remembered.

Umbecca's pleasure, which a moment before had been at its height, was at once a little diminished. Umbecca valued her invitation to the ball sufficiently to keep it on the tea-table on permanent display. She liked to think of it as a rare privilege, vouchsafed to none other, as if she were set to attend some vast, glittering gathering at which she would also, by some strange ecstatic doubling of possibility, be the only person there. Impossible, of course. Officers, their wives, and every person of quality for many leagues around had also received the summons; Umbecca's invitation was one of many. She knew this; of course she did. But the knowledge that her niece, and even her nephew, were also considered of sufficient rank to attend was, in certain moods, distressing to her. A harlot and a Vexing? Whatever next? Would Nirry be invited, too?

The insensible Ela was dealt with easily; her aunt wrote the refusal in her own hand. Jem, alas, was another matter. The chaplain, she supposed, would expect him to attend.

Had the boy put on his new blue suit?

There was a polite *tap-tap* at the chamber door. Already

Umbecca recognized the familiar tattoo. She grabbed the maid's arm. 'Nirry! Quick! The hat! My gloves! He must see me in my full glory.'

A final preening before the glass came next; then Umbecca, pushing her maid aside, called airily in the direction of the door, 'Come!'

'My dear Mistress Rench!' The chaplain mimed the action of a man stopping in his tracks. 'What is this vision?' He cast himself to his knees; reached for her hand.

Yes, he noted: the new carpet was *most satisfactory*.

Eay Feval rose. He walked around the fat woman, a full circuit of her considerable bulk; and when he had completed it, peered at her curiously.

She looked almost alarmed.

'Chaplain? Is something wrong?'

But secretly she was thinking that the chaplain must now remark, he must surely remark, on the astonishing transformation in her figure. He must merely be seeking the appropriate phrases. On the brink of laughter, she was almost tempted to offer him her own choice. An old buck who had besieged Ruanna's virtue for the full length of a season had complimented her persistently on her *sand-timer shape*; the phrase drifted pleasantly through Umbecca's mind.

'Wrong? Oh no, my good woman.' Feval laughed frivolously, and as he laughed Umbecca was aware that his eyes had rested, with an intentness that unnerved her, on the exposed cleavage of her breasts.

She coloured.

'Not wrong,' he said. 'Missing. But missing no more.'

A hand slid into a pocket of his uniform and Umbecca's eyes grew wide as the chaplain held before him, horizontal on his white palm, a small, flat, velvet-covered box. Slowly he raised the lid.

Umbecca gasped. 'They're beautiful!'

'From the mines of Tiralos. The finest.'

Umbecca flushed with pleasure as the chaplain fastened the diamonds at her neck.

He stepped back. 'The commander's token.'

'The commander's?' Umbecca's voice wavered, just a little.

'Indeed. And perhaps I might confide in you,' said the chaplain confidentially, 'that the commander has expressed an especial fondness for – how should one put it? – the *fuller-figured* woman.'

'He has?'

Umbecca staggered in her tight stays.

'But our carriage waits below. Come.' The chaplain crooked his arm. 'The boy is ready, I trust?'

'Jem!' Nirry called, trotting to his alcove. She hoped he had dressed. The poor boy had become so dreamy!

'And may I enquire after your niece?' the chaplain asked pleasantly, as he escorted Umbecca from the chamber.

It seemed like good form.

'Lying in a senseless stupor, as usual!' replied the fat woman, with more vehemence than she intended. But then she turned back and smiled demurely at the chaplain.

The bitter words might never have been spoken.

❈ ❈ ❈ ❈

Her aunt was gone at last.

Ela raised her head from the soft roll of her pillow. She brushed back her tangled hair. Her bleary eyes seemed to clear. A lamp was burning on the table by the window. For a moment, Ela leaned back on her elbows, breathing deeply, taking in the clutter that filled her apartment: the strewn offcuts of Bluejacket blue; the torn remnants of lace; the jagged cuts of cloth; the beads and buttons and knives and scissors and pins and needles that lay about or were stuck about on the table or the chairs or the sofa or the hideous new carpet. In the looking-glass, the lamplight made a golden, empty haze.

Ela lolled back her head, humming to herself. On the little table beside her bed, the bottle of sleepy-treacle lay untouched, as it had lain untouched since the Bluejackets came. Streaks of the mixture, long-dried, had stuck the stopper to the lid. Ela had to laugh. How arrogant her aunt had become! The old bitch noticed nothing.

Giving up had been worse this time than last. It had been an agony; and an agony that was worse because it was secret. Only Nirry had guessed the truth. While Umbecca guzzled tea and cakes by the fire, or paraded vainly before the looking-glass, from time to time the maid had slipped over towards the curtained bed, wiping the brow of her young mistress or ensuring that she had fresh water to drink. Sometimes the maid would just stroke Ela's arm, and tormented eyes would gaze up at her gratefully. Dear Nirry! She was a common, ignorant girl, but she had been Ela's nurse and even her companion, her true companion, while Aunt Umbecca had failed in duty, as in humanity, again and again. In the nights, when the fat woman slept at last, Nirry had returned to Ela's chamber. Straining over her sewing in the light of a single candle, the maid had sat loyally by the side of her young mistress, and sometimes, when Ela shuddered or moaned, Nirry would reach out and grab her hand. 'My poor lady!' the maid would whisper. 'Be brave! Be strong! It will be over soon.'

It was over now. Ela swung her legs from the bed and reached for her shawl. She slipped her feet into slippers, wary of treacherous pins. Quickly, she crossed the carpet. First, she took the lamp in her hand.

She crossed to the wainscot.

In the last moment, as she was about to vanish through the secret panel, there was a creak at the door of the apartment. Ela turned.

It was Nirry.

But the maid only smiled knowingly, happily, as the young mistress disappeared into the wall.

Chapter 51

TOMATO

The carriage swept through the village, bearing them to the ball. It was evening, but the village was ablaze with light. Lamps hung from the trees all around the green.

Crushed into a corner beside his aunt's bulk, Jem looked disconsolately at the changes in the village. Something about them had begun to disturb him. Time, too much time since the Season of Theron, had become for the boy merely a half-remembered haze. But he had forgotten nothing that had gone before. He knew what was happening, but was helpless. Slowly but violently, piece by piece, the world of his childhood was being destroyed.

In the castle, the Bluejackets had driven back almost wholly the rot and decay that had come to seem part of its very fabric. Making his way quietly about on his crutches, concealed behind archway and arras and armour, Jem could only watch in mute distress as ruined chambers he had explored with Barnabas were turned over violently by the men in blue. Shouted commands rebounded from the walls. Bonfires burned brightly each night in the yards, heaped high with mouldering books and rotting fabrics and wormy, rickety chairs.

It was the same all over the village. Fresh thatch burgeoned proudly on once-bedraggled roofs; sturdy beams, cut from Wildwood trees, propped up ceilings that had sagged, ready to crash. The smell of whitewash hovered on the air. Hacking and hammering, sawing and sanding, were everywhere to be heard. Everywhere there was a new clarity, an access of light. In the tombyard, tangling weeds were removed by the roots and the long grass scythed.

The carriage slowed to a crawl as their destination loomed near. The lane to the Lectory had been made much wider, but tonight was still too narrow for the crush of carriages and horses and milling, excited crowds. The curfew loomed near, but still hordes of peasants waited eagerly to glimpse the arriving guests, exclaiming over the magnificence of equipages and gowns. If a few would still mutter darkly of the Bluejackets, most were dazzled by the wealth and splendour that suddenly, on this magnificent evening, seemed on the verge of enveloping them all. Sentries, muskets at the ready, lined the Lectory walls.

The guard on the gate hissed urgently over his shoulder, 'The chaplain's party!'

The intelligence passed rapidly along a line of men, all the way back to the brilliantly lit house. Officer cadets in dress uniform rushed to assist the party from the coach, smilingly helping down the lady and the cripple.

'A chair for the boy!' Eay Feval snapped his fingers, but Jem held tightly to the grips of his crutches. He gave the chaplain an earnest glance and the chaplain relented.

The party swept imperiously towards the gates, Umbecca with her arm crooked in the chaplain's, Jem swinging himself confidently behind. The crowd pushed close, only kept back by the soldiers. There were gasps at the sight of Umbecca's costume; gasps and a ripple of derision, swiftly suppressed.

Umbecca did not hear it.

'Give them a little wave,' the chaplain murmured.

Jem's aunt was about to comply. Indeed, she was turning back in the open gate, lifting her veil demurely as Ruanna had done, on the brink of entering a royal reception; Umbecca was about to raise a gloved hand, as if in benediction, when suddenly a ripe tomato exploded against her breasts!

She screamed.

She shrieked.

Hoots of laughter erupted from the crowd as soldiers quickly bundled Umbecca through the gates. Strong hands gripped Jem, hauling him away, but in the moment before he

407

was plucked from the scene he thought he glimpsed, in the corner of his eye, a ragged girl who looked back for an instant as she darted away through the crowd.

There were shouts.

There were shots.

❉ ❉ ❉ ❉

Inside the house, as his tearful aunt was sequestered in a retiring-room, Jem's memory flung up a second glimpse of the girl. The face became clearer: broad, high-cheekboned, split wide in a mischievous grin.

Then it was gone.

Jem looked about him. They had left him in the hall. His crutches beside him, he was sitting on one of several stiff-backed sofas. The arms and legs were painted in gold; the velvet seat was blue.

As he was borne rapidly towards the house, Jem had registered the carpet that lined the path, cutting a swathe of bruised purple-green through the clipped, illuminated garden. He knew now that the carpet had been blue, only altered by artificial light. Inside the house, everything was blue. Blue, 'Ejard Blue', ran in thin stripes down the walls and churned in bright whorls on the floor at his feet. Blue was the colour of the fabric that draped from ceiling to floor, in the windows and before the high interior doors that would open into the ballroom. Blue was the colour of costume after costume, not only of soldiers but of arriving guests; and blue, Jem thought glumly, was the colour of the stiff, hot velvet of his new knickerbocker suit. The lace at the collar and the cuffs was white.

The boy sat looking at the blue backs of tail-coats and bustles passing into the ballroom. Above the doors, in a ponderous frame that looked as if it might fall and kill someone, was a picture of the king. Jem looked at it. He had once seen an engraving of Ejard Red; Ejard Blue looked just the same, but dressed in a different colour. There was a white marble bust of him in a window-nook, too. It occurred to Jem

408

that perhaps this had been meant to be Ejard Red, and now they were only saying it was Ejard Blue. That was the advantage of having Twinned kings, one after the other. It was a curious thought. Jem looked back to the painting, then again at the bust. Another thought began to stir in him, and one still more curious; but he did not pursue it. People were talking close by, and Jem wanted to listen.

'Who was that fat old bag?' an officer's wife was saying.

'Shh! From the castle. The local quality.'

'Quality!' The officer's wife let out a hoot.

'Darling, *shhh*.'

'But that dress! By the Lord Agonis! Why ever is the chaplain squiring her about?'

'Darling, please. We *are* in the provinces.'

'Dear lady, don't let it distress you!' said the chaplain. 'I implore you, do not permit this vulgar incident to ruffle for one moment your charming demeanour, or spoil your pleasure in this illustrious occasion. The missile was directed at me, not at you. There are undesirable elements in any town; one must expect some limited, initial opposition. But there! It is nothing, nothing.'

Umbecca dried her tears.

There was no need to cry. With the tact and finesse he had shown all along, the chaplain had procured from one of the officers' ladies a starched lacy handkerchief which, with just a fold here, a tuck there, he had pinned into position on the stained front of her gown.

'There! Who will know now?'

He turned her to a looking-glass. Umbecca beamed. The embroidered facing was just what the gown needed. Why had she not thought of it before?

The chaplain returned the diamonds to her neck, and bore her into the ballroom.

Chapter 52

THE BALL

Jem's head was buzzing.

Where had his aunt gone?

Incapable of dancing or standing unassisted, the boy was enduring a miserable evening. The atmosphere in the ballroom was intolerably close. Fires burnt brightly in many hearths and thousands of candles flickered overhead; the crush of bright uniforms and trailing gowns generated its own rising, moist heat. Not even in Temple were there so many people; Jem had not, indeed, considered that the world contained so many.

He had, at least, found his station for the evening. He had set himself up on a chair by the far wall, in a neglected corner between the orchestra and the drinks table. It was most convenient.

What exactly it was that the ladies and gentlemen were drinking, Jem was not quite sure; he only knew that to drink it seemed a good idea. Repeatedly the gentlemen would repair to the corner table, ladling out a colourful liquid from a huge glass bowl. Usually they took not one glass, but several.

Jem, with his crutches, could not quite manage this. He regretted it, but was close enough to manoeuvre himself up and down frequently. Sipping the curious liquid, which was strangely bitter and sweet at the same time, the boy occupied himself in observing the orchestra.

This also was a good idea. The music boomed satisfactorily loudly in his ears, drowning the hubbub of laughter and conversation. It diverted him to watch the scrapings of the bows across the viols, and the lutenist's fingers as they darted back and forth. The bass keys of the harpsichord thundered behind his head.

'A lonely lad?'

Jem looked up. A portly gentleman gazed at him benignly. Across the gentleman's girth glittered a golden fob-chain. He wore a wig of particular splendour. The gentleman leaned close, a roll burning in his hand. A single, round eyeglass was fixed in one of his eyes; or rather, appeared to be attached to the side of his nose, which – particularly in its contrast with his red, veined cheeks – had about it a curiously wooden appearance. Yes. Wood: painted wood. It was, for all that, a magnificent nose.

Jem smiled politely.

'Alas, I have no daughters,' the gentleman said.

Jem wondered why. Not why he had none; why he had said so.

'Now Colonel Rextel of the Blue Irions, I can tell you for a fact, has five beautiful young fillies—'

'Horses?'

'Daughters! Daughters, my boy! The magic word for a young lad. You'd be, what, just a little too ... *short* in the tooth for your first commission, I dare say, but you're a fine-looking lad and make no mistake. I think it wouldn't do you any harm at all to have a little introductory dalliance, this very evening, with the gorgeous Miss Vyella Rextel. Think about it. Hm? Now, if I had any juices that could still be flowing, my boy, I'd be taking up this offer. Say the word, lad, and your future is assured. Come! Say you want to dance with Miss Vyella Rextel.'

Jem looked glumly on to the crowded dance floor. The Jarvel-roll pointed and as it pointed, seemed to magic into being the undoubted presence of Miss Vyella Rextel. Yes. That was her: a horsy creature, many years Jem's senior, at that moment being put through her paces by a young lieutenant of her father's regiment. She pranced back and forth in the Quadrant Dance.

'I'm a cripple,' Jem said.

The gentleman laughed. 'Ho, boy! I felt the same, I assure you, when first I encountered the charms of the sex. I reared and whinnied like a shy young colt. But look you, boy, feast your eye, feast your eye on the luscious Vy . . .'

Then the gentleman noticed Jem's crutches beside him, and *hem-hemmed* loudly.

'But perhaps you are right, boy. Perhaps you are too young. *Squander not the heart, squander not the flesh*: old saying from the province of Midlexion, and one, alas, to which I did not attend. You see before you the ruin of a man, merely patched and poulticed. Treasure your innocence, lest like me you should end your life racked with regret, sick from venery and its attendant ills.'

The gentleman nodded politely, and took his leave.

'Oh! Chaplain!'

A familiar voice.

'You have done for me! I can dance no more.'

The Quadrant Dance was over and Jem, joining in the applause, switched his attention from the departing gentleman to the wobbling bulk of his aunt. Coming to rest on the chaplain's arm, she had stationed herself just a little distance from her nephew, but did not see him sequestered in his corner, screened intermittently by this uniform, or by that gown, as the guests mingled about.

The orchestra struck up a Holluch reel.

'Chaplain, tell me: and when is our host to show himself?'

'To show himself! You make it sound as if he were concealing himself! He shall be making a little speech forthwith, as is his wont.'

Another voice: 'Mistress Rench!'

It was unmistakable.

It was eager.

'May I say, my good woman, that my wife and I have long admired you, but never so much as we have done this evening. I declare, you are the belle of the ball!'

'Chaplain, you are familiar with Goodman Waxwell?'

'Indeed.' The chaplain bent his neck stiffly in greeting. 'But I can hardly compete with such gallantries. You will excuse me, madam?'

Could it be, Jem wondered, that a certain chill had entered the smooth voice? Peering from behind the bustle of a shimmery ball-dress, Jem saw the chaplain's departing immaculate form and in its place, the familiar crook-backed physician, dressed in a new blue suit that sat on him more than a little ill.

It occurred to Jem that he had never, until now, seen the physician in anything but Agonist black. This attempt at the costume of a gentleman of fashion was a regrettable affair. The golden quilted waistcoat! The floral buttonhole! The silken sash across his chest was particularly ill-advised; as he spoke, the physician kept plucking at it, then pulling at it, with one nervous hand, as if first it were too tight, then too loose, and the ideal arrangement could not be found. A new white wig slipped awkwardly over his skull.

Waxwell said, 'It's been a time since you came to see us, my good woman, and I have to admit, it has begun to disturb me. I have asked myself if anything has happened. I have asked myself if anything is wrong. I have asked myself, has there been any wavering in your faith?'

'My faith?' Umbecca said coldly. 'Goodman, you have seen me in Temple each Canonday, have you not? I rather wonder from where your doubts arise.'

The surgeon plucked his sash with particular force. 'The Canonical, my good woman, is a splendid thing; but I am sure you know how easily it can become but mere *form*. I am sure you know, too – in your heart – that mere appearances, after all, are *but* mere appearances. That outward displays are but outward displays.'

'Goodman, what are you suggesting?'

The physician moved closer. Jem strained to hear. Was there a hint of reproach in the wheedling, whining voice?

'Sometimes, those not firm enough of heart will permit

certain . . . *setbacks* to drag them down. Oh, it is foolish of them! To those who offer up their hearts to the Lord Agonis, the way can only be clear, inevitably clear. But doubt's insidious burden weighs heavily on their hearts. Down, down they slide like sticks into a drain. I should hate to see that happen to you, my . . . *my dear.'*

Umbecca was silent, and Jem, intrigued, gathered that Goodman Waxwell had now, in some way, offended her. Perhaps she would walk away; perhaps she would make some outburst.

She did neither.

When she spoke, she spoke quietly, deliberately. 'Yes, Goodman, I have had my doubts—'

'I knew it!'

'No! Not of our intentions. They were good. They were honourable. But what we did. What we almost did. Something in my heart revolted against it, Goodman. I have meditated long and hard on this, and I am bound to say that, had the boy not found his own way from our clutches, I should certainly have released him before the time of reckoning. Oh, Goodman! The boy's escape was the judgement of the Lord Agonis upon us. Our scheme was foolish, surely you see that? It was excessive. It was superstitious. It was . . . Goodman, it was *provincial.'*

A butler in a billowing frock-coat swept past, bearing glittering drinks on a tray. The Holluch reel was over. There was a round of delighted applause.

'Oh, I see! I see exactly what the picture is now!' Bitterness surged in the physician's voice. His twisty face had turned a deep shade of red. 'I see that there is one in our midst who has sold the truth of faith for the gaudy baubles of this world!'

The physician stepped back; and with a mighty pluck the ill-advised sash came away in his hand.

But Jem by this time was no longer watching. He was no longer listening. In his buzzing head a tide of memory had surged up and crashed.

He remembered.

He grabbed his crutches, struggling upright. All at once the orchestra was deafeningly loud and the heat of the room was stifling him.

He had to escape.

Umbecca closed her eyes. The physician, mercifully, had slipped away; but where was the chaplain? All through the evening he had been close by. If he were not himself her partner, for this dance or that, he was squiring her to and from the arms of the handsome young officers whose names had appeared, as if of their own volition, in her programme. Umbecca looked around her, suddenly aware of the heat, the crush. Dazzling gowns intruded upon her awareness. Smooth, swan-like necks. Sand-timer waists. For the first time in the evening, Umbecca was alone.

But it lasted only an instant.

'Mistress Rench?'

The young man bowed low.

'All evening I have sought your acquaintance; that I have failed until now in this noble quest is a commentary not upon my ardour, I assure you, but upon the equal ardour of others, which has kept, as well it might, a woman of such singular charms so regularly engaged.'

Umbecca smiled. It was a gallant speech; dimly she remembered one just like it in her sister's novel, *Marital and Martial*. Ruanna, if she remembered correctly, had placed it in the mouth of the sly, greasy Eustan Vyles; but now the speech issued from a charming young officer in a superb dress uniform. Such lovely curls!

Something about him was familiar.

Indulgently, the young officer glanced towards the hunched back of Goodman Waxwell. Departing, the physician had been experiencing difficulty in passing between the stiff, hooped gowns of two fine ladies. Nervously he *hem-hemmed!* as they stood with their backs to him.

'A charming gentleman, Goodman Waxwell.'

'Oh, indeed!'

'He has been one of the pillars of this community through all its darkest years.'

'Indeed.'

'Irion has much cause to look on him with gratitude – as do I.'

Recognition spread over Umbecca's face.

'Poltiss Waxwell?'

So much time had passed since she had seen the physician's young ward that Umbecca was startled by the transformation in him. He was splendid! With a fresh clarity, she saw the falsity of Goodman Waxwell. The man was suffering from something. Delusions. It had to be. He said the boy had gone to the bad!

The young officer inclined his curly head, and smiled, 'Poltiss, indeed, my dear lady; but Waxwell no longer. Veeldrop. Poltiss Veeldrop.'

'Veeldrop?'

A sensation at once distinct yet indescribable enfolded Umbecca's heart. She saw now that the young officer – how Poltiss had grown! – was even more familiar than she had thought at first. Umbecca closed her eyes and memory welled in her.

'Mistress Rench?'

The enquiry expressed a polite concern. Poltiss took her arm. The wheeling music of the ball had ceased and the chink of a spoon against a fluted glass rang high over the room.

Umbecca did not look up.

On the podium where the orchestra had played, the chaplain handed the glass to an aide. He held up his gloved hands, palms outward. His face creased into an indulgent smile as the hubbub of the great bright room was slowly stilled.

'Gentlewomen and gentlemen of the Tarn,' the chaplain began, 'it is an auspicious occasion on which we gather here tonight. Tonight, we enjoy the most glittering festival to have been seen in these valleys in all the time since their glorious liberation from the hated tyranny of the Redjacket Pretender. In this festival, it is my belief, we may see at once a culmination and a confirmation, a denouement and a declaration.

'The space of four moonlives now has passed since the glorious day when the United Regiments of the Tarn returned to assume their rightful place here. In that time we have seen this village transformed from the abject condition in which once it languished, into a place which, I feel it hardly rash to declare, already seems likely to grow into a city that shall be the envy and awe of all the Agonist lands.'

Eay Feval was pleased with himself. This was shaping up to be one of his best speeches. He only hoped that the old man, waiting behind the curtain at the back of the podium, would not stumble as he made his way forward. It was so important to make a good impression.

'Think of the renewal we have seen here, and the glory of that renewal. To renew! To repair! To renovate! To restore – revitalize, rejuvenate! It is a noble undertaking; but to see it only as a physical one, my friends, would be wrong. In the rebirth of these valleys, may we not find a fit symbol of that renovation of the heart which we who follow in the path of the Lord Agonis must seek to bring to this ruined world?'

The chaplain looked benevolently over the gathering, and noted, with a faint wrinkling of his forehead, that Mistress Rench appeared a little distressed; the fat woman, evidently, was in the grip of some emotion.

Dear me.

She had much to learn.

Umbecca had retreated into the cavern of her memory.

She had returned to the heady days just after the Siege, when all the world was alive with possibility. Could it be, now, that those days had returned? She had barely dared to hope. And yet, was not everything, now, as it had been before? She recalled the courtyard below her window filled with milling, blue-jacketed forms. They had returned. She recalled the rumbling carts and the cawing cries of prisoners; she recalled the hangings on the green and the waving flags and the music. They had returned. She recalled the day when she had met the Bluejacket commander. *Sister Becca, this is Commander Veeldrop*, the Archduke had said. Had he returned, too? Umbecca had stopped herself thinking about him. She had never wanted to think of him again – but she found herself thinking of him now. His height. His handsomeness. His hair. His hands. His magnificent, curling moustaches!

No, she had never wanted to think of him again!

'And so,' Eay Feval was saying, 'it remains only for me to introduce the man who is alone responsible for the astonishing renewal we have seen here in the Tarn. You know him as – *ahem* – one of the *greatest heroes* in all the long annals of the Agonist lands; you know him as a man who liberated you before, as he has liberated you now. Gentlewomen and gentlemen of the Tarn, if I have any sorrow in my heart as I give him to you now, it is only in that I cannot introduce him by the title which, you shall all agree, should rightfully be his – no, not just Commander, but *Lord* Veeldrop!'

Applause, like thunder, burst through the ballroom, and slowly, flickeringly, as one returns from a deep dream, Umbecca opened her eyes. She gazed, astonished, on the broken old man, watching unbelievingly as he swayed for some moments, leaning heavily on a bejewelled stick, before collapsing into a chair without speaking.

In rapid succession, the chaplain led a round of applause, and the orchestra struck up the Canticle of the Flag.

Chapter 53

THE ORCHARD IN DARKNESS

Jem was trembling.

In the orchard, the air was chilly, but the boy was not shivering. He was frightened; frightened, but puzzled, too, that he should feel such fear. The danger, after all, had been averted. He had escaped.

Jem had laid his crutches beside him and was leaning over the bowl of the fountain called The Foretelling. He pressed down heavily on his crossed arms, gazing up at the figures that rose, mysterious in the moonlight, above the welling water. The statues had been cleaned of their green crust of moss. Silver water burgeoned round their feet like a shimmering, crystal flower, and rippled brimmingly into the vast bowl beneath. Once, Jem reflected, it had been evil-smelling, festering with slimy life. He looked down into the clear coolness of the water and saw, in the depths, the phantom of the moon, locked inside the lattice of reflected leaves and branches.

Above him, the neatly pruned trees creaked lightly.

Plop!

The moon dissolved. Spots of water splashed Jem's face. Something had fallen from the trees. An apple? He looked down as the moon shimmered back into being.

Then, a moment later, it happened again.

Carefully, keeping his grip on the rim of the bowl, Jem tried to turn. To twist himself.

'Is someone there?'

No reply.

But this time, when the moon reappeared in the water, Jem saw that a face had appeared there, too. He saw the familiar tangle of dark hair and the broad, high cheekbones. The deep, intent eyes.

Jem had remembered something.

Now he remembered everything.

'Cata!' He laughed aloud.

'Why do you laugh?'

There was a loud crash of leaves and the girl was beside him.

'Why?' she said again.

But Jem could not stop laughing; and had he done so, he could never have explained. He understood now why he had been so afraid. He had been afraid he would never see Cata again. He had buried not one memory, but two.

The first because it made him so sad.

The second because it made him so happy.

It was happiness that made him laugh now; and it was happiness that made him swing out recklessly from the side of the fountain, grabbing for his crutches; it was happiness that made him miss them, and made him clutch absurdly at the fountain again, as his crutches clattered down the marble steps.

He gasped, breathless between the laughter, 'Cata, help me!'

He reached for her hand, but then Jem's joy turned to astonishment as the girl suddenly, angrily, pushed him away. He slumped, hard, to the marble platform.

'I hate you!' she burst out.

She jumped up, swinging back into the branches.

'Cata?'

Jem lay on his back, looking up. He should have felt helpless, hopeless, but strangely, at this moment, he felt calm. Very calm. He gazed into rustling leaves and bobbing, pendulous apples. A regular, choking rhythm was sounding from above.

Cata was sobbing.

She gulped, 'I looked for you. Oh, how I looked for you! Now there you are in your fine clothes, and you just laugh at me.'

'Oh, Cata!' said Jem. 'You're wrong! I wasn't laughing at you.'

There was a pause; and soft sniffling.

'Then why were you laughing? You wouldn't tell me.'

'I couldn't! Cata, I was laughing because I was happy.'

Loudly, Cata wiped her nose. She flung back, 'What have you got to be happy about? You're still a cripple.'

Jem almost laughed again. But he checked himself. 'I've got you,' he said shyly.

'What?'

He didn't much want to say it again. But he closed his eyes and said, very calmly, 'I'm happy because of you. I was never so happy as when I was with you. I'm happy because you're here.'

There was a long silence from the apple tree; there was not even snuffling. But at last a small voice came, 'Really?'

'Really,' said Jem.

This time the girl slipped down sinuously, silently, from the tree. At one moment she was above; at the next, she was beside him.

She looked down at him.

She held out her hand.

Jem's hand linked with hers; and that was when something extraordinary happened. As if a force, as if some secret power had passed between them, Jem felt himself moving upwards into the force of her grip; at first imperceptibly, then with a rush of power, he knew that the impossible had happened again.

He was standing.

❄ ❄ ❄ ❄

Later, Jem would look back on that moment as the time when his life had first assumed definition. For so long, he had lived without purpose. He had not known why he lived. From that moment on, he knew he had a destiny; though quite what it was, he could not be sure.

But Cata was a part of it.

She had to be.

They walked around The Foretelling, their hands clasped hotly; tentatively, they crunched along the cinder-path; they ventured under the trees. But only when Jem, in sudden excitement, tried to run ahead, and fell, did they realize the curious nature of the magic that had enveloped them.

Jem could walk: but only when Cata held his hand.

Poltiss Veeldrop breathed deeply, relieved to have escaped the foetid air of the ball. He strolled through the topiary of his father's formal gardens.

The music had started in the ballroom again and the frothy strains of a Varby waltz drifted elegantly on to the air. The evening had been a great success. Polty had danced with some of the finest beauties of the province, and the eyes of all the ladies, it was clear, had been upon him. Had he rushed back into the ballroom at that moment, and offered his hand even to the luscious Miss Vyella Rextel, she would have accepted him. Of course she would.

Polty did a little twirl on the crunching path. Women! They disgusted him. He had become a creature of beauty, but he had been ugly for too long not to feel, with a sharp pang, the bitter ironies of beauty. The eyes that lingered admiringly over him now only filled him with contempt. The same eyes, he knew, would once have looked on him with loathing. Women were fools, dazzled by bright baubles. They were hypocrites, finding virtue in the dwelling-places of their lust.

Even the old bag from the castle was stuck on him, he could tell. Umbecca Rench! A ridiculous woman, rigged out in a curtain with a snotty handkerchief stuffed down the front. All the fine ladies were sniggering behind their hands.

But the chaplain had some sort of plan for her, it seemed; she had to be kept on side. Polty would be very good, from now on, at keeping people on side.

He had changed his outward form.

He had not changed his heart.

Polty laughed softly to himself. He listened to the distant sounds from the ballroom. There would be only a few moments now until the Lexion Revels. He had promised the dance to the lovely Vy; but it would do her proud heart no harm to wait, just a little. He should like to see some spots of colour in those icy cheeks!

Idly he passed through the gate that led into his father's orchard. Here, he did not walk on the path but instead on the grass verge. It amused him to be silent. He was careful not to rustle against the leaves of the trees.

That was when he heard the voices, intent and low beneath the burbling of the fountain. Polty could not make out all the words. But he knew that something was going on. Something interesting.

His gaze pierced through the curtaining leaves. For an odd moment, the voices seemed to issue from the statue above the fountain, that shimmered palely in the moonlight through the trees. Polty recalled that the statue was called The Foretelling: the Lord Agonis and the Lady Imagenta, naked and holding hands.

Sentimental rubbish.

Then he saw the darker, smaller figures close by. A girl and a boy, standing.

Embracing.

The girl, he could tell at once, was no lady of fashion. She appeared to be dressed in rags.

'But how can I see you again? When?'

'Come to me in the Wildwood—'

'I can't! They wouldn't—'

'You go to Temple, don't you?'

'I couldn't get away—'

'You'll find a way. There's a place in the tombyard. Near

the big yew. A hole in the wall, almost covered by brush-wood. Like a wall of sticks. But you can push your way through—'

'A wall of sticks?'

'I'll be waiting.'

Then the girl kissed the boy for a last time and shinned swiftly, lithely, up the trunk of a tree.

She was gone.

Some peasant slut, breaking curfew? She must have climbed over the wall.

But who was the boy?

It was only when the boy turned to come away that Polty saw, to his astonishment, the answer to this question.

Crunch, drag, went the crutches on the cinder-path.

Crunch, drag.

But for a moment, had it not seemed that the boy was standing? It was the strangest thing.

Polty hissed silently to himself.

Chapter 54

UMBECCA IN THE JUNGLE

'Chaplain, one feels one is in a jungle!'

Fronds of ferns stroked Umbecca's arms. Draping vines swished past her face.

'It is called the Glass Room, dear lady—'

'The Glass Room? How remarkable.'

But Umbecca knew. Of course she did. How many times had she sat in this green chamber, gazing like a fool at Lector Wolveron?

She shuddered.

She did not want to think of Silas now.

'Here we are.' The chaplain held the foliage apart like a curtain as Umbecca stepped, a little tentatively, on to the green carpet. She was, it appeared, the first to arrive. A tea-table, laden admirably with pastries, was set invitingly in the centre of the carpet, surrounded by a circle of spindly chintz chairs.

Three of them.

'Dear lady, do take a seat.'

Umbecca began to colour a little, gazing at the chaplain with a nervous smile. 'You're not expecting a *large* party, then, Chaplain?'

'Dear lady, no! The commander prefers a certain . . . *intimacy* at tea.'

'Ah. My, what lovely pastries!'

A surge of greed fought in Umbecca with a strange alarm. She was wondering if she had misjudged the occasion. Again she was wearing her ball dress, cut down and suitably altered, its magnificence not so much diminished as *adapted* for afternoon wear. She had hoped to give the impression that she had many beautiful gowns; but also that they were all in the loyal colour of blue.

Yes.

That was what she had wanted; for after all she had hardly imagined an occasion like the present. As she had remarked to her maid, in the course of one extensive fitting, 'In the world of fashion, Nirry, there is no such thing as a *mere* invitation to tea. You should view this, indeed, not so much as what *you* might understand as tea, Nirry – a rapid slurping followed by a satisfied sigh – but rather as what, perhaps, you dimly apprehended of the ball . . . the ball resumed at an earlier hour. And all eyes, Nirry, shall be upon me. You do understand me, don't you, girl?'

But the wretched girl had only grunted, her mouth full of pins. The new panels in the side-seams had caused particular difficulties, and the maid was more than usually unhappy.

Drat the girl!

❈　❈　❈　❈

It had not been the chaplain this time, but Poltiss Veeldrop who had brought Umbecca her invitation. She had gazed at him with a little smile, for certainly he was the most handsome Bluejacket she had seen; but a shyness prevented her from asking the questions she longed to ask. Ever since she had seen the commander again, Umbecca had felt a strange, throbbing apprehension.

The apprehension was strong in her now, as she gazed about the Glass Room. Umbecca's eyes roved across the unrustling, strangely sinister ferns and vines and flowers. There were huge bright lolling tongues and fruity, hunched assemblages of needle-like quills and spikes. Dreadful plants; the sort of things that came, she understood, from southern climes such as those of the Agonist Deliverance. How appalling to be surrounded by such monstrous growths! Umbecca was glad to be an Ejlander.

Her gaze travelled to the huge desk, with its heavy column-like legs and the little, dainty volumes lined neatly on the top. Behind the desk, the high curved back of the green leather chair was turned away towards the plants, as if perhaps its occupant had left in a hurry.

Where was the commander?

Umbecca could not help but wonder why the old man should have chosen this place as, evidently, his centre of command. Had such a room been part of her house, Umbecca would certainly have had it knocked down. The place was repellent, perverse; precisely, she reflected, the characteristics of the man who had built it. Dimly, Umbecca understood that Silas Wolveron, in this dreadful chamber, had endeavoured to express his divided nature, at once of the Wildwood, yet not. The massive desk was a rampart against the primitive greenness, and yet the greenness had been there all about him. Insisting. Encroaching. Oh, it was disgusting! There would be flying things in some of those plants. Nasty little burrowing bugs. Worms! With a shudder Umbecca thought that some of them might even have crawled into the carpet.

She shifted her feet.

'Tea?' smiled Eay Feval.

It seemed they were not to wait for the commander.

The tea-pot was an ornate affair of porcelain flummery. The painted design that ran round the sides featured amorous swains, milkmaids, various cows and sheep, a windmill and a burbling stream. With admirable precision, Eay Feval upended the spout over a dainty cup, bearing the same design. The service was a fine specimen of 'Varby Pastoral'. Such a set, Umbecca knew, was both expensive and rare. Her spirits lifted a little, and then it occurred to her, with a peculiar pang, that such a set had featured prominently in one of her sister's novels. Yes: it was in *The Prickly Path to Wedlock*, in which the purchase of a 'Varby set' had sparked off such long-running complications in the courtship of Meroline and Colonel Fonnel.

That was when Umbecca glanced back to the huge rampart of the desk and registered the line of small, dainty volumes. It was not just any set of books.

It was a set of Ruanna's books.

'A pastry, dear lady?' offered the chaplain.

Umbecca smiled. Her fat stomach gave an appreciative rumble. It was pleasant, after all, to be sitting here with the chaplain! The richest cream of the valleys oozed through her fingers.

She attempted small talk.

'It must be a splendid thing,' she remarked, 'for the commander to be reunited with his son.'

'Oh, indeed. Young Captain Veeldrop is a good boy, and has been a great comfort to his lordship. Do you know, I should not be surprised if the young captain were himself one day to become a great man like his father?'

'I have no doubt about it.'

The young man, after all, resembled the commander greatly. With a little more maturity, a little more gravity, Poltiss would be the very image of the commander as he had been. He might almost have been designed to be a reminder of the past. Dear Poltiss!

Umbecca looked uneasily at the empty chintz chair. 'The commander is busy with his duties, I assume?'

But Eay Feval did not answer the question. 'More tea, dear lady?'

It was not until Umbecca had consumed several cups of tea, and most of the remarkably delicious pastries, that she was to divine at last the purpose of her visit. Its purpose, in the event, would only puzzle her more.

The conversation had rambled from one inconsequential pleasantry to the next, and seemed merely to be wandering in the direction of another, when the chaplain said:

'You have not remarked, dear lady, on a certain phenomenon. A phenomenon which, I thought, might have interested you.'

Umbecca followed his gesturing hand; and saw that the chaplain's white glove was indicating – yes, it was clear – the familiar gilt edges of the 'Agondon Edition'. If Umbecca had said nothing about her sister's books, it was because they made her uncomfortable. To be reminded of Ruanna's success had always galled her. Besides, why ever should she remark upon them? In the eyes of the world, they were nothing to her.

'The books, chaplain?'

'The "Agondon Edition",' he returned. 'The definitive set, is it not, of the writings of a certain young lady? A lady now said to be taken, one gathers, from our midst?'

Umbecca, sipping her tea, assumed a disinterested air. 'A "Miss R——," was it not? I heard of her – oh, long ago. My niece has one or two of her books, I believe. I did look into them – oh, once, twice. But novels are such trash, don't you find? I can't say I thought "Miss R——" an exception to the rule.' She gave a little laugh; but she had coloured, she knew, and had failed to keep the welling emotion from her voice.

The chaplain, too, had assumed an air of disinterest. He was standing, and with apparent idleness had taken one of the volumes from the line on the desk. He looked at the title. '*Marital and Martial*,' he said. 'Do you know it?'

'Hm – I can't say I've seen that one.'

The chaplain picked out a page at random and held the book towards Umbecca. He said, with an uncharacteristic prefatory *hem!*, 'I don't suppose, dear lady, you would read just a little? The print is small, and vanity, I am afraid, makes me eschew eyeglasses. Besides, I think a lady's voice . . . *hem!*'

All at once, Umbecca was alarmed again. The disturbing sense came to her that the chaplain was playing some sort of game; that he was tormenting her in a way, and for reasons, she could not quite understand. What did he know? What did he want? Umbecca, for all her pretence of refinement, was a woman of crude, powerful emotions. The chaplain, she began to realize, had in him a subtlety which frightened her.

In another life, Umbecca might at this moment have refused the volume; she might have seized it from the chaplain's hands and flung it down angrily. In this life, she had no choice, it seemed, but to comply with his request. She took the volume from him meekly.

Her hands were trembling.

She looked up. Clouds drifted like ghostly, vast ships in the pallid sky overhead as, wonderingly, striving to keep her voice level, Umbecca read:

LETTER TWENTY-ONE.

My dearest friend,

Oh, monstrous! What am I to say, what can I say, to this concerning news? I am at a loss to speak, and can barely write. That such threats, such imprecations should pass within the bosom of a respectable family! Write to me again at once, my dear, and tell me all that fell out when your hot-headed brother confronted at last your attempted ravisher. And that they still threaten you with so odious a suitor! It is not to be borne! How often, my dear, have I thought back to that tearful parting when you left for Agondon, and wished only that I could take you from the house of your hated parents and return you to these valleys, where together we could live in rustic innocence? What a world is this in which we live, that the most virtuous of her sex should come to such a trial?

But hold! Mama is at the door, and I must break off.—

Umbecca broke off, almost sobbing. She looked up, uncertainly. Her attempt to keep the emotion from her voice had failed signally. She gazed, uncertainly, in the direction of the chaplain. That was when she saw that a third figure had joined them. He had been there all the time, concealed from her, in the averted green chair behind the desk.

Now the commander made his way towards her, leaning painfully on his bejewelled stick. The old man had pushed up the visor from his eyes and gazed on Umbecca with an ardent rapture. She staggered upright, the dainty volume falling from her lap, almost crying out as the commander lurched forward and caught her hands in his.

'My dear lady! My dear, dear lady! How good of you to come! You'll come again tomorrow, I hope?'

Chapter 55

THE WALL OF STICKS

And to his first-born he gave a crystal coloured like night,
glowing purple-black with a light that was like darkness.
Ork. Juv. II. 38/13–14

'Women and men of Irion, let us consider this most curious thing. A crystal, it is written, that was coloured *like night*; a light, it is written, that was *like darkness*. Now, I know what some of you are thinking. Oh, I do: for I have heard such thoughts before. No, don't look so worried, my man – *that's* not what I meant.'

Titters.

'Think of it! This curious thing: this dark crystal; this light that *glowed like darkness*. Now, I say to you, I know what you are thinking. How do I know, you ask? I say to you, I have heard such thoughts before. Where have I heard them? Where? Where?'

Eay Feval's voice had dropped to a whisper. Looming over the lectern, he was pleased to note that the congregated had, in their place, inclined their heads forward, as if to be certain of catching his words. He delivered them slowly, carefully, as if they were a confidence vouchsafed privately to each of his hearers, to each one alone.

It was an admirable technique.

'Women and men of Irion, I must tell you that the place where I have heard these things is a place of the most intimate and personal nature. It is a place to which, by its very nature, one retires to be alone. I should say, indeed, that it is the most intimate place I know.'

Jem glanced at his fascinated aunt, sitting beside him. A blush, red and burning, had spread across her cheeks.

'Of where do I speak? Oh my friends, is it not clear? The place of which I speak is *my own heart*.' The chaplain reeled back. He flung out his blue-robed arms and cried, 'For yes, my friends, I too have been burdened, as a beast is burdened, by the weight of doubt which assails you now! In the dark chambers of my own heart, have I not wandered, as in a labyrinth? I have! For how, I have asked myself, could it be, how could it happen, how could it come to pass ... that a *light* should be produced from *darkness*?

'My friends, let us think on this dark crystal. For it is written that the dark crystal was given by the dying god to his first-born son. And who, let us ask ourselves, was his *first-born* son?'

The chaplain's eyes darted over the faces of the congregated. Yes, the techniques were working well now. They were working admirably.

'Koros!' he thundered. 'Koros, god of the Vagas!'

Jem was restless.

When he had first begun to attend the Canonicals, the boy had felt a certain awed respect. There was something in the chaplain that disturbed him, it was true; something, perhaps, in the contrast between the private and the public face. Was not the chaplain, perhaps, a little frivolous? Was his manner really that of the guardian of sacred truth? But Jem had not doubted that the chaplain must be in possession of such truth; it was only his conduct of his role that seemed puzzling.

Now it was more. Jem was, in many ways, a simple boy, but he was never a fool. He was able to think.

And to think is to doubt.

It was, perhaps, at the moment when Eay Feval shouted out the name of Koros that Jem first realized the purpose of the Canonical.

The secret purpose.

The darkness, claimed the chaplain, was the darkness of the Vaga-kind, severed from the light of the Lord Agonis; the light from the darkness, he claimed, was the active evil that shone, as a blackening, negative light, from the Vaga-kind in all their works and ways.

That was when the gnawing, nagging feeling, which Jem had been almost alarmed to find inside him, was suddenly clear to him.

Then he knew:

They want us to hate the Vagas.

They want us to hate the Vagas so we won't hate them.

Jem thought about the El-Orokon. The sacred book, he knew, dated back long ago; so long ago that no one was quite sure when it was written, or who had written it. Perhaps it was false. Perhaps it was true. But Jem knew one thing: it may as well have been written specially by the Bluejackets, to justify their regime.

That was how they used it.

He turned to his aunt and looked at her, as she gazed up, enraptured, at Eay Feval. She gazed at him now as she had once gazed at Waxwell. For a time, after the night of the ball, Jem had hated his aunt. Fuming inwardly, he imagined that he would tell her everything he knew. Suddenly he would burst out with the fact of his knowledge. Then he realized that he would not, and realized that he did not hate Aunt Umbecca.

He pitied her.

He twisted his head and his eyes roved over the upturned faces of the officers' wives, of the respectable tradesmen, of the peasants at the back. Eay Feval would call them his flock, and Jem saw, indeed, that that was what they were.

A flock of sheep.

Jem could sit politely no longer. He raised himself on his crutches and made his way down the aisle.

'Excuse me. Excuse me.'

'Jem! Are you sick?' his aunt whispered.

Jem did not reply. Later, he would tell her that indeed he had been sick, though he would not say what it was that made him so; now he only dragged himself down the aisle as fast as he could, while Eay Feval, faltering just a little, thundered of the bound duty of the Agonists to stamp out Vaga-evil wherever it was found.

To stamp out the Vagas.

❉　❉　❉　❉

The air in the tombyard was crisp and clean.

The guards in the portico looked at Jem as he made his way awkwardly down the temple steps. Jem knew what they were thinking.

The cripple-boy from the castle.

Harmless.

He crunched slowly around the path between the graves. It was neat and well-weeded now. Strangely, all at once Jem found the Canonical had vanished from his mind. In the temple, outrage had consumed him. Now it was gone; it was all gone. He looked up at the overcast sky; he looked down at the tomb-slabs and the hacked grass that surrounded them. Where was he going? He just wanted to wander amongst the graves, that was all.

No he didn't.

He turned back. No guards watched him. No one could see him. He heaved himself off the path and made for the corner of the tombyard. The grass was still long here, and billowed in the wind. From the temple, far off, he heard the heft of the organ and the voices rising in Final Canticles. The mingling sounds, drifting over the tomb-slabs, made Jem feel peculiarly alone.

'I am alone,' he said aloud.

'No, you're not.'

Of course she was there. Jem had come to the place in the far wall, the place where she had told him to come.

The gap.

The breach.
The wall of sticks.

Jem was gazing into the strangest eyes.

It had to be an illusion, of course; there could be no eyes that were quite like this. At one moment they were golden; at the next, they were black. At one moment they glowed like flat, opaque discs; at the next they were possessed of the most profound depths. When they were black, it seemed to Jem that he might sink into those eyes as into a bottomless pool. But he would not drown. He would not die. He would only go down and down, and somewhere, deep in the darkness, would be light.

Wood-tiger turned and flickered away.

It was over; it was over. Deep in the Wildwood, Jem was lying in a bower of white petals.

Cata lay beside him.

End of Part Four

PART FIVE

The Burning Verses

Chapter 56

A WILDWOOD TREE

Jem's life had changed.

When he was younger, he had left the castle only in a cart or carriage, and only ever in the company of his aunt. Alone, he had heaved himself about the interior of the castle, but to have ventured beyond the bailey walls would have seemed a feat beyond him. Now he would be bolder. He had entered his fourth cycle; and as if this had been a sign of new strength, the boy hazarded expeditions first a little down the road from the crag, then further.

Then further.

Soon, in the intervals when the weather was clear, Jem would take himself off for long, lonely walks. He made his way about the streets and lanes of the village, and beyond. Sometimes, as he swung perilously through puddles or snow-slush, or struggled back up the rocky, steep road to the crag, a merchant in a cart or a soldier on horseback might call to him, politely asking if he needed assistance. Jem, resolute in his stubbornness and pride, always shook his head. He did not want pity and he did not want help.

Jem did not feel afraid of walking about the domain of the Bluejackets. On the contrary, he felt safe. To the soldiers, the sight of the 'crippler', as they called him, would become a familiar one; for some, he would become an object of inarticulate, deep affection.

'Halt!' an unfamiliar sentry demanded one night, as Jem was hauling himself back across the drawbridge. Dark had drawn in and the curfew had sounded. In the clouded moonlight the figure propped on sticks, with its hanging, twisted legs, might have given a momentary impression of malevolence. The sentry, raising his musket, demanded Jem's purpose.

'Morvy! Don't be silly!' A second figure stepped out of the shadows of the gate. 'It's just the poor crippler, can't you see? He lives here.'

Another time, Jem heard a fellow say, 'Leave the crippler be. He's only a simpleton.'

This, he realized, was what they all thought. It disturbed him; but he thought about it and then he decided it was good. It was a source of power.

❋ ❋ ❋ ❋ ❋

Jem was already a familiar spirit in the village by the time he could walk to the Wall of Sticks. For the length of a first, then a second moonlife, he could not quite bring himself to go so far. Then one day he slipped from the path in the tombyard and swung rapidly, recklessly towards the gap. He passed beneath the yew-tree. All the snow had melted that morning and hanging, dripping leaves spattered his face.

Would she be there?

He leaned against the impacted wooden wall, breathing deeply. No one had seen him come here; he was certain of that. Would she come?

Of course not.

It was foolish, absurd. How long had passed since they were together? Was she to spend her life waiting here for him? Jem was aware of a deep, secret torment. The girl had done something to him, changed him. Sometimes he found himself hating her for it. What they had done in the woods that day had seemed at the time a perfect thing, complete in itself. It had seemed like the end of something: a culmination. The boy had not reckoned with his desire to do it again. Alone at night in his alcove in the castle, Jem dreamed of the scene replaying itself. Again and again he imagined the girl.

He wanted her.

Fluid burst from him, sour-sweet and hot, and cooled to flaky stiffness on his blankets and his hands.

Thoughts of these things crashed forlornly through his mind as he waited for her, that first day. His heart boomed longingly in his chest. Between his thighs, the ache of the nights had returned.

She was not there; but the next day, and the day after, Jem returned to the Wall of Sticks. He would push his way awkwardly through the concealing screen and stand, trembling, on the Wildwood side.

On the fourth day she was there.

He said, 'I knew you'd come.'

But he had not. He had known nothing.

'I watched you.' There was defiance in her eyes. 'I watched you in secret.'

'You knew I was here?' The boy could not look at her. His own gaze was cast down. Desire had gone from him and he was trembling with cold.

Drip, drip, came the water from the leaves.

She tossed back her head. 'I wanted to see how much you wanted it.'

It was a challenge. There was cruelty in her voice. Jem could not bear it. Slowly his crutches slipped from beneath his arms. With little twistings of his body, awkward little grabbings at the wood-wall sticks, he was sinking to the ground.

He held out his hand.

'Take it. Please.'

She did not.

He lay in the mud and leaves, shivering. His eyes were closed. He could hear her feet stirring, stirring at the twigs and mouldering leaves. Had she turned to go? Let her go; he would not come here again. Not think of her again. Some other object would be found in time, to prompt the harsh, hot burstings of his body.

She lay beside him.

She touched him.

What they did that day had nothing in it of bliss. She did not kiss him. The raw animal need rose in him again, unbidden and urgent, responsive only to the actions of her hands. She ripped open his breeches; she pushed him on to his back and squatted on top of him, pulling up her shift. He jabbed at her sharply, swiftly.

He cried out; it was pain, not pleasure.

She scrambled up. She vanished into the trees and he heard her running, running, breathlessly away.

The boy was still shivering, and sobbing now, too. It had been too much. It had been too much.

But he came back the next day, and so did she.

Something was over.

Something was decided.

Now Jem's days were consecrated to Cata. The warm days of the Season of Viana were creeping back slowly, uncertainly over the valleys, and as the sweet brief swelling of life came to the trees, Jem would repair each day to the Wildwood. Sometimes the girl would not be there, waiting for him at the Wall of Sticks, but when she was, she would take his hand. Power surged through his twisted limbs again. Then he would conceal his crutches beneath a vine that draped long and heavily over crumbly, moist sticks, and together they ran deeper into the greenness. Their hands entwined, they leapt and laughed; they sported and played in the Wildwood light. Under this tree, or that, they would fondle and kiss; each tree would seem like a holy place, and each tree would seem like the only one.

How he loved her!

Sometimes he would glimpse her in a fleeting, captured moment – the flash of eye beneath a hooded, slanting lid; the fall of shadow on a jutting cheekbone – and it would seem to him that in these moments the whole of her was there. Then he would long to possess her utterly, only so that then he could possess that light, that shadow. Later, he would recall the eyelid, the cheekbone, and the massiveness of love and desire would sweep over him again. Away from her, the burstings of his need were unremitting, goaded to new heights by his spit-moistened hands; but it was different now. It was because she was his, and because he was hers, and because his desire for her could never stop.

Together, they entered an eternal realm. They fondled, embraced; they clashed their mouths together hungrily, ardently. They tore off their clothes. In the Circle of Knowing, stripped to the naked reality of their need, they sank in ecstasy to the petal-strewn earth.

She was wilful, perverse. She laughed at him and toyed with him and pulled his hair; she dug her teeth and nails into his skin. She rolled on top of him, pinned him down; denied him satisfaction when he burned with longing. She took her pleasure alone, with darting fingers, with circling palm. When he longed to share in it, she pushed him away.

'I hate you, I hate you!' he would sometimes sob.

But it was a sweet torment. Sometimes he would end it, seizing his swollenness in his own hand, spattering the hot fluid on to his belly. Then she would creep back to him, and her hot tongue licked it clean.

How he loved it when she yielded to him utterly! Then she let his body pin her to the ground, her moistening thighs spread wide beneath him. Then, with savage thrustings, he took his revenge; his awkwardness, his boyish shyness gone and forgotten. All else was scattered; there was only the explosive force of his passion and a reckless, onrushing quest for pleasure.

She moaned beneath him, the slave of his desire.

But he was her slave, too.

Intoxicated, enraptured, the boy surrendered to her; to the sweet mysterious darkness of her skin and the blackness and pungency of her long, entangling hair. He loved the smooth firm ripeness of her limbs, the curve of her belly, the tender swellings of her breasts; he loved the succulent depths of her interior moistness. Her touch, her taste, her smell consumed his senses. His fingers explored every curve, each crevass; his mouth and her mouth mingled their spittle, twisted their serpent-tongues raveningly together. Again and again his desire unfurled, sticky, aching and demanding satisfaction. There was nothing else in the world and there could be nothing else. It was as if the flow of common time had halted; nothing existed, nothing was real, but their joyous love, their lust. He loved her; he wanted only to be with her, to do these things, to feel like this, to explode like this into cascades of gushing white heat.

Again and again.

With her.

For ever.

Chapter 57

THREE WOMEN

Umbecca sighed with satisfaction.

Gazing into the looking-glass in the afternoon sunshine, she saw before her a light, airy figure in the palest of pale-blue muslin tea-gowns. The gown was printed in a charming floral design. Delicate silvery threads across the bodice created a most diverting effect of shimmering. The skirts seemed to fall so lightly, so loosely, that the word *diaphanous* sprang at once to mind. That, at least, was what the chaplain had said, and the chaplain's judgement was always right in these matters.

As in all others.

Delicate trimmings completed the effect, fashioned from the finest Varby lace. Just the thing for the Season of Theron! Umbecca gave a little twirl before the glass.

The gown, this time, was not the work of Nirry, but had been sent from Agondon at the chaplain's request. It was only one of many magnificent new costumes he had given to Umbecca: ball-gowns, tea-dresses, morning wear . . . He was so kind. So considerate. How Umbecca loved the magnificent parcels wrapped in ribbon that he would bring to her; how she loved the crispness of the paper inside and the pungency of the cloth as she drew it forth, exclaiming. 'Oh, Chaplain!' Umbecca would gasp; and sometimes, more intimately, 'Eay!'

Much of her day was now spent in dressing.

A knock, a light *rat-a-tat*, sounded at the door; the knock seemed as much a thing of air and light as the magnificent blue skies outside the open casement and the – yes – *diaphanous* vision in the glass. Birdsong sounded sweetly on the air.

'Girl?' said Umbecca, as she turned to go.

Nirry appeared, as if from nowhere.

'You don't think my nose is shining, a little?'

'Perhaps just a little, ma'am.'

Nirry applied the powder-puff; then, at a further prompting, just a little more rouge. Umbecca, of course, was not a vain woman, nor a woman given to the cosmetic arts; indeed, as she had remarked to the admiring chaplain, there was nothing that she deplored more than a painted woman. The mere sight of that green-gartered old harridan from the Lazy Tiger, she added sweetly, was enough to cause a shudder in the breast of any virtuous woman. The chaplain had agreed fulsomely; but a virtuous woman, he had said, was nonetheless a woman, and what woman should forgo the enhancements which, so all the great world agreed, were the birthright of her sex? Umbecca had smiled then, and at once concurred, for when the chaplain spoke of the *great world,* she knew, he was speaking not of the world, *the world,* in all its uninteresting and vulgar enormity, but rather of the highest and most exclusive circles of Agondon society.

He was speaking of the court itself.

Umbecca gave her glass a final admiring glance. What a figure she made! It was the figure, she said to herself, not of a woman of *mature years* – the phrase conveyed quite the wrong impression – but rather of a woman in the *prime of life.*

Yes.

That was something else the chaplain had said.

Umbecca sailed – *diaphanously,* of course – towards the door, where a handsome young Bluejacket guard stood respectfully. Could it be, she fondly wondered, that the *rat-a-tat* of his hand might be echoed, at this moment, in a *rat-a-tat* at his heart? She gave a little laugh, just a little laugh, as he handed her into the carriage, and essayed the *enigmatic* smile she had been practising, of late, before the glass.

How Umbecca's life had changed! Sometimes she dated it from the day the Bluejackets came; sometimes from the ball; sometimes from the first tea she had taken in the Glass Room. She knew only that she was happy, with a happiness that seemed to grow and spread with every day that passed. A carriage had been put at her personal disposal, and each afternoon she would repair to the Lectory, there to take tea with the commander.

And the chaplain.

At first, it was true, Umbecca had been just a little disappointed at a certain aspect of these afternoons. Even now it might be said that she was happier, just a little, on those occasions when the commander was indisposed, with his duties or his gout, and she was free to speak to the chaplain of the latest patterns in chintz, or the Tiralos carpets at Lady T——'s, or the remarkable masquerade for which Lady S—— had taken over the entirety of the Ollon Pleasure-Gardens. All Agondon still spoke of it, the chaplain said.

Yet, for all this, Umbecca no longer found it distressing to read from Ruanna's novels. After the first day, the chaplain had intimated that she should begin at the beginning of the 'Agondon Edition', reading 'Miss R——' in sequence. So it was that they had started with *Becca's First Ball*. That novel alone took the length of a moonlife to read each afternoon, aloud, at tea. By the end of it, Umbecca was regularly laughing and sobbing at the experiences of her namesake. Day by day the beautiful young Becca negotiated the waters of the great world, threatening often to sink, but coming at last to safe harbour in the arms of Lord Elgrove. Little by little, piece by piece, Umbecca found that something in her heart had cracked. Perhaps she was beginning to admit to herself that Ruanna, after all, had never despised her; that Ruanna had never been anything but kind. Perhaps she saw, if only dimly, that even the title of Ruanna's first novel was a gift, a kindness, to her plainer sister. For what was 'Becca', after all, but everything Umbecca wanted to be? In the pages of fiction, Ruanna had reversed all the disappointments of her sister's actual life. Was not the fictional Becca, indeed, in many ways rather like the real Umbecca? Both were women of ardent faith. Both were women of infinite refinement.

Umbecca's readings became more sprightly; Becca's voice became her own.

'She's so like you,' said the commander one day, reaching unexpectedly for Umbecca's hand. She had just concluded the moving passage in which Lord Elgrove had offered his heart, and poor Becca was overcome with feeling. She had thought he had believed all the slanders against her. Now she saw that he was a finer man than she had ever known – a finer man, and a man who loved her.

The passage had prompted tears all over Ejland, a generation ago; now there were tears again in Umbecca's eyes, and tears, she could see, in the commander's too. As he bent his old head, kissing her hand, Umbecca gazed above him to the smiling chaplain. They exchanged a meaningful, lingering look. How charming a tableau, Umbecca thought. How charming that two virtuous young people, united in the love of the Lord Agonis, could bring this simple happiness to a gentleman of quality, stricken in years! It was, indeed, exactly like the courtship of Meroline and Colonel Fonnel in *The Prickly Path to Wedlock* . . .

With a sweet sadness it came to Umbecca that once, in his days as a valiant hero, she would gladly have given the commander her hand. But then Umbecca's sadness was gone, and she thought not of the past but of the future. For had not every one of her sister's heroines been forced to give up a previous attachment, before at last she achieved her happiness? Had not a sweet sadness of renunciation been always the prelude to a final fulfilment?

Umbecca had loved the commander, it was true. But now her heart was differently engaged. A virtuous woman, the chaplain had said, was nonetheless a woman; a Received man, Umbecca thought, was nonetheless a man. The thought had sometimes come to her – just a fleeting, fugitive thought – that it was a pity that a man like the chaplain should be, as he must be, sworn to celibacy. Then she reflected that Received men had, after all, received Dispensations. In the highest circles in Agondon, she gathered, it had been rather common; and the chaplain, after all, was nothing if not a man of the highest circles.

Lovingly, she looked into the chaplain's eyes.

❋   ❋   ❋   ❋   ❋

'It's the tithes, I suppose?'

The girl was sullen and did not reply.

'Don't have much to say for yourself, do you, dearie? Well, never mind. The face is pretty enough. You don't look like the tarty sort, if I may say. I expect it's the tithes. One sees many a tithe-girl in my line of work. I say, there's the tithe-girls and there's the tarts. And I think a gentleman respects a tithe-girl just that little bit more, don't you? After all, we can none of us pay the tithes. All the money I make, and I can't pay the tithes! I'll have you know, I've been in my time a respectable married woman. Alas, my poor Ebby was not a respectable married man.'

As she spoke, the old woman was holding the girl by the chin, turning the young face back and forth in the flickering lamplight. A pretty girl.

But.

And something would have to be done about that dress.

Music and laughter drifted up the stairs as Goody Throsh called on her professional expertise. 'Come here, dearie,' she said kindly, and took the girl by the hand. 'Let's have a look in the box of magic tricks, hm?'

'M-Magic?'

The girl's eyes were troubled; standing before the chest at the end of the bed, she pulled suddenly from the old woman's grasp. She stepped back.

Goody Throsh turned. Her old face furrowed; then all at once she laughed. 'Oh dearie, you are a green one, aren't you! You quite had me going there. Still, there's many a gentleman likes a bit of innocence. Likes to feel he's the first. Even if ... well, never mind. There's no magic here! Look, dearie, it's just my old dressing-up box, see?'

The old woman opened the chest. The girl peered inside.

All at once her face was overspread with wonderment. She gasped. Reaching forward, she ran her hands through the sea of glistening fabric. She turned to the smiling old woman and whispered, 'Are you a Vaga?'

'A Vaga!' burst out the old woman. 'Well, I like that, coming from you!'

But then she returned, a little more kindly, 'There's no saying what I might be, my dear. Any more than you. Hm?' She reached into the chest, pulling out a long, rustling skein of red. 'Ah, yes. Just the trick.' She laughed. 'Shall we make the green girl red? Now take off that old rag, hm?'

The girl complied silently, donning first the bright red dress, then the white stockings, then the leather shoes, painted red like the dress, that the old woman dredged from deeper in the trunk. But when the girl was dressed, Goody Throsh looked at her with uncertain eyes.

'There's something not quite right.' She stepped forward, fingering the girl's dark hair. 'You could get a lot for that, my dear, don't you know? There's them who'd pay a pretty price.'

The girl stepped back, her eyes suddenly sharp.

Oh dear! Goody Throsh took a deep breath, and smiled kindly, 'No, no, my dear! Never you mind! Just advising you on your assets, that's all. And a pretty set of choppers, too, if I may say. Little pearls. But come. The finishing touch.'

And diving into the glistening sea once again, this time almost disappearing into the bright depths, Goody Throsh emerged with what might have been the pelt of a shaggy yellow animal. The girl's eyes widened; but swiftly, before she had time to protest, the old woman had bundled up the girl's long hair and pushed the tight wig firmly over it.

She propelled the girl to the looking-glass, and as the girl stared, astonished, at her transfigured form, the old woman leaned close to her and whispered, 'There's our magic, hm, my dear? What is green, we make red! What is dark, we make light! By the way, dear, what's your name? I think we'll call you – hm – "Dolly". Yes, Dolly! A lovely name!'

It was over.

It was decided.

But the old woman remembered one other thing. How could she forget?

'You'll need these, of course, my dear.'

Uncertainly, the girl took the green garters.

Aron Throsh was miserable. Nothing had been the same since the day the chaplain had come and taken Polty. Now Polty had changed completely, and so had life at the Lazy Tiger.

One evening he confronted his mother. She was sitting before her looking-glass, adjusting her wig. Pots of paint and powder lay before the glass. There were combs and brushes and cloths and squashy, discoloured puffs. In a cloud of subsiding white powder, carefully the old woman glued a large black spot to her cheek.

Business was booming, after all.

'You look like you've got the plague.'

'It's a beauty spot, Aron. All the ladies of fashion wear them. But then, you don't know much about fashion, do you, Aron? Or about ladies.'

'I know what you're doing, Ma.'

'Aron, have you brought in that barrel of Squincy?'

'Yes, and three more.' Aron toyed with his mother's hair-brush. Strands of her several wigs streamed out, mingling. It was human hair. Red, brown, black, blonde. Tonight she was wearing the blonde.

A little slap. 'Aron, leave my things alone.'

'I want it to stop, Ma.'

'Hm? Stop what, Aron?' The old woman got up from the dressing-table, and Aron caught her arm.

'Ma, I know what you've been doing.'

'Doing? Putting a roof over your worthless head for four full cycles is what I've been doing, Aron Throsh. Now, out of my way. We're opening the doors any minute. I know what your trouble is, boy.' She shook free of his arm.

'What?'

'You're miffed, that's your trouble.'

'Miffed? What do you mean?'

'Come on, Aron! Because you're not Master Kingpin here any longer. That's it, isn't it? Oh, don't look like that! What with your old dad being what he was, little Aron was Master Kingpin as soon as he could walk! Wasn't he?'

Aron had no idea what his mother meant. All he had been since he could walk, so far as he knew, was a dogsbody, the unpaid help at the Lazy Tiger.

But now it was so much worse.

'Well, Aron, times change,' his mother was saying. 'If there's one thing I've learnt in my long life it's that. You're a funny boy, Aron. I always thought there was something funny about you, and now I know. I thought you'd be glad that the business is going well! I thought you'd be glad we're expanding!'

'Expanding? You've turned this place into a brothel!'

Goody Throsh turned and slapped her son's face.

'Don't you give me your filth, Aron Throsh! I've employed some nice girls to serve behind the bar! I've kept my customers happy! What do you want the soldiers to do? Ogle *you*? You're a skinny little beanpole, Aron, and if you haven't noticed – which I suppose is possible – you are, after all, meant to be a boy!'

Suddenly Aron was flailing at his mother. 'I hate you! I hate you!' He twisted her in his arms, forcing her back to the looking-glass. He dashed at the glass brutally, smearing away the layers of powder, like fine dust, that diffused the sharp lines of his mother's reflection. 'Look at you! Your awful withered cheeks painted like a doll and this – this stupid thing!' He pulled the old woman's wig from her head, exposing the thinning white strands beneath. Aron fell on to his mother's bed, sobbing. 'You're just an old harlot, and this place is a whorehouse!'

There was a rapping, firm but friendly, at the side-door below. Goody Throsh ignored her sobbing son. With quiet dignity she replaced her magnificent new wig and stepped across to the curtained windows. She glanced out surreptitiously, then, with a little gasp of pleasure, fled the room. Aron heard her clumping down the stairs, then a bolt drawing back, and the sound of happy voices:

'Master Polty! You're a little early tonight, don't you know!'

The smack of a kiss. 'Can't keep away, Wynda, now, can I? Not from a pretty little girl like you.'

'Ah, gallantry! The smooth-tongued deceiver! Come in, Master Polty, let me get you a little something.'

'Something, Wynda? Oh, and what might that be?'

'Saucy boy! Actually, Master Polty, I have something very special for you tonight. A little something in green. Or perhaps I mean red. Or perhaps I mean yellow.'

'I don't know what you mean, Wynda.'

Laughter. 'I think you do, Master Polty, I think you do! Ooh, stand back again and let me look at you! I do declare, I always knew you were destined for greatness.'

❋　❋　❋　❋　❋

Next morning, Aron Throsh stood before Sergeant Bunch. The sergeant looked him up and down; he felt the muscles in a spindly arm.

'You're a bit of a beanpole, lad. Still, we'll build you up. Come on, let's get your uniform.'

Chapter 58

OROKON DESTINY

'Shh!'

The beast rippled silently out of the entangling foliage, the taut muscles moving beneath its stripy sides. A shaft of light caught its eyes and they flashed mysteriously, like golden discs. In the golden flash there seemed to be some special, mysterious knowledge.

Jem gazed, fascinated, at the creature.

'Wood-tiger?' he whispered.

'It is he.'

Cata had descended cautiously to her knees; the fingers of her hand were entwined in Jem's and he, very slowly, descended too.

'Shh. Shh.' Cata closed her eyes. She stretched her fingers forward, and Jem, linked with her, felt compelled to do the same. In the green shadowy light of the Wildwood, crouched in reverence before the wild beast, they offered themselves up to a strange communion.

They were naked, their bodies bruised and aching from their love, but the communion seemed only an extension of their love. Jem was becoming a creature of the Wildwood. Imperceptibly, as their days together unfolded, Cata had taught him the secrets of the trees, the birds, the animals. In the touch of her hand, in the pressure of her lips, in the mounting and discharging of their wild ecstasies, the boy felt that all of the forest looked on. They were the Wildwood. It flowed through them, it filled them. They were sinking, drowning joyfully, in its green intensity.

Cata whispered, 'Wood-tiger, speak.'

But the tiger would not speak: Jem, holding tight to the

girl's hand, was aware of no change in its pressure, its heat. She could see nothing, he sensed, but the purple-blackness that glowed behind the lids of her closed eyes.

'Come to me,' she said.

The tiger did not; yet for a time, they could tell, the creature lingered, gazing at the crouched children with its intent, strange eyes.

Then it was gone.

Jem felt a slow, sad plunge of knowledge. At the time he did not know why, and soon it was forgotten as desire possessed him again. But later, he wondered if the creature had not spoken after all, spoken even to him. Perhaps, in its very being, there was a mournful wisdom. They had thought the wood-tiger had nothing to say. But perhaps, in the eyes that flashed golden, then were dark, perhaps, in the darkness and brilliance of its stripes, was lesson enough for those who could learn.

Heat was borne down through the treetops with the light. The urgent, crude bursting of the Season of Viana had forced itself already into a brash Season of Theron, that burnt too brightly and would end too soon. Perhaps Jem knew, even then, that the idyll in the Wildwood, like the season, could not last.

❋ ❋ ❋ ❋ ❋

That day, as they parted at the Wall of Sticks, all at once Jem broke from Cata's kiss and blurted, 'Let me stay.'

The thought had never come to him before. Now it gripped him with a sudden, pained intensity. Why should he return? He was at one with the woods, with the fish in the river, with the sleek otter and the damask owl.

But he was not.

She pushed him away. He gripped at the stick-wall, unable to stand.

She turned from him. 'You can't stay.'

'Cata, why?'

He had grabbed for his crutches, hating them, as they

received the burden of his body's uselessness. He gazed through the cracks in the Wall of Sticks. The tombyard light was a blue-white shimmer. He said, very quietly, 'Out there, I'm just a cripple. In here, I can walk. Run.'

'Only when I hold your hand. I can't always hold your hand. Can I?'

Her voice was not cruel; it was only flat.

The boy's face fell. The tears came to him quickly, unself-consciously. Cata had turned from him, her face set firm. Only when he had vanished through the tombyard wall, dragging himself with a laboriousness she had not seen before, did the girl feel her own tears press hotly at her eyes. She plunged back urgently into the concealing woods.

She ran, sobbing, back to the cave. Why had she said what she had said? The girl could not explain. But the instinct in her that knew that Jem must go was stronger than the longing in her that he should stay.

'Papa!'

She buried her face in the old man's robes. She had told him nothing of her meetings with the boy. She had told him nothing of other things, too. It had not mattered: the old man had known, of course he had known. He cupped his rough hand round his daughter's head, stroking her hair in a trembling benediction.

'The order of things must work itself out, child. We are all of us part of the order of things.'

❋ ❋ ❋ ❋ ❋

Jem, in the tombyard, had his own encounter.

It was a day of blazing heat. Beneath the yew-tree's shade in the far corner, a party of Bluejackets sat about a tomb-slab, drinking from a keg of ale and playing at cards. They had removed their hats and jackets and lolled drunkenly. Every so often they laughed uproariously.

What they were doing was forbidden, the gaming as well as the violation of the tombyard; but the heat had induced a lackadaisical atmosphere. With the connivance of the sentries

and a certain bold contemptuousness that seemed to infuse
the little party, what was forbidden became what was done.
Besides, they were officers.

'Hey!'

They saw Jem.

'What's he been doing, then?'

'Looks a bit guilty if you ask me.'

'Tossing himself off, most likely. Dirty little beggar!'

'Look who's talking!'

'Hey! Cripple-boy!' There was a beckoning finger.

Jem pretended he did not understand.

A red-headed officer lurched towards him, drunkenly. A
captain, he appeared to be the leader of the little party, the
source of the contemptuousness that rose from them like
rancid fumes. At another time he might have been a handsome man, but drunkenness made him ugly. His flaming hair
fell about his face in tangles.

'Hey! Dribble-face! Toss me off, too?' The captain leered;
his hand gestured obscenely. Behind him, his cohorts were
collapsing in laughter.

Jem struggled to pass them quickly, swinging his legs in
rapid heaving strides from the clutter of the graves to the
cleared, weeded cinder-path.

A crutch slipped in the dirt, and he fell.

There was applause.

Whooping.

Jem breathed deeply, lying on the ground. He had cracked
his head against a mossy stone and a sharp pain was coursing
round his skull.

'Cripple-boy?'

Jem looked up. Laboriously, the drunken captain was
bending over him, and it seemed in that moment that something registered in him, that something beyond the curiosity
of cruelty flickered in his face.

Something registered in Jem, too. The image of Captain
Veeldrop filled his awareness; and though Captain Veeldrop
was now lean and muscular, for a moment Jem saw him as

he had been before, as he had been when he had just been Polty: the belly rolling hugely over the waist of the breeches; the doughy sphere of the head with its jagged, cropped hair. It was as if Polty had disguised himself, and what Jem saw, just for a little, was the truth beneath the disguise. The ugliness. Jem did not consider that this was impossible. He was only aware of the loathing that filled him like nausea, threatening to spill. But when he spoke, his voice was quiet, controlled, directed to Polty alone: 'Shut up, you fat pig. Just shut your fat face.'

The face flushed crimson. There was silence.

'Polty?' came a questioning voice.

Slowly the red-haired officer straightened up, flinging casually over his shoulder to his companions, 'I think that ale's gone through me something awful. Know what I mean, lads?'

He fumbled at the front of his breeches.

'Polty, stop it.' A lanky lieutenant was there suddenly, gripping the captain's arm. 'It's not funny.'

'You were laughing!'

'It's not funny now.'

His own face flushed and hot, Jem kept his mouth pursed tight as the lanky lieutenant clumsily helped him up.

'There? All right now?'

Jem was shaken by the incident. Until now, the soldiers had been good to him. If he had despised their blue jackets, he had not despised the men who wore them.

But this was different.

As Jem went on his way, he heard Polty blustering drunkenly, 'You're so wet, Bean! To think, I got you your commission, too! You always were such a wet, weak girl.'

❋　❋　❋　❋　❋

On the slab that marked the grave of Cata's mother, cards depicting figures of wizards, beggars and horsemen were scattered about promiscuously amongst the glinting coins and ale-mugs. The soldiers had been playing a game called Orokon Destiny. They played it only for money, not comprehending its meaning. Had they done so, their manner might have been different. The game of Orokon Destiny mimed the implacable secret chains by which time brings us all to confront our separate fates. It turned upon the strangeness of the choice, the free will, that seemed to exist in any moment, yet in retrospect seemed never to have existed at all.

There is a time in the life of each young person when destiny begins to show its hand. Certain incidents are preludes, clearings of the way. The encounter with Polty that day was the first of three that Jem would have, before his way would be revealed to him at last.

Chapter 59

FLAMES IN THE ALCOVE

That night, the fervour of Jem's lust was in abeyance. Breathing slowly, he lay motionless in the alcove as a single candle burnt slowly down. The heat was intense and the window was open; no breeze stirred the candle-flame. The boy pondered hard on what Cata had said. A heavy sadness weighed on his heart. He had thought that what he had discovered with the girl was an end; now he began to see that it was not an end but a beginning. So soon, he had thought, so early, he had found the place where he wanted to be. But he could not be in that place. Inevitable as the dissolution of the burnt-out season would come his ejection from the happiness of the Wildwood. He could see it now.

Let me stay.

What a fool he had been!

Jem's eyes lingered over the objects in the alcove, the crumbling books, the mouldering garments, the Redjacket shield he had turned to the wall. The Jarvel-box, set in the nook above the hearth, glinted dully. It was an empty box. It had always been empty, it must have been; and the thought came to Jem that perhaps this was appropriate.

Sadly he reflected that these things in the alcove, retrieved from the old ruined rooms, were all that remained of the castle as it had been, in the days before the Bluejackets came. Sadness deepened in him then; for he had lived amongst these objects, these things that had been saved from so great a wreckage, and been for so long oblivious to them. As he surged, enraptured, on a tide of desire, all his precious things had gone for nothing. A sickly shudder passed through his frame. He thought back to the childhood evenings in this alcove, when he had drifted into sleep to the sound of the hurdy-gurdy. He thought of poor Barnabas. What had become of him? Jem saw the picture of the pale highway. It was still there; it had just been disregarded. But Jem could never go back to what he had once been, and again he wondered if what he had thought before could be true, that Cata had destroyed something in him, damaged him.

But it was not Cata.

It was time.

❋ ❋ ❋ ❋ ❋

There was a book that Jem had long kept beside his bed. It was tattered and old, with a flaking spine. Once, it had seemed the biggest book in the world, as he sat with it open on his knees in the evenings. With a sad smile he remembered the stories of Princess Alamane, and of the Swine-Warrior of Swale; with a sadder smile he remembered the story of Nova-Riel.

Carefully Jem reached for *The Mytholegicon*. If he dropped the book, or jarred it, he expected it to dissolve. It had not always been this way. Once it had seemed almost magical. Now it seemed sadly faded, diminished. The book was not so big as it had seemed before.

Carefully, in the dim light, Jem turned the pages. His eyes roved over the familiar pictures: the man bedecked with flowers, riding a cow; the boy with fish where his eyes should be; the dog with the face of a man. But Jem knew what he was seeking. He was looking for the bird-boy, who rose into the air on the dark stormy night.

Yes.

There he was.

Tears came to Jem's eyes, and for a moment he thought he could almost hear again the strange undulations of the hurdy-gurdy. For how long, Jem wondered, had he puzzled over this story, in the days when Barnabas had just taught him his letters? Brushing his eyes, he began to read again; but in the dim light of the single candle, the old print was hard to make out. It soon began to blur, and Jem kept losing his place.

. . . For Sassoroch was the last of the Creatures of Evil; and the evil one, desperate as he was devious, was determined that nothing should drive him back into the horror of the Realm of Unbeing . . .

. . . Now there was much fear and trembling in the castle as the tenth return of the monster drew nigh . . .

. . . Riel had fallen beneath a moving carriage, crushing his legs beneath the rolling wheels . . .

THE MARK OF RIEL

. . . Yet each time he was slain, he returned stronger than before; for when he had been slain once, he returned twice as strong and doubled in size; when he had been slain twice . . .

HIS POWER SHALL BE A HUNDREDFOLD

. . . It is the boy who shall save the castle. On the night after next, there shall come a great storm . . .

THE POWER OF THE OROKON

What was happening?

It was the strangest thing. Perhaps it happened because Jem was tired, perhaps because he had strained his eyes. The words on the page were shifting, changing, and the new words that replaced them seemed not to be old and dulled and grey but graven into the book as if with fire.

But it was a dark fire.

Jem had been lying stretched on his bed, the book propped on his chest. Now he hauled himself upright. The book was on his knees and seemed bigger, heavier. He screwed up his forehead, struggling to read the new, bright words. At first, there were only further flashes. Jem read: HE SHALL BEAR HIS TRUE NAME and COME AGAIN FROM UNBEING and, again, THE MARK OF RIEL.

On instinct, Jem turned the page. He gasped. On the next page, the words did not flicker; the words did not flash. The next page was alive and leaping with purple-black flames.

Through the flames the words blazed out with a light that seemed at once brilliant, yet black as darkness. This is what Jem read:

> THE CHILD WHO IS KEY TO THE OROKON
> SHALL BEAR THE MARK OF RIEL
> & HAVE IN HIM THE SPIRIT OF NOVA-RIEL:
> BUT HIS TASK IS GREATER AS THE EVIL ONE IS GREATER
> WHEN THE END OF THE ATONEMENT COMES

There was more, but Jem could barely comprehend the words. It had to be an illusion. It had to be. The last thing Jem heard before he lost consciousness was the ghostly echo of the hurdy-gurdy, sounding on the air.

The book fell from his hands and the spine cracked apart. Crumbling pages cascaded over the floor.

'Jem, Jem,' the voice came softly.

A hand shook his shoulder.

Jem woke slowly, heavily. There was no melody; only the dull insistent rhythm of rain beating, beating at the narrow, high window. It was the middle of the night. The alcove was in darkness, but there was a flicker of flame. It was a candle, cupped in a hand, and as the hand moved Jem could make out the figure above him. The figure was dressed in white. All at once Jem was not frightened but astonished.

'Mother!'

'Jem!'

She handed him his crutches and Jem might still have been dreaming as he swung himself now, smoothly and swiftly, behind his mother's white, billowing form. The castle was silent but for the falling rain and the distant thunder that rumbled on the air as Ela, at the door to her apartment, turned back to her son. She clasped his arm, standing close to him as she whispered hotly, 'He said you mustn't know. Jem, he didn't want you to see him like this. But I had to tell you, Jem. You had to know.'

Jem did not know what she meant. What she was saying, it seemed to him, was just words, hollow and empty as the drumbeat of the rain. He knew nothing, but at the same time, Jem knew so much. He was standing and his mother was standing, and he registered, for the first time, how tall he had grown. He had reached the height of a man.

The candlelight flickered in his mother's wan face, and Jem knew, too, how ardently he loved her; but knew also that, now that he was grown, something had ended decisively between them. Something was over. He gazed on his mother with a desperate sadness. His eyes filled with tears. She was mad, of course.

'Mother, I don't understand.'

She ruffled his hair. 'You look just like him.' She reached up quickly and kissed his lips. 'I love you, Jem.'

She turned the doorknob and the door swung open. Jem followed his mother into a dim lamplit haze; for now, this world that he had known so well, where his aunt had endlessly taken tea and tormented the maid and flirted so pathetically with her gentlemen callers had been transformed.

It was another world.

In the wall with the wainscot, a panel was open. Their visitor sat by the fire, wrapped in blankets; the hollow-eyed, skeletal figure of a man. Jem approached him slowly. It was a man who seemed immensely old; a man whose taut skin might have been made of parchment. It was a man who seemed so weak that at the merest touch he might crumple to fragments, crumple to dust.

It was a dying man.

It was Tor.

Chapter 60

THE WHITE PETALS

Jem would not know, not then, exactly what had happened
to his uncle. He knew only that Tor had been wounded and
had made his way back to the castle with the last of his
strength. If, dimly, the boy knew, also, that his uncle had
come home to die, it was an awareness he suppressed. Tor
was sick, Jem thought; and if the fire and the force that he
had loved had gone, the boy told himself that these things
would return. The Red Avenger would rise again! Didn't he
always rise again?

Astonishment at Tor's reappearance consumed any surprise that Jem might have felt at the existence of the secret
panel in the wainscot. It was a secret, he gathered, that his
mother and Tor had shared; one that their mother had shared
with them. It might have seemed almost unfair to Jem that
he had not known, and an irony, too, that he and Barnabas
had explored so much of the castle, yet never found something so exciting and so strange. Once, his mother said, she
had intended that a day would come when she would show
Jem this secret, but then her days had for so long been
shattered, as much by her treatment as by her illness. The
days that had passed could not be called back and Jem knew
that for almost two cycles his mother, whom he had seen
every day, had been lost to him as much as was the distant
Tor. In times to come, Jem would often reflect sadly on this.
That first night, as he sat reverently at his uncle's feet, he
thought only, when he looked up at his mother, that she was
a beautiful and noble woman, cruelly abused by a wicked
world.

And a wicked aunt.

He was sorry only that his mother had held back, for so long, the truth about Tor. To think, that for all these moon-lives Tor had languished in the castle and his mother's life, in secret, had been consecrated to his care! Even Nirry had known! At this, Jem felt aggrieved, but he was aware, too, of a nagging, irrational feeling that he had not been worthy of the knowledge. When he thought of how he had filled his own days, shame overcame him.

With downcast eyes, he told his mother that he would no longer leave the castle each day, but dedicate himself, as she had done, to the care of Uncle Tor. His mother hugged him and kissed him again, but said that their days must proceed as they had always done. There must be no changes. Everything must be as it had been before.

The Bluejackets must suspect nothing. If they found Uncle Tor, they would kill him.

❉   ❉   ❉   ❉   ❉

The next day Jem had half-thought, more than half-thought, that Cata would not be there. But she was waiting already at the Wall of Sticks. They did not speak of what had happened between them the day before; nor did Jem tell her what had happened in the castle. But both knew that something was coming to an end. It would not end today, perhaps not for many days; but it would end soon, like the season, and a different time would come.

In their hearts, they knew it would be a sadder time.

Today there was a peculiar tenderness between them, a silent acknowledgement of the awareness they now possessed. In the Circle of Knowing they were almost shy again, as they had been on their first time together. There were no games, no abandoned riots. Breathing deeply, they rolled together in the white petals, clinging close until each had achieved a noiseless, trembling release.

I love you, Cata, Jem wanted to say.

But he could say nothing.

He lay looking upwards, his eyes open, aware only of a

pale radiance, descending and bathing him. The awareness was a kind of pain.

Cata scooped up a handful of petals; then slowly, tenderly, one by one, began to place them upon the boy's face. She fixed each petal in place with the moist, mingled juices that flowed from between her thighs, that coated his. It was the task for an age. When she was finished, an eternity later, the boy wore an aromatic, stiff white mask. He lay unmoving, limp; but then, understanding, he turned on his side. He scooped up petals; and he did to her what she had done to him.

They kissed.

Then it began.

The sounding of the horn was at first so far away as to be scarcely a sound at all, merely one stirring among the many stirrings of the Wildwood: the distant cawings of birds; the tickings of beetles in bark; the slitherings of worms in the warmth beneath the ground.

Then came the barkings of the dogs.

'Listen!'

The kiss was to have been eternal, too; now Cata broke off, rising to her haunches. She swept her hair to the back of her neck, her head swivelling, intent, alert. There was a sharp cry and one scattered bird, then another, flapped urgently into the bower.

Then silence.

Cata turned to Jem. 'Can you hear it? Hounds. Horses.'

He could hear nothing.

She saw that he was frightened. She reached for his hand and he stood beside her, clinging to her, in the fragrant centre of their secret place. All Jem could hear was his own blood, booming massively in his chest and ears. Then it came to him that this was what was wrong. Something was different in the woods outside. All the susurrus of ordinary sounds was gone. It was quiet, too quiet. The Wildwood had paused, tensed. It was holding its breath.

Then it happened.

It was upon them in a moment, bursting around them like the rushing of a tide. In a convulsion of rage it exploded on to the air, a frenzy of hate as if all that had passed in the petal-strewn bower had called forth, at last, its destructive dark side. Jem and Cata were concealed in the bower, but outside, beyond the curtaining vines, the Wildwood was in tumult. First the barking overwhelmed the air in a possessed, wild chorus. Paws, hooves, crashed through the under-growth. Shouted voices; a whipcrack.

Boom!

Boom!

Birds rose, shrieking.

Jem's knuckles were white as bone and his nails dug too deeply into Cata's shoulder, sinking into little welling pools of blood. Oblivious, she was shaking, sobbing soundlessly. The girl's fear was no less than the boy's; neither had ever heard the sounds of the hunt.

There was a pause; not silence, but restless circlings of the trained animals, little tramplings of the grass and ferns. Little roarings, snorts.

'Where's it gone?'

'Damn it to Koros!'

The first voice was high, awkward, twisting off into a breathless laugh; the second, a malevolent, guttural gnashing. All the imperiousness of the human heart was there, thwarted and determined on violent discharge.

A sleekness of fur brushed Cata's calves, then Jem's. Behind them, the vines had parted soundlessly. Struggling steps, soft on the bower's thick floor, added no new sound.

Only drippings of red.

The wounded wood-tiger lay at their feet, stretched calmly in this protected place. A spreading pool began to stain the white petals, slipping slowly, slowly, down the tiger's striped side.

Voices, beyond the curtain:

'It's gone.'

'Useless bloody dogs!'

'What's wrong with them?'

'I'm getting it!'

'Polty, we've lost it!'

'We nearly had it!'

'Polty, it's gone! Come back!'

An urgent whisper, 'Shut up! It's somewhere here, I tell you!'

'Polty, come back!'

Cata moaned, sinking; she heard nothing, saw nothing, but the deeply breathing tiger. Outside, the horses and the dogs moved away; she did not even register the sounds of their going. She closed her eyes. But her hand, distracted, lay still in Jem's; so it was that it was Jem, still standing, the stiff petal-mask white against his face, who would be the first to gaze defiantly at the intruder who found himself suddenly, unexpectedly, on the other side of the vines.

He entered sideways, creeping, rifle at the ready.

Polty gave the smallest gasp. He stiffened. 'Who are you?' His voice was still a whisper; this strange place, perhaps, cowed even him.

But only for a moment.

Cata had stood now, rising to confront him, her hand still twined tightly in Jem's.

Through her mask, her eyes blazed fire.

'I see. A Vaga-whore, up to her tricks. Filthy little bitch. What's wrong with your faces? Why have you got that stuff on your faces?'

They said nothing.

'Hey, skinny-ribs! You know she's got the pox, don't you? They all have, these Vaga-sluts. Reeking of it, I tell you.' Polty hawked a gob of phlegm. His rifle jabbed the air, gesturing at the tiger. 'I've come for him. He's mine.'

'He's not yours,' Cata murmured.

'I've come to finish him off.'

Polty took aim.

'He's not yours,' Cata said again.

That was when she did an extraordinary thing. Keeping

hold of Jem, she led him closer to Polty, walking directly into the rifle's path.

'Hey!'

Polty did not shout; nothing was shouted in the Circle of Knowing. Everything they had said, everything that they would say, had been in voices that were almost whispers. Now Cata began to whisper still lower, her lips close, too close, to Polty's ear.

He lowered the rifle, just a little.

'Why do you whisper?'

'We're the whispering people.'

'What?'

'You asked why our faces look this way. We're not like you. We live here in the woods. And we whisper. But we can shout. And if we should shout, you would die. If we should shout, all the blood in you would burst from your ears. You can't kill the tiger! Kill him and we shall cry out loud. Kill him and the blood in you shall flow without stopping, spurting redly from your eyes and nose and mouth.'

'Polty! Where are you?'

The spell was broken. It was a voice from outside. Brutally, Polty pushed Cata aside. She staggered; her hand was torn from Jem's. The boy crumpled, a helpless cripple.

Polty's head swivelled; for a moment he would have called to his companion, but didn't bother.

He aimed again.

Cata lunged at him. He struck her and would have fired again, blasting his shot at close range into the wounded beast. He would have bashed open its skull with his rifle-butt, just to be sure it was dead. He would have ripped open its stinking guts with his hands, tearing out the heart and holding it aloft, triumphant.

He would have done these things, but all the time, as the beast had lain there, it had been only readying itself to rise again, renewed. The blood that flowed from its side had stopped; the wound had knitted over; now, of a sudden, fast

470

as lightning, a huge golden-black streak of muscle, fangs and claws was rearing up, blazing-eyed, ready to spring.

A hunter braver than Polty would have gone ahead and fired, but Polty, terrified, cried out and fled, bashing back through the curtain of vines.

On the bloodied petals, Jem and Cata crawled back slowly into each other's arms. The tiger had vanished. Later, Cata would recall something Papa had said, long ago, about the creatures that men had killed – the ones they had killed entirely so that none remained. She had not understood it then. He had said that one of the dead things, just one, always lived on, and could not be killed, for all that men would do.

Now they heard the voices on the other side of the vines.

'Polty, there you are! What happened?'

'Happened? Nothing.'

'You cried out.'

'Shut up. I didn't.'

'I heard you!'

'A spider-web. I hate spiders.'

'Polty?'

'What now?'

'I thought I heard the tiger.'

'What?'

'You didn't.'

'It roared.'

'Bean, do shut up. You're such a girl, you really are!'

The voices faded away.

Chapter 61

MYSTERY OF THE AVENGER

The light through the ceiling of the Glass Room was no longer so bright as it had been before. The season had begun to fade, and as clouds collected and the darkness came sooner, the chaplain installed the ornate lamp from the quilted coach on the edge of the commander's desk. Soon the lamplight bathed Umbecca as she read, its hissing, diffuse goldenness mingling strangely with the green of the carpet and the thick foliage and the blue and red and purple and black that shifted so slowly, mysteriously above.

At first, the lamp was lit only when the light through the ceiling was weak; but soon, it seemed, the commander liked to have it lit all the time, even when the sky was still bright.

The old man liked the sound it made.

Hiss.

❀ ❀ ❀ ❀ ❀

Umbecca had begun the first volume of *A Beauty of the Valleys* when a curious incident occurred. Turning a page, she was surprised to find that a piece of yellowed, loose paper fell from the book into her lap; of course, in the moment of distraction she could not help but glance at it.

It was a letter, or rather a note. The note had once been folded, it was clear, but had now been flattened in the pages of the book. The note, too, was a very short one, and as it had fallen upright on the side with the handwriting, it was quite impossible for Umbecca not to read it. What she read made her face suddenly flush. *Tor, I love you*, were the words the note contained; the handwriting, Umbecca knew, was Ela's.

How had it got here?

What did this mean?

The chaplain arched an eyebrow. 'Something is wrong, dear lady?' he whispered.

'Oh no.' Umbecca struggled to form her enigmatic smile, and resumed her place. The commander's visor was down, after all, and she should not like him to raise it. When his visor was down, it was almost as if she were alone with the chaplain. Sometimes, one was not certain if the old gentleman were sleeping.

Sometimes he was, but usually, when it was time to leave, he would push back his visor and offer some gallantry.

The note lay in Umbecca's lap as she finished that day's reading; though it was only a piece of paper, the merest scrap, she was aware of its presence against her person as something outrageous. A violation. It scorched through the pale fabric of her tea-gown. It spread across her lap like a stain.

The words of the fair Evelissa, it seemed, were filled that day with more than the usual admixture of emotion. It was one of Umbecca's most brilliant readings. When it was over, the commander exclaimed fulsomely over the gifts of his fair guest. He held her hand for rather longer than usual.

But in the instant before the old man pushed back his visor, the chaplain did an extraordinary thing. He snatched the note from Umbecca's lap.

It vanished into his coat.

Of course, it was done in the most elegant, the most accomplished, of swift, single movements. The action had in it everything of tenderness and respect, and nothing, not a hint, of coarseness or vulgarity.

The incident was over, but Umbecca's feeling of violation had not gone away. For the first time her happiness, which had grown greater each day, seemed instead to have shrunk. To have shrivelled, just a little.

That night, she stood for long moments gazing at Ela. As usual, the bottle of sleepy-treacle lay beside the girl. Now the soldiers had come, it seemed that Nirry could procure a constant supply. Really, it was disgusting.

Umbecca hardly spoke to her niece these days. During Ela's groggy mornings, Umbecca was too busy deciding upon the day's costumes to pay much attention to her. Some fine ladies, the chaplain had intimated, changed *every* item of their apparel as many as five times *every* day. The two women might have conducted their lives in separate houses, not merely at opposite ends of a single cavernous chamber. In the early afternoons, Ela slept. She took her tea when Umbecca was out and was usually sleeping again when Umbecca returned. At night, Umbecca retreated to her cell.

Once, Umbecca would hear regular reports from Nirry. Lady Ela did this; Lady Ela said that. I'm a bit worried about Lady Ela. Now, moonlives had passed and Umbecca had heard no such reports. Perhaps she had just not been listening. Only one thought of her niece had occupied her of late. It concerned the question of accommodation. Ela's apartment was large, but Umbecca's new possessions filled it more and more. To Umbecca, Ela's apartment was at once dressing-room, morning-room and drawing-room. What was it to Ela but a place to slumber away her days? She was hardly, in any real sense of the word, a *fine lady*. Umbecca's cell would be more appropriate for an invalid. She would have the soldiers give it a fresh coat of whitewash. In Ela's apartment, Umbecca would have privacy. Really, it was appalling to have no privacy!

Only two things prevented Umbecca from carrying out this plan. The first was a certain look which came into Nirry's eyes when Umbecca had mentioned it; a wild look, such as Umbecca had seen seldom, but had indeed seen before. In truth, Umbecca was a little frightened of Nirry, though she would never have admitted it to herself. She was also a little frightened of her niece, and that was the other reason why the plan was still in abeyance.

It had to be said for Ela that she was usually no trouble, unless one counted the fact that she existed at all. But though she would lie in her loathsome stupor for moonlives on end – there was nothing more disgusting than an addiction to drugs, Umbecca thought – she did nonetheless have the capacity to rouse herself, upon occasion, to fearsome heights of emotion. It was regrettable; and it was dangerous. Goodman Waxwell had always warned that a haemorrhage was possible. Just like the one that killed Mother. A terrible business; all her bedding had had to be thrown away afterwards. Umbecca had said the mattress could at least be saved; but Ruanna said no.

If Ela were to wake and find herself in the cell, there was no telling what might happen. Perhaps the whitewashing could be deferred, until the girl had grown accustomed to the new arrangements. A good thought; but still, the plan was in abeyance, and the fact of its abeyance only made Umbecca resent her niece more. She was such a selfish girl.

Now, thinking of the note that had fallen from the commander's 'Agondon Edition', Umbecca's annoyance had risen to new heights. *Tor, I love you.* What had her niece been playing at? What had Tor? She turned from Ela in exasperation. The chaplain had snatched the note deliberately, decisively. *I know what it says*, that gesture seemed to say. *I know what it means.*

In the four words of the note, and the place in which they had been, Umbecca saw a world of mystery. That this mystery might be working its way towards her, insinuating itself, slitheringly, into the heart of her happiness, was too much for Umbecca to bear. The old, familiar thudding began in her temples again.

The chaplain, as he handed her back into the coach that evening, had not alluded to the matter.

He would return to it some days later.

Rain was pattering lightly on the glass above them. The

sky was grey and the lamp on the desk burned unusually bright. It was one of those charming evenings on which the commander, laid more than usually low by his gout, was unable to join them. Fondly, Umbecca imagined the poor old gentleman floating dreamily at this moment on a haze of sleepy-treacle.

Umbecca's happiness had returned. In the brick wall that joined the strange chamber to the house, the foliage had been cleared back sufficiently to expose the hearth of an ample fireplace. A cheerful fire leapt in the grate. The chaplain smiled at her across the marquetry table as he gracefully performed the ceremonies of tea. An enormous, heaped plate of strawberry tarts lay before them. Umbecca's mouth watered as she eyed the rich red jam.

'Tart, dear lady?'

'Oh, chaplain, perhaps just one. A lady must watch her figure, you know.' Umbecca essayed the enigmatic smile again, and popped the tart, unbitten, into her little mouth.

Some days earlier, the chaplain had begun telling her the most diverting story about a certain gathering at the town-house of Lady M——, in which false rumours had circulated that the king was to attend. Umbecca was about to press – delicately, of course – for a return to this theme, when the chaplain began instead, 'You have been wondering, perhaps, dear lady, about a certain small incident?'

'Chaplain?' Umbecca's hand, at that moment conveying a second of the delicious tarts to her mouth, was momentarily stayed.

It was at this point that the chaplain, reaching into the interior of his coat, produced again the note which had so disturbed Umbecca. It lay before them on the marquetry table, between a cup and the cream-jug of the 'Varby set'.

'*Tor, I love you*,' the chaplain quoted. 'A charming message, would you not say? It appears to be written in a lady's hand; and "Tor", if I am not mistaken, is a pet-name for – what would you suggest, dear lady?'

'"Torby"?'

'Hm.' The chaplain appeared to consider this. 'You may well be right. But "Torby" is a slightly . . . *vulgar* name, would you not say?'

'Oh, indeed.' Umbecca flushed slightly. Her father's name had been Torby.

'Yes. "Torby",' the chaplain went on, 'is a name seldom found above the middle rank. But there is a rather more . . . *aristocratic* name which springs to mind, is there not?'

Umbecca looked upwards. She saw her reflection and the chaplain's inverted in the grey, rain-washed ceiling. 'Perhaps "Torvester"?' she offered airily. 'Though one must consider the context of such a missive. To express one's love on a scrap of torn paper . . . well, it is hardly the behaviour of a woman of the upper echelons, unless of course she were abandoned to all virtue and shame. I should say there was nothing of aristocracy in this little note, chaplain. The hand, one must admit, is elegant and clear, the spelling true; but there is many a good little charity-school where a girl might learn such arts. No, chaplain,' – Umbecca gave her little laugh – 'this is surely the passion of some Dolly Mop for her hulking Torby!'

As if to aid her in her little speech, Umbecca had taken up the note in her hand and, as if to demonstrate her contempt for its vulgar provenance, had turned it over, glancing down at it, in the moment of her laughter. It was the first time Umbecca had held the scrap of paper; it was the first time she had seen the verso. The paper, though yellowed now and crumpled, was of high quality. It was torn from a book. On the verso was a scrap of printing, and a name in ink. The printing was the last letters of a title. The signature, small and neat, in what must once have been the top corner of the page, was unmistakable:

Ruanna Rench.

HE VALLEYS

Ela, after all, had kept her mother's books.

'Remarkable, isn't it?' said the chaplain, smiling. 'But I can clear up one part of the mystery at once. You may have heard, dear lady, of a certain individual who goes by the name of "The Red Avenger"?'

Umbecca's eyes roamed, but impassively now, over the plate of jam tarts. She considered, for some moments, the enigmatic smile, but instead gave a little, just a little hum of assent.

'All Agondon society regards him as the most vulgar person,' the chaplain was saying. 'For a time he led a little band of men; there was, I gather, a most distressing altercation on the coast of Xorgos Island. You know Xorgos Island, dear lady? A most useful place to deposit those of the lower orders who have forgotten their place . . .'

Umbecca raised her eyes. 'It is so important,' she began expansively, 'for the lower orders to remember their place!'

'I could not agree more, dear lady. And yet, is it not even more important, some might say, for their betters to set an example?'

'Chaplain, but of course—'

The chaplain sighed. 'That is why His Imperial Agonist Majesty is so very disappointed in The Red Avenger. To think, that a young man of good family . . . well, it is said that for a time he travelled with a party of . . . *Vagas*, in the guise of a harlequin. Early on, one gathers, he would carry out his atrocities whilst dressed brazenly in the uniform of the red king; later, the particoloured harlequin became his preferred guise. The red, after all, was concealed amongst many other colours . . .'

Umbecca was becoming decidedly uneasy. Was this a game the chaplain was playing? Everyone knew The Red Avenger's name. Everyone knew he was the Archduke's son. The fire made a loud crackling. In the lamplight, there appeared to be a curious glitter in the chaplain's eye. For the first time, for just the flicker of an instant, the thought came to Umbecca that he was cruel. Just a little.

His words washed over her.

'You may not be aware, dear lady,' he was saying, 'that the campaigns of The Red Avenger were of particular virulence during the late Zenzan wars. Little news was made known, even in Agondon, but it might truly be said that without the evil of The Red Avenger, the liberation of our benighted neighbouring kingdom would certainly have been accomplished with much greater ease.'

He leaned forward in his chintz chair. His tone became confidential and at first Umbecca thought, to her relief, that he had changed the topic. But he was only approaching it from another angle.

He nibbled at a tart.

'Have you ever wondered, dear lady, why a gentleman of the eminence of Commander Veeldrop has not yet been made a lord? One might expect him to be a marquis, at least! Have you ever wondered, indeed, why it should be that he should rule – if you'll pardon me, dear lady – the *Tarn*, and not the fattest of the southern provinces? Have you ever wondered why he wears an embroidered visor, and why his manly form has so terribly declined?'

Umbecca, indeed, had wondered all of these things. She gazed at the chaplain, wide-eyed.

'The answer, dear lady, may be given in three words. The Red Avenger!'

Umbecca gasped. She began to tremble.

The chaplain finished his tart and took another. He gestured for Umbecca to do the same; she did so only with reluctance.

'The Late War of the New Divulged Destiny had been in progress for but a few seasons when already, it seemed, our time had come,' the chaplain went on. 'The commander's forces were at the gates of Wrax. In a matter of days, it seemed, he would have battered through their defences. Zenzau would be ours! Word was sent rapidly to our base on the coast. In Agondon – I recall it well – it was even thought that victory was assured already. Did I ever speak of

Lady W——'s Grand Victory Ball? The embarrassment, dear lady, oh, the shame of it! There we were, toasting what we called already – it had such a pleasing sound – the "Victory of Veeldrop", at the very moment when a rider from the front brought new and different intelligence. Poor Lady W——! She has never quite recovered from it!

'For indeed, victory had seemed ours for the taking. We had thought The Red Avenger dead, the Resistance dispersed. Who could suspect that, all the time, the traitor was working in secret inside the city, making ready a monstrous new weapon?'

Umbecca laid down her tart. She had only nibbled the rim.

'The Red Avenger had become, in the course of the late war, a bitter enemy of the commander,' said the chaplain. 'Many times he was thought to be dead – absolutely, decisively; many times, just as decisively, he seemed to rise again. Now, as the commander is wont to say, it is only when The Avenger is swinging from a gallows that we shall know he is truly dead. And what, after the Atrocity of Wrax, could more alleviate the commander's pain than to give the order for that long-delayed hanging?

'The commander is of the view that some evil Vaga-magic assisted The Avenger in the atrocity of that day. Certainly, the power The Avenger unleashed went beyond anything seen in all the wars of Ejland. All the commander can say is this: that at the moment he attacked at last, and was about to batter down the walls of Wrax, a force greater than the firing of any cannon was unleashed, scattering his ranks. Hundreds of men died. Thousands were wounded. It was the work of a moment! What could it be, this strange power? I have asked the commander to describe it many times, but he can say only that it was a blinding flash. His eyes have never recovered; nor has his heart.'

'His heart?'

'One cannot forget, dear lady, that the commander is a proud man. There was a time when he was celebrated as our greatest hero. There was a time when he was reviled, wickedly, as a traitor. But always he was acknowledged as a man of power. Now, on the brink of glory, he was forced into retreat, his command in disarray. Though the extraordinary weapon was not deployed a second time, the commander could not regain the impetus he had lost.

'Soon after, his health gave way, and he had no choice but to retire from the front. Back in Agondon, the commander found that he had fallen rapidly from favour. The "Victory of Veeldrop" that never was, was spoken of now in terms of bitter irony. "Veeldrop jokes" were bandied about in drawing-rooms. Jokes, about the victor of the Siege of Irion! Jokes, by fops with milk-white hands! The First Minister himself, who could be said to owe his present status wholly to the commander, was known to say now that Veeldrop could not be trusted; that Veeldrop's day was over; that Veeldrop was worthy only of the most vulgar of provincial postings! The commander was even denied the elevation to the peerage that had seemed certain to cap his long career. It was an outrage. There were some who said his elevation should have come after the Siege of Irion and were appalled that the First Minister had denied him then, but now, all the great world turned from the commander. A peerage? They said he had never deserved it. Was not the Archduke the real hero of Irion? What, after all, had the commander done, but lie in wait to take the king away? Oh, perfidy! Such is the fickleness of human affection.

'Meanwhile, it was left to Commander Michan to become Liberator of Wrax, and, in due course, Lord High Governor of that most desirable of possessions. "Michan!" the commander will sometimes moan. "And to think, he was once a mere stripling, under my command!" Now, were the commander to meet Michan, he should have to bow to him, and call him "my lord"!'

'Oh, the poor, poor gentleman!'

By now, tears flowed freely down Umbecca's face. It was an affecting display of feeling, but her feelings were not only for the commander.

The chaplain swept on, 'I am glad to see that you are sensible, dear lady, of the sufferings of this great man. He is old, and soon must die; to relieve all his afflictions is now impossible. Only if we could call back time could we restore the commander to all he has been. And yet, dear lady, there are things that we may do.'

'Chaplain?'

'It was said that The Avenger had damaged himself; that the magic he had unleashed had taken some terrible toll, not only upon others but upon himself. After the explosion at the walls of Wrax, his distinctive handiwork was not seen again. Once again, rumour had it that he was dead.

'But there has been intelligence that he has been in hiding, first in one place, then another; always on the move, always just out of reach. Moving, we have concluded, in a certain direction. Perhaps, we may ask, there is a place where he wishes to end his days?

'Oh, dear lady! Think of it, just think of it, if the commander could take The Avenger now! To see him hanging from the gallows on the green would be a sight to bring tears of joy to those noble, faded eyes! And when the traitor's head was borne back to Agondon, could even the First Minister deny that Olivan Tharley Veeldrop had indeed, in the end, vindicated his name? And would not that name be sure to be changed, as it should long ago have been changed? "Commander Veeldrop" he would be no more! Now, "Lord Veeldrop", as he should always have been!'

Umbecca broke down. She had been sobbing, at first silently, then freely, gutturally. Now she slumped forward, almost collapsing into the tarts.

'Oh, Tor, Tor!' she moaned, stricken.

It was worse, it was all so much worse than she could have thought. Umbecca, isolated in the provinces, could have had no knowledge of the extent of her nephew's perfidies. She had loved the boy, but now, when the chaplain said that Tor must die, Umbecca had no choice but to agree. She thought back to the commander, as he had been after the Siege. She thought of the commander, as he was now. Oh, it was monstrous what Tor had done!

But why had the chaplain tormented her thus?

'Chaplain, you are cruel!' she burst out. 'Do you expect that I shall defend The Red Avenger? Don't you think I have suffered, suffered every day, at the shame of this connection? Dear Torvester was such a sweet, such a charming boy! But to have betrayed his father! To have betrayed his king! And now, to have brought such agony to the commander! To think, that once I dandled that monster on my knee! I had thought his sister brought shame on my family, but her harlotry is as nothing to the wickedness of that boy!'

Umbecca had almost slipped from her chintz chair. The chaplain sank to his knees on the floor, embracing her.

'Dear, dear lady! Please, do not imagine that I do not grieve at, indeed share in, your terrible suffering! And please, do not let the thought even cross your mind that you are yourself an object of suspicion! No one impugns you! No one blames you! Everyone loves you and wants you to be happy!'

Umbecca snuffled, looking into the chaplain's face.

'Everyone?'

This might have been a scene from Ruanna's books; the chaplain might, at this moment, have made his declaration.

He took her hands.

'Dear lady, I must say to you but one thing. *I love you—*'

Umbecca's heart bounded. *Oh, chaplain!* she might have shrieked at that moment, but all power of speech was taken from her. Yes! It was all as she had dreamed! The chaplain would ask for a Dispensation, and he would be hers!

She crushed him in her arms.

After some moments, and not without difficulty, the chaplain extricated himself. The woman, clearly, was overwrought. He helped her back to her chair. She sat with her shoulders hunched, as if in the grip of some mortifying realization. Her face hung forward, scarlet, and she took up a fistful of strawberry tarts.

The chaplain paced about the carpet, and quoted again, '*I love you, Tor*. Now, this scrap of paper was found inside a coat, known to have been discarded by the renegade. Where did it come from? Perhaps, dear lady, it is a remnant of long ago, that the renegade has always kept close to his heart. But perhaps, too, it is a sign of something else. A sign that the renegade has a contact. A contact, dear lady, very close at hand.

'Your niece, you have told me, possesses the novels of "Miss R——". Could it be, perhaps, that your maid had torn this scrap from a volume, and penned a message to her lover?'

'Nirry?' Now Umbecca almost forced out a laugh. There had been none of those excellent little charity-schools in the Tarn. Nirry could neither read nor write. As for the thought that Tor would have an affair with her, this was too much. Not even Tor would sink so low . . .

Umbecca checked herself.

Now the chaplain swooped close to her ear. His voice was a hot, passionate whisper. 'Dear lady, the commander has reason to believe that The Red Avenger may be in the valleys, hiding somewhere. The renegade, as we know, is an adept in certain nefarious arts. On our journey here, the commander's men were about to take him when all at once, The Avenger made himself disappear. But his powers must be weakened, of that we are certain. He may be close to death. Could it be that he has returned to his homeland? Could it be, even now, that someone is harbouring him?

'Dear lady, I repeat that you shall never, could never, be an object of suspicion. Yes, you dandled the boy on your knee. It is a tragedy that one so dear, so virtuous, should have been so vilely abused. But what is a virtue that has not been tested? All I ask of you is this: should any knowledge come to your awareness, I beg you, dear lady, not to withhold it. Oh, I know what a struggle such a decision would occasion in your heart! Dear lady, I am a man of feeling! But your nephew is no longer the boy you dandled on your knee. He has ruined himself, cast away his character and his name. He—'

Umbecca leapt up. Strawberry tarts scattered to the floor. The scene that had begun so sweetly had turned into one of bitter humiliation for her, but now she saw how all might be redeemed.

'Chaplain, it is enough!' she cried. 'My heart is breaking! I say only this: that whatever shadow of love still lingers in me for that base deceiver, it is as nothing compared to the allegiance I owe to virtue! Fickle man! Are you deaf? Are you blind? Can you have known me for so long – so immeasurably, so illimitably long – and yet known nothing of the noble heart that beats within this breast? Can you imagine that any selfish impulse could hinder this heart, for the merest flicker of an instant, in the prosecution of its duty? O, vile calumny! Know ye not, weak, doubting man, that you stand in the presence of a woman of virtue? Know ye not that there is no act which a woman of my virtue could begin to meditate which should not be consecrated to the greater glory of the Lord Agonis, and her king! Doubting man, grovel at my feet and beg forgiveness!'

Eay Feval did so, restraining his laughter. To Umbecca, it sounded as if he were sobbing.

❈ ❈ ❈ ❈ ❈

It was, thought the chaplain later, Umbecca's finest moment; or rather, her finest so far. She was improving. She was definitely improving. The speech was taken, word for word, from *Marital and Martial*.

When she was gone, the commander rose from the averted chair behind his desk. There were aspects of the conversation which had by no means pleased him, but he recognized their necessity. They had prompted feeling in the lady's heart; that much was clear. He pushed up his visor and his eyes were wet. 'A most affecting scene. What is your view, Chaplain?'

The chaplain adjusted his gloves. 'We cannot be certain if she knows his whereabouts, sir. But if she does not, I suspect she will, soon enough.' Rain was still pattering on the glass roof. 'And when she does, she will give him up.'

The old man gave the chaplain a rare smile. It was a pitying smile. The poor chaplain was no man of feeling! 'I should like to say that you surprised me, Chaplain. But of course, you do not.'

'Sir?'

'She has shown herself a woman of virtue. But what else should we expect? We know who she is, do we not?' The commander sighed fondly, and gazed at the line of books on his desk.

The tooled spines glittered in the lamplight.

❊ ❊ ❊ ❊ ❊

A number of dingy old books languished, unregarded, in Ela's apartment. It was a long time since Ela had looked at them, and a longer time since Umbecca had done so. That night, as she was removing her finery before the glass, Umbecca caught sight of the little bookshelf, just visible in a corner of the reflection. She turned and crossed to it. Umbecca eyed the volumes with distaste. They were distressingly shabby; not at all like the commander's beautiful 'Agondon Edition'. That would be an ornament to any polite home.

Her fingers settled, easily enough, on *A Beauty of the Valleys*. She drew the little volume forth, her nose wrinkling in distaste as a cloud of dust settled on her petticoats. It was in the corners of a room, Mother had often said, that one could tell if the servants did their work. One could see that Nirry did none at all. Umbecca opened the book.

But of course.

A BEAUTY OF T

declared the title-page.

It was not that there had been any doubt; there had been

none. Umbecca fingered the jagged, torn edge. Wonderingly, she gazed at the insensible form on the bed. Ela's breath rose and fell slowly. Umbecca's heart thudded hard.

She wondered.

Wondered.

That was when a new thought began inside her. It began with the message that had been scrawled on the note: *I love you, Tor.* Then it took in what she had told the chaplain, that no woman of virtue would send such a note. Then it took in the chaplain's suggestion, that perhaps the maid had been writing to her lover.

But no. Not the maid.

For the first time, a terrible suspicion entered Umbecca's heart. She was moved to no sudden cry, no violence. Quietly, she made her way back to her cell. In darkness, she lay down in all her petticoats and wept into her pillow, silently and long.

What a fool she had been.

What a wicked, wicked fool.

Chapter 62

THE TOMBYARD SLAB

The Season of Theron had burnt out already when Jem had
his third encounter with Poltiss Veeldrop. Jem's destiny was
about to unfold.

That day, the sky above the village was damp with grey
clouds, threatening rain. Jem had been to the Wall of Sticks,
but Cata was not there. In his time with the girl, there had
always been something impassive, something blindly acqui-
escing in his love. He had accepted that on some days she
would not come. He would not ask why. He would only be
saddened, dimly and quietly. Now, as the chill skies bespoke
the return, so soon, of the Season of Agonis, Jem felt a sharper
ache of grievance. Already he had felt a murky foreboding,
knowing that things could not continue as they were; now,
particular ways stood out in sharp relief. When snow lay
deep on the ground and fluttered perpetually from the sky,
how should he then make his way down from the crag? He
had thought he was on the brink of a great expansion of life;
now, he saw, there were things he had done that soon he
would be able to do no longer.

Jem cursed his helplessness. How he had come to need the
touch of Cata's hand! What she conferred on him, it seemed,
was life.

He returned to the tombyard. On the blustery afternoon it
was empty and grey. A deep weariness overcame him. He
had longed to run and leap in the Wildwood; instead, he
dragged himself to the corner beneath the yew-tree where
the soldiers had been. Evidence of their revelry still lay about:
a curve of smashed glass, glinting between the tangled roots

of the yew; the ballad-sheet of a bawdy song; a green garter, symbol of a soldier's bravado.

The tomb-slab stretched supine in the shadow of the yew. Soft-edged, furred with moss, it lay like a flattened, low rock amongst the grass and returning weeds. The inscription could barely be read. Vegetable slitherings and pinprick yellow spores had blurred the balanced characters, but Jem, tracing their ghosts, could just make out the homage they paid to the memory of a woman called Catayane. It was some moments before the boy considered that this, an old Juvescian name, must be what Cata was called, too.

Awkwardly, Jem eased himself down. He laid his crutches beside him and sat, huddled, on the edge of the slab. He looked at his feet. Only then, in the weeds beside the grave, did he see the playing-card, face-down and crumpled, spilt from the pack by an unsteady hand. He reached for it: the dark god, Koros. Black, misshapen, presaging death, the dark god seemed for a moment to gaze into Jem's eyes. The boy shuddered and let the card fall.

Huddling into his coat, he stretched over the slab. He lay back, gazing through the twisted mesh of branches to the sky. The merest mist of rain began slowly to fall. He closed his eyes. Blackness; but then, from the caverns of the world inside his skull, swirling into shape on the purple-black, came the face from the card, suddenly huge, as if the dark god were leaning over him, gazing down at him from the burdened, impending sky.

Then came the flash of the burning verses:

FOR SASSOROCH SHALL COME AGAIN FROM UNBEING
& HIS POWER SHALL BE A HUNDREDFOLD:
BUT NOW HE SHALL BEAR HIS TRUE NAME & TRUE VISAGE
THAT WERE HIDDEN FROM THE WORLD
WHEN HE WAS SASSOROCH

Jem's eyes snapped open.

He was shaken. He had forgotten the strange dream that had come to him in the alcove. He remembered now that he had been reading from *The Mytholegicon* but his eyes had drifted shut and he had dropped the book to the floor. He had broken its spine. What terrible sorrow, what emptiness had overcome him later, when he saw the scattered, crumbling pages on the floor! The dream meant nothing, of course; it was only nonsense. But the sorrow returned to him now, as he lay on the tombyard slab. Jem knew only that he was possessed of a great longing he could neither understand nor define. He had thought that what he had done with Cata was enough, or could be enough. Now, perhaps, there was a void opening in him that nothing could fill.

Sassoroch!

Did he want to be Nova-Riel?

But lightning, as his aunt had said, did not strike twice.

The ways of fate are mysterious, and it is not for us, mere pawns in its unknowable hands (as we are and must inevitably be!) to question its intricate and inexplicable designs. But though only the torments of Unbeing can punish the base deceiver Porlond, and only in The Vast can my dear Evelissa now be restored to me, yet I shall grieve not, and take comfort – as I trust, my dear, shall you – rather in the illimitable blessings which have yet been visited upon your (yes!) happy Anna, who now (by the time you receive this, my dearest living friend!) must forevermore sign herself

LADY QUINMIRE

It was too much.

The volume fell from Umbecca's hands. She collapsed, sobbing. The commander sobbed, too. They had reached the end of *A Beauty of the Valleys*. And to think, there were those who said this last work marked a decline in the genius of 'Miss R——'! It was a calumny. The novel was a masterpiece.

The chaplain smiled indulgently at the sobbing figures before him, then made his way quickly through the foliage to the doors.

Ah, good.

The guards were waiting.

The reading had gone on late this evening, as indeed it had been designed that it should. But the lady was captivated by the last pages of the novel. There had been no need to persuade her to stay; even though, the chaplain thought wryly, she had received a more meagre tea than usual. Only a carrot-cake, a seed-cake, and a plate of butter scones. Poor, dear lady! She must be hungry! Ah, well; she would receive her reward soon enough.

Umbecca looked up, in surprise and almost alarm, as the guards filled the room.

'Chaplain?' she asked, her voice uncertain.

But it was the commander who answered her question.

'Dear lady!' The old man caught her hands. 'Over these last moonlives you have given us such rich pleasure, such copious enjoyment! May we not be permitted to repay you now?'

Umbecca gazed wonderingly at the milling guards. First they whisked away the little low tea-table, replacing it with a higher, more imposing table. For an instant the polished surface gleamed darkly in the lamplight, then vanished beneath the billowings of a crisp white cloth. Then came the salvers and the plates and the cutlery. An intoxicating aroma drifted on to the air.

Umbecca turned. It was like a dream. On a trolley, rumbling forward through the parted foliage, was a whole sucking-pig, slick with oozing fat, with a baked apple stuffed in its mouth! It rested on a bed of roasted onions and carrots and parsnips and pumpkin and potatoes, all swimming, drowning, in the oily, running rivulets. Boats of steaming gravy followed behind. Umbecca swooned, but the chaplain was in attendance, plucking a glittering glass from a tray and conveying it, with a smile, to the lady's hand.

'I take it, dear lady, you're staying for dinner?'

491

Jem's eyes must have drifted shut again; he must, in his weariness and wretchedness, have slept. When he woke, it seemed to him that he had been far, far away. Strange, dark shapes had twisted through his mind. There was a confused jumble of memory and dream: the velvet curtain, fluttering in his alcove; the face of the dark god, purple-black and huge.

Then, once again, the flash of burning words:

    & BEFORE THE RETURN OF THE EVIL ONE
A TIME OF SUFFERING SHALL DESCEND UPON THE EARTH
    & THIS SHALL HERALD THE END OF ATONEMENT:
      & ONLY THE POWER OF THE OROKON
  SHALL DEFEAT THE EVIL THAT THEN SHALL COME

What was wrong with him?

If only this nonsense would go away!

Awake again, Jem was aware of an aching coldness; like a fool, he had lain out in the rain. His clothes were damp all through and the impotence of his legs seemed for a moment to have crept through all his body, upwards to his thighs, through his chest, down his arms and to his fingers.

His teeth chattered.

He forced his eyes open and the darkness was not dispelled. Then he saw that it was the sky through the mesh of branches that was dark, silvered just a little by the moon behind the clouds. Jem struggled up on to his elbows. The tombyard was silent but for the stirrings of the wind; but for the drippings of the wet leaves.

A viscous, slow alarm spread through Jem's chest. How much time had passed? He had missed the curfew and his strength was gone; there would be Bluejackets posted at the tombyard gates and milling drunkenly, perhaps, on the green, spilling from the doors of the Lazy Tiger. Jem thought of all that Tor had told him. He had not been frightened of the Bluejackets before; now he was very frightened indeed.

He heard voices.

He flattened himself against the slab again; he did not know why. His hand clutched at the mossy edge, feeling for his crutches. Did the sentries patrol the tombyard at night? The slow alarm in Jem's chest had turned into a cavernous thud of fear. An owl hooted, far away, over the wall that kept out the Wildwood.

The voices came closer. They were not the voices of sentries.

'I can't! I can't! Oh, come back, do.'

'Don't hold out on me. It was you, I know it was.'

'You're mad! I don't know what you mean.'

'Take me there! Take me there now.'

The first voice was a man's; the second a woman's. Each was low and urgent, and in each there was pleading; but the man's plea, it was clear, threatened at any moment to be something more.

To be something violent.

'Come on, Dolly!'

'Let me go!'

Jem turned his head and through the darkness he could see them, weaving through the graves to the gap in the wall. The man, muffled in a greatcoat, held a lantern aloft; he pulled at the woman's resisting arm. Garish in the lantern-light, her figure stood out, yellow-haired and in a bright red dress. Her face, what Jem glimpsed of it, was a mask of fear. She struggled to break away. The figure in the greatcoat grabbed her.

She cried out.

'Shut up, bitch!'

She kicked him.

He lurched; he dropped the lantern. It rolled across the grass, the arc of its rays revolving wildly through the air.

'You stinking, pox-ridden little slut!'

She had twisted away from him again and would have run, flailing, from the tombyard, but could not.

She was cornered.

The man loomed immensely. He stepped forward, lit hideously from below by the guttering lantern. He had been wearing a furry hat and now it had fallen from his head; but it was hardly necessary, after all, to see the angry redness of his hair. The wheedling malevolence of the voice was unmistakable.

'Come on, Dolly! I pay for it, don't I?'

'You can't. Not this.'

'Can't? That's where you're wrong, Dolly. I can have just what I want, and I can have it the way I want. I thought you'd know that by now, Dolly.'

'Just leave me. Please. Go!'

She held up her hands. Stumbling, she backed away towards the yew-tree, and the slab where Jem lay.

'Oh, Dolly!' Polty chuckled. He hawked a gob of spit on to his hand and held it upright, the fingers shaped into a sharp point. He jigged it up and down, leering repulsively. 'If you won't take me, I'll have to take you.'

Appalled and fascinated, Jem rolled from the slab and lay, breathing heavily, in the weeds beside it, peering up over the edge. The back of the red dress came closer to him, billowing. On the woman's feet, he saw, she wore leather pumps, painted to match her dress.

His hands closed about his carved, heavy crutches.

It happened suddenly. It was the simplest thing; the heel of a pump, turning on a stone.

'My ankle!'

'Stinking little bitch. Dirty, dirty little Vaga-whore!'

Polty was upon her. There was scratching, biting. He slapped her. He ripped her dress. In a madness of rage he flung her on to the tomb-slab. She cried out again as he grabbed her ankle, wringing it wildly, wrenching back her leg.

'Little bitch, I'll have you!'

He tore open his breeches.

The lantern was failing. There were wild flashes, then darkness. The flashes, searing on to the night like bursts of lightning, disclosed first the figure of Jem, rearing up on his knees beside the tomb-slab; then Polty, crumpling; then Jem, the twinned thicknesses of his crutches flung back above his head, about to smash down.

Again.

Again.

Then there was darkness. The body, senseless, rolled into the grass.

Jem slumped forward.

'Cata?'

He had known, of course; not at the beginning, but at the end he had known.

'Oh, Cata, what have you done?'

'No, Jem. What have *you* done?'

The boy said nothing. A hushed wind shivered through the yew-branches; grey clouds drifted hazily over the face of the moon.

'You've killed him, Jem.'

The sucking-pig had been only the prologue; the merest hint of all that was to come.

Then had come the jellied eels.

Then had come the partridges.

Then had come the venison in cherry-wine sauce.

Then had come the pheasant. The goose, the duck, the swan.

Then had come the succulent, bloody side of beef.

It was a banquet more splendid than any even Umbecca could have imagined. The best wines not only of Varl but of Orandy and Lexion had accompanied each course; there had been basket after basket of piping-hot bread-rolls; and the guards had served everything with such elegance and refinement!

Dessert was an enormous apple pie with a crisp golden crust, a huge, steaming plum-pudding, flamed in brandy and swimming in custard and a cheesecake baked to perfection and topped beyond extravagance with the rarest fruit preserves from the Zenzan forests and white, whipped mountains of cream. They washed it down with pots of Zaxos coffee, accompanied by the best and most exotic liqueurs of Tiralos. Boards of the best cheeses from Varby and Holluch stood by at the ready, to satisfy any remaining hunger.

Only as she sat back, replete at last, sipping at another cup of Zaxos Black and popping a mint-flavoured chocolate into her mouth, did Umbecca take in the scene that surrounded her. Beaming with pleasure, her gaze roved over the ornate golden candlesticks that lined the table, the brilliant arrangement of flowers in the centre and the tight, budded rose that lay, like an offering, before her own place. It was a red rose. Umbecca looked down at it, then looked up, and saw that a series of looking-glasses had been moved into a circle around the table. The candle-flames, the flowers, the faces of her friends, were doubled and redoubled in a haze of reflection.

'Ah, good,' said the chaplain with a smile.

Now the guards were bringing something else. It was not food this time; it was not flowers; it was not another looking-glass. It was a curious wooden figure with a blank, round face. It was a dressmaker's dummy, padded out to the size of Umbecca. The dummy wore a white gown, the most magnificent arrangement of lace and gauze and ribbons that Umbecca had ever seen.

Understanding dawned on her only slowly, and at first what she understood was not quite the truth.

'Oh, chaplain . . .' she began.

But it was the commander who blundered up from his chair, sinking to the floor and catching her hands. 'Dear, dear lady! What is this? Surprise? Ah, the modesty of a virtuous woman! But how could I not have loved you from the first? How could I not love you, when you – don't deny it! – when *you* are "Miss R——"?'

He crushed her in his arms and a horrified Umbecca could only gaze wildly over the old man's shoulder, into the reflection of the chaplain's face.

His mouth had twisted into an enigmatic smile.

Cata kicked off her harlot's shoes.

'My ankle!'

It was swelling already.

Jem could only look at her blankly in the tarnished moonlight.

'Why, Cata?' he breathed.

She knew what he meant and she looked down sadly, rubbing the hideous paint from her face. 'It was the tithes. They were going to take Papa! I had no gold but the harlequin's coin – I had to do something, Jem.'

'Oh, Cata!' Jem bunched a hand into a fist, grinding the knuckles deep between his eyes. Emotions filled him that he could scarcely understand: jealousy and envy and a strange wonderment, passing in waves; then a horrified pity. How could he have guessed? How could he have known?

'I couldn't tell you, Jem.'

She gestured to the body, lying on the ground. 'That day in the Circle of Knowing. He knew it was me. I said it wasn't, but he knew. He said I had to take him there.' The girl shuddered, on the verge of tears. 'He would have destroyed it! But now we've destroyed it.'

'Cata, what do you mean?'

Heavy boots crunched along the cinder-path.

'Ho!' came a voice.

Then another, 'Who's there?'

Jem gripped Cata; Cata gripped Jem. For moments they had seemed to hover, suspended above time, oblivious to the staccato drip-drip of leaves and the blustering wind and the movement of clouds across the wan moon.

Then time came back.

'They're coming!' Jem breathed.

'They'll kill us,' said Cata.

'Can we make it through the wall?'

She gripped Jem's hand; but this time something was wrong. She could not stand, and nor could he.

Jem bit his lip. He offered desperately, 'Cata, lean on me. Quick.'

But no. There was a sharp splitting. A gasp of wild grief escaped the boy as his crutches collapsed beneath him, twin splintered sticks. He looked about him wildly. He saw the spreading pool of blood from Polty's head. He saw the lantern approaching, swinging back and forth, flashing through the mesh of the yew's entangled branches.

That was when Cata said, 'I know a way. Quick. Get off the slab.'

Cata scrambled in the grass and weeds, her hands clawing at the sides of her mother's tomb-slab. She had almost flung Jem aside and he lay prostrate, desperately weak, and desperate in his weakness. A tangled yew-root dug painfully into his belly.

'Cata! I don't understand! What is it?'

The mechanism was old, choked with moss and weeds; but it worked well enough.

Jem gasped.

Soundlessly, the heavy tomb-slab rose up like the lid of a Jarvel-box. The lantern flashed on the other side of the tombyard; the sentries, inspecting each shadowy corner, had been already to the north, east, and west.

They turned.

They were coming.

It could only have been the recklessness of a rush of love that permitted Cata, in that moment, to bear down hard on her agonized ankle. She gathered Jem from the ground. For a moment they stood clutched together, swaying and ready to fall. As the moonlight glinted in Cata's eyes, Jem saw that they were flooded with tears.

He blundered, 'I love you, Cata.'

'We've destroyed it all, Jem. Someone must pay. It's what Wood-tiger tells us. The black stripes; the gold. You understand, don't you? Jem?'

He did not.

Then he did.

'No!' he whispered, in an access of horror, but his horror was not for the gaping tomb.

It was the separation.

The sacrifice.

Then it was over. Then all her power was gone from her; she was slipping.

One moment remained. It was the moment when she flung Jem into the chasm before them and the lid of the tomb descended upon him.

'Cata!' His voice was not a whisper then, but a shout.

It was too late. As swiftly as it had opened, the slab had shut, obliterating all sound, all sight, all sense.

When the lantern-light fell upon her, an instant later, Cata was crouched across her mother's tomb, a sobbing Vaga-child in a ripped red dress.

'By the Lord Agonis!' cried a man's voice. 'Look!'

She was tiny. So small.

But what had she done?

Chapter 63

THE BLACK PETALS

First it was oblivion; then something else.

Lying in utter blackness, at first Jem felt not even sorrow, not even pain. It was as if the darkness about him, like blotting-paper, had soaked up all prospect of feeling. Here, even the crudest sensations seemed things that had been taken from him, sapped away. How far had he fallen? Was he hurt? If Jem had cracked a rib, he did not feel it. If he had bruised his arm, he did not feel it. If he had a knife and were to cut his heart open, he would not feel it.

Cata was gone and he did not feel it.

Long moments passed before Jem was aware both of his pain and of his predicament. What had Cata done? She had sacrificed herself, given herself up for Polty's death. She would die on the gallows on the village green.

Meanwhile, she had left Jem to die here, slowly and horribly, in this darkness. She had condemned him, too. She had put him in a box where he could not be found.

'Cata, why?'

Now Jem sobbed.

Why could she not have let them die together?

Only slowly did Jem come to consider the place in which he found himself. He was lying neither on the hard stone he might have expected, nor the crumbling bones he might have feared. Beneath him, the bottom of the tomb was soft.

Straw?

No.

A curious, heady incense filled the black place. Was it the smell of death? As soon as he was aware of it, it seemed more intense. Rich and strange, but familiar, too, the smell burgeoned in his nostrils, filling his senses.

Then he knew.

His fingers ran through the softness beneath him. He swung out an exploratory arm, brushing a wall of fluttering, tiny tongues. The place was filled with flowers, many-petalled flowers grown from wreathing vines. But how could flowers grow down here, in a place that was sunless and black?

Tentatively Jem crawled forward, feeling for the limits of his new domain. Until now, his eyes had been closed, as if the dark interior of his skull were at least to be preferred to the darkness around him. Now his eyes were open, perhaps in readiness for a sliver of moonbeam, spilling through a crack in the slab above, to offer him the merest glimpse of the flowers.

There was no crack. No moonbeam.

But there was a light.

It was not bright, not blazing, not a beam of fire; at first it could barely be seen at all. It was only the faintest refulgence of purple, dark and deep, brushed so faintly on to the background of black that Jem could not even be sure it was there.

It faded.

It was gone.

It might have been a trick his mind was playing. To Jem, the light had seemed remote, like the glimpse of a flickering, far-off aurora. Impossible, of course, within the narrow walls of a tomb, but the boy had sensed already that his black prison was not so small as it may at first have seemed.

The light came again, and this time the phosphorescence lingered a little longer; this time it was a faint, pulsing lambency that enabled Jem, for the first time, to see where he had fallen. He lay not in a narrow, high box, but at the end of a broad, low tunnel. The tunnel was lined with flowers, and the flowers, he saw, were black.

Dark, purple-black, like the strangely glowing light.

The source of the lambency he could not yet see; now, all he knew was that he must move towards it. In the strange light, drawn forward by a force he could not understand, the crippled boy began to crawl across the floor of black petals.

Dimly he recalled a conversation with his aunt, far away and in another life. She had been talking about cross-tunnels, the tunnels that had been built, long ago, beneath the earliest of the Agonist temples. Could there be one beneath the Temple of Irion? She had said not.

But she was wrong.

Cross-tunnels, Jem knew, had been designed to ensure that no part of a temple's sacred grounds, or the earth in which the dead should lie, should fail to partake of the sacred unction. From a central point beneath the temple's altar, the extended, deep cellar would stretch its five arms to each corner of the tombyard. In later times, the cross-tunnels were thought a mere superstition, and they were no longer built. Those which had been built were usually sealed. Often they were forgotten.

Had Cata known? She must have known!

Jem crawled onwards, and as he crawled, the purple-black light became strangely stronger, blazing not brighter but more intensely. Flame-like, it flickered through the aromatic air; it gleamed and glimmered on the blackness of the flowers, becoming stronger, ever stronger, while all the while remaining a light that burnt from blackness.

Still Jem could not see what made the light; but the place to which he crawled, from where the luminescence came, was the centre of the five arms of the cross. As he approached it, the vegetation, swathing the tunnel's walls, grew in greater profusion. Black tendrils and vines draped his path; petals shook down on him as he pushed his way through. The vines which bore the black flowers all radiated, he saw, from this central place.

The central place was a larger, pentagonal chamber, and in the thickening of the vines Jem did not at first see that the ceiling of the tunnel, as it neared its end, was higher; nor did he know that his own figure, ineluctably, as if in response to this increase of height, was rising slowly from its crouched position. He was crawling no longer.

When Jem reached the centre, he was standing.

He turned, slowly. It was not like a dream; he was intensely, but strangely conscious. In five directions leading away from him, he looked down a tunnel. In the central chamber, wreathing vegetation obscured almost entirely the crumbling curve of staircase which once had led down from the temple above. There was no way out now, but Jem did not think of this.

Marvelling, he remained in the centre of the strange light, slowly turning, turning; moments had passed before it came to him that even here, in this central place, he could not see what it was that made the light. He stood inside it and the dark candescence hovered, surrounding him, like a sphere of mist; it might have been propagated spontaneously from the air.

Or from him.

Jem looked down at the legs and feet that now, miraculously, bore his weight. The place where he stood was a raised mound in the petal-strewn floor. His turning feet had disturbed the petals that lay scattered thickly on the mound, as elsewhere.

The mound was the great central root of the vines. They were all the same plant, these vines, and grew from this place; looking at the criss-cross of root-limbs, impossibly ancient and thick and firm, Jem could see that they had pushed their way up from the earth underneath the tunnel floor.

Then he saw the rock.

In the purple-black light it could barely be seen, lying entangled in the twisted roots. There was no reason why the rock should excite him; it was the least exciting thing in the tunnels. It was nothing: a hard, ugly chunk of impacted black clay, caught in the implacable strange roots that had forced their way up around it from below. It was the size of a man's fist, perhaps a little less. It did not sparkle. It did not shine.

Jem's heart began to beat very slowly.

Very slowly, he sank to his knees.

To wrench the black rock from its entrapment in the roots would have been effort too great for a powerful man. There was no reason to try, but the impulse that possessed Jem was deeper than reason. It was deeper than thought. He gripped his hands about the roots and pulled.

Impossible; they might as well have been made of metal.

He tried again.

It was dark again; the purple-black light above him had dispersed.

But Jem was not afraid.

There was nothing to fear.

Everything until now, he sensed, had been illusion. That was when the new light, the real light, began. That was when the rock began strangely glowing as the air had done, at first with the same penumbral phosphorescence, then with the same mysterious black intensity.

Jem watched, entranced, and though as he watched he understood nothing, he knew that his life had been leading him to this moment. He knew that his destiny was suddenly upon him; though what that destiny was, and what it meant, he could not say. It was a benediction that might make him cry out with joy; a burden that might make him break down in tears. Regret, and a wild elation, surged through his heart.

The thick roots parted, easily now, beneath Jem's hands as he reached for the rock.

No. Not the rock. The crystal!

Now Jem understood.

Now Jem knew.

& THE CHILD SHALL FIND FIRST THE CRYSTAL OF DARKNESS
FLUNG TO THE SKIES BY THE FATHER OF THE GODS:
& HE SHALL QUEST THROUGH THE LANDS OF EL-OROK
FOR THE CRYSTALS OF EARTH FIRE WATER & AIR
THAT HE MAY UNITE THEM IN THE OROKON

Jem cried out; first with joy, then pain, then joy and pain. The blazing darkness of the crystal scorched his hands. He tore it free, holding it aloft; he rose to his feet as if rising after it. His clothes fell from him, seared by black heat. His coat, his shirt, his breeches, fluttered away to powdery ash. He was naked and his skin was black. Hot tears streamed down his face and Jem, in his ecstasy, could barely see that all around him, equally, down each of the five tunnels, a rippling dissolution was running wild. The vines withered rapidly, as at the action of savage flames, collapsing first into ash, then powder.

Then they were nothing.

The crystal was all!

    & IF HE SUCCEEDS A NEW AGE SHALL DAWN
    & ALL THE LANDS OF EL-OROK SHALL LIVE IN PEACE:
    & IF HE FAILS THE HORROR THAT HAS PASSED
        SHALL BE AS NOTHING TO THE HORROR
            THAT SHALL COME

Greater and greater grew the heat that was not heat, the light that was not light. Higher and higher the crystal rose. Now Jem was stretched to the extreme of his height; now the crystal was bearing him aloft; now all the world was the purple-black light. Wild images, visions, dreams, flashed up and down the tunnels of the cross, borne on the buckling, fusing waves.

The explosion, when it came, was a thousand thousand thunderbolts, discharged all at once in a world without light.

Chapter 64

THE JARVEL-BOX

Turning, turning.

The face of the moon was immensely close, aching in the brightness of its golden light. The light was so bright as to sear the world; the light was brighter than the light of the sun.

But one side was black. East? West? The moon was revolving in the sky like a wheel; the hazy line between the dark and the light was turning, turning slowly. Below, the curtains of the clouds had parted; admist the velvet darkness the figure who was turning, turning in the sky could look down at the brightness of the subsiding blast.

It turned slowly to black; turning, turning.

Jem's eyes opened.

It had all been a dream.

The tombyard was gone and the tunnel was gone. There were no vines; no purple-black flowers. No crystal. Cata was in the Wildwood, and by her mother's tomb-slab, Poltiss Veeldrop was not lying dead.

Jem was in the castle and his legs were crippled.

They would always be crippled. Had they ever been anything else? He had thought so; but it seemed to him now that this had been a mere illusion, forced into life from the intensity of his need.

He raised his head a little and saw his legs now, the bowed and the buckled, their contours familiar beneath his blankets. The objects in the alcove surrounded him impassively, grey and unglinting in the overcast light. Rain slithered slowly down the high slit-window. There were clatterings, voices, from the corridors and courtyards. The morning, it was clear, was far advanced.

The morning, in fact, was over.

Jem sank back. He was naked beneath the blankets, and cold. There was no fire in the alcove.

'Master Jem! Still in bed?'

The curtain billowed back.

'Nirry!' He had seen her only the day before, but all at once the sight of her seemed strange. He gazed up at her as she looked down at him, her face a study in bemused dismay.

'Look at you! Sleeping into the afternoon! And you're so dirty! Look at your face! I tell you, Master Jem, she won't have it. She was out late last night but she looked in here, and where were you? She'd have talked about nothing else, I tell you, if it hadn't been for all the rest that's happened.'

The maid was bustling about the boy's bed, rolling up discarded stockings, a crumpled tunic, a stiffened, stained kerchief. The stench in the alcove was abominable.

'The rest? What rest?' Jem rubbed his eyes.

'Come on, Master Jem, you must have heard it, wherever you were! They've blown up the temple! They say it was Vaga-magic!' Nirry's eyes widened. 'Wiggler – he's my particular friend – says there'll be a big crowd gathered on the green today!'

Jem's head was whirling. All he could say, as he gazed stupidly at Nirry, was, 'Crowd?'

'The Vagas, Master Jem!' Nirry mimed the pulling of a noose about her neck. Her tongue lolled; then she snapped back into life. 'Them Vagas are really going to get what's coming to them now. Remember what they did to you in the woods? The whole village is up in arms this time! Wiggler says they're rounding up the ringleaders. Now come on, Master Jem, you must get up. I'd consider myself lucky if I were you. As it is, it's bad enough. She *knows*, Master Jem!'

'Knows?' Jem struggled up in his bed. Hadn't Nirry alarmed him enough? 'Nirry, what does she know?'

The maid flung back, 'You know!'

'I don't!'

Nirry gripped the edge of the curtain, gazing on the boy with exasperated love. She bit her lip. Flushing scarlet, she burst out, 'She's seen your blankets, Master Jem!'

Jem's laugh was sudden and wild, and rang behind Nirry as she retreated down the corridor.

It frightened her.

The laugh subsided and Jem lay back. Could it be true, about the hangings on the green? His head ached; he felt so weak! He flopped an arm from the bed, reaching for his crutches where they always lay. His hand pawed about the floor, back and forth. He rolled over, hanging from the side of the bed. That was when something small and very light, that must have been caught in his tousled hair, detached itself and fluttered to the carpet beneath him. Jem picked it up.

It was a black petal.

The alcove lurched, suddenly; the petal flickered and fizzed out of being.

Jem almost cried out. He turned over his hands: though he felt no pain, he saw that the palms were deeply marked, seared with scars, as if, long ago, they had gripped a burning orb.

He flung back the blankets from his bed, his heart pounding.

How could it be?

His legs were bowed. Buckled.

Everything had changed and nothing had changed. A sob escaped him, bitter and harsh.

There was a commotion in the corridor.

'Please, girl! I must see your mistress! I must!'

'You can't! Oh, how did you get in here? Please, go!'

The second voice was Nirry's; the first had been a man's. It was venerable and trembling, but its owner, evidently, was possessed of strength. A strength of desperation. Urgently, Nirry endeavoured to restrain him as he pushed his way past her to the door of Ela's apartment.

Who could it be?

Then Jem knew.

The astonishment that filled him was almost enough to make him forget what had happened, moments before. He beat, distracted, at the sides of his bed. Oh, if only he had his crutches! He wanted to see the meeting that was about to take place as much as the maid wanted to prevent it.

He had to see it.

He had to know.

He rolled on to his side. He stared ahead, blankly. Down the corridor, he could hear his aunt's voice, booming out her demand for the meaning of this disturbance.

Blank-eyed, he gazed at the objects in the alcove: at the stuffed toy piglet, mildewed and threadbare, that had looked on impassively through all his nightly riots; at the tarnished goblets and the candlesticks and the picture of the pale highway. In the low mantel-nook above the hearth was the Jarvel-box, just where it had always been, in the place where Barnabas had put it. But something was odd. The box, Jem could tell, had been moved, just a little. Taken out and replaced.

The crippled boy thudded from his bed to the floor, crawling across to the empty, chill hearth. With trembling hands he drew forth the box, gazing almost incuriously at the ornate, carved lid.

Yes.

He had known.

His fingers felt for the secret catch.

Inside, the crystal shimmered and pulsed with its strange, dark light; Jem, taking up the mystic object, found that the light was coursing up his arms and down his body, surrounding and enfolding him in its empurpled aura.

Jem rose slowly from the floor where he lay. Weightlessly, his back brushed against the ceiling.

He hovered from the alcove.

The door of his mother's apartment was flung wide. Protected from view by the aura of darkness, Jem, like a spirit from the Realm of Unbeing, looked on at the scene that was unfolding within.

But could only look on.

Chapter 65

ERMINE

Umbecca, when the commotion came, had been sitting by the fireside, knitting a scarf. She was dressed in a simple, plain blue gown. She was happy. Soon, her carriage would arrive. She was to take tea in the Lectory before the hangings that afternoon; in the meantime, plum cake and butter scones would suffice to keep body and spirit together.

Earlier, Umbecca had been troubled. She had been tormented. It was not the explosion of the temple that had caused her distress; to Umbecca, this was, for the moment, mere background noise in the drama of her own emotions. Like Meroline, after she received her proposal from the broken-down General Etzcombe, Umbecca had spent that morning in an *agony of indecision*. The commander's declaration had come as a shock; there was no denying it had been a terrible shock. But slowly, Umbecca's horror had subsided. Of course, she was disappointed. It was only natural; nor could she forgive the chaplain for sporting, as he had clearly done, with her virtue. But she was a strong woman. She had borne many disappointments before.

Besides, unlike Meroline, she had come to see the merits in the proposal. One, in particular, was glowingly clear. This very afternoon, she would open her heart to her intended on a topic of a most intimate and personal nature. Tearfully, she would inform Olivan that it was now quite beyond her to tend any longer to her poor niece; that Ela from now on would require care that was more constant. More secure. Olivan must arrange it.

Umbecca sighed with happiness upon making this decision. Yes! She would be free! In a surge of thankfulness she mumbled out a litany-line: *Lord Agonis, tomorrow I shall serve you more truly.* Yes, she would serve him! She would serve him as no one had served him before! As the commander's wife, with decent servants and without Ela to hold her back, Umbecca would have untold opportunities to exercise her benevolent influence in the world. Her virtues had been hidden; now they would burst triumphantly forth.

She looked about her. Since the chaplain had come, Ela's apartment had been much improved. The new blue carpet and the matching blue curtains had been a great boon, it was clear. But there was still so much to be done! Now, it would never be done; not here, not in this apartment. Soon it would be emptied; then it would be closed up; in due course, perhaps, it would be turned over to the soldiers. All trace of Umbecca's long life here would be gone. For a moment, she was forlorn. She gazed at the casement; at the wainscot; at the bed where Ela, unsuspectingly, lay. Then Umbecca's happiness flamed out again. It was the happiness of a triumphal victor. She thought of Ela lying in that bed, day after day; she thought of the stretches of her life that had been consumed in looking after an ungrateful, mad harlot.

No more!

No longer!

'How came this man here?'

'Please mistress, he was just here! He just appeared!'

'Vaga-magic, I suppose! You evil man!'

'Umbecca, listen. Please, just listen.'

In an instant, Umbecca's happiness turned to rage. She flung down her knitting. Her face flushing, she reared up from the sofa and stood before Silas Wolveron. The encounter had in it something shocking, as if two worlds that must be kept apart had clashed suddenly and violently together. In his robes, with his cowl and staff, the old man might have been some ancient figure from The Juvescence, intruded bizarrely into a time that was not his and a place in which he should never have been.

On the bed, Ela stirred.

Drab, grey rain pattered steadily at the casement.

'Please sir, won't you go?' Nirry tugged again at the old man's sleeve.

'It is my daughter!' he burst out. 'She has been arrested!'

'Arrested?' Umbecca, by the fireside, displayed no confusion. 'As a Vaga-whore, no doubt. That girl is an affront to all decent, respectable people. Silas, how you have the effrontery to come here I shall never know.'

'But I come to appease you, Umbecca. I come with an offer.'

'Offer? Appease? How can you ever appease me, Silas Wolveron? After all that has happened. After all that you have done. To come to me!'

Umbecca spoke low and rapidly. Her words were not loud, not shrill, but thick with the bitterness that welled in her like bile. The wicked man! How she had been deceived in him! What a world this was, where those who seemed virtuous could turn out, in truth, to be vice incarnate! She felt for her glittering Circle of Agonis, clutching it as she continued her denunciation.

'Corrupted, depraved man! The virtue of this village lay in your care! How many others fell when you fell? Would my beloved niece have become a harlot in her turn, had it not been for your debauching of Yane? Would my dear nephew, Torvester, have been tempted into treachery? Silas, it is our duty to conquer our nature! Did you not teach me that, when I came to you in the temple? I trusted you! I believed in you! In you, I believed, my faith found its reflection. Can you begin to understand what you did to this village? To me? Oh, Silas, to fall so hard, so catastrophically! Faith, trust, cast to the wind like chaff! Duties, vows, flung contemptuously aside!'

'Umbecca, Umbecca! Blind, foolish woman!'

'Blind? You call *me* blind?'

'Because you see nothing! Umbecca, you are younger than I, but you are growing old. Have you not learnt, in all your years, that there are obligations higher than those of this world, its conventions, its institutions? It is those that are the chaff! I lied to myself when I was Lector of Irion. Yane was my destiny.'

'Destiny? You were a member of the Order. You call it your *destiny* to seduce a young girl?'

'Poor Umbecca! You shall never understand. Yane and I indulged in no guilty passion. No temple sanctioned our union, but of all the marriages that have been celebrated in this valley, ours was among the only true ones. We were married in the Wildwood, in a bower of white petals. It is a place more sacred than the Temple of Irion; the place where my darling now lies, though her monument is elsewhere.'

But Umbecca seemed scarcely to be listening any more.

'Oh, leave me, Silas! You weary me as much as you disgust me. Tell me no more of your catalogue of depravity.' She shuddered, turning to the fire. 'To think that I entrusted you with the secrets of my heart! To think that I sat alone with you, so many times!'

The old man might almost have laughed. 'Oh, you were safe, Umbecca! I had no lust for you!'

There was a silence. Umbecca, by the hearth, was twisting her hands. When she turned back, long moments later, her face and neck were so gorged with blood that they might almost have burst, showering the room in scarlet cascades. She said quietly, 'Nirry, call the guards.'

'No. Nirry, stay.'

It was Ela's voice. Stiffly, slowly, but not so slowly as might have been expected, the pale invalid was rising from her bed.

'Ela!' Umbecca's voice was a hoarse whisper. Her little eyes blazed. But the fat woman was more outraged than astonished, rather as if someone had insulted her. Slapped her. The fresh outrage was almost too much. How could it be that her niece was rising? Ela's role was to lie passively on her

514

bed, saying nothing and doing nothing; soon she would not even have that role. Olivan would punish her; punish her as she deserved to be punished.

Umbecca struggled to command herself. For a moment she was silenced.

'Old one, you said you had an offer for my aunt,' said Ela. 'Tell us what it is. Tell us why you have come.'

Wolveron turned to her. His cowl had been disturbed in the drama of his entrance, and as he turned it slipped back from his head, exposing the hideousness of his mutilation. For a pained moment, Ela closed her eyes.

Then she opened them.

The old man bowed his head.

'My Lady Elabeth,' he said quietly, 'I come here not to torment your aunt. Nor do I come to make peace with her at last, for though I might offer it, I know she would reject it. What I seek may be stated simply. The Bluejackets have taken my beloved daughter, suspecting her of a part in the affairs of last night. The commander, in the name of his justice, has seen fit already to pronounce her doom. Five Children of Koros are said to be her accomplices. She is to be hanged with them when evening falls.'

Ela gasped, 'Hanged?'

Nirry gasped, 'Hanged!'

'A fate,' Umbecca said tartly, 'that any person *with eyes* could long ago have foreseen.'

Already the fat woman had regained her composure. Would Ela triumph over her? She would not! Gleefully Umbecca contemplated the fate that lay in store for her niece. Olivan would have her put away! In Agondon, there were special hospitals. Very special hospitals. She licked her lips. It would be almost as good as having *Ela* hanged. After all, her niece was no better than the blind man's slut of a daughter.

'Aunt, be silent—' Ela attempted.

'No, niece, I shall not! Must I listen to this? So! A harlot is to be hanged. And what would you have me do, blind man?

Go to the commander and plead for her worthless life?' A scoffing laugh erupted from the bloated face.

'Umbecca, I said that I sought no favour of you,' Silas Wolveron said calmly, 'and nor do I. You say that I have betrayed your sacred trust. Since that time, you have looked on me with loathing.

'I told you I had come to appease you, but I seek not an appeasement in love. It is your hatred I wish to appease. I offer you, freely, the vengeance you have sought.

'The commander, though he condemns my daughter, will not speak to me. I am turned from his gates. Umbecca, he will listen to you. Go to him, I beg you, and tell him of my guilt. Tell him that it is I, in my fastness in the Wildwood, who has schemed and plotted and committed every outrage that the triumphant Bluejackets might wish to ascribe to me.

'Dear Umbecca! Dear, foolish woman! Can you see now what I ask? Can you see now what I give you? I am an old man. I have lived too long, and when I could see, I saw too much. Only let my beloved child go free, and my life may then be that much chaff in the wind. I place it in your hands, Umbecca. Cast it away!'

In the course of this speech, the old man had sunk to his knees before the imperious fat woman, clinging for support to his upraised staff. She was not moved. She looked on him implacably. When he had finished, a smile flickered for an instant across her face. Then her mouth set hard. She flung herself away. Her refusal, when it came, was violent and contemptuous.

'Vile, lustful old Vaga-man! Do you imagine I shall do as you ask? It is wrong! It is wicked! You forget, Silas, that I am consecrated, as you once were, to live in the love of the Lord Agonis. What you would fling to the winds is truth itself! And for what? For a ruined child?'

'Enough, Aunt! Enough!'

Ela had listened, and been silent, for too long. The voice that broke from her now was a shout.

Umbecca span, startled.

The old man, his calmness gone, had collapsed, sobbing, in the centre of the floor. Ela went to him. She took him in her arms. She held him, kissed him. She stroked his hair, his face; she ran her fingers tenderly about the seared pits of his eyes. The scars puckered horribly with the bitter, dry sobbing.

Umbecca looked on, incredulous and disgusted. A shuddering, horrified perception of the old man came over her: of the lice and fleas in his filthy robes; of the pustular sores on his head and arms; of the rank stench that rose from him like garbage. She had loved him, worshipped him; and he had run away to live like a beast in a stinking cave, rolling with a harlot in a sty of lust. Had he come any closer to her now, she would have screamed. She would have seized the poker from the hearth and struck him down.

Slowly, Ela rose from the old man's embrace. When she spoke again, it was with calm authority.

'Nirry, get my coat. My shoes.'

'M'lady?'

'Niece, what are you saying?'

'Isn't it obvious, Aunt? I'm going out. I've done it before. Just not for a while, that's all. Nirry?'

'Niece, you're not well!' Umbecca burst out. 'You're delirious! Please, get back into bed before you hurt yourself.'

'Nirry?' Ela said again.

'Nirry! Keep away from that chest!' The fat woman lurched forward, grabbing the maid's arm.

'Ouch! Stop that!' Nirry wrenched away. She stood between the two women, rubbing her arm, her eyes darting uncertainly from the one to the other.

'Nirry, do as I say,' Ela said icily. 'Have you forgotten, it is I who am your mistress? This woman whom you seem so eager to obey is nothing more than my maiden aunt. My "companion", though a dreadful one she has proved to be. Whatever my shame in the eyes of this vile world, I was and I am the daughter of the Archduke. I am Lady Elabeth Ixiter of Irion, a noble of this realm, and it is as such that I shall see Commander Veeldrop now.'

'See the commander? Niece, what are you talking about? She's raving, Nirry, can't you see? Oh, help me with her!'

But Nirry had repaired already to the chest at the end of the bed; now she was helping Ela into a large coat. Worn directly over the invalid's nightdress, the coat was musty and more than a little moth-eaten. It was of red velvet, with ermine trim. There was a matching hat. Fixed into the hat was a gold brooch, representing the Redjacket arms.

'I go neither to sacrifice the life of this poor old man,' Ela was saying, 'nor my own. No one is to die: not you, Aunt, not you, Nirry, not me, not Jem, not Lector Wolveron here. And not Yane's child.

'Oh, how I have cursed the weakness that has bound me here! From my bed I have listened, half-aware, as this castle, this village, this kingdom has been overtaken by horror! I am weak and sick and I have borne much, too much; but some things cannot be borne. Aunt, do you imagine I'll let Veel-drop get away with this? Hanging Yane's child by the neck on the village green? Veeldrop, indeed! A dirty little piece of jumped-up, murdering scum!'

'Niece, you are speaking of the saviour of our kingdom!'

'Saviour? Its destroyer!'

'Come, m'lady. I'll go with you. Father shall drive us to the Lectory.' Nirry had taken Ela by the arm, but all at once Umbecca's bulk was barring the door.

'You can't go. I won't let you go.'

'You have no choice in the matter, Aunt. Let me pass.'

'He won't listen to you! Do you think . . . *Olivan* will listen to you?'

'Olivan?'

'It's his name. Olivan Tharley Veeldrop. You see, I know him . . . I know him very well.'

'Congratulations, Aunt. Is that what you want me to say?'

'Yes, niece. That's it, precisely. You see, Olivan and I are going to be married.'

'*What?*'

'He loves me! He loves me and he has asked me to marry him! That's how I know he'd never listen to you.'

'Marry him? And you're going to? You pathetic, sick woman! Don't you know who he is? What he's done?' With an outflung arm, Ela gestured to the prostrate form of Silas Wolveron. 'Don't you know who it was who put out his eyes? Your Olivan, that's who!'

But Umbecca's face registered no horror. 'Yes, he did! And do you know why? Because I told him to, that's why! Silas Wolveron was a danger to us all. He was an apostate and a traitor and he deserved to die. I told Olivan everything that depraved man had done. I said he had smuggled Bluejacket secrets into the castle during the Siege. It was true, I know it was! I saw him!

'But I said he had once been a good man, too. That's why he wasn't executed. Because of me! That's why he was treated with compassion.'

'Compassion!'

'Yes, compassion! And he thinks I hate him! I pity him, that's all.'

'And I pity you, Aunt. Our time together is over. Marry your precious Olivan, then! Can he stop me leaving this village? Can you? I have been punished for too long. I have mourned for too long—'

'Mourned? Mourned what?'

Ela ignored her, rushing on:

'It's all over, Aunt. I'm going to Veeldrop now, but when I come back, I'm taking Jem and Nirry and Stephel and ... and we're leaving for Agondon and I don't care if we all starve so long as we get away from you!'

It was wild talk; it was almost raving; but Ela seemed possessed of a strength and fury now that had nothing in it of reason. Nirry clung to the young mistress, her face fixed into a steely resolve. But Jem, as he watched, could almost read what the maid was thinking: *What about Lord Tor?*

Ela pushed past her aunt. 'Now get out of my way. Move!

Do you want me to slap your face? Do you want me to push you down the stairs?'

The fat woman let out a jeering laugh. 'Yes, slap your old aunt, that would be a fine thing, wouldn't it? Daughter of the Archduke, indeed! You're no better a noble lady than that wretched old man was Lector of Irion. You filthy little harlot! Do you think I care if you die in a gutter? You, and your sick, perverted little brat? As for Olivan, don't you think he knows all about you? He'll laugh at you, that's all. Noble lady? You're nothing but a crazy, drug-addicted whore!'

Ela slapped her aunt's face. 'Out of my way, you evil-minded old bitch!'

She pushed past the fat woman, almost gasping for air, desperate to be liberated from the oppression of her presence, but now Umbecca was gripping Ela's arm, clawing Ela's coat, desperate to wound her niece as cruelly, as harshly, as she could.

She fought for the words, the worst she could find, 'I know about Jem!'

'Jem? Leave Jem out of this! What have you done but patronize him and torment him and fill his head with your slavering Agonist drivel? I am just glad he has a strong spirit and can see through you!'

But her aunt was not dissuaded. 'I know about him, I tell you! Don't you think I haven't worked it out, you filthy whore?'

'Worked out? What have you worked out?'

'I know who his father was!'

Ela swung back. 'His father? What do you know?'

'A "soldier in the Siege", that's what you said, wasn't it? Yes, that was a good story, wasn't it? We all thought there must have been so many soldiers, you didn't know which one! We all thought you were a soldier's harlot! But that was better than the truth, wasn't it? You didn't want us to know that, did you? That was even worse!'

'Truth? What do you know of the truth of anything?'

'I didn't see it at first, how could I? The chaplain made me see it. He is experienced in the ways of the world. How could I, a virtuous woman, even imagine such depravity? How could I imagine that my beloved niece should not only bear a bastard child, but the bastard child of *her own brother*?'

There was silence.

In the silence, Umbecca's hands dropped slowly from the collar of Ela's coat, where they had almost ripped away the ermine lapels.

In the silence, Ela staggered back, her face fixed in shock.

In the silence, Nirry's jaw was hanging, almost drivelling.

And in the silence, a panel in the wainscot slid back.

Tor staggered forth.

He was huddled in a blanket, and as he advanced, the blanket slipped from him. Beneath it, he wore the garb of a harlequin.

Umbecca's red face was suddenly white.

'You're wrong, Aunt,' Tor said softly. 'I love my sister, but she was not my lover. You call her a whore and a harlot. You say she was a fallen woman. My poor, foolish aunt!'

'Oh, Tor, Tor!' Umbecca whispered. She was barely listening to the words he said. She stepped forth, hands outstretched as if to embrace him; then she snatched back her hands and covered her face. She swayed, almost crashing to the floor. Her teeth were clenched. 'What is he talking about?' she muttered. 'What does he mean?'

'You just didn't see, did you, Aunt?' said Tor. His voice was still soft, almost ethereal. He gestured to Silas Wolveron, who had retreated to the window and leaned on his staff, his head bowed in sorrow. 'You thought Lector Wolveron was smuggling secrets into the castle, and so you betrayed him. You were wrong. He came to the castle during the Siege. But why did he come? He came to perform a marriage. He came to marry my sister to her lover.'

'What?' Umbecca was barely breathing.

'Tor—' Ela began. She was trembling so much that she could barely support herself.

'Sister, she must know. Our aunt has been a vain and foolish woman; but I know that, in her heart, she possesses goodness. Only if she knows the truth can we recall her to the higher duties she has forgone.'

Umbecca was gazing wonderingly at her nephew now; Tor's wasted face stared intently into her eyes.

'Dear Aunt,' said Tor, 'Jem is no Vexing. A common soldier was not the father of the boy, and nor was I. No, my sister's virtue was never squandered; it was saved only for the highest and noblest of suitors.'

All through this, Tor's voice had been low; now it dropped to a whisper, and he stepped close to his aunt.

'You call my sister a harlot; but Aunt, you are speaking of your Dowager Queen. Yes, Aunt: Jemany is the son of Ejard Red, and the rightful heir of this kingdom!'

Tor swayed, about to fall.

'No!' Umbecca broke from his gaze and cried out, blundering back, as her nephew almost collapsed into her arms; it was left to Nirry to catch him as he fell.

There was a knock at the door, a polite *rat-a-tat!*

Umbecca's carriage had arrived.

Chapter 66

THE IRION FIVE

'But – it's outrageous!' Morven whispered. 'Five men? Innocent men? Vagas, yes, but there are principles of justice—'

Crum sighed. His friend was beginning to repeat himself. Indeed, he had been repeating himself for some time. Straggling at the end of a line of guards, the two young men were trudging up the muddy lane to the Vaga-camp. It was a way they had gone before, on the day of their secret mission. But then the weather had been warm and bright, and they had been by themselves. This was the first time they had been on Vaga Patrol – a bad enough business, Crum thought, without Morven suddenly discovering a conscience!

'Think of Vytoni's *Discourse on Freedom*. The third epistle, "On Political Liberty": *Only the rod of justice is fit to rule, and only with mercy can that rod be wielded* ... For what did that great philosopher write, if we are to acquiesce in—'

'Morvy?' Crum hissed.

'Yes, Crum?'

'Shut up.'

Crum was angry. Justice? Mercy? These things had never bothered his friend before. If he was not on duty, Morven was always reading in the barracks while the hangings took place on the village green. His mind floated perpetually in the world of his books. Now, because he had been reading about justice and mercy, he decided that no one had thought of them before.

Or the lack of them.

Morven could not resist adding, 'Think of Jelandra's great Soliloquy on Power – the very speech that contains the Great Caesura!'

'You men! Fall in step!' barked Sergeant Bunch.

The sergeant was in one of his no-nonsense moods. Things in the village had reached a sticky pass. There had been talk before that all the Vagas should be rounded up. They would probably have to do it now, and a wretched task it would be. Without Vagas, who would the villagers have to hate? The Bluejackets, that's who! Bunch could only hope these five would be enough.

And the girl.

Morven and Crum trudged on in silence, their heavy muskets clanking at their sides. Then after a moment, Morven broke out again, 'I don't understand how it's allowed, Crum. The commander's a cultivated man – he was at college with Professor Mercol! Surely he's read . . . Crum, do you think he can *know* what's going on?'

'Morvy, of course he does! He ordered it, you fool!'

'*What?*'

'You men, shut up!' bellowed Sergeant Bunch.

They turned a corner and the Vaga-camp was upon them, more miserable and degraded than it had seemed before. A ragged little Vaga-brat burst into tears at the sight of the soldiers. It had begun to rain again.

Morven said bitterly, 'I don't know how you can call me a fool, Crum. If anyone's a fool, it's you. Just obey, and no questions asked! Well, isn't that typical of the military mind? Have you never heard of a thing called integrity?'

'Morvy, I wouldn't recommend it round here.'

Ahead of them, Sergeant Bunch was choosing the Vaga-traitors who would be hanged as Cata's accomplices. Crum had thought there might be a struggle. Perhaps shots. But it was easy. The Vagas came in silence. Suddenly Crum felt a horrible, sick feeling in the pit of his stomach. He remembered the day of their secret mission; then the Vaga-fairs of his childhood in Varl. He wanted to throw up, but swallowed hard.

'You don't know much about politics, do you, Morvy?' he said. 'You call me a fool, and yes, I haven't read all your clever books. How could I? They don't teach reading to the likes of me. But you forget, I come from Varl. I've seen all this before, Morvy. Oh, I know exactly how your precious commander thinks. Yesterday, somebody blew up the temple. Who did it? Who knows? It could take you a whole season to find that out. You might never find out. But somebody's got to be blamed, don't they?'

Morven was abashed. 'Somebody?'

'Very well, these'll do,' Sergeant Bunch called.

The Vagas were chained about their ankles and necks. Now the patrol would march them back to the green. Crum was falling back into step when Morven caught his arm and hissed urgently, 'Somebody? Anybody?'

It was as if he still could not quite believe it.

Crum shrugged. 'That's politics.'

He shook his arm free. He hoped the scene was over. Poor Morvy! Crum felt a rush of compassion for his friend. He should have stayed in his comfortable college.

Morven stood blank-faced, his jaw hanging open. He did not move; for a moment he could not. Something was working through him, coursing through him like an elixir.

'Morvy,' Crum urged, 'fall back in!'

But that was when something alarming happened. Morven had known, of course he had known, that evil had engulfed the kingdom of Ejland. He had known that he, Plaise Morven, had become an instrument of that evil. But until now, evil had been only a word to him. Now it was a reality. Hot tears burst from his eyes as he watched the Vagas being marched away. Morven sank to his knees in the mud. He clasped his hands in prayer, gazing up in anguish at the ominous sky. A sense of his childhood flooded over him and he saw himself kneeling in the Great Temple of Agonis, offering up his earnest prayers in the days when his faith had been simple and strong.

'Blessed Lord Agonis, forgive me, forgive me—'

'Morvy, stop it—' Crum began, appalled.

Too late.

'You! Recruit Morven!' Sergeant Bunch had had enough for one day. Angrily he sloshed across the muddy ground and kicked the young soldier viciously in the ribs. Morven doubled over, sobbing, clawing the ground. Was the man mad? These clever ones were always more trouble than they were worth. 'Get up, you fool! What do you think you're doing, grovelling in the dirt?'

Crum could only look on, white-faced with shock. The rain was falling harder.

※　※　※　※　※

Umbecca had composed herself. But only just. Rumbling down the crag in the Bluejacket carriage, she shuddered with horror at the scene she had left. Had the guard noticed anything? What should she do?

To think, she had been happy but a short time before!

Of course, she believed not a word of Tor's story. The boy had always been the most vicious liar and deceiver, and had invented this latest absurdity only as a cover for the guilty truth. Besides, the boy was mad. And yet, what a beautiful boy he had been! Umbecca had loved him so!

It was Ela who had corrupted him, that much was plain. Yes, Umbecca could see it now. Ela had lured her brother into the foul sty of incest. Rapidly, after that, his moral character had rotted away, and the poor boy had been lost to all virtue and shame.

Ela was sick.

Ela was mad.

She was like an infection, let loose in the world.

Umbecca doubled over, moaning, inside the coach. Until now, she had never quite considered just how much she detested her niece, how much she loathed her. She loathed madness and she loathed weakness.

A desire overcame her, frightening in its intensity. It was a desire to hurt Ela, so much and so irretrievably, that the girl should never recover from it; Umbecca felt a frustrated impotence because, it seemed, she had no such way.

Nothing would be enough.

Jem was flying.

Liberated from the confines of the castle keep, with its lowering arches and thick-beamed ceilings, he had soared up suddenly and dazzlingly into the pallid, rain-wet sky. Gripping tight to the crystal, he could look down on the castle far beneath him, at the carts and the horses and the barrack-room roofs and the cabbages and marrows in the kitchen gardens and the geese and rooting pigs in the yards. Higher, higher, Jem rose, wheeling far above the fluttering flags and the watchmen on the high walls and battlemented towers. His gaze took in the drawbridge and the swift-flowing moat; he glimpsed the white mountains that were curtained by the clouds and the houses and fields of the village below.

He felt at once an immense power, and a powerlessness greater than ever before.

In his mother's chamber, billowing against the ceiling, Jem had at first felt a heady, secret exhilaration. He might have been one of the gods from The Vast, gazing from on high at this ruined world. To be unseen, and yet to see others: that was power. To be unheard, and yet to hear others: that was power. If he screwed his forehead tight and looked piercingly into their eyes, it seemed to him that even their thoughts were revealed to him, startling and terrible in their clarity and truth.

This was power. This was knowledge.

Yet there was nothing he could do but look. Time and again, as his aunt assailed first Old Wolveron, then Ela, Jem had burned to attack the fat woman. To punch her face. To smash her teeth. To kick her in the backs of her fat legs. Without warning or mercy, he would swoop down from the ceiling, striking her to the floor.

He could not even touch her, not flick her ear, not poke

her eye, not jiggle his finger at a protruding nose-hair. The dark aura protected him, and lifted him up, but imprisoned him also in a dimension of loneliness.

So it was that each new revelation flung from his aunt's lips, or his mother's, seemed to reverberate on the air a hundred times, bouncing back and forth between the women and the wainscot, before it could quite mean anything to Jem. He was not only outside space but time, never quite present, never quite real.

He whirled through the sky.

Boom!

The signal.

The command.

The cannon-fire, drifting up from the village green, recalled Jem to the present. Now he heard the thud-thud of drumbeats. Looking far below through the drizzling air, he saw the dun-coloured, huddled crowds gathering about the scaffolds, and the stiff-backed Bluejackets ranged in lines. The pale afternoon would soon be gone; soon the dark would come. On and on went the sinister thudding; it would relent only when the executions were over.

It would relent only when Cata was dead.

An ardour and a longing swirled through Jem's mind as he struggled now to direct his flight down, down, following his mother; now it seemed to him that it would only be his mother who could tether him to the earth. Without her, he would fly off for ever; he would drift into the high clear sky above the mountains and never come back.

He could see her.

The scarlet brilliance of her coat flamed out. She was standing in the back of Stephel's rackety cart, holding tight with one hand and with the other waving wildly, urging on the driver. Standing beside her, his cowl flung back and his robes fluttering on the wind, was Old Wolveron. The back of the cart was a clutter of straw and empty ale-bottles; for many seasons it had been Stephel's bed. Now Stephel swung his whip through the air, flaying the old grey cart-horse. Nirry had been left behind to tend to Tor.

Thundering over the drawbridge, the vehicle, shabby as its driver, looked as if it might collapse at any moment. Careering crazily round the curves of the crag, it was always on the verge of hurtling off the road, tumbling and crashing to the depths below.

Jem's mother led the charge like a hero into battle; as if only now, reckless in her red coat, she would unleash at last, in one mighty burst, all the anger and the energy and the passion and the pride that had lain sleeping for so long, that had been so spurned and squandered.

The village was close now. Tumbling through the air, Jem took in the yellow thatch of the roofs – here Blossom Cottage, there the Lazy Tiger – and the glowing glass of the chamber of command. He took in the tomb-yard with the Wildwood over one wall and, over the other, the clipped Lectory gardens; he took in the marble white wreckage of the temple with the gaping blackness of the crater at its centre. For an instant the explosion filled his mind again, sweeping him up once more in all the mighty force of its advent.

Boom!

Standing at the head of her chariot, going at last into battle for her king, pride welled in the Dowager Queen's heart, and burst from her lips into song. They were all singing, even Old Wolveron, but only as Jem struggled back to the present, and plummeted closer, could he hear the words they sang. It was an old campaign song from the days of the Siege, when some believed, wrongly, that the Bluejacket yoke could yet be lifted from the realm of Ejland.

> *We raise our voices and proudly sing*
> *Ejard Red is the rightful king!*

He shall return in glory and bravery
He shall release us from Bluejacket slavery
Ejard Red is the—
Ejard Red is the—

A delayed, slow horror gripped Jem's heart. *His mother was mad.* Shame overspread him, red as her coat. Years of sleepy-treacle had turned her wits. She could not save Cata; she could not save herself.

Rain fell again and the light was fracturing. Jem closed his eyes, turning and turning through the broken, bright air. *Thud, thud,* came the drumbeats from below, but the story the drumbeats told was not the only one there could be. Too high and locked in the dimension of loneliness, Jem could know nothing of the events that time had readied: of the stones and bricks that would hurtle through the air; of the fleeing human forms; of the urgent shouts and the bursting chains as bright-garbed figures on the green below made their sudden and violent bid for freedom.

The Crystal of Koros glowed in his hands, casting its rays on the scene below.

❋　❋　❋　❋　❋

Later, none would know how the Vaga-riot had begun. It was an event so unexpected that it could not be explained. No one, not Veeldrop, not the Bluejacket soldiers, perhaps not even the villagers who had massed for the hangings on the green, believed that it had been Vagas who blew up the temple. The Vagas, and Cata, the dirty little half-caste, were convenient scapegoats, as usual. Half-excited, half-appalled, Irion would watch as they went to their deaths. There was no question of justice. It was ritual slaughter – but they were only Vagas.

For all the time that had stretched before, the Vagas had been the despised of the earth. After that day they would remain despised; they would even suffer worse than they had suffered until now. But in the long cycles that lay ahead,

530

the memory of that day, when they had risen up suddenly as one, would live on in their memories as a beacon of freedom; slowly at first, then faster and faster, word of that day, called Irion Day, would spread through the lands where the Vagas travelled, and something in the heart of each Vaga would change. What this day would say, in story, song, and dream, was that injustice and oppression could not last for ever; that in time their reign would be out, and freedom would come to the Children of Koros.

Some said the rising had begun with the captives. Awaiting execution, the party of Five had been held in a tent behind the scaffold. They should have been watched more closely. One of the Bluejackets, some said, had been lax; later, there would be a full investigation. How it could happen no one quite knew; but the story went that one of the Vagas, just one of them, had slipped his chains. Swiftly he managed to free the others. Then the Five – the Irion Five, as they would be called in time – burst from the tent, and for crucial moments they overwhelmed the guards.

A strange, special power seemed to burst from the Five then. Later, some who were there would speak of a glowing light; though quite what sort of light it might be, they could not say.

That was one story of how it began. Another story told of the bands of Vagas who had assembled, that afternoon, round the edges of the green. Soon, all the Vagas from the camp had come. The villagers were uneasy and so were the Bluejackets. It was unexpected. Vagas never came to the hangings; but the hangings, after all, were long before curfew. *They weren't doing anything wrong*, Sergeant Bunch would later whine. But this was no excuse. After all, the Vagas had never been doing anything wrong.

Even the light had conspired against them that day, Bunch would try to explain. The maddening whiteness of the sky; the slither, slither of the rain from the leaves; the watery *plink! plink!* on to the timbers of the scaffold: all had fed the unease and strange foreboding that hung above the scene like impending doom.

The Vagas looked on in silence.

There was no expression on their faces.

Then the Vagas had begun to sing. It had been as if some peculiar magic, something not quite willed, had taken them over. The songs they sang were not the merry, familiar ditties of the Vaga-booths, hewn coarsely for the ears of Ejlanders. Instead, they were meandering, mysterious Vaga-airs, doleful and half-chanted.

The singing – the chanting – was at first intermittent, and would stop every time a guard loomed near. Soon the Blue-jackets were all on edge. Some of them said they could not stand it. Perhaps that was why a guard, suddenly snapping, had struck an old Vaga-bitch who let fall the merest hinted chant from her lips.

A passion of violence had surged in the guard. It had happened before; it would happen again. Up in the camp, the Vaga-bitch would have been struck repeatedly while she lay on the ground, beaten about the head with the butt of the soldier's musket. Other Bluejackets would have just turned away, pretending nothing was happening, while the Vagas cowered in fear.

But today it was different.

The Vaga-bitch hit back, and hit back hard.

Soon the uproar consumed the green. Soon the Bluejackets had lost control.

The Vagas surged forward.

And so did the villagers.

Plaise Morven stared blankly into the fray. He was trembling; he was feverish; for a moment he could barely hold his musket. Blood was flowing from his split upper lip.

Why had he struck the Vaga-woman?

'You, man! Do something!' cried Sergeant Bunch.

Chapter 67

DEATH AND BIRTH

Moments earlier, Umbecca had faced Commander Veeldrop.

With a shudder, she would think back later to how narrowly she had avoided the outbreak of the Vaga-riot. She might have been caught at its very heart! Rounding the green in her Bluejacket carriage, Umbecca had looked with an indulgent smile at the scene that appeared to be arranging itself. The order was impeccable: the gallows at the ready; the neat lines of soldiers; the drumbeats methodically measuring the time. Even the peasants seemed sombre and devout: the impending spectacle had not, Umbecca was pleased to note, brought out any bent in them for vulgar revelry. Some of them had even made an effort with their attire: a neatly-knotted kerchief here; here, a nice white bonnet; there, a freshly-laundered pinafore. If even the lower orders could spruce themselves up, it showed that standards were indeed improving.

Dear Olivan! He had made life so much better for all!

Umbecca had never attended a hanging before and was unaware that the Vagas were not usually present. She only observed that they, too, seemed remarkably well behaved, standing neatly at the periphery of the green; which was, she assumed, where they belonged.

It was a pity about the rain.

Then the coach passed the tombyard gates and the ruins of the temple loomed into view, gaping and jagged as an enormous wound. At once, all pleasant musings were gone from Umbecca's mind. Her expression fixed itself into a sour resolve and she was not even able to feel her usual pleasure when the handsome young guard on Olivan's gate handed her down from the carriage.

'I must see the commander urgently,' was all she said.

❊　❊　❊　❊　❊

In the Glass Room, Commander Veeldrop sat barricaded behind his enormous desk. Slumped back in his chair and puffing at a Jarvel-roll, he might have been gazing at the glass above him, studying the raindrops and the fractured air.

But the embroidered visor covered his eyes and all the commander could see was blackness.

'You're ready, Chaplain?'

'Ready, sir.'

' "People of Irion", or "People of the Tarn" – what you will. "I speak today as the embodiment in your midst of the love and mercy of the Lord Agonis; and I speak, too, under the full, consecrated and constituted authority of our most excellent commander" – and so forth.

'So: "Since the commencement of our government here in Irion, we of the United Regiments of the Tarn, upholding the divinely and legally sanctioned reign of His Imperial Agonist Majesty, King Ejard of the Blue Cloth" – and so on, and on – "have sought to enforce standards of justice, decency, mercy and reason that would shine as a beacon throughout this province, illuminating each nook that once was dark, each cranny in which wickedness might yet take refuge, each hole-in-corner for the impulse of injustice, illuminating even . . . even . . ."'

'The Vagas, sir?'

'I'm coming to them. I meant the Zenzans.'

'Perhaps "the benighted hosts of Zenzau", sir? I always find that useful.'

'Hm.'

The chaplain sat on his blue chintz chair, one leg carefully crossed over the other. On a small tablet, resting on his knee, he took down the commander's words with rapid, casual scratches of his pen. Only seldom did the chaplain lean towards the edge of the commander's desk, dipping the pen into the open inkpot; to an observer, indeed, it might have seemed that Eay Feval wrote far fewer words than the commander was saying.

This was untrue. The chaplain had devised a private short-hand. He had found it useful in remembering the wishes, and other things, of his ladies in Agondon. Returning home from the drawing-room of Lady A——, say, or the bedcham-ber of Lady B——, the chaplain had always taken it upon himself to record, as precisely as possible, all the knowledge that had been vouchsafed to him. Lady A——, after all, had such a bad memory; Lady B—— was such a busy woman. One never knew when she would want to be reminded of this, or that, or the other.

Eay Feval restrained a sigh. His situation did not disap-point him, not in the least. But (dear me!) it was a pity, wasn't it, to waste his skills on the old boy's maunderings? Besides, when he was on the scaffold the chaplain would just improvise. He always did.

It was a pity about the rain.

'Now: "It seemed much to hope that before the elapsing even of a cycle, we should see this once-proud village ..." Town?'

'Community?' suggested the chaplain.

'Hm. "This once-proud community restored to the bless-ings of—" And so on, and so on. Ejlander justice, envy and glory of all the world. The usual ...'

'We've done that, sir, haven't we? Sir?'

Was the commander falling asleep? His head was drooping forward. Eay Feval rolled his eyes; then, recalling the feeling he had had before, that the old boy could see him through the embroidered visor, wished that he had not.

The commander continued, '"But in all this, we reckoned without that viper in our midst, that foul betrayer of morality and virtue who has for long, too long, been tolerated in our empire ..."'

The old man drew back on his Jarvel-roll. The developments of the last day had disturbed him. He was most annoyed. To think, at the moment when 'Miss R——' had come to him, that he must waste his time on nonsense like this! It was not as if it would do his career any good to hang a few more dirty Vagas. Anyone could hang a Vaga. Or five. Why couldn't they leave the wretched temple alone?

He thought again of the tremendous explosion that had so disrupted his sleep last night. *Vaga-magic*, they were all saying. Vaga-magic, so Vagas must die. But could there be something more to it than that? He thought back to the explosion in Zenzau.

The Red Avenger!

Could it be?

Eay Feval wondered again if the commander had fallen asleep. 'We might put in something about the dark god Koros at this juncture, sir,' he offered. 'How his evil is working through the Vagas. The dark god, that's the best approach; then something on the cheating, money-grubbing ways of the Vaga. There's no one in the audience who hasn't been cheated by a Vaga, let's face it. Get them worked up about it, I say! That way, they forget all the fun they had at the f—'

There was a crash of foliage and Umbecca burst suddenly on to the scene.

Tears sprang from her eyes.

'Olivan,' she blurted, 'I have to talk to you! Alone!'

Jem's eyes had opened.

Turning, turning, in the pallid sky, he looked down on the chaos below. Wet with rain, the green shone brilliantly. Against its emerald-brightness he saw the fleeing figures of the Vagas and the Bluejackets in pursuit; he saw the peasants joining in the fray, flinging stones and planks and bricks; he saw the flashes of musket-fire and the clouds of rising smoke.

Some things were dark and some were bright; some things hazy and some clear. Jem saw them all; but most of all he saw his mother's coat, scarlet and dazzling and moving fast. Still careering wildly, the cart was cutting over the green; then Ela had leapt out and was running, running, flailing in her flapping coat towards the Lectory gates.

Musket-balls and bricks and missiles rained around her. Jostling human figures pushed into her path. But nothing could obstruct her. Nothing could stop her.

The world came back.

Suddenly, Jem was disconnected no longer. All at once, with a rush of knowledge, he saw that his mother's very presence that day was one of the things that made the Vaga-riot happen; she was its spirit, and she was protected.

He felt no fear.

Then he knew, with a blaze of certainty, that Cata would not go to the scaffold. It would not happen. It could not happen.

She would live.

She would be free.

That was when Jem felt a desperate love, more ardent than any he had known before. Like the rays from the crystal it burst from his body, reaching out in its passion and longing to envelop his mother, as she rushed across the green; to envelop Tor, in his fastness in the castle; to envelop Old Wolveron and Nirry and her father and Barnabas, his lost friend, wherever he might be. In a vertiginous moment Jem saw that it embraced even all the enemies he had made: Aunt Umbecca and Goodman Waxwell and poor, dead, carrot-haired Polty; it embraced the forces of Ejard Blue as it embraced those of Ejard Red; it embraced the Vagas and it embraced the Zenzans and all the other races of the mysteri-ous, vast world. It embraced the creatures of the Wildwood and the fish in the river and the birds of the air; it embraced all the living as it embraced the dead, lying in the warm darkness under the earth.

Reaching out like the vines from the crystal, the love widened and deepened and grew to include the whole of the abused and ruined world that lay, stretched and suffering, beneath Jem's flight; and the source of all this love, Jem knew, the deepest love that mastered and controlled all else, was his love for Cata.

It was a desperate madness.

It was everything.

The world was back!

Jem turned, turned. But as the first ecstasy of his love subsided, that was when he saw the strange light of the crystal in his hands subsiding, too.

It was fading.

The rain, that had fallen so softly all day, was falling harder now, and now Jem could feel it. Its wetness flowed across his eyes and lips and chilled his clutching hands.

It was just at the moment when his mother, far below, pushed her way through the Lectory gates that Jem realized that the crystal was gone. It had vanished from his hands and he was falling.

Below, those who raised their eyes above the fray would have seen a dark form like a shadowy, stricken bird spinning down slowly through the greying haze of sky. Jem's careening vision took in the ruined temple and the tombyard and the Lectory gardens; it took in the high Lectory chimneys and the glowing glass roof of the room at the side, spattered and flowing with the falling rain.

❋ ❋ ❋ ❋ ❋

Eay Feval had been pacing in the ballroom in the last moments before it all began. His steps were measured and precise and soft, almost shuffling, as if he had been practising a solitary dance. The wet evening was closing in, impending at the edges of the darkening, drawn curtains.

He was waiting. First he had waited in the long corridor that led to the Glass Room; then in the hall, where his gloved hand had flicked a speck of dust or two, idly, from the king's marble shoulder; now here, in the scene, he reflected, of the first social triumph of a certain Mistress Rench. How swift her rise had been!

If, at that moment, an observer had remarked that the

chaplain was annoyed – that he was even, perhaps, furious – Eay Feval would not have demurred. That the old man had dismissed him from the Glass Room was indignity enough; what was worse was that Mistress Rench had intimated nothing to the chaplain in advance, not a jot, as to the motive which lay behind her abrupt, tearful entrance.

Ladies did not treat Eay Feval this way.

Of course, had it not been for the relentless tread of a guard, in too great a proximity to the Glass Room door, Eay Feval might have known a little more, as it behoved him to know, of precisely what was passing within. As it was, he had heard only the beginning. Some confession, that much was clear. Some revelation.

Then it came to him.

Of course! The Red Avenger!

The chaplain breathed deeply. His heart was lightened. Salvation! An imaginary orchestra seemed to swell out of the darkness and Eay Feval found himself humming under his breath. He took a little step; then another.

One-two-three, *one*-two-three . . .

Eay Feval thought back to the night he had squired Umbecca to the ball; he thought back to her hideous dress and her monstrous hat and the number of times she had trodden on his feet as they made their leaden way about the floor. She was ridiculous; all the officers' wives, all of them, had been laughing behind their hands. In the best society they would have laughed openly, unable to restrain themselves. They would have thought she was a comic turn, Eay Feval's joke, like the monkey in mourning that had so delighted all at Lady M——'s; like the loincloth he had worn to Lady E——'s famous Jungle Evening.

But Umbecca Rench was no joke, he knew; the joke was on those who thought of her as such. The Lectory Ball did not matter. A rustic barn-dance! Next time Umbecca Rench went to a ball, it would be a ball of a very different calibre. And no one would dare to laugh.

Eay Feval had an instinct about women. Mistress Rench

was raw yet, that was all; but her provincialism was merely of the surface. For now, she had distanced herself from the chaplain. She had felt herself slighted by him. This was provincialism and this would pass. Mistress Rench would be hurt, insulted; but Lady V—— would see that Eay Feval was the best friend she would have.

For surely it would come to pass. Umbecca Rench was no fool. She had only to give up The Red Avenger and all she had ever wanted would come to her. Veeldrop's reputation would be restored. Umbecca's marriage would be brilliant, and widowhood, best of all, would follow soon enough. Agondon society would lie at her feet!

And there, at her side, would be her spiritual adviser.

Eay Feval danced on the darkened floor, shuttling in a circle like a clockwork toy.

It happened quickly.

In his darkened bastion, Eay Feval did not at first hear the noises that sounded along Tombyard Lane. In the ballroom, the shouts were whispers; the breaking glass was birdsong; but when the shots came, they were shots even here. There was a slamming door and the sound of guards, urgently making their way to the Glass Room.

Something was happening. The orderly preparation for the executions, it was clear, had been disrupted. The chaplain's waltz came to a halt and he crossed to the doors of the empty ballroom. With pursed lips, he stepped into the blue hall. Those wretched guards had tracked mud across the carpet; it really was too bad. Eay Feval glanced to a window, glimpsing the rain on the cinder-path.

There was a crunch of footsteps.

The chaplain was lingering uncertainly by the door when it burst violently open. He staggered back, startled by the scarlet apparition.

The Red Avenger!

A moment of terror passed before the chaplain saw that

this was not, after all, the fearsome renegade, but Lady Elabeth, risen from her bed.

'Where is he?'

'My Lady Ela, really!'

She flung away his arm. 'Where's Veeldrop? Tell me where he is!'

Eay Feval had never much liked the look of Lady Ela. He did not think *she* would have been one of his ladies. Stammering, he waved her in the direction of the Glass Room, and as he rushed in the wake of her billowing coat he looked back to see, to his horror, two old men, a wizened servant and a filthy old Vaga, who were, evidently, Lady Ela's party. They were following behind.

No, she was not one of Eay Feval's ladies!

In the Glass Room, the commander had risen behind his desk, swaying painfully on his bejewelled stick. Before him, Umbecca still knelt on the carpet, her face awash with tears from some trauma of revelation. The guards who had broken into the scene were staggering back, cowering, as the force of the commander's anger burst around them like thunder.

'What? The Vaga-scum? What? What?'

'Veeldrop!'

It was not an appeal; it was a command.

'Ela!' Umbecca's face swivelled, astonished. She had left her niece sobbing over the collapsed form of Tor; never, for a moment, had she imagined that Ela would carry out her wild threat to confront the commander. And she had brought Silas! And Stephel!

The scarlet form swept forward. It was the form of a rightful queen, burning with imperious rage and hate and love. For one eternal moment the tableau was held, the confrontation between the red and the blue; and Eay Feval, terrified, saw that he had been wrong. No, Lady Ela could never be his; but yes, The Red Avenger had come, the spirit of Resistance incarnate in this room!

Then the sky fell in.

There was a flash, then another, lighting up the rain-washed ceiling. For stabbing instants, the greying panels were suddenly luridly, blindingly white.

Then came the thunderclap.

The ceiling exploded.

The commander collapsed beneath his desk. Umbecca flung herself to the floor again. Ela twisted, stumbling, falling. The guards reeled back, shielding their faces, as glass showered the room.

Rain poured in.

And there was something else.

Something had fallen into the centre of the floor.

'Vaga-magic!' Umbecca breathed, gaping in horror at the naked human form. It was huddled in a ball; about its wet flesh there lurked the last glimmerings of a fading, purple-black aura. Slowly, in a circle beneath the shattered ceiling, crunching over the broken glass, all who were there now gathered to look on the vision that confronted them.

Only one did not rise. One lay where she had fallen, in a scarlet heap.

And a scarlet, spreading pool.

Goodman Waxwell, then, had been right about one thing at least. In a mighty, crimson eruption, all the blood from Ela's body, it seemed, had gushed from her mouth. The haemorrhage, long-predicted, had come at last. Stephel collapsed, sobbing, over his queen. But there was nothing he could do.

The figure on the floor, for a time, was oblivious. Only slowly did the face turn upwards to the faces that looked down; slowly, in the rain that cascaded through the roof, the naked figure rose, trembling, to its feet.

'Jem!'

Umbecca would have staggered forward, perhaps to embrace the boy, perhaps to strike him. But a guard's hand pulled her back, as if from danger. Bluejacket muskets were trained on the boy, poised perilously on the brink of firing as he turned his dripping face to the commander and intoned, levelly, 'It wasn't Cata. I did it. I did everything.'

Chapter 68

A BEAUTY OF THE VALLEYS

The commander slumped back, leaning against his desk. Pain contorted his empurpled face and it seemed for a moment that he could not speak.

The lapse was momentary.

Sergeant Bunch burst through the foliage; then stood, astonished, at the scene before him, his words checked on his lips. His eyes looked as if they might burst from his head.

The commander reared up. 'What is it, man?' he boomed.

'S-Sir!' The fat sergeant clicked to attention. 'The r-riot is quelled, sir!'

'Quelled?'

'Th-three of my m-men are injured, sir, and one hit by a b-brick.'

'And the Vaga-scum?'

'S-Sir?'

The sergeant, for all his efforts, was finding that his eyes kept straying irresistibly to the glowing vision in the centre of the room. Later, he would struggle to understand what had happened. Without warning, it would seem to him, his very identity as soldier and sergeant had been pushed to the brink of collapse. When he was a boy, his black-garbed grandmother had taken him on a pilgrimage to the Great Foretelling, with the Lady Imagenta who wept real tears. Not since then had the fat sergeant risen out of himself, as he rose now, in the awed knowledge that the world was not, after all, the dull round of matter-of-fact, ordinary things that his life, like a confidence-trick, had taught him to believe.

He struggled back into himself.

'We've p-potted some Vagas, sir. And a c-couple of

p-peasants who were throwing s-stones ... and ...' The sergeant trailed off; his eyes strayed again.

The commander approached him; almost strode to him. The old man was barely leaning upon his stick. Instead, he might have been about to swing it back above him, striking the fat sergeant. 'What's wrong with you, man?' he boomed. Then, 'And the rest of the Vaga-scum? You've rounded them up?'

The sergeant gasped:

'S-Sir, a f-few have escaped into the w-woods—'

The stick swung back. 'Then you are a fool, Bunch! There shall be a full investigation into this, do you understand? You were in charge of today's operations, and I hold you personally responsible for what has happened here! Do you understand? Our position here depends on a savage control. If you cannot keep that control, then you are not fit to keep your command. Now get out of my sight! Round up every bit of Vaga-scum you can find and kill it without question. Do you understand?'

'Sir!'

The commander turned back, furious, to the room. The crisis had brought out something in him; something that had been sleeping. Roused from his lethargy, he had taken on again the fearsome mantle of the hero of the Siege; and Silas Wolveron, hearing the pitiless, barked commands, hearing the stick that struck the sergeant, knew that he was again in the presence of his torturer.

The blind man's staff fell from his grip and all at once he had dropped to his knees, pleading suddenly, barely coherently, for the life of his daughter. It was a startling exhibition; none could have imagined that such desperation and fear could erupt from the heart of the old hermit. In his appeal, in its keening wildness, the Vaga-heritage of the former Lector of Irion was shockingly evident. Perhaps it was not so much a plea as a lament, drawn from immemorial depths of sorrow. His cowl slipped from his head, exposing his mutilations.

Eay Feval had removed his left glove and was studying his

nails; they were neatly filed, with admirable half-moons. There was nothing for him to do; he had found already his theme for the address he was sure he would soon be called upon to deliver, denouncing the boy's depravity.

Nakedness. That was the angle.

The shamelessness of wanton lust.

The chaplain permitted himself a glance at the boy. The sight filled him with a certain aesthetic pleasure, it could not be denied, but swiftly, he turned his eyes away. Indifference was best in these matters, he had found.

If only the old Vaga would shut up! Really, one was appalled at such vulgarity.

'What a wretched old fellow you have become, Silas Wolveron,' the commander was saying, his voice raised, riding over the keening. 'Or should I say, "Eyeless Silas"?'

He looked about him and the guards sniggered dutifully.

'As it happens, my man, with an arrogance and spiritual pride which is, if I may say, typical of you, you underestimate the justice, the mercy, the compassion and clemency of my rule. Were I the monster you imagine me to be, would you have had these twilight years of your useless life to enjoy, basking in the glow of your daughter's regard? You would not! Vile-hearted old traitor! What atrocities will you not impute to me? How dare you imagine for one moment that I should see fit to send to the scaffold a poor, abused girl? Abused, I suspect, not least of all by you? For the sake of the Lord Agonis, man! What do you take me for?'

The commander snapped his fingers and a guard stepped forward, smashing Silas Wolveron over the back of the head.

Excitement hammered in Umbecca's heart.

Rage burnt in Jem's. He burst forward, rushing for the commander. His hands clasped about the old man's throat. Could he have killed Veeldrop then with his bare hands, Jem would have done so.

'Stop him, stop him!' Umbecca shrieked.

It was over in an instant, and Jem was struggling in the grip of the guard who had struck Silas Wolveron.

'The boy has gone feral!' choked the commander, staggering back. He was clutching at his throat, purple-cheeked, as if he were swallowing back a tide of vomit. He gulped hard, gasping, 'Are you mad, boy? Do you know what you do? Boy, if your Vaga-evil will let you vanish at this instant, then I suggest you do so. What other wicked things you've done, I don't know, but the action of that moment has cost you your life! Take him away!'

'No!' Umbecca cried out.

But the commander ignored her. Leaning forward over his desk, he was breathing hard, a huge stricken beast. He gritted his teeth.

'Olivan?' Umbecca was at his side.

'I'll take care of this, Father,' came a voice.

Jem gasped. A shiver passed through him. Held in the grip of the Bluejacket guard, only slowly could he turn his head to see the figure who now joined the circle, stepping carefully, on slippered feet, round the broken glass at the rim. A blue robe enfolded the lean, muscular form; a white bandage, like a turban, concealed the flaming hair.

Poltiss Veeldrop stepped close to Jem. With a critical air, he gazed up and down at the naked boy. 'Shouldn't someone get something to cover him? He has exposed enough of his moral vileness without treating us to the vileness of his body, I should have thought.'

'Poltiss!' The commander spoke through gritted teeth. 'Go back to bed, you're not well.'

'Nor are you, Father. But you, I fear, shall become only worse. I shall be better, soon enough – no thanks to this boy here. I had his splintered crutches brought to me. Quite a sight. Had I taken the full force of his assault, I should be dead by now for certain. It was no doubt his intention. As it was, after the first blow he seems to have vented his fury more upon the tomb-slab of the harlot, Yane Rench, than upon my skull – which is perhaps appropriate. Yane Rench, I understand, was a woman with a lot to answer for. One might say she began that chain of evil which led to this boy's own pathetic, joyless little course of moral turpitude.'

'Poltiss, please!' said the commander; but whether he was appealing for his own parlous health, or that of his son, was unclear.

His son made the former interpretation. 'Father, sit down, do! Here, let me help you. Goodman Waxwell shall be joining us shortly. He is just making sure the girl takes her medicine.'

'Girl?' Jem burst out. 'What have you done to her?'

Polty turned incredulously to the company. 'Do you hear? Oh, the shamelessness of it! He asks me – *me* – what I have done to the girl!'

'What are you talking about?' Jem cried. 'I love her!'

'Love!' Polty let out a burst of laughter. 'See where the corruption of his heart has led him? Oh, at first one could barely believe that a simple little cripple-boy was capable of such vileness!'

Eay Feval studied his nails, a little irritated, as young Captain Veeldrop, becoming expansive, now used, as if deliberately, a large slab of the material that the chaplain had been saving for his own address.

'We all like to think, of course we do, that in outward deformity we may glimpse the deformity within,' Polty said. 'In the lesson of the body, we like to think, we may read the lesson of the heart. But we quell this awareness, don't we? We curb it, we check it, we muzzle it, we bridle it – as if in shame! Where there is disgust, we would have compassion. Where there is antipathy, we would have tolerance. But what of the revulsion, the repugnance and horror which yet wells from our hearts as naturally as water from a spring?

'For how long did we watch him, heaving himself about the village on his crutches? Poor little cripple-boy, we all said! Leave him alone, he's harmless, we said! Who could have predicted that, in the secrecy of his heart, this boy should have sold himself to the dark god?'

There was a further disturbance of the foliage, and a new voice intruded, 'I believe that I may answer that question;

because I, after all, had made that prediction. It was my conviction that moral pollution would spread from his lower limbs, as from the site of an infection, and, if I may say, I have been proved right. That the Vexing is now even able to disguise his deformities shows, indeed, just how right I have been.'

It was Goodman Waxwell, with his twisty smile, insinuating forward on crabwise steps. But Jem had no eyes for the shabby physician. Before him, high against his chest, Waxwell clutched his instrument bag; but behind him, the physician led by the hand a strange, but strangely familiar figure.

At first Jem was confused, for when Polty had said that the physician was tending to a girl, naturally Jem had assumed that it was Cata.

But who was this girl?

She was dressed in a shiny white gown, buoyed up on layers of petticoats that rustled as she advanced. Embroiderings of lace encircled the high collar and flared in neat petals from the tight wrists. The girl's dark hair was piled high on her head, swept clear from her forehead and tied with a blue bow. She was very clean.

From a chain around her neck hung an amethyst ring. Then Jem sensed that, beneath her petticoats, the girl was limping.

'What have you done to her?' he cried.

Cata's head hung low and her shoulders drooped; when she looked up, gazing quizzically at Jem, there was no life in her eyes.

At that moment, as if summoned back into awareness by his daughter's presence, Old Wolveron stirred. But when he raised his mutilated head he only whimpered, only moaned, like a creature who was lost.

He did not sense Cata.

He did not sense her at all.

'Oh, Cata, Cata,' Jem was sobbing.

'A fine show of contrition!' said Polty, disgusted. 'He

pretends to the noble and refined passion of love, when all the time he has sought only to lure this innocent girl into the snares of his depraved lust.'

'No! Jem!' Umbecca cried.

'I'm afraid so, Mistress Rench.'

Sweepingly, Polty gestured towards the strangely altered Cata, and as the handsome young man stood, gazing at the girl as if with love, a fantastic story poured smoothly from his lips.

Jem stood amazed.

Polty began, 'Oft had I heard of this lonely girl, who lived in the green simplicity of the Wildwood, learning no lessons but those of the trees, knowing no time but the rhythm of the seasons. Many would shun her as one beyond the reach of mercy and love; yet I saw that, severed as she was from the Lord Agonis, as from all benefit of society, this child yet possessed in her heart the instinct of virtue. Could she but be taken from her Wildwood ways, I knew, she might yet be received into the communion of our temple. She is not a wicked child, but only one requiring teaching. With proper education of the heart and mind, I saw, this girl might be redeemed; and, in her redemption, we might find fit symbol of that renovation of the heart which we, of the forces of His Imperial Agonist Majesty, have sought to bring to this benighted province.

'I endeavoured to bring forth this girl from her darkness. Over long moonlives, with bright trinkets and sweetmeats, I would lure her from the woods, hoping that I might gain her trust; then, slowly but inexorably, draw her after me into light that is the love of the Lord Agonis. So it was that, shyly at first, as a young faun blunders on its spindly legs, this girl would come to me in the soft light of evening, and eat of the spiritual bread of my hand.'

Polty's voice had dropped to a mournful caress; now, all at once, it was a stern declamation. He turned suddenly, facing Jem, pointing an accusing finger.

'But I reckoned not with the viper in her path; for all the

time, as I sought to claim her spirit, little did I know that there was one who sought her flesh! Little did I know that, all this time, this depraved boy craved, in this innocent girl, a cistern for his lusts!'

'Oh, Jem, Jem,' Umbecca sobbed.

Polty rushed on, 'The girl, I am convinced, has remained virtuous; but had it not been for my intervention, her ruin would have been certain! For a time, her natural simplicity had protected her; ignorance, and not the scruples of conscious virtue. But this could only inflame this boy's lusts, and he became yet more ardent in the siege he laid to her innocence. In the end, frustrated by the failure of his designs, he resorted to the end of all base seducers and sought to accomplish by force what he could not achieve by fraud. In a pretended ceremony of remembrance for the dead, he dressed the girl in the mantle of a harlot, and, taking her to the tombyard under cover of darkness, he would at last have achieved his vile ends, across the tomb-slab of her dead mother!'

'Oh, monstrous!' burst out the commander, rearing up, forgetting his pain in a rush of righteous anger; for the wicked acts his son had described were exactly those visited upon the fair Evelissa in the pages of *A Beauty of the Valleys*.

'The girl has been saved,' said Polty piously, 'and shall not return to the Wildwood now. She shall become the charge of my dear adoptive parents, who cared for me in my tender years before I found my father. In Blossom Cottage, she shall be protected alike from base seducers and the mad hermit who has abused her so grievously; and there, it shall be my delight to be her frequent visitor. For it is my belief that in time she shall become an ornament to this village, as happiness replaces her present sorrows, and recollection of this evil boy is expunged from her heart.'

Eay Feval gnawed at a hangnail. The irritation that had churned in him had become something more. For long moments, he had felt himself superseded. And to think, so short a time ago, he had dressed the young captain in his new, fine clothes! The commander's son learned quickly, that was for certain.

The chaplain's hangnail tore away.

The commander had risen to his feet again now and was looking with admiration on Polty.

'Ah, my son, my son! I had wondered if you were a true Veeldrop, and now I see that indeed you are. With this girl, you have shown your compassion and the depths of your trust in human virtue; with this boy, you have shown the anger which must burn in us when that trust is abused. This poor girl I take to my heart, and shall look on as a daughter; as for this boy, nothing remains to say. He has expelled himself from the human community; for his crimes are crimes against innocence, and thus too abominable to forgive. In his presence, the flame of compassion dies. Before him, the waters of forgiveness freeze. He has passed beyond hope of redemption. Guards! Take him to the scaffold!'

'No!' Jem cried out. 'Cata! Tell them, please!'

But Cata, sunk deep in a haze of Waxwell's medicine, could say nothing, feel nothing; she could only look on blankly as the guards began to drag the resisting boy from the room. With that, it might all have been over; but for Umbecca, her huge bulk shaking with sobs, who clawed suddenly, wildly at the commander's sleeve and cried:

'Olivan, no! You can't! You're wrong—'

Eay Feval looked up from his fingernails, arching an eyebrow as the commander turned, lowering, on his bride-to-be. The purple rushed back to the old man's face.

Oh dear! This was worrying.

This was dangerous.

'Wrong? Woman, do you forget yourself? Do you know what you're saying?'

'Please, Olivan! Jem is not a wicked boy—'

'What? You've seen what he's done, and you say he's not wicked?'

'I know he's not wicked!' Umbecca cried. 'Look at him! He stands before us now in the garb of depravity; that I do not deny. But is this his natural garb? Is this the suit he must wear? Olivan, your son has put the case for this girl. But might not equal eloquence be turned to this boy? Do we not see in my poor Jemany, too, a story of innocence abused?'

Eay Feval gnawed at another nail.

'Think of the life he has lived! Can we not see that this poor boy was cast into this world without hope? Deformed! – conceived between incestuous sheets! – a harlot for a mother, a traitor for a father! I tried my best with him, but what chance had I, a weak woman, against such odds? Remember, too, that through his early years there was not even a temple here in Irion where I might take him, so severed was this province from all benefit of society. What hope was there that this boy could follow the Lord Agonis, whose light alone may redeem us from the depravities of this world? It was inevitable that this poor boy should fall, and fall hard.

'We see him now, lost to all human dignity and shame, writhing in the grip of the dark god Koros. Oh, Olivan, I can't deny that there is in my own heart a lust for vengeance! When the boy, in his madness, launched himself at your neck, I burned to strike him down; I cursed the womanly weakness which restrained me. But Olivan, I beg of you, as you love me, save my poor Jemany! His crimes are not those of his parents. He's not evil. He's sick. He needs treatment.'

Through all this, Goodman Waxwell had been listening with a special attention; and now, stepping forward, he smiled his twisty smile at Umbecca and remarked, 'I'm glad to see, my good woman, that you've come round to my view.'

'Your view, Goodman?' The commander turned to him, as to an expert witness.

Umbecca went pale.

'Indeed, my Lord. If, as a man of science, I might offer you my professional opinion, I must say that I have long believed the Vexing to require not moral censure but surgery. From the first I have been apprised of his case; though not, I am afraid, of all the facts. Had I known him to be the spawn not only of bastardy, but of the vile abomination of incest, this should only have deepened the conviction I had formed.

'His birth explains the extent of the hideous deformities which, through the operation of Vaga-magic, the Vexing contrives at present to mask from our view. When the Vexing was younger, I had hoped that, by removing the deformed parts, the remaining fabric of his being might be saved. Had the procedure been carried out then, much that we have seen might have been avoided. It is my fear that the infection has now spread too far; and yet, if there is to be any hope for the Vexing, I would urge that you permit me to operate at once.'

'No! Please, Olivan!' Umbecca burst out, but this time the commander would not hear her.

He raised his hand, staying her. 'You have spoken well, Goodman. The "Vexing", as you call him, is a mere child, and if there is a way to save him, then save him we must.'

He turned to Umbecca. 'Calm yourself, my dear. You must see that Goodman Waxwell's way is the best; for he is a servant of science as well as of the Lord Agonis, and has shown us how these ways may be reconciled. I had thought that only in wrath could we have done with this boy; I see now how science may offer a path of mercy.

'Very well, Goodman. You may take the boy.'

Chapter 69

THE COMPANION

The world was a blur of blackness and rain.

For long moments Jem had felt himself suspended, held as firmly by the Bluejacket guards as he had been held in the purple-black light. Then, all at once, everything was movement; and then, all at once, everything was over. He would remember the bright, deluged room, suddenly wheeling as the guards dragged him forth; he would remember the green impendings of the plants and the golden glitterings of the smashed ceiling; he would remember the commander, looming blue and massive, and his aunt, sobbing in black, and Cata's father, insensible, in his dun-coloured robes; he would remember the red of his mother's corpse and, in the middle of everything, dominating his awareness, the blank, destroyed whiteness of Cata, sinking obliviously into Poltiss Veeldrop's arms.

Like echoes, as from a vault, Jem heard his own cries, desperate with horror and longing and love; then the guards were slapping him to keep him quiet, then gagging his mouth, then binding his hands and feet, then enveloping him in a cape that smothered him like a shroud.

They bundled him into a coach.

'Come quick! There must be no delays this time! We must ready him for surgery!' Waxwell's cries rang on the rain-swept air. The coachman cracked his whip and the rhythm of galloping hooves sounded, slamming and urgent, beneath the discords of the storm.

The rain cascaded down in torrents now, and Jem's imprisoned form was jogged heavily, flung from side to side as the coach careered onwards. Wildly his vision veered between the lashing storm outside and the hideous, hated figure of Waxwell, bouncing grotesquely in the opposite seat. Desperately the boy tried to cry out, but could not; he longed to lash out with his fists, but could not; to kick, but could not. A thick wadding of cloth filled his mouth, forcing back his tongue; the ropes that bound his limbs were drawn tight and cut into his wrists and ankles like wires.

Lightning flashed across the sky, exposing Waxwell's twisted face, leering forth now in all its monstrous evil. Eagerly, with the ardour of a lover, the physician gazed on the bound, gagged boy. He lurched forward, swooping close to Jem's stricken eyes.

'Oh, Vexing, Vexing! Soon you shall be cured!'

He jumped up, thumping at the padded ceiling.

'Faster, man, faster!'

Spit flew from Waxwell's drooling lips; his wig had juddered off, exposing a scabby head; his eyes rolled wildly, whitely.

'Faster! Faster!'

The rhythm of the coach was like a rhythm of love, leading him at last, in a rising ecstasy, to the bloody consummation of all his longings.

They ripped into the lane that led to Blossom Cottage.

That was when it happened.

It was the work of an instant. All the time the storm had been rising, rising, in time with the madness of Waxwell's passion; now came the crescendo in a monumental crash, a sudden, dazzling incandescence of light. There was a terrified neighing and the coachman's cry as the vast tree-trunk smashed across the road.

Mutely, beneath his gag, Jem screamed.

First he was flung against the carriage-window; then further, wider, into the ferocity of the air as the coach splintered into fragments like tinder.

It was over.

But no. Not quite.

Lightning struck twice.

As he lay, bound tightly and soaked with rain, in the undergrowth on the brink of the Wildwood, three impressions were burned on Jem's brain: the coachman's neck, snapped back like a stalk; the horses tearing free and galloping away; and Waxwell, his legs crushed beneath the tree-trunk, screaming and screaming against the storm.

Then came the second incandescence from the sky, and the ruined coach was an explosion of flame.

Goodman Waxwell would scream no more.

Crum was snoring.

Crum was always snoring; sometimes it drove Morven to distraction. Lying in the bunk beneath his friend, Morven would reach up, thumping his hand on the creaking slats above him, or scramble up and shove a pillow over Crum's nose and mouth. But tonight Morven barely noticed the piggish grunts. The sound of the storm was loud.

The storm inside Morven was growing louder, too.

His upper lip was swollen, slashed by a ring on the Vaga-woman's hand. Morven was in pain, but he treasured his pain. It was the beginning of something. Shame suffused him, and horror, when he thought of what he had done that day, striking a wizened crone, starting a riot. But then he thought, *I wanted her to hit me back. I wanted it.*

In the riot, Morven had acquitted himself well. After the first moments, he had sprung into action. He had fired shots, he had run about urgently, he had spluttered reports of movements, numbers, to the harassed Sergeant Bunch. It was as if something hard, something mechanical inside him had taken over; an impulse, perhaps, of self-preservation.

I must not sacrifice myself, Morven thought. *Not yet.*

Later, Sergeant Bunch would think that Recruit Morven was not so bad, really not so bad. Just needed knocking into shape, that was all.

He did not know who had started the riot.

In the barrack-room, the night was black as pitch. Morven

turned fitfully on his hard bunk; he might have wondered if he would ever sleep again. From the moment – it seemed so long ago – when he had fallen to his knees in the mud and prayed, Morven had been aware of a sense of evil, beating, beating at his temples like a drum. He saw the evil as growing, spreading, filling the world; and the Bluejackets, he knew, were the agents of that evil.

The storm subsided at last and Crum's grunting snores filled the darkness above Morven's head. Poor Crum! Morven felt a rush of compassion for his friend; then for all the soldiers who lay around him, uneasily sleeping, in the long, cold room.

Some of the men had died that day.

Morven sat up, his face in his hands. He knew despair: for his part in the riot, but more than this, for the whole system, the whole order of the world. What could he do? What could anyone do? He saw himself as infinitely small, infinitely helpless, a tiny fly caught in a vast spider's web.

And the spider was creeping closer.

When a sliver of light entered the barrack-room at last, Morven reached for the book beneath his pillow. It was Vytoni's *Discourse on Freedom*. He read, straining his eyes, until the bugle sounded.

Jem lay gazing into the violent sky.

It was not until the storm had died down that the boy became aware of the figure looming near him, looking down at him. The figure had approached not from the lane but from amongst the trees. At first it was no more than a presence to Jem, a soft, silent knowledge of enveloping benevolence; then, penetrating the tormented clouds came a gleam of Eastmoon light, and Jem turned his head and looked, as he had known he would look, into the mysterious, familiar eyes. They flashed once, then were dark again.

Wood-tiger.

Tenderly the creature laid its paw on Jem's chest and as he

continued gazing into the depths of the eyes Jem could see forming, in the darkness of each eye, twinned, strange impressions of colour and slow movement. The colours shifted, deep in the darkness, like the turning image of the kaleidoscope; and then the turning colours became something else. Something more. It was the image of a human form, writhing and twisting strangely, and as the image became more distinct, Jem saw that the form was dressed in the garb of a harlequin. Transfixed, he lay watching the harlequin's dance, and drifting on to the air came the echoes of a song from long, long ago.

> *Hey, ho! The circle is round!*
> *Where can its start and its end be found?*

❄ ❄ ❄ ❄ ❄

When Jem awoke, he was aware only of the persistent *drip! drip!* of the leaves by his face and the first glimmerings of early dawn through the high, damp branches above. Swiftly he jerked his head, looking for the wreckage of the physician's coach. It was not there. He was deep in the Wildwood. Then he saw that he was free of his bonds and dressed in the green-brown garb of a peasant.

He sat up.

'It's what you'll need to wear,' came a voice. 'At least, for the first part of the journey you must take.'

Jem turned his head.

It was the harlequin, long-limbed and lean, in his particoloured costume and his silver mask.

'Tor! Is it you?' Jem stood swiftly, brushing twigs and leaves from his peasant's tunic. 'What do you mean, the journey I must take?'

'Come, Jem, have you forgotten? You must see it! Your time in this village has come to an end; indeed, all your life up until now, all the manners and ways you have known, have slipped irretrievably into the past. Your childhood is over, Jem. It has become a place to which you cannot return.

'Now, if the Bluejackets are not to take you, you must make your way south. There is no risk that they shall seek for you – not now, not at once. They shall assume that your remains are to be found, mingled with others, in the charred ruins of the physician's coach. Still, for a time you must keep to the woods, but follow the route of the pale highway. In a day or so, you shall meet with a party of Vagas, disguised as you are, and you may travel with them. In Agondon, Vagas are still tolerated as entertainers; that is where they shall head.'

'Am I to become a Vaga?' Jem asked, marvelling.

'No, Jem; for in the great city of Agondon, that sprawls across the delta of the River Riel, you shall find a street called Davalon Street; and there, in that luxurious thoroughfare, is a house with golden scrolls above the doors and windows. It is the house of a gentleman who is known as Lord Empster. You are to go to him, Jem, and he shall receive you.'

'But Tor! How shall he know me?'

'He shall know you, Jem.'

Jem's eyes sparkled as he turned to the harlequin. The harlequin had told him that his childhood was over, but all at once a dream came back to him, spinning back from the days when he was small.

'Tor! The Resistance?'

Was the dream to come true?

They were walking through the dim early light of the Wildwood, brushing briskly though the ferns and long grasses. It was the harlequin who had led the way, and Jem, naturally, had fallen into step beside him.

The harlequin did not quite answer Jem's question.

'Jem, in time you shall understand much that now must remain unclear to you. But first, there is the journey ahead of you. It is a hard road you face, and the Crystal of Koros cannot help you again. When you found the crystal, it burnt with power and enveloped you in the aura of its power. But now you shall have only the powers of this world. You shall walk, but you shall not fly, and the crystal shall appear to be only a dark, dull stone. Thus it shall be until the end of your quest, when the crystal is united again with its fellows.'

'Quest?' For a moment, Jem did not want to believe it. Could all these things be true?

'Jem,' said the harlequin, 'you must understand by now that you were a child who was marked for destiny.'

Jem stopped; he laid a hand on the harlequin's arm. How thin the harlequin felt, how frail! Birds stirred in the branches above them, and a grey squirrel flashed across their path. 'There was something mother said. Just before—'

The words choked on Jem's lips.

The harlequin had turned back to the boy, smiling sadly; now he moved on.

'Yes, Jem,' he said. 'But you are more than the son of Ejard Red; just as the evil which looms over us now is more than the evil of Ejard Blue. The times in which you have been born, Jem, are times that have seen much, but all that we have seen until now is but a prelude. The Time of Atonement is ending, Jem, and even now, the one who was once known as Sassoroch is girding himself to break forth from the Realm of Unbeing. There shall be a time, Jem, when you understand more; now, you need know only that you are the Key to the Orokon. And that all that is foretold in The Burning Verses shall come to pass in this time.'

Jem looked down thoughtfully. 'But Tor, what of Cata? Am I to leave *her*?'

'Jem, there is nothing you can do for her. Now, she is entangled in the machinations of evil, but this, like all times, is a time which shall pass. Child, you must permit her to find her own destiny.'

'But I love her! I can't!'

'Jem! Hush, child, please.' The harlequin had turned again, catching the boy in his frail arms. 'I have said that now you must leave her, but Jem, I promise you, you shall meet again. I have said that she must find her own destiny, and this is so. But know this: that her destiny is entangled with yours.

Much time shall pass, Jem, as much time must: but in the end, you shall find that it is so.'

'But Tor, how do you know these things?' Jem pursued.

There was no reply. The harlequin relinquished the boy's embrace, pushing rapidly through the crisp woods again; but after a moment, some way ahead, he turned back suddenly.

'Did I say I was Tor?'

Jem raced ahead. 'I don't understand!'

But this time the harlequin only laughed.

Their brisk walk led them to a place Jem knew. It was the Wall of Sticks; and at first Jem was confused, for the harlequin had told him he must leave the village, and yet had led him back to its very brink.

'Jem, we have come to the place where I must leave you. Embrace me now, my child, for long seasons must pass before you are destined to see me again. But know this: in your heart I go with you, and where you are, I shall always be.'

Tears pricked at Jem's eyes.

'But Harlequin! Won't you come with me?'

'It cannot be, my child. Now, Jem, you must hurry.' The harlequin's long hand gestured to the gap in the tombyard wall. 'One more time, Jem, you must go this way. As yet, it is barely light, and you shall be safe in the garb you wear.'

Jem gazed, puzzled, into the silver mask.

'Harlequin, what is it?'

'You mean you have forgotten? Jem, there is a companion that you cannot travel without; the companion who awaits you in the centre of the green.'

'Harlequin?'

Then a sudden excitement burst over Jem's face. Of course! What a trickster the harlequin was! The trick he had played this time was cruel; but all Jem could think of was the joy that rushed over him.

'Cata? Can it be? Oh, Harlequin! How?'

But this time Jem did not wait for an answer.

He burst through the gap in the tombyard wall. Eagerly he

ran ahead, through the morning grey, past the mossy tomb-slabs and the twisted yew and the crater where the temple had once proudly stood. Jem had listened with awe to the harlequin's words; but as he heard of the quest he faced, and the trials and dangers of the times that lay ahead, the boy had felt, too, a welling, secret fear, and a sorrow for the childhood he must leave behind. Now, his fear was gone, his sorrow flung to the winds. With Cata beside him, there could be no fear; there could be no sorrow that could not be redeemed. He could go anywhere, he could do anything, enfolded in the special dimension of their love.

The boy flung himself through the tombyard gates, skidding in the mud from last night's rain. The green was before him; then Jem staggered and almost fell, for the sight that was disclosed to him was not what he had expected.

It was a sight of horror.

Corpses lay where they had fallen in the mud. There were bodies of Vagas; there were bodies of villagers; there was even, here and there, a sprawled figure in blue. Trembling, Jem trudged across the churned, dark earth. There was an overturned cart; there was broken glass; there was canvas from a ripped tent, flapping in the wind. Here, Jem saw a dead dog, its head smashed open by the blow of a brick; there, a white handkerchief, lost to its owner and trodden underfoot.

Jem stooped, picking up the crumpled fabric; how heavy it was, from the clinging mud! 'Why, why?' he whispered, almost sobbing; as he took in a choking breath he gazed up, arching back his throat, into the reaches of the painful dawn. First, and most obscurely, he saw the white mountains, barely visible behind the grey, impending clouds; then the dark crag of the Rock of Ixiter, where the vast edifice of the castle hovered over the village. Then he lowered his eyes back to the scene before him and slowly took in what he had not seen before.

In the centre of the green, the harlequin had said, Jem's companion awaited him, but what Jem saw in the centre of the green was nothing but a long, shadowy figure, hanging, swinging from the scaffold by a noose. So there was, then, one hanging that had gone ahead last night; one execution of Veeldrop's justice that neither policy nor fate had forestalled.

And now a new, urgent terror consumed Jem's heart; for there was something familiar, too familiar, in the size and the shape of the hanging form.

Slipping, stumbling, he made his way towards it.

He sank to his knees.

That was when Jem recalled his aunt's face when Tor had staggered forth from the panel in the wainscot; the struggle, even then, that had been visible in her. Tor had thought that she could be no danger. For all the confusion and bitterness in her heart, his aunt, Tor had thought, was not wholly abandoned. Now Jem knew that Tor had been wrong; Jem knew that Tor had been terribly wrong. Umbecca Rench had struggled; but it was a struggle, Jem saw, that she had lost.

The suit of motley had been dragged through the mud.

Tears coursed freely from Jem's eyes now as he gazed into the loved, familiar face that hung, grey and sagging, beneath the broken neck.

'Oh, Tor! Tor!'

The sky glimmered redly, and as Jem knelt by the scaffold in the mud, he saw in the new access of light that a strange, twisting vine had emerged from the ground beneath. Slowly but inexorably it wreathed its way around the grim wooden edifice. Black, tender petals rustled on the wind.

Then Jem understood.

With clawing hands he parted the thick roots of the vine, digging into the clay of the dirt beneath the scaffold. This time, as the harlequin had said, the crystal was only a dark, dull stone; but Jem drew it forth and clutched it to him.

Before he went back through the tombyard gates, Jem turned and looked behind him. He looked up at the castle; then down at the village. He would have lingered; but he heard the boots of a Bluejacket patrol, trudging, trudging, on the other side of the green.

He hid the crystal inside his tunic and ran back into the Wildwood.

Here ends the First Book of THE OROKON.
In the Second Book, *The King and Queen of Swords*,
Jem embarks upon his quest in earnest,
as the greater evil that has lain in wait is
unleashed upon the world.

Appendix:

TIME IN THE OROKON

It is perfectly possible to visit the world of THE OROKON, because it is not distant from our own: it *is* our world, but in another dimension. At certain 'weak points' in the dimensional fabric, we may easily step through into the 'earth' of THE OROKON, as into many other alternative worlds.

Accordingly, time in THE OROKON is not, as we may at first think, wholly different from time in our own world. In the measurement of time, there are units which are real and units which are arbitrary. The length of a year is real, and shall not change, if by 'a year' we mean the time taken for the earth to travel around the sun. The length of a day is real. A week, on the other hand, is an arbitrary unit. There is nothing special about the cycle of seven days; it is only a matter of culture and tradition. In El-Orok, the 'real' units of time are the same as ours. What differs are the ways in which they are measured.

These ways vary through the various lands of El-Orok. What follows relates principally to the kingdom of Ejland, and to the notions of time indicated in *The Harlequin's Dance*.

There are five major levels on which the Ejlanders measure time. These are *seasons*, *cycles*, *moonlives*, *phases*, and the various divisions of the day; they are explained below:

SEASONS

The year falls into five seasons, named after each of the five gods. There are two seasons which correspond to winter in our world: the *Season of Agonis*, which ends the annual cycle, and the *Season of Koros*, which begins a new one. The Agonis-season is the time of the Festival of Agonis, the principal religious celebration in the Agonist lands. This season corresponds to Christmas in our own dimension, while the Koros-season represents the early months of the new year (traditionally seen as the bleakest period of winter in the northern lands of our world).

The associated gods of each season follow the order in which the gods were created, according to the El-Orokon. The full cycle of the seasons is given in the table below, with appropriate months keyed to our own northern hemisphere. We should note, however, that the cycle of the seasons in El-Orok is being progressively disrupted. In Ejland, the cold seasons are becoming longer and harsher and the warm seasons ever more fleeting. Here is the traditional pattern:

Season of Koros: winter (= January, February, March).
Season of Viana: spring (= April, May).
Season of Theron: summer (= June, July, August, September).
Season of Javander: autumn (= October, November).
Season of Agonis: winter (= December).

THE CYCLE

In peasant communities, time is conceived mainly in terms of the seasons and their associated rural activities. The major formal unit of time in Ejland, however, is a unit of five years known as a *five-cycle* or *cycle*. Individual years are not numbered on the principle of 1998, 1999, 2000, etc. Rather, a number is attached to each cycle, and the years of the cycle differentiated only as *a, b, c, d, e*.

The Harlequin's Dance begins in Atonement Cycle 997*a*; that is, the first year of the 997th cycle of The Atonement. Therefore, the actual number of years since the beginning of The Atonement is not 997 but 4,981.

The belief that The Atonement is ending is fuelled by the impending thousandth cycle.

Human age is similarly calculated in terms of cycles rather than years. Thus when Cata is a 'five-cycle old' she is five years old. By the end of *The Harlequin's Dance*, when Jem has 'entered his fourth cycle', he is fifteen years old, and will be considered to be 'in his fourth cycle' between his fifteenth and nineteenth years.

Both Jem and Cata were born in 996*a*. In our terms, they will therefore be twenty years old at the beginning of the thousandth cycle; in their terms, the thousandth cycle of Atonement corresponds to the fifth cycle of their age.

Cycles are gathered into longer units known as *gens* and *epicycles*. A *gen* (the closest thing to our 'decade') represents 5 x 5 cycles, or 25 years; an *epicycle* (analogous to our 'century') is 5 x 5 gens, or 125 years.

THE MOONLIFE

In the Lands of El-Orok, the 'month' as we know it is generally known as the *moonlife*. As in our dimension, the lunar cycle takes 29.5 days, and the solar cycle approximately 365.25 days. The essential problem for calendar-makers, therefore, has always been how to construct a coherent, recurring pattern of months which reconciles the solar and the lunar cycles (the solar cycle is roughly eleven days longer than twelve lunar months). In El-Orok, this problem has been made to seem more vexing by the failure of the year to fall consistently into patterns based on the sacred number five. There are five seasons; but they are not even in length, and there are not five moonlives in each season.[1]

[1] The 'imperfection' of the annual cycle has been a source of much commentary by theologians and men of science alike. Some maintain that the cycle was perfect in the time of The Juvescence, and has fallen into ruin since the gods departed the earth. Others note that though the Ur-God Orok, according to the El-Orokon, 'ordered the

In the provinces, the lunar cycle remains a literal thing: a moonlife is literally the time of the moon's life. In Agondon, however, the moonlife has been regularized – although in such a way as to sever it from any relationship to the actual cycles of the moon. In the Agonist Reformed Calendar (ARC), the year has been divided into twelve 'moonlives', each of thirty days. These have the names given in the table below, derived from the ancient tongue of The Juvescence and indicating a rather romanticized notion of the traditional attributes of the given times of the year.

ARC Moonlives (each of thirty days)

Ichios	= snow	(January)
Evos	= rain	(February)
Vyand	= wind	(March)
Sendal	= seed	(April)
Evanos	= blossom	(May)
Pesdior	= pasture	(June)
Harion	= harvest	(July)
Fend	= heat	(August)
Luxor	= fruit	(September)
Vendal	= vintage	(October)

----

times and seasons of the world', nonetheless he was essentially repairing, as best he could, the chaos of the 'Korosan Creation'. Time, in this view, was always ruined. At Temple College in Agondon, debate has long raged as to whether Orok was *unable* to create a perfect system of time (the 'Unablist' position) or whether the Ur-God *could have done so* had he so wished (the 'Deliberatist' view), but left time in a ruinous state in order to indicate from the beginning the fallen, compromised condition of the earth. The Unablists are seen as heretical by the Deliberatists, and vice versa: to the Deliberatists, it is outrageous to assume that Orok was not all-powerful; to the Unablists, the heresy lies in proposing that the Ur-God would not have made creation perfect had he been able to do so. Nothing is known as to what awareness of time existed (at least among the women and men of earth) during The Juvescence. Some believe that a quite different (and superior) consciousness of time must have prevailed then.

Nos	= fog	(November)
Aros	= ice	(December)

As the year is of the same length as our own, it is therefore necessary to include five additional or *intercalary* days (known as 'Meditations') at the end of each year – six in leap years. These are inserted between Aros and Ichios, and are named for each of the gods, in the order of their creation. In leap years, the extra day is named for the Ur-God Orok, *viz.*

    (i)   Meditation of Koros
   (ii)   Meditation of Viana
  (iii)   Meditation of Theron
  (iv)   Meditation of Javander
   (v)   Meditation of Agonis
  (vi)   Orok's Day: *leap years only*

THE PHASE

The notion of a *week* is unknown in the Lands of El-Orok. Within each moonlife, there are five *phases*. In the provinces, these phases literally represent the phases of the moon; under the Reformed Calendar, the connection between nature and time as measured on the calendar has been severed. However, under the traditional reckoning, the 'new moon' which initiates each moonlife is known as *Blackmoon*. The moonlife therefore lasts from one Blackmoon to the next, a period of either twenty-nine or thirty days, and the time between Blackmoons is divided into five phases, named after the principal element or attribute of the moon's cycle in each phase:

Day 1. *Blackmoon*. New moon.
Days 2–6. *Waxing*. Crescent moon on western side of disc.
Days 7–12. *Westmoon*. Half-moon on western side.
Days 13–18. *Hornlight*. Full moon.

Days 19–24. *Eastmoon*. Half-moon on eastern side.

Days 25–29 or 30. *Waning*. Crescent moon on eastern side.

In Ejland, Blackmoon and the beginning of the second, third, fourth and fifth phases (that is, Days 1, 7, 13, 19 and 25) are designated the *Canonday*, in which attendance at Temple has traditionally been commanded (analogous to Sunday in the Christian countries of our own dimension). The first day of the moonlife may therefore be known with equal correctness both as *Blackmoon* and *First Canonday*.

There are no individual names for subsequent days, which are numbered according to their place in the lunar phase. The second day of the moonlife is therefore *First Waxing*, followed by *Second Waxing*, *Third Waxing*, etc.

Days 7, 13, 19 and 25 are *Westmoon Canonday*, *Hornlight Canonday*, etc., with *First Westmoon*, *First Hornlight*, etc., then counted from Days 8, 14, 20 and 26.

To express these dates in writing, it is conventional to use abbreviated forms: thus, First Waxing would be written as *1Wa*, Westmoon Canonday as *CWe*, Third Hornlight as *3H*, Fourth Eastmoon as *4E*.

In some parts of Ejland, it has been customary to number the Blackmoons of each season: therefore it would be possible to give a date such as 'Second Blackmoon, Javander', and the number of the Atonement Cycle. Traditionally, no more precise dating was required, but under the Reformed Calendar, attempts are being made to introduce a much more rigorous system.

Divisions of the Day

In Ejland, a day is divided into fifteen 'hours' or *fifteenths*. This derives from an ancient system, common in Ejland and Zenzau, in which each unit of the day (the working day, the period after the working day, and the sleeping-time), was divided into five parts. Though sometimes associated with the use of shadow-clocks, this 'system' was often derived merely from observation of the sun. As such, it is still widely in use among peasant folk.

The fifteenths which are measured so precisely by the clock in Blossom Cottage represent a regularization, made necessary by the invention of the mechanical clock. Each fifteenth is therefore equivalent to 1.6 hours in our own world, or one hour and thirty-six minutes. Conversion between Ejlander time and the time of our own world may therefore be reckoned as follows:

Midnight–1.36 a.m.	= First Fifteenth
1.36 a.m.–3.12 a.m.	= Second Fifteenth
3.12 a.m.–4.48 a.m.	= Third Fifteenth
4.48 a.m.–6.24 a.m.	= Fourth Fifteenth
6.24 a.m.–8.00 a.m.	= Fifth Fifteenth
8.00 a.m.–9.36 a.m.	= Sixth Fifteenth
9.36 a.m.–11.12 a.m.	= Seventh Fifteenth
11.12 a.m.–12.48 p.m.	= Eighth Fifteenth
12.48 p.m.–2.24 p.m.	= Ninth Fifteenth
2.24 p.m.–4.00 p.m.	= Tenth Fifteenth
4.00 p.m.–5.36 p.m.	= Eleventh Fifteenth
5.36 p.m.–7.12 p.m.	= Twelfth Fifteenth
7.12 p.m.–8.48 p.m.	= Thirteenth Fifteenth
8.48 p.m.–10.24 p.m.	= Fourteenth Fifteenth
10.24 p.m.–Midnight	= Fifteenth Fifteenth

Within fifteenths, time is divided into *fives* (five equal sub-units, each of a duration of 19.2 minutes); and then into smaller units corresponding to the minutes and seconds common in our own world. These smaller units were only introduced with the mechanical clock, invented by the great Ejlander mechanist Plaise Olton in AC 951*c*, and are known as *oltons* and *mechons*, or *mechs*.

A five is divided into fifteen *oltons*. The *olton* corresponds to our minute, but its duration is in fact 76.8 seconds. As there are 75 oltons in a fifteenth, so in each olton there are 75 mechs. In Chapter 40 of *The Harlequin's Dance*, 'A Ticking Clock', the clock therefore ticks once every 1.024 seconds of our own time.

Time is written down as 1/15, 2/15, etc., when it is necessary to specify only the fifteenth: thus, when Umbecca is invited to the ball, the invitation is for 13/15, or 8.48 p.m. in our terms. The Vaga-curfew is for the same time: that is, 'after the passing of the twelfth fifteenth', or by the beginning of the thirteenth.

More precise indications of time are still uncommon in Ejland, but would be expressed according to the following formula: first the fifteenth; then the fifth; then the olton if necessary. Usually, some such formulation as 6:3/15, indicating the third fifth of the sixth fifteenth (in speech, 'Six Three') would be sufficient. (In our terms, this would indicate a time roughly analogous to 'nine o'clock in the morning' – actually, 8.57 and six seconds.)

A particularly precise time would be expressed as, for example, 12:4:5/15 (in speech, 'Twelve Four Five'); for us, 6.36 p.m. (and 52.4 seconds).

Also available from Victor Gollancz

The King and Queen of Swords
The Second Book of The Orokon

TOM ARDEN

Once there were five evil kings, each with an evil queen. But most feared of them all were the King and Queen of Swords. Now they are only painted faces on playing cards. Or are they?

Jemany Vexing, true Prince of Ejland, sets out on the second stage of his quest, seeking the long-lost crystals of the gods. On the run, Jem is making for the city of Agondon. There, he hopes his mysterious new guardian will guide him to the green Crystal of Viana. But Lord Empster is not all he appears to be.

Meanwhile Cata, Jem's lost love, is caught in the schemes of the evil, ambitious Aunt Umbecca. The wild girl has been turned into a lady. Cata recalls nothing of her powers – or of Jem. But her memory is beginning to stir.

ISBN 0 575 06371 8
hardback

A glorious fantasy trilogy

REBECCA BRADLEY

Lady in Gil
Scion's Lady
Lady Pain

Tigrallef is a Scion of Oballef, a direct descendant of the first priest-king of Gil, forced to change from memorian to hero . . .

'Compelling . . . Bradley's lucid prose slips down a treat' *Starburst*

'Tightly plotted, fast-moving fantasy' *Infinity*

'Snappy prose, nicely drawn characters' *SFX*

'Bradley's view of humanity is upbeat. She tells her story clearly, with great pace, and a vivid and subtle imagination' *The Times*

Lady in Gil ISBN 0 575 60190 6 (pb)
Scion's Lady ISBN 0 575 60161 2 (pb)
Lady Pain ISBN 0 575 06430 7 (hb)

Other Vista Fantasy titles include

The Three Damosels Vera Chapman 0 575 60108 6

Golden Witchbreed Mary Gentle 0 575 60033 0

Ancient Light Mary Gentle 0 575 60112 4

The Tough Guide to Fantasyland Diana Wynne Jones
0 575 60106 X

Minor Arcana Diana Wynne Jones 0 575 60191 4

A Sudden Wild Magic Diana Wynne Jones 0 575 60197 3

Deep Secret Diana Wynne Jones 0 575 60223 6

Hawkwood's Voyage Paul Kearney 0 575 60034 9

The Heretic Kings Paul Kearney 0 575 60186 8

Terry Pratchett's Discworld Quizbook David Langford
0 575 60000 4

Eric Terry Pratchett 0 575 60001 2

The Discworld Companion Terry Pratchett
and Stephen Briggs 0 575 60030 6

The Gates of Noon Michael Scott Rohan 0 575 60032 2

Cloud Castles Michael Scott Rohan 0 575 60023 3

The Lord of Middle Air Michael Scott Rohan 0 575 60234 1

VISTA books are available from all good bookshops or from:
Cassell C.S.
Book Service By Post
PO Box 29, Douglas I-O-M
IM99 1BQ
telephone: 01624 675137, fax: 01624 670923

VISTA